OXFORD WORLD'S CLASSICS

THE WILD IRISH GIRL

SYDNEY OWENSON (1776?–1859) is often said to have been born on the Irish Sea, but in her *Memoir* she claimed Dublin as her birth-place. Her father was an actor and an Irish Catholic whose patriotic love of all things Irish, including Gaelic songs and legends, he passed on to his daughter. After the death of her English Protestant mother, Jane Hill, Owenson was sent to boarding-school with her younger sister, Olivia. In her mid-twenties she turned to governess-ing but soon began her long and productive career as a writer. She wrote four highly successful Irish novels which helped to establish the terms of nationalist discourse later in the century: *The Wild Irish Girl* (1806), *O'Donnel* (1814), *Florence Macarthy* (1818), and *The O'Briens and the O'Flahertys* (1827). Much sought after in English and Irish high society, Owenson took up residence with the aristocratic Abercorns in County Tyrone in 1809 and married the family physician, Sir Charles Morgan, three years later. Thereafter, she signed her works Lady Morgan, a title by which she is often known today. A passionate advocate of democratic ideals not only in Ireland but throughout Europe, Owenson continued to write con-troversial works later in her career, including *Italy* (1821), a book Lord Byron praised, and *Woman and Her Master* (1839), a feminist history. Throughout her adult life her writing made her financially independent, and in 1837 she became the first woman to receive a literary pension from the British government, £300 a year.

KATHRYN KIRKPATRICK is Associate Professor of English at Appalachian State University. She has also edited Maria Edgeworth's *Belinda* and provided the Introduction to Susan Ferrier's *Marriage* for Oxford World's Classics.

OXFORD WORLD'S CLASSICS

*For almost 100 years Oxford World's Classics have brought
readers closer to the world's great literature. Now with over 700
titles—from the 4,000-year-old myths of Mesopotamia to the
twentieth century's greatest novels—the series makes available
lesser-known as well as celebrated writing.*

*The pocket-sized hardbacks of the early years contained
introductions by Virginia Woolf, T. S. Eliot, Graham Greene,
and other literary figures which enriched the experience of reading.
Today the series is recognized for its fine scholarship and
reliability in texts that span world literature, drama and poetry,
religion, philosophy and politics. Each edition includes perceptive
commentary and essential background information to meet the
changing needs of readers.*

OXFORD WORLD'S CLASSICS

SYDNEY OWENSON, LADY MORGAN

The Wild Irish Girl

A National Tale

Edited with an Introduction and Notes by
KATHRYN KIRKPATRICK

OXFORD
UNIVERSITY PRESS

Oxford University Press, Great Clarendon Street, Oxford OX2 6DP

Oxford New York
Athens Auckland Bangkok Bogotá Buenos Aires Calcutta
Cape Town Chennai Dar es Salaam Delhi Florence Hong Kong Istanbul
Karachi Kuala Lumpur Madrid Melbourne Mexico City Mumbai
Nairobi Paris São Paulo Singapore Taipei Tokyo Toronto Warsaw

and associated companies in Berlin Ibadan

Oxford is a registered trade mark of Oxford University Press

Published in the United States
by Oxford University Press Inc., New York

Editorial matter © Kathryn Kirkpatrick 1999

First published as an Oxford World's Classics paperback 1999

British Library Cataloguing in Publication Data
Data available

Library of Congress Cataloging-in-Publication Data
Morgan, Lady (Sydney), 1783–1859.
The wild Irish girl : a national tale / Sydney Owenson, Lady
Morgan ; edited with an introduction and notes by Kathryn
Kirkpatrick.
(Oxford world's classics)
Includes bibliographical references.
1. Ireland—Social life and customs—19th century—Fiction.
I. Kirkpatrick, Kathryn J. II. Title. III. Series: Oxford world's
classics (Oxford University Press)
PR5059.M3W5 1999 823'.7—dc21 98–47831
ISBN 0–19–283283–2

1 3 5 7 9 10 8 6 4 2

Typeset by RefineCatch Limited, Bungay, Suffolk
Printed in Great Britain by
Cox & Wyman Ltd., Reading, Berkshire

CONTENTS

ACKNOWLEDGEMENTS

I would like to thank James Casey for his contributions to the Note on the Text and Burt Carbia for her valuable help with the Explanatory Notes. Amy Greer prepared the manuscript with graciousness and efficiency. Rosemary Horowitz, Tina Groover, and Tom McLaughlin listened patiently to travails. My editor at Oxford, Judith Luna, made important suggestions for revision. As always, William Atkinson provided support and insight every step of the way.

INTRODUCTION

The Wild Irish Girl is a novel about origins. Written in the decade following Ireland's parliamentary union with England, Sydney Owenson's book seeks to provide a genealogy for a separate Irish identity at a historical moment when that identity seemed lost. Indeed, in the context of the 1800 Act of Union which formalized Ireland's status as a colony, politically and economically controlled by England, the novel's subtitle, 'A National Tale', made a particularly defiant rhetorical gesture. And the terms in which Owenson represents Irishness in *The Wild Irish Girl* are defiant too. Drawing on the work of antiquarians of the Celtic Revival, she retrieves an ancient Gaelic history and culture as the origin of Irish identity and thereby excludes as non-Irish the Anglo-Irish Protestant Ascendancy whose members had held most of the power and most of the land in Ireland since the English confiscations and plantation settlements of the seventeenth century. On this level, *The Wild Irish Girl* performs a figurative act of retribution: to be Irish was to be Gaelic or native Catholic; all others in Ireland were interlopers.

Sydney Owenson's origins, too, were of her own making. Her mother was an English Protestant from Shrewsbury whose strictures on piety, and negative assessment of Ireland as 'the land of potatoes and papists', were flatly rejected by the young Sydney. Instead, Owenson embraced her Irish Catholic father's country and culture. Known for his rendition of Irish songs and his efforts to establish a national theatre in Ireland, Robert Owenson claimed kinship with the ancient families of Galway and could recite the genealogies of the Gaelic tribes of that region. Raised in a family where she was forced to choose between English and Irish cultures, Sydney Owenson made no secret of her preference. 'My father was a Celtic Irishman,' she wrote in her *Memoirs*, 'my mother was a Saxon; and "I had the good fortune," as Paddy O'Carrol says, "to come over to Ireland to be borned." '[1] But though Owenson usually claimed to have been born in Dublin on Christmas Day, both the year and the location of

[1] *Lady Morgan's Memoirs: Autobiography, Diaries, Correspondence* (London: William H. Allen & Co., 1863), i. 40.

her birth were a matter of intense speculation by others. Among Robert Owenson's actor friends a tradition grew up that his daughter had been born on the Irish Sea while his wife, Jane Hill, was making the crossing to Ireland. Sydney Owenson sometimes made the same claim herself.[2] Moreover, the year of her birth she kept a mystery all her life, though one vicious critic of her politics and writing established a Royal Commission and even offered money to find out her age.[3]

Owenson's mystification of the details of her birth allowed her to construct and perform an identity—'what she called her "flimsy, fussy, flirty Celtic temperament".'[4] Indeed, her conflicted cultural heritage and her uncertain class background provided both the opportunity and the need for self-definition. Unlike her famous Anglo–Irish contemporary, Maria Edgeworth, whose family were landed gentry, Owenson's family existed in an unstable class position, her mother with 'a moderate but independent fortune', her father's acting work itinerant. Because her mother's family had found her actor father an unsuitable husband for their daughter, Robert Owenson and Jane Hill had eloped and throughout their married life they were far from financially secure. Yet Robert Owenson always struggled to provide his daughters with middle-class respectability. After his wife's death in 1789, he packed off Sydney Owenson and her younger sister, Olivia, to a boarding-school to save them from the impropriety of lives in the theatre. Although her father wished to rescue her from a profession still regarded in the late eighteenth and early nineteenth centuries as disreputable for women, Sydney Owenson practised the art of performance her whole life. For if we regard performance in Wolfgang Iser's terms as a form of play which allows us to prepare for future actions or permit 'real limitations to be overstepped', then performance and staging become ways of 'crossing boundaries'.[5] By constructing and performing roles for herself, Owenson became adept at

[2] Lionel Stevenson, *The Wild Irish Girl: The Life of Sydney Owenson, Lady Morgan (1776–1859)* (New York: Russell & Russell, 1936), 3.

[3] Mary Campbell, *Lady Morgan: The Life and Times of Sydney Owenson* (London: Pandora Press, 1988), 1.

[4] Qtd. in Campbell, *Lady Morgan*, 100.

[5] *Prospecting: From Reader Response to Literary Anthropology* (Baltimore: Johns Hopkins University Press, 1989), 260.

crossing boundaries between classes, cultures, and gender roles.
When her father's theatre went bankrupt, she became at 25 the
family breadwinner and for a time turned to governessing. But
inspired by what she had read of Fanny Burney's financial success as
an author, within the year Owenson began her first work of fiction,
creating a role she was to perform for forty years, the first Irish
professional woman writer. She published seventy volumes—
including poetry, novels, travel books, sketches, articles, pamphlets, a
comic opera, a biography, a women's history[6]—and her writing made
her financially independent. Even after her marriage to Sir Charles
Morgan in 1812, an alliance which provided her with the elevated
social role of titled wife,[7] she continued to control all her earnings.
Towards the end of her career, in 1837, her achievement was
crowned: she became the first woman writer to receive a pension,
£300 a year, from the British government. Thus, by constructing for
herself the role of professional writer, Owenson crossed boundaries
of class and gender, rescuing herself and her immediate family from
penury and enjoying a professional and economic success usually
reserved for men. Moreover, it was through her fiction, particularly
The Wild Irish Girl, that Sydney Owenson also constructed a cultural
identity. In her first Irish novel she created a Gaelic character who
provided her with another public role she would perform for much
of her life. Her name was Glorvina.

The Wild Irish Girl thus provided both Ireland and Sydney
Owenson with myths of origin. Intended to persuade English
readers that the true Irish were Gaels, Owenson's novel along with

---

[6] See Colin and Jo Atkinson's 'Sydney Owenson, Lady Morgan: Irish Patriot and
First Professional Woman Writer', *Eire-Ireland: A Journal of Irish Studies*, 15 (1980),
60–90.

[7] Biographers have suggested that Owenson's aristocratic patrons, the Abercorns,
knighted the family physician Charles Morgan in 1811 to encourage Owenson to marry
him. Other critics have suggested that Owenson's use of the title 'Lady Morgan' after
her marriage was an effort to make use of 'masculine models of authority' (see Jeanne
Moskal, 'Gender, Nationality, and Textual Authority in Lady Morgan's Travel Books',
in Paula R. Feldman and Theresa M. Kelley (eds.), *Romantic Women Writers: Voices and
Countervoices* (Hanover, NH: University Press of New England, 1995), 171–93). However, though Owenson certainly did not refuse the social prestige her title conferred, it is
safe to say that she wore the title lightly. After all, she had already established herself in
London high society before her marriage, and after her marriage she continued to write
radical and controversial political books that did not in general express the views of
English aristocrats.

its extensive footnotes provided instruction in the Irish language, music, history, and legend. And just as Owenson suppressed Anglo-Irish elements in her representation of Irish identity, so she suppressed Englishness in the representation of her own. Adopting the name and dress of her Gaelic heroine, Owenson made popular in London and Dublin 'Glorvina's harp, brooch, cloak and coiffure—all supposedly authentically Celtic'.[8] As Owenson describes the staging of her Celtic identity in London high society:

I found myself pounced on a sort of rustic seat by Lady Cork. I was treated 'en princesse' and denied the civilized privileges of sofa or chair, which were not in character with the habits of a 'wild Irish girl'. So there I sat, the lioness of the night, exhibited and shown off like 'the beautiful hyena that was never tamed' of Exeter change, looking as wild and feeling quite as savage.[9]

Owenson's father had made his name as an actor playing the Stage Irishman in productions like Richard Cumberland's popular *The West Indian* where the Irishman was stereotyped as rashly courageous, good hearted, and comic: 'A brave, unthinking, animated rogue, | With here and there a touch upon the brogue.'[10] Playing her own version of this role on the London social circuit, Sydney Owenson witnesses to the price paid for the reduction of identity to a unitary Celtic origin. Depicting herself as an exotic animal caged for viewing, Owenson at once revels in, mocks, and chafes at the role. She is both captive and captivator, able to gain admission to such circles precisely because of the exaggerated difference she represents but isolated and contained by that difference.

The public persona of Glorvina thus required Owenson to stage herself as 'other' for an English audience. In this Owenson re-enacted her heroine's own relation both to the English narrator of her tale and the novel's English readers. In *The Wild Irish Girl*, the Princess of Inismore, 'descended from the Kings of Connaught', makes her home in the ruined castle of her ancestors on the remote west coast of Ireland. Raised in isolation and educated by a learned

---

[8] Robert Lee Wolff, 'Introduction', *The Wild Irish Girl* (rpt. New York: Garland Publishing, 1979), p. viii.

[9] Qtd. in Campbell, *Lady Morgan*, 86.

[10] Richard Cumberland, *The West Indian*, in *Plays of the Restoration and Eighteenth Century* (New York: Henry Holt & Co., 1931), 748.

Catholic priest, she appears to Horatio as Rousseau's unspoiled and natural woman, uncorrupted by the pettiness and artifice of civilized life in London. Described by the 'decent old man' Horatio finds tending his father's Lodge, Glorvina is noble by birth and noble by nature:

I cannot well tell you what the Lady Glorvina is, for she is like nothing upon the face of God's creation but herself. I do not know how it comes to pass, that every mother's soul of us love her better nor the Prince; aye, by my conscience, and fear her too; for well may they fear her, on the score of her great learning, being brought up by Father John, the chaplain, and spouting Latin faster nor the priest of the parish: and we may well love her, for she is a saint upon earth, a great *physicianer* to boot; curing all the sick and maimed for twenty miles round. (p. 41)

This portrait predates by a century the figure of the Irish Queen Yeats would make popular in the Countess Cathleen, beloved by her subjects and reciprocal in the loving attention she gives them. And with such a character, living beyond the pale of propriety codes regulating most women's lives, Owenson was able to enlarge dramatically the scope of a woman's pursuits beyond the confines of the early nineteenth-century domestic realm. For unlike the traditional heroines of either the domestic novel or the gothic romance of this period, Glorvina is truly learned. Besides the usual female accomplishments of music, dance, and languages, she is widely read in history and philosophy, studies classical texts in Greek and Latin, and practises medicine. In fact, Glorvina is described by Horatio as a genius, and by the priest as so intellectually accomplished that she has transformed her relation to him from student to friendly rival. And rather than adopting a deferential role towards Horatio, she becomes his tutor in the Irish language, culture, and history. When he does find something he can teach her, painting, Glorvina attends to his instruction only when she feels inclined.

But if Glorvina's identity as a secluded Irish princess allowed Owenson radically to expand upon traditional early nineteenth-century representations of women's capacities, she had also to instil in Glorvina those Gaelic traits which her English audience would read as exotic, the traits of a 'wild Irish girl'. Thus, Glorvina possesses a 'natural impatience and volatility', 'an union of intelligence and simplicity, infantine playfulness and profound reflexion', which

Horatio describes as 'both *natural* and *national*' (pp. 92, 120). Other aspects of the Irish 'national character' appear in her father, the Prince, who speaks on no subject 'with coolness or moderation; he is always in extremes', 'in rapture', or 'melancholy pleasure' (p. 63). Indeed, besides providing instruction for Horatio and the English reader on Irish history and culture, *The Wild Irish Girl* also gives a complete catalogue of qualities intrinsic to the Irish character, repeatedly reinforcing the idea of a 'purely national, natural character' (p. 65).

This conflation of the 'national' and the 'natural' performs another kind of marginalization of the Irish. No longer savage barbarians in Owenson's text, the Irish are none the less 'wild' and 'untamed'. And these qualities still operate within and fulfil the terms of a colonial discourse which 'establishes the colonized as the repressed and rejected "other" against which the colonizer defines an ordered self and onto which all potentially disruptive psycho-sexual impulses are projected'.[11] Moreover, by continuing to define the Irish in essential, if essentially positive terms, Owenson's text reveals the dangers of becoming complicit with the same ideological strategy she wishes to oppose: the repression of difference which in turn requires an 'other' to bear multifariousness and heterogeneity. By constructing an originary national Irish character for an Irish national identity, Owenson's text plays out the politics of nationalism. And 'nationalism', observes the historian E. J. Hobsbawm, 'requires too much belief in what is patently not so'.[12]

We can see the boundaries of national character firmly drawn towards the end of Owenson's novel when her English narrator, Horatio, travels to the north of Ireland with the Priest of Inismore, Father John. Horatio's host, the Prince of Inismore, agrees to part with Horatio because he thinks the trip will provide 'new sources of observation' for his guest, in particular, 'an opportunity of viewing the Irish character in a new aspect; or rather of beholding the Scotch character engrafted upon ours' (p. 173). The botanical metaphor used by the Prince suggests that the Gaelic roots of the northern inhabitants of Ireland are intact. 'That *exotic* branch is not very

---

[11] David Cairns and Shawn Richards, *Writing Ireland: Colonialism, Nationalism and Culture* (Manchester: Manchester University Press, 1988), 8.

[12] *Nations and Nationalism Since 1780* (Cambridge: Cambridge University Press, 1990), 12.

distinguishable from the old stock,' he claims. But the narrative does not bear him out. Instead, Owenson sets up a dramatic contrast between north and south, Scots and Irish, by comparing one evening during the journey spent at the home of an Irish family in Connaught and another spent at an inn in Ulster. The priest prepares Horatio for the Irish hospitality he will receive in Connaught, observing 'We poor Irish . . . find the unrestrained freedom of an inn not only in the house of every friend, but of every acquaintance however distant' (p. 180). Indeed, at the home of their Irish hosts, Horatio and the priest are greeted with the warmth of 'ten thousand welcomes', fed a 'plenteous dinner', and entertained with music and conversation; 'the ease of the guest seemed the pleasure of the host' (pp. 194–5). But in Ulster the narrative instructs readers in a different history and a different culture. Describing the six counties of the north as 'a Scottish colony' settled by favourites of James I, the priest portrays the Scots character as one in which 'the ardor of the Irish constitution seems abated, if not chilled. Here the *cead-mile falta* of Irish cordiality seldom lends its welcome home to the stranger's heart' (p. 198). Bereft of 'convivial pleasures', Ulster is instead presented as a region of industry and trade where material prosperity is had at the expense of heartfelt sociality. As if to give the northern Irish character visual representation, Horatio and the priest conclude their trip to the north with a visit to one of the last Irish bards, the *mon wi the twa heads*, so named because of an enormous growth on the back of his head. (Owenson describes the wen in a footnote to her text as 'hanging over his neck and shoulders, nearly as large as his head' (p. 201).) Father John laments the impoverished circumstances of this old Irishman who sleeps in bed with his harp: 'Who would suppose that that wretched hut was the residence of one of that order once so revered among the Irish' (p. 203). Not only are the values of true Irishmen neglected in this region, but the representatives of authentic Gaelic culture languish and even, perhaps, mutate. Thus, Owenson's narrative trip to Ulster closes with a monstrous and pathetic human manifestation of the cultural graft with which the Prince of Inismore heralds the journey. Readers are left to suppose that his Irish generosity gets the better of his judgement in his assessment of the Scots.

Contemporary scholars have criticized this kind of essentialist thinking about national identity in *The Wild Irish Girl*, and they have linked such thinking with the Troubles in the North. Elmer Andrews has argued that in the nationalist discourse of the 1970s and 1980s in Belfast or Derry

> you hear played out ... the old clamant sound-track of Romantic Ireland, the old ancestral myth of origin, a spiritual heroics ... expressive of the Hegelian notion of an inner essence or spirit which has lent itself to and become the justification for nothing less than a declaration of war. For at the heart of the conflict in the North ... is a political theology, the paradigms of which were laid down in Lady Morgan's originative literary stereotyping of a myth of Irishness.[13]

But of course Sydney Owenson did not create Irish stereotypes. The English had long been in that business. Rather, she sought to make the stereotypes more positive. In *The Wild Irish Girl*, the Irish are represented as loquacious, generous, passionate, courteous, and kind. And if on one level Owenson's novel perpetuates a dangerous typology of intrinsic national character, on another her text reveals the conditions under which such national codes of character are formed. Indeed, her narrative demonstrates that nations require myths of origin and that these myths can be violent in their exclusions. Thus, the construction of essential national identities depends on identifying insiders in relation to outsiders, not only outside the literal borders of a country but, as we have seen, inside as well.

Practised in this way, nationhood is a hereditary clique that relies on a degraded other. As Homi Bhabha describes the formation of national identities: 'the very fact that such identities depend constitutively on difference means that nations are forever haunted by their various definitional others. Hence, ... the nation's insatiable need to administer difference through violent acts of segregation, censorship, economic coercion, physical torture, police brutality.'[14] This list, of course, reads like a description of the English policy in Ireland under the Penal Laws, many of which were still in place during Owenson's lifetime. Irish Catholics were banned from living within the limits of incorporated towns; from holding public office, military, civil service, or teaching posts; from publishing newspapers or books; from buying land from Protestants or passing on estates

---

[13] 'Aesthetics, Politics, and Identity: Lady Morgan's *The Wild Irish Girl*', *Canadian Journal of Irish Studies*, 12 (1987), 8.

[14] *Nation and Narration* (London: Routledge, 1990), 5.

intact;[15] in short, from all the forms of bodily and emotional security that the enfranchised possess and the disenfranchised do not. What Owenson's novel so poignantly reveals is how easily a challenge to Ireland's role as England's definitional and degraded other could become a nationalism that required its own others. But while *The Wild Irish Girl* narrates this kind of nationalism, it also plays out other choices. By charting the progress of an English narrator who gives up his prejudices towards Ireland and the Gaelic Irish, Owenson suggests that difference might be loved rather than hated.

For Owenson's English narrator in *The Wild Irish Girl*, the Irish initially and predictably serve as degraded others. Horatio's prejudices are represented as those his own culture has taught him, for without ever having visited Ireland, he is certain of what he will find there: ferocity and barbarity. That he visits the country at all is a measure of his own dire straits: his father banishes him from London because, instead of attending to his training in law, he has embarrassed himself and the family with dissipated habits and gambling debts. Yet in his early objections to Ireland, Horatio's prejudices are represented as more complex than an aversion to an uncivilized culture. Rather, through contact with the English, the Irish have begun to lose their usefulness even as 'others'. They will not be, Horatio predicts, 'other' enough to interest him:

Had he banished me to the savage desolations of Siberia, my exile would have had some character; had he even transported me to a South-Sea Island, or thrown me into an Esquimaux hut, my new species of being would have been touched with some interest . . . But sent to a country against which I have a decided prejudice—which I suppose semi-barbarous, semi-civilized; has lost the strong and hardy features of savage life, without acquiring those graces which distinguish polished society—I shall neither participate in the poignant pleasure of awakened curiosity and acquired information, nor taste the least of those enjoyments which courted my acceptances in my native land. (p. 10)

Here Horatio reveals the dual psychological function of the colonial other to the colonizer: the other serves not only as a reminder of the colonizer's superiority but also as an exotic alternative to, and respite from, the dominant culture. Yet, ironically, Horatio reveals that the process of colonization, of transforming the other into the image of

---

[15] Noel Ignatiev, *How the Irish Became White* (New York: Routledge, 1995), 34.

the self, destroys the other's usefulness as an object of tourism. Indeed, historian E. J. Hobsbawm argues that, during this age of nation formation in the early nineteenth century, nationalities that posed no real threat to competitor nations were often valued for their exoticism and encouraged to be markedly different:

The small people, language and culture fitted into progress only insofar as it accepted subordinate status to some larger unit or retired from battle to become a repository of nostalgia and other sentiments—in short, accepted the status of old family furniture.[16]

But Sydney Owenson's novel does not present a people willing to be small or to accept the status of old family furniture. In fact, both English and Anglo-Irish readers found Owenson's portrait of Gaelic culture so compelling that officials in Dublin Castle feared the book could convince even wealthy Protestants in Ireland that their allegiance to England might be misplaced. Dublin publishers had recoiled from the manuscript, and even Phillips in London who had published Owenson's earlier novels and prided himself on his radical politics suspected the novel's 'sentiments' were 'too strongly opposed to the English interest in Ireland'.[17] In the preface to the 1836 edition of *The Wild Irish Girl* Owenson recalls the restive years in Ireland after the Union, which had, after all, been achieved by bribing an exclusively Anglo-Irish Parliament, and without the consent of the native Irish: 'At the moment *The Wild Irish Girl* appeared it was dangerous to write on Ireland, hazardous to praise her, and difficult to find a publisher for an Irish tale which had a political tendency.'[18] And yet, what Owenson's novel attempted, and, judging from the novel's popularity among English readers, succeeded in doing was to name English crimes of colonization in Ireland, present the native Irish as wholly unworthy of such treatment, and encourage a reconciliation modelled by a marriage. Indeed, like her contemporaries in Ireland and Scotland, Maria Edgeworth and Susan Ferrier, Sydney Owenson represents marriage between the English and the colonized other as a solution to the impasse of colonial relations.

By marrying Glorvina and Horatio, Owenson dramatically

[16] *Nations and Nationalism Since 1780*, 36.
[17] Qtd. in Campbell, *Lady Morgan*, 63.
[18] Ibid. 3.

undermines the essentialist definition of Irishness her novel appears to endorse. For the emphasis on pedigree that informs her representation of an Irish national identity is radically challenged by a marriage which will produce children of mixed English and Irish ancestry. That the love affair is forwarded through deception and disguise suggests that 'national' animosities are far from 'natural': with his ancestral baggage stowed, Horatio inspires the feelings of a lover in Glorvina and the love of a father in the Prince of Inismore. And Horatio's own national prejudices against Ireland and the Irish are no match for actual travel in the country and interaction with its people. Confronted with the Irish boatmen before he reaches the Irish coast, Horatio's jaundiced views quickly receive 'some mortal strokes'. By the time he gets to Dublin, he is commenting upon the 'warmth and cordiality of address' he finds among the Irish. Later, during his travel to the west, Irish peasants open their home to him and Horatio is filled with guilt: 'How did my heart smite me, while I received the cordial rites of hospitality from your hands, for the prejudices I had hitherto nurtured against your characters' (p. 30). This guilt deepens while Horatio stays at the Castle in Inismore: 'I wish *my* family had never possessed an acre of ground in this country, or possessed it on other terms' (p. 42).

As Horatio confronts his prejudices, Owenson's first-person narrative catalogues the psychological moves that make colonization possible. In order to assuage the guilt he feels while visiting the family at Inismore, a family deprived of their land by his own ancestors during the Cromwellian wars, one of their patriarchs murdered by one of his own, Horatio tries, through his half-knowledge of the family, to assume them savage and inferior so that he will feel less remorse over the wrongs done to them. The prince he fancies 'a ferocious savage', the princess 'a pedant and a romp', and the priest 'bigotted and illiberal'. These stereotypes, he admits, soothe his 'conscientious throes of feeling and compassion'. But his dreams predict the nature of his own ignorance and the direction the narrative will take in educating him. For he dreams Glorvina is a gorgon, and awakes to have his vision corrected by her actual face. Horatio must, of course, reclaim the violence of his own history and take back the negative projections his culture has encouraged him to displace.

Surrendering his preconceptions about the Irish at last, Horatio decides to do what Owenson clearly encouraged for her English readers—learn the Irish language and history, and judge Ireland and the Irish fairly. And as if to suggest that the process of coming to terms with Ireland is also the process of knowing himself, Horatio finally acknowledges his own otherness by describing himself as foreign, '*one* stranger, who is willing to offer up his national prejudices at the Altar of Truth' (p. 87). But for all the full-blown sentiment in her romantic narrative, Owenson does not sentimentalize the price paid for telling and hearing the truth. When Horatio and his father's identity are revealed at another altar, the marriage altar, Glorvina is faced with marriage to her family's murderers. Though hers is indeed a history to turn men and women to stone, she looks it in the face and accepts the alliance.[19] Thus, if Sydney Owenson's novel originates and predicts an Irish nationalism that perpetuates the violence from which it was born, it also suggests a possible solution: a violent forgiveness.

[19] For another reading of this marriage, see Julia Anne Miller's 'Acts of Union: Family Violence and National Courtship in Maria Edgeworth's *The Absentee* and Sydney Owenson's *The Wild Irish Girl*', in *Border Crossings: Irish Women Writers and National Identity* (Tuscaloosa, Ala.: University of Alabama Press, forthcoming).

NOTE ON THE TEXT

AFTER negotiations with rival publisher Joseph Johnson, Sydney Owenson sold *The Wild Irish Girl* to Richard Phillips for £300 in 1806. The novel was published that year with immediate popular success, running through nine editions in England and America during its first two years. Phillips published the first four British editions, and the first American edition was produced by Alsop, Brannan and Alsop in New York in 1807. In the same year, T. S. Manning of Philadelphia published the second and third American editions, while Richard Scott of New York and S. F. Bradford of Philadelphia were responsible for the fourth and fifth editions, respectively. A sixth American edition appeared in 1808 from J. Greenleaf of Boston. Longman of London published a fifth edition in 1813, and the novel was included among H. Colburn's Standard Novels in 1846 and 1850. An 1822 edition appeared in Philadelphia from J. Conrad, and S. Andrus & Son of Hartford published editions in 1850 and 1855. Haverty of New York produced editions in 1857 and 1867. After the publication of P. J. Kenedy's 1883 edition in New York, Owenson's novel did not appear again until Garland Publishers' reprint of Phillips's 1806 edition. In 1986, *The Wild Irish Girl* was included among Pandora's Mothers of the Novel series, and in 1995 a facsimile reprint of Phillips's third edition was published as part of Jonathan Wordsworth's Revolution and Romanticism series. This edition reproduces the text of the first edition, 1806 (which has a number of archaic spellings).

SELECT BIBLIOGRAPHY

Biography

Campbell, Mary, *Lady Morgan: The Life and Times of Sydney Owenson* (London: Pandora Press, 1988).

Dixon, W. Hepworth, and Jewsbury, Geraldine (eds.), *Lady Morgan's Memoirs: Autobiography, Diaries, Correspondence*, 2 vols. (London: W. H. Allen, 1862; revised, 1863).

Fitzpatrick, W. J., *Lady Morgan: Her Career, Literary and Personal* (London: C. J. Skeet, 1860).

Stevenson, Lionel, *The Wild Irish Girl: The Life of Sydney Owenson, Lady Morgan (1776–1859)* (New York: Russell & Russell, 1936; 1969).

Criticism

Andrews, Elmer, 'Aesthetics, Politics, and Identity: Lady Morgan's *The Wild Irish Girl*', *Canadian Journal of Irish Studies*, 12/2 (Dec. 1987), 7–19.

Atkinson, Colin B., and Atkinson, Jo, 'Sydney Owenson, Lady Morgan: Irish Patriot and First Professional Woman Writer', *Eire-Ireland*, 15 (Summer 1980), 60–90.

Dunne, Tom, 'Fiction as "the Best History of Nations": Lady Morgan's Irish Novels', in Tom Dunne (ed.), *The Writer as Witness: Literature as Historical Evidence* (Cork: Cork University Press, 1987), 133–59.

Ferris, Ina, 'Narrating Cultural Encounter: Lady Morgan and the Irish National Tale', *Nineteenth-Century Literature*, 51/3 (Dec. 1996), 287–303.

Flanagan, Thomas, *The Irish Novelists 1800–1850* (New York: Columbia, University Press, 1959).

Leerssen, J. Th., 'How the Wild Irish Girl Made Ireland Romantic', in C. C. Barfoot and Theo D'hean (eds.), *The Clash of Ireland: Literary Contrasts and Connections* (Amsterdam: Rodopi, 1989), 98–117.

Lew, Joseph W., 'Sydney Owenson and the Fate of the Empire', *Keats-Shelley Journal*, 39 (1990), 39–65.

Newcomer, James, *Lady Morgan the Novelist* (Lewisburg, Pa.: Bucknell University Press, 1990).

Tracy, Robert, 'Maria Edgeworth and Lady Morgan: Legality versus Legitimacy', *Nineteenth-Century Literature*, 40/1 (June 1985), 1–22.

Williams, Julia McElhattan, *Love Beyond the Pale: Sydney Owenson's The Wild Irish Girl, Maria Edgeworth's The Absentee, and the Boundaries of Colonial Power* (Boston: Northeastern University Press, 1991).

Irish History, Culture, and Politics

Cairns, David, and Richards, Shawn, *Writing Ireland: Colonialism, Nationalism and Culture* (Manchester: Manchester University Press, 1988).

Canny, Nicholas, *Kingdom and Colony: Ireland in the Atlantic World, 1560–1800* (Baltimore: Johns Hopkins University Press, 1988).

Chuilleanain, Eilean Ni, *Irish Women: Women and Achievement* (Dublin: Arlen House, 1985).

Foley, Timothy P., and Ryder, Sean (eds.), *Ideology and Ireland in the Nineteenth Century* (Dublin: Four Courts Press, 1998).

Hadfield, Andrew, and McVeagh, John, *Strangers to that Land: British Perceptions of Ireland from the Renaissance to the Famine* (Gerrards Cross: Colin Smythe, 1994).

Kelly, Gary, *Women, Writing and Revolution, 1790–1827* (Oxford: Clarendon Press, 1993).

Kelly, James, 'The Origins of the Act of Union: An Examination of Unionist Opinion in Britain and Ireland, 1650–1800', *Irish Historical Studies*, 25 (1987), 236–63.

Lloyd, T. O., *The British Empire, 1558–1983* (Oxford: Oxford University Press, 1984).

McCormack, W. J., *Ascendancy and Tradition in Anglo-Irish Literary History from 1789 to 1939* (Oxford: Clarendon Press, 1985).

MacCurtain, Margaret, and O Corrain, Donncha, *Women in Irish Society: The Historical Dimension* (Westport, Conn.: Greenwood Press, 1979).

McDowell, R. B., 'Ireland in 1800', in T. W. Moody and W. E. Vaughan (eds.), *A New History of Ireland*, iv. *Eighteenth-Century Ireland, 1691–1800* (Oxford: Clarendon Press, 1986), 657–710.

Orel, Harold (ed.), *Irish History and Culture* (Lawrence, Kan.: University Press of Kansas, 1976).

Weekes, Ann Owens, *Irish Women Writers: An Uncharted Tradition* (Lexington, Ky.: University Press of Kentucky, 1990).

A CHRONOLOGY OF SYDNEY OWENSON

1776   Born on Christmas Day, first child of the Irish actor Robert Owenson and Jane Hill. Because Sydney Owenson was secretive about her age, this date has sometimes been in doubt. American Revolution begins.

1782   Parliament in Dublin seeks and is granted independence from England, making Ireland a separate kingdom sharing a monarch with England.

1789   Death of Sydney's mother. French Revolution begins.

1789–92 Sydney and her sister Olivia attend Mme Terson's Academy in Clontarf followed by Mrs Anderson's finishing school in Earl Street, Dublin.

1791   Founding of United Irishmen, a revolutionary group seeking complete independence from England.

1794   The Owensons spend time in Kilkenny, where Robert establishes a theatre.

1798   Armed rising led by Wolfe Tone and the United Irishmen with aid from the French; the revolt fails.

1800   Visiting her father's cousins in Sligo, Sydney meets Myles McDermott of Coolavin, on whom Glorvina's father in *The Wild Irish Girl* is based. Act of Union dissolves Irish Parliament.

1801   *Poems, Dedicated by permission to the Countess of Moira*. Sydney becomes governess with the Featherstonehaugh family, Bracklin Castle, County Westmeath, and later with the Crawford family, Fort William, County Tipperary.

1802   *St Clair; or, The Heiress of Desmond*, Sydney's first novel, inspired by Goethe's *Sorrows of Young Werther*.

1803   Robert Emmet's plot to seize Dublin Castle and lead a revolution fails.

1805   *The Novice of Saint Dominick*, set in sixteenth-century France, anticipates the historical fiction of Sir Walter Scott. *Twelve Original Hibernian Melodies*, a collection of Irish songs translated from Gaelic.

1806   *The Wild Irish Girl: A National Tale* launches Sydney as a literary celebrity.

1806–7 Sydney visits Croftons in Connaught.

1807   *The First Attempt, or Whim of a Moment*, a comic opera set in Spain in which Sydney's father makes his last stage appearance. *The Lay of an Irish Harp: or, Metrical Fragments; Patriotic Sketches of Ireland*, written in Connaught and addressing political and social problems in Ireland.

1808   Sydney visits London where she is lionized as the new name in Irish writing.

1809   *Woman, or, Ida of Athens*, a novel portraying Greek, Irish, and women's political oppression. Sydney takes up residence with the Marquis and the Marchioness of Abercorn at Baron's Court, County Tyrone, where she meets Charles Morgan, an Englishman and her patrons' physician.

1810   Sydney's portrait is painted by Sir Thomas Lawrence during a visit to London.

1811   *The Missionary: An Indian Tale*, a novel admired by Percy Bysshe Shelley. Charles Morgan is knighted.

1812   Sydney marries Sir Charles Morgan. Robert Owenson, Sydney's father, dies. The Morgans give up residence with the Abercorns.

1813   The Morgans take up residence at 35 Kildare Street, Dublin.

1814   *O'Donnel, A National Tale*, is highly successful: the first British novel to portray a governess as a romantic heroine and an Irish Catholic gentleman as hero.

1815–16   The Morgans sent to France by Sydney's publisher, Henry Colburn, after Napoleon's defeat at Waterloo.

1817   *France*, a controversial travel book promoting pro-Revolutionary ideas.

1818   *Florence Macarthy: An Irish Tale* portraying an Irishwoman who supports herself as a novelist.

1819–20   The Morgans visit France and Italy.

1821   *Italy*, a book whose radical politics drew praise from Byron and censure from the King of Sardinia, the Emperor of Austria, and the Pope.

1822   *The Mohawks: A Satirical Poem* (with Sir Charles Morgan).

1823   Daniel O'Connell forms the Catholic Associate of Ireland to campaign for Catholic emancipation.

1824   The Morgans visit England. *The Life and Times of Salvator Rosa*, a biography of an Italian painter Sydney much admired.

1825   *Absenteeism*, an essay on Ireland.

1827   *The O'Briens and the O'Flahertys: A National Tale*, Sydney's least optimistic novel about Ireland.

1829   *The Book of the Boudoir*, a collection of autobiographical sketches. The Morgans visit the Low Countries and France. Catholic emancipation in Ireland.

1830   *France in 1829–30.*

1832   The Morgans visit England.

1833   *Dramatic Scenes from Real Life*, set in Ireland.

1835   *The Princess, or, The Beguine*, the last novel.

1837   Sydney becomes the first woman to receive a literary pension from the British government, £300 a year. Suffering disillusionment over events in Ireland, the Morgans move to Belgravia in London.

1838   *Historic Sketches.*

1839   *Woman and Her Master*, a critique of women's treatment through the Middle Ages, planned as the first in a series on women's history.

1841   The Morgans visit Germany. *The Book Without a Name*, collected essays written with her husband.

1843   Sir Charles Morgan dies.

1845–51 Potato famine; with mass starvation and emigration, the population in Ireland falls from 8 to 6.6 million.

1858   Founding of Fenian Brotherhood, the revolutionary organization from which grew the IRB and IRA.

1859   (16 April) Sydney Owenson, Lady Morgan, dies. *Passages from My Autobiography.*

1862   *Lady Morgan's Memoirs: Autobiography, Diaries, Correspondence.*

THE WILD IRISH GIRL

A National Tale

'Questa gente benche mostra selvagea
E pur gli monte la contrada accierba
Nondimeno l'e dolcie ad cui l'assagia.'

'This race of men, tho' savage they may seem,
The country, too, with many a mountain rough,
Yet are they sweet to him who tries and tastes them.'

Fazio Delli Uberti's Travels through Ireland
in the 14th Century*

INTRODUCTORY LETTERS

THE EARL OF M——

TO THE HON. HORATIO M——, KING'S BENCH

Castle M——, Leicestershire,
Feb. ——, 17——

If there are certain circumstances under which a fond father can address an imprisoned son, without suffering the bitterest heart-rendings of paternal agony, such are not those under which I now address you. To sustain the loss of the most precious of all human rights, and forfeit our liberty at the shrine of virtue, in defence of our country abroad, or of our public integrity and principles at home, brings to the heart of the sufferer's dearest sympathising friend a soothing solace, almost concomitant to the poignancy of its afflictions, and leaves the decision difficult, whether in the scale of human feelings, triumphant pride or affectionate regret preponderate.

'I would not,' said the old Earl of Ormond, 'give up my dead son for twenty living ones.' Oh! how I envy such a father the possession, and even the *loss* of such a child: with what eagerness my heart rushes back to that period when *I* too triumphed in my son,—when I beheld him glowing in all the unadulterated virtues of the happiest nature, flushed with the proud consciousness of superior genius, refined by a taste intuitively elegant, and warmed by an enthusiasm constitutionally ardent; his character indeed tinctured with the bright colouring of romantic eccentricity, but marked by the indelible traces of innate rectitude, and ennobled by the purest principles of native generosity, the proudest sense of inviolable honour, I beheld him rush eagerly on life, enamoured of its seeming good, incredulous of its latent evils, till fatally fascinated by the magic spell of the former, he fell an early victim to the successful lures of the latter. The growing influence of his passions kept pace with the expansion of his mind, and the moral powers of the *man* of *genius*, gave way to the overwhelming propensities of the *man* of *pleasure*. Yet in the midst of these exotic vices (for as such even yet I would consider them), he continued at once the object of my parental partiality and anxious solicitude; I admired while I condemned, I pitied while I reproved. * * * * * * * * * * * * * *

The rights of primogeniture, and the mild and prudent cast of your brother's character, left me no cares either for his worldly interest or moral welfare: born to titled affluence, his destination in life was ascertained previous to his entrance on its chequered scene; and equally free from passions to mislead, or talents to stimulate, he promised to his father that series of temperate satisfaction which, if unillumined by those coruscations* *your* superior and promising genius flashed on the parental heart, could not prepare for its sanguine feelings that mortal disappointment with which *you* have destroyed all its hopes. On the recent death of my father I found myself possessed of a very large but encumbered property: it was requisite I should make the same establishment for my eldest son, that my father had made for me; while I was conscious that my youngest was in some degree to stand indebted to his own exertions, for independence as well as elevation in life.

You may recollect that during your first college vacation, we conversed on the subject of that liberal profession I had chosen for you, and you agreed with me, that it was congenial to your powers, and not inimical to your taste; while the part I was anxious you should take in the legislation of your country, seemed at once to rouse and gratify your ambition; but the pure flame of laudable emulation was soon extinguished in the destructive atmosphere of pleasure, and while *I* beheld you, in the visionary hopes of my parental ambition, invested with the crimson robe of legal dignity, or shining brightly conspicuous in the splendid galaxy of senatorial luminaries, *you* were idly presiding as the high priest of libertinism at the nocturnal orgies of vitiated dissipation, or indolently lingering out your life in elegant but unprofitable pursuits.

It were as vain as impossible to trace you through every degree of error on the scale of folly and imprudence, and such a repetition would be more heart-wounding to me than painful to you, were it even made under the most extenuating bias of parental fondness.

I have only to add, that though already greatly distressed by the liquidation of your debts, at a time when I am singularly circumstanced with respect to pecuniary resources, I will make a struggle to free you from the chains of this your present *Iron*-hearted creditor, though the retrenchment of my *own* expences, and my temporary retreat to the solitude of my Irish estate, must be the result; provided that by this sacrifice I purchase your acquiescence to my wishes respecting the destiny of your future life, and an unreserved abjuration of the follies which have governed your past.

Your etc. etc.

M——

TO THE EARL OF M——

My Lord,

Suffer me, in the fulness of my heart, and in the language of one prodigal and penitent as myself, to say, 'I have sinned against Heaven and thee, and am no longer worthy to be called thy son.' Abandon me then, I beseech you, as such; deliver me up to the destiny that involves me, to the complicated tissue of errors and follies I have so industriously woven with my own hands; for though I am equal to sustain the judgment my own vices have drawn down on me, I cannot support the cruel mercy with which your goodness endeavours to avert its weight.

Among the numerous catalogue of my faults, a sordid selfishness finds no place. Yet I should deservedly incur its imputation, were I to accept of freedom on such terms as you are so generous to offer. No, my Lord, continue to adorn that high and polished circle in which you are so eminently calculated to move; nor think so lowly of one who, with all his faults, is *your son*, as to believe him ready to purchase *his* liberty at the expence of *your* banishment from your native country.

I am, etc. etc.

H.M.

King's Bench.

TO THE HON. HORATIO M——

An act to which the exaggeration of *your* feelings gives the epithet of banishment, I shall consider as a voluntary sequestration from scenes of which I am weary, to scenes which, though thrice visited, still preserve the poignant charms of novelty and interest. Your hasty and undigested answer to my letter (written in the prompt emotion of the moment, ere the probable consequence of a romantic rejection to an offer not unreflectingly made, could be duly weighed or coolly examined), convinces me experience has contributed little to the modification of your feelings, or the prudent regulation of your conduct. It is this promptitude of feeling, this contempt of prudence, that formed the predisposing cause of your errors and your follies. Dazzled by the brilliant glare of the splendid virtues, you saw not, you would not see, that prudence was among the first of moral excellencies; the director, the regulator, the standard of them all;— that it is in fact the corrective of virtue herself; for even *virtue*, like the *sun*, has her *solstice*, beyond which she ought not to move.

If you would retribute what you seem to lament, and unite restitution to penitence, leave this country for a short time, and abandon with the haunts of your former blameable pursuits, those associates who were at once the cause and punishment of your errors. I myself will become your partner in exile, for it is to my estate in Ireland I *banish* you for the summer. You have already got through the 'first rough brakes' of your profession: as you can now serve the last term of this season, I see no cause why *Coke upon Lyttelton* cannot be as well studied amidst the wild seclusion of Connaught* scenery, and on the solitary shores of the 'steep Atlantic,' as in the busy bustling precincts of the Temple.*

I have only to add, that I shall expect your undivided attention will be given up to your professional studies; that you will for a short interval resign the fascinating pursuits of polite literature and belles lettres, from which even the syren spell of pleasure could not tear you, and which snatched from vice many of those hours I believed devoted to more serious studies. I know you will find it no less difficult to resign the elegant theories of your favourite *Lavater*,* for the dry facts of law reports, than to exchange your duodecimo* editions of the amatory poets for heavy tomes of cold legal disquisitions; but happiness is to be purchased, and labour is the price; fame and independence are the result of talent united to great exertion, and the elegant enjoyments of literary leisure are never so keenly relished as when tasted under the shade of that flourishing laurel which our own efforts have reared to mature perfection. Farewell! my agent has orders respecting the arrangement of your affairs. You must excuse the procrastination of our interview till we meet in Ireland, which I fear will not be so immediate as my wishes would incline. I shall write to my banker in Dublin to replenish your purse on your arrival in Ireland, and to my Connaught steward, to prepare for your reception at M—— house. Write to me by return.

Once more, farewell!

M——

TO THE EARL OF M——

My Lord,

He who agonized on the bed of Procrostus* reposed on a couch of down, compared to the sufferings of him who, in the heart he has stabbed, beholds the pulse of generous affection still beating with an invariable throb for the being who has inflicted the wound.

I shall offer you no thanks, my Lord, for the generosity of your conduct, nor any extenuation for the errors of mine.

The gratitude the one has given birth to—the remorse which the other has awakened, bid equal defiance to expression. I have only (fearfully) to hope, that you will not deny my almost forfeited claim to the title of your son.

H.M.

TO J.D. ESQ. M.P.

Holyhead

We are told in the splendid Apocrypha of ancient Irish fable, that when one of the learned was missing on the Continent of Europe, it was proverbially said,

'*Amandatus est ad disciplinum in Hibernia.*'*

But I cannot recollect that in its fabulous or veracious history, Ireland was ever the mart of voluntary exile to the man of pleasure; so that when you and the rest of my precious associates miss the track of my footsteps in the oft-trod path of dissipation, you will never think of tracing its pressure to the wildest of the Irish shores, and exclaim, '*Amandatus est ad,*' etc. etc. etc.

However, I am so far advanced in the land of *Druidism*,* on my way to the 'Island of Saints,' while you, in the emporium of the world, are drinking from the cup of conjugal love a temporary oblivion to your past sins and wickedness, and revelling in the first golden dreams of matrimonial illusion.

I suppose an account of my high crimes and misdemeanours, banishment, etc. etc. have already reached your ears; but while my brethren in transportation are offering up their wishes and their hopes on the shore, to the unpropitious god of winds, indulge me in the garrulity of egotism, and suffer me to correct the overcharged picture of that arch caricature *report*, by giving you a correct *ebauche** of the recent circumstances of my useless life.

When I gave you convoy as far as Dover on your way to France, I returned to London, to

> —— 'Surfeit on the same
> and yawn my joys——'

And was again soon plunged in that dreadful vacillation of mind from which your society and conversation had so lately redeemed me.

Vibrating between an innate propensity to *right*, and an habitual adherence to *wrong*; sick of pursuits I was too indolent to relinquish, and linked to vice, yet still enamoured of virtue; weary of the useless, joyless inanity of my existence, yet without energy, without power to regenerate my worthless being; daily losing ground in the minds of the inestimable few who were still interested for my welfare; nor compensating for the loss, by the gratification of any one feeling in my own heart, and held up as an object of fashionable popularity for sustaining that character, which of all others I most despised; my taste impoverished by a vicious indulgence, my senses palled by repletion, my heart chill and unawakened, every appetite depraved and pampered into satiety, I fled from myself, as the object of my own utter contempt and detestation, and found a transient pleasurable inebriety in the well-practised blandishments of Lady C——.

You who alone know me, who alone have *openly* condemned, and *secretly* esteemed me, you who have wisely culled the blossom of pleasure, while I have sucked its poison, know that I am rather a *mechant par air*,* than from any irresistible propensity to indiscriminate libertinism. In fact, the *original sin* of my nature militates against the hackneyed modes of hackneyed licentiousness; for I am too profound a voluptuary to feel any exquisite gratification from such gross pursuits as the '*swinish multitude*' of fashion ennoble with that name so little understood, *pleasure*. Misled in my earliest youth by 'passion's meteor ray,' even then, my heart called (but called in vain), for a thousand delicious refinements to give poignancy to the mere transient impulse of sense.

Oh! my dear friend, if in that sunny season of existence when the ardours of youth nourish in our bosom a thousand indescribable emotions of tenderness and love, it had been *my* fortunate destiny to have met with a being, who—but this is an idle regret, perhaps an idle supposition;—the moment of ardent susceptibility is over, when woman becomes the sole spell which lures us to good or ill, and when her omnipotence, according to the bias of her own nature, and the organization of those feelings on which it operates, determines in a certain degree our destiny through life—leads the mind through the medium of the heart to the noblest pursuits, or seduces it through the medium of the passions to the basest career.

That I became the dupe of Lady C——, and her artful predecessor, arose from the want of that 'something still unpossessed,' to fill my life's dreadful void. I sensibly felt the want of an object to interest my feelings, and laboured under that dreadful interregnum of the heart, reason and ambition; which leaves the craving passions open to every invader. Lady C—— perceived the situation of my mind, and—but spare me the detail of a connexion which even in memory, produces a *nausea* of every sense and feeling. Suffice it to say, that equally the victim of the husband's villany as the wife's artifice, I stifled on its birth a threatened prosecution, by giving my bond for a sum I was unable to liquidate: it was given as for a gambling debt, but my father, who had long suspected, and endeavoured to break this fatal connexion, guessed at the truth, and suffered me to become a guest (*mal voluntaire**) in the King's Bench.* This unusual severity on his part, lessened not on mine the sense of his indulgence to my former boundless extravagance, and I determined to remain a prisoner for life, rather than owe my liberty to a new imposition on his tenderness, by such solicitings as have hitherto been invariably crowned with success, though answered with reprehension.

I had been already six weeks a prisoner, deserted by those gay moths that had fluttered round the beam of my transient prosperity; delivered up to all the maddening meditation of remorse, when I received a letter from my father (then with my brother in Leicestershire), couched in his usual terms of reprehension, and intervals of tenderness; ascertaining every error with judicial exactitude, and associating every fault with some ideal excellence of parental creation, alternately the father and the judge; and as you once said, when I accused him of partiality to his eldest born, 'talking *best* of Edward, but *most* of me.'

In a word, he has behaved like an Angel! So well, that by Heavens! I can scarcely bear to think of it. A spurious half-bred generosity—a little tincture of illiberality on his side, would have been Balm of Gilead* to my wounded conscience; but with unqualified goodness he has paid all my debts, supplied my purse beyond my wants, and only asks in return, that I will retire for a few months to Ireland, and this I believe merely to wean me from the presence of an object which he falsely believes still hangs about my heart with no moderate influence.

And yet I wish his mercy had flowed in any other channel, even though more confined and less liberal.

Had he banished me to the savage desolations of Siberia, my exile would have had some character; had he even transported me to a South-Sea Island, or thrown me into an Esquimaux hut, my new species of being would have been touched with some interest; for in fact, the present relaxed state of my intellectual system requires some strong transition of place, circumstance, and manners, to wind it up to its native tone, to rouse it to energy, or awaken it to exertion.

But sent to a country against which I have a decided prejudice— which I suppose semi-barbarous, semi-civilized; has lost the strong and hardy features of savage life, without acquiring those graces which distinguish polished society—I shall neither participate in the poignant pleasure of awakened curiosity and acquired information, nor taste the least of those enjoyments which courted my acceptances in my native land. Enjoyments did I say! And were they indeed enjoyments? How readily the mind adopts the phraseology of habit, when the sentiment it once clothed no longer exists. Would that my past pursuits wore even in *recollection*, the aspect of enjoyments. But even my memory has lost its character of energy, and the past, like the present, appears one unvaried scene of chill and vapid existence.

No sweet point of reflection seizes on the recollective powers. No actual joy woos my heart's participation, and no prospect of future felicity glows on the distant vista of life, or awakens the quick throb of hope and expectation; all is cold, sullen, and dreary.

Laval seems to entertain no less prejudice against this country than his master, he has therefore begged leave of absence until my father comes over. Pray have the goodness to send me by him a box of Italian crayons, and a good thermometer; for I must have something to relieve the *tedium vitæ** of my exiled days; and in my articles of stipulation with my father, chemistry and belles lettres are *specially* prohibited. It was a useless prohibition, for Heaven knows chemistry would have been the last study I should have flown to in my present state of mind. For how can he look minutely into the intimate structure of things, and resolve them into their simple and elementary substance, whose own disordered mind is incapable of analyzing the passions by which it is agitated, of ascertaining the reciprocal relation of its incoherent ideas, or combining them in different proportions (from those in which they were united by chance), in order to join a new and useful compound for the benefit of future life? As for belles lettres! so blunted are all those powers once so

> 'Active and strong, and feelingly alive
> To each fine impulse,'

that not *one* '*pensèe couleur de rose*'* lingers on the surface of my faded imagination, and I should turn with as much apathy from the sentimental sorcery of *Rousseau*,* as from the voluminous verbosity of an high German doctor;* yawn over 'the Pleasures of Memory,'* and run the risk of falling fast asleep with the brilliant *Madame de Sevigne** in my hand. So send me a FAHRENHEIT, that I may bend the few coldly mechanical powers left me, to ascertain the temperature of my wild western *territories*, and expect my letters from thence to be only filled with the summary results of meteoric instruments, and synoptical views of common phenomena.

Adieu,

H.M.

THE WILD IRISH GIRL

LETTER I

TO J.D. ESQ. M.P.

Dublin, March —— , *17* ——

I remember, when I was a boy, meeting somewhere with the quaintly written travels of *Moryson** through Ireland, and being particularly struck with his assertion, that so late as the days of Elizabeth, an Irish chieftain and his family were frequently seen seated round their domestic fire in a state of perfect nudity. This singular anecdote (so illustrative of the barbarity of the Irish at a period when civilization had made such a wonderful progress even in its sister countries), fastened so strongly on my boyish imagination, that whenever the *Irish* were mentioned in my presence, an *Esquimaux* group circling round the fire which was to dress a dinner, or broil an enemy, was the image which presented itself to my mind; and in this trivial source, I believe, originated that early formed opinion of Irish ferocity, which has since been nurtured into a *confirmed prejudice*. So true it is, that almost all the erroneous principles which influence our maturer being, are to be traced to some fatal association of ideas received and formed in early life. But whatever may be the *cause*, I feel the strongest objection to becoming a resident in the remote part of a country which is still shaken by the convulsions of an anarchical spirit; where for a series of ages the olive of peace has not been suffered to shoot forth *one* sweet blossom of national concord, which the sword of civil dissention has not cropt almost in the germ; and the natural character of whose factious sons, as we are still taught to believe, is turbulent, faithless, intemperate, and cruel; formerly destitute of arts, letters, or civilization, and still but slowly submitting to their salutary and ennobling influence.

To confess the truth, I had so far suffered prejudice to get the start of unbiassed liberality, that I had almost assigned to these rude people scenes appropriately barbarous; and never was more pleasantly astonished, than when the morning's dawn gave to my view one of the most splendid spectacles in the scene of picturesque creation I had ever beheld, or indeed ever conceived; the bay of Dublin.

A foreigner on board the packet, compared the view to that which the bay of Naples affords: I cannot judge of the justness of the comparison, though I am told one very general and common-place; but if the scenic beauties of the Irish bay are exceeded by those of the Neapolitan, my fancy falls short in a just conception of its charms. The springing up of a contrary wind kept us for a considerable time beating about this enchanting coast: the weather suddenly changed, the rain poured in torrents, a storm arose, and the beautiful prospect which had fascinated our gaze, vanished in mists of impenetrable obscurity.

As we had the mail on board, a boat was sent out to receive it, the oars of which were plied by six men, whose statures, limbs, and features, declared them the lingering progeny of the once formidable race of Irish giants. Bare-headed, they 'bided the pelting of the pitiless storm,' with no other barrier to its fury, than what tattered check trowsers, and shirts open at the neck, and tucked above the elbows afforded; and which, thus disposed, betrayed the sinewy contexture of forms, which might have individually afforded a model to sculpture, for the colossal statue of an Hercules, under all the different aspects of strength and exertion.[1]

A few of the passengers proposing to venture in the boat, I listlessly followed, and found myself seated by one of these sea monsters, who in an accent and voice that made me startle, addressed me in English at least as pure and correct as a Thames boatman would use; and with so much courtesy, cheerfulness, and respect, that I was at a loss how to reconcile such civilization of manner to such ferocity of appearance; while his companions, as they stemmed the mountainous waves, or plied their heavy oars, displayed such a vein of low humour and quaint drollery, and in a language so curiously expressive and original, that no longer able to suppress my surprize, I betrayed it to a gentleman who sat near me, and by whom I was assured that this species of colloquial wit was peculiar to the lower classes of the Irish, who borrowed much of their curious phraseology from the peculiar idiom of their own tongue, and the cheeriness of

[1] This little marine sketch is by no means a fancy picture; it was actually copied from the life, in the summer of 1805.

manner from the native exility of their temperament; 'and as for their courteousness,' he continued, 'you will find them on a further intercourse, civil even to *adulation*, as long as you treat them with apparent kindness, but an opposite conduct will prove their manner proportionably uncivilized.'

'It is very excusable,' said I, 'they are of a class in society to which the modification of the feelings are unknown, and to be sensibly alive to *kindness or to unkindness*, is, in my opinion, a noble trait in the national character of an unsophisticated people.'

While we spoke, we landed, and for the something like pleasurable emotion, which the first on my list of Irish acquaintance produced in my mind, I distributed among these 'sons of the waves' more silver than I believe they expected. Had I bestowed a principality on an Englishman of the same rank, he would have been less lavish of the *eloquence* of gratitude on his benefactor, though he might equally have felt the *sentiment.*—So much for my voyage *across* the *Channel*!

This city is to London like a small temple of the Ionic order, whose proportions are delicate, whose character is elegance, compared to a vast palace whose Corinthian pillars* at once denote strength and magnificence.

The wonderous extent of London excites our amazement; the compact uniformity of Dublin our admiration. But as dispersion is less within the *coup-d'œil** of observance, than aggregation, the small, but harmonious features of Dublin seize at once on the eye, while the scattered but splendid traits of London, excite a less immediate and more progressive admiration, which is often lost in the intervals that occur between those objects which are calculated to excite it.

In London, the miserable shop of a gin seller, and the magnificent palace of a Duke, alternately create disgust, or awaken approbation.

In Dublin the buildings are not arranged upon such democratic principles. The plebeian hut offers no foil to the patrician edifice, while their splendid and beautiful public structures are so closely connected, as with *some* degree of policy to strike *at once* upon the eye in the happiest combination.[1]

In other respects this city appears to me to be the miniature copy

---

[1] Although in one point of view, there may be a policy in this close association of splendid objects, yet it is a circumstance of general and just condemnation to all strangers who are not confined to a *partial* survey of the city.

of our imperial original, though minutely imitative in show and glare. Something less observant of life's prime luxuries, order and cleanliness, there is a certain class of wretches who haunt the streets of Dublin, so emblematic of vice, poverty, idleness, and filth, that disgust and pity frequently succeed in the minds of the stranger to sentiments of pleasure, surprize, and admiration. For the origin of this evil, I must refer you to the supreme police of the city; but whatever may be the cause, the effects (to an Englishman especially) are dreadful and disgusting beyond all expression.

Although my father has a large connexion here, yet he only gave me a letter to his banker, who has forced me to make his house my home for the few days I shall remain in Dublin, and whose cordiality and kindness sanctions all that has ever been circulated of Irish hospitality.

In the present state of my feelings, however, a party on the banks of the *Ohio*, with a tribe of Indian hunters, would be more consonant to my inclinations than the refined pleasures of the most polished circles in the world. Yet these warm-hearted people, who find in the name of stranger, an irresistible lure to every kind attention, will force me to be happy in despite of myself, and overwhelm me with invitations, some of which it is impossible to resist. My prejudices have received some mortal strokes, when I perceived that the natives of this barbarous country have got goal for goal with us, in every elegant refinement of life and manners; the only difference I can perceive between a London and a Dublin *rout* is, that here, even amongst the first class, there is a warmth and cordiality of address, which, though perhaps not more sincere than the cold formality of British ceremony, is certainly more fascinating.[1]

It is not, however, in Dublin I shall expect to find the tone of national character and manner; in the first circles of all great cities (as in courts), the native features of national character are softened into general uniformity, and the genuine feelings of nature are suppressed or exchanged for a political compliance with the reigning modes and customs, which hold their tenure from the sanction and example of the seat of government. Before I close this, I must make

---

[1] 'Every unprejudiced traveller who visits them (the Irish), will be as much pleased with their cheerfulness as obliged by their hospitality; and will find them a brave, polite, and liberal people.'—*Philosophical Survey through Ireland by* Mr YOUNG.*

one observation, which I think will speak more than volumes for the refinement of these people.

During my short residence here, I have been forced, in the true spirit of Irish dissipation, into three parties of a night; and I have upon these occasions observed, that the most courted objects of popular attention, were those whose talents alone endowed them with distinction. Besides amateurs, I have met with many professional persons, whom I knew in London as public characters, and who are here incorporated in the first and most brilliant circles, appearing to feel no other inequality, than what their own superiority of genius confers.

I leave Dublin to-morrow for M—— house. It is situated in the county of ——, on the north-west coast of Connaught, which I am told is the classic ground of Ireland. The native Irish, pursued by religious and political bigotry, made it the asylum of their sufferings, and were separated by a provincial barrier from an intercourse with the rest of Ireland, until after the Restoration;* so I shall have a fair opportunity of beholding the Irish character in all its *primeval* ferocity.

Direct your next to Bally——, which I find is the nearest post town to my *Kamscatkan palace*; where, with no other society than that of Blackstone* and Co. I shall lead such a life of animal existence, as PRIOR gives to his Contented Couple—

> 'They ate and drank, and slept—what then?
> Why, slept and drank, and ate again.'—

Adieu,

H.M.

LETTER II

TO J.D. ESQ. M.P.

M—— House

In the various modes of penance invented by the various *penance mongers* of pious austerity, did you ever hear the travelling in an *Irish post-chaise** enumerated as a punishment, which by far exceeds horse-hair shirts and voluntary flagellation? My first day's journey from Dublin being as wet a one as this moist climate and capricious season ever produced, my berlin* answered all the purposes of a *shower bath*, while the ventilating principles on which the windows were constructed, gave me all the benefit to be derived from the *breathy* influence of the four cardinal points.

Unable any longer to sit tamely enduring the '*penalty of Adam, the season's change*,' or to sustain any longer the 'hair-breadth scapes,' which the most dismantled of vehicles afforded me, together with delays and stoppages of every species to be found in the catalogue of procrastination and mischance, I took my seat in a mail coach which I met at my third stage, and which was going to a town within twenty miles of Bally——. These twenty miles, by far the most agreeable of my journey, I performed as we once (in days of boyish errantry) accomplished a tour of Wales—on foot.

I had previously sent my baggage, and was happily unincumbered with a servant, for the fastidious delicacy of Monsieur Laval would never have been adequate to the fatigues of a pedestrian tour through a country wild and mountainous as his own native *Savoy*.* But to me every difficulty was an effort of some good *genius* chacing the dæmon of lethargy from the usurpations of my mind's empire. Every obstacle that called for exertion was a temporary revival of latent energy; and every unforced effort worth an age of indolent indulgence.

To him who derives gratification from the embellished labours of art, rather than the simple but sublime operations of nature, *Irish* scenery will afford little interest; but the bold features of its varying landscape, the stupendous attitude of its 'cloud-capt' mountains, the impervious gloom of its deep embosomed glens, the savage desolation of its uncultivated heaths, and boundless bogs, with those rich veins of a picturesque champagne, thrown at intervals into gay expansion by the hand of nature, awaken in the mind of the poetic or pictoral traveller, all the pleasures of tasteful enjoyment, all the sublime emotions of a rapt imagination. And if the glowing fancy of Claude Loraine would have dwelt enraptured on the paradisial charms of English landscape, the superior genius of Salvator Rosa* would have reposed its eagle wing amidst those scenes of mysterious sublimity, with which the wildly magnificent landscape of Ireland abounds. But the liberality of nature appears to me to be here but frugally assisted by the donations of art. Here *agriculture* appears in the least felicitous of her aspects. The rich treasures of Ceres* seldom wave their golden heads over the earth's fertile bosom; the verdant drapery of young plantation rarely skreens out the coarser features of a rigid soil, the cheerless aspect of a gloomy bog; while the unvaried surface of the perpetual pasturage which satisfies the eye of the interested grazier, disappoints the glance of the tasteful spectator.

Within twenty miles of Bally—— I was literally dropt by the stage at the foot of a mountain, to which your native *Wrekin* is but an hillock. The dawn was just risen, and flung its grey and reserved tints on a scene of which the mountainous region of Capel Cerig will give you the most adequate idea.

Mountain rising over mountain, swelled like an amphitheatre to those clouds which, faintly tinged with the sun's prelusive beams, and rising from the earthly summits where they had reposed, incorporated with the kindling æther of a purer atmosphere.

All was silent and solitary—a tranquillity tinged with terror, a sort of 'delightful horror,' breathed on every side.—I was alone, and felt like the presiding genius of desolation!

As I had previously learned my route, after a few minute's contemplation of the scene before me, I pursued my solitary ramble along a steep and trackless path, which wound gradually down towards a great lake, an almost miniature sea, that lay embosomed amidst those stupendous heights whose rugged forms, now bare, desolate, and barren, now clothed with yellow furze, and creeping underwood, or crowned with mistic forests, appeared towering above my head in endless variety. The progress of the sun convinced me that *mine* must have been slow, as it was perpetually interrupted by pauses of curiosity and admiration, and by long and many lapses of thoughtful reverie; and fearing that I had lost my way (as I had not yet caught a view of the village, in which, seven miles distant from the spot where I had left the stage, I was assured I should find an excellent breakfast), I ascended that part of the mountain where, on one of its vivid points, a something like a human habitation hung suspended, and where I hoped to obtain a *carte du pays*:* the exterior of this *hut*, or *cabin*, as it is called, like the few I had seen which were not built of mud, resembled in one instance the magic palace of Chaucer, and was erected with loose stones,

'Which, cunningly, were without mortar laid,'

thinly thatched with straw; an aperture in the roof served rather to
admit the air than *emit* the smoke, a circumstance to which the
wretched inhabitants of those wretched hovels seem so perfectly
naturalized, that they live in a constant state of fumigation; and a
fracture in the side wall (meant I suppose as a substitute for a casement) was stuffed with straw, while the door, off its hinges, was laid
across the threshold, as a barrier to a little crying boy, who sitting
within, bemoaned his captivity in a tone of voice not quite so mellifluous as that which Mons. de Sanctyon ascribes to the crying children of a certain district in Persia, but perfectly in unison with the
vocal exertions of the companion of his imprisonment, a large sow. I
approached—removed the barrier: the boy and the animal escaped
together, and I found myself alone in the centre of this miserable
asylum of human wretchedness—the residence of an *Irish peasant*.
To those who have only contemplated this useful order of society in
England, 'where every rood of ground maintains its man,' and where
the peasant liberally enjoys the *comforts* as well as the necessaries of
life, the wretched picture which the interior of an *Irish* cabin presents, would be at once an object of compassion and disgust.[1]

[1] Sometimes excavated from a hill, sometimes erected with loose stones, but most
generally built of mud; the *cabin* is divided into two apartments, the one littered with
straw and coarse rugs, and sometimes (but very rarely) furnished with the luxury of a
chaff bed, serves as a dormitory not only to the family of both sexes, but in general to any
animal they are so fortunate as to possess; the other chamber answers for every purpose
of domesticity, though almost destitute of every domestic implement, except the iron
pot in which the potatoes are boiled, and the stool on which they are flung. From these
wretched hovels (which often appear amidst scenes that might furnish the richest
models to poetic imitation) it is common to behold a group of children rush forth at the
sound of a horse's foot, or carriage wheel (regardless of the season's rigours), in a perfect
state of nudity, or covered with the drapery of wretchedness, which gives to their
appearance a still stronger character of poverty; yet even in these miserable huts you will
seldom find the spirit of urbanity absent—the genius of hospitality *never*. I remember
meeting with an instance of both, that made a deep impression on my heart: in the
autumn of 1804, in the course of a morning's ramble with a charming Englishwoman, in
the county of Sligo, I stopped to rest myself in a cabin, while she proceeded to pay a visit
to the respectable family of the O'H——s, of Nymph's Field: when I entered I found it
occupied by an old woman and her three granddaughters; two of the young ones were
engaged in scutching* flax, the other in some domestic employment. I was instantly
hailed with the most cordial welcome: the hearth was cleared, the old woman's seat
forced on me, eggs and potatoes roasted, and an apology for the deficiency of bread
politely made, while the manners of my hostages betrayed a courtesy that almost
amounted to adulation. They had all laid by their work on my entrance, and when I
requested I might not interrupt their avocations, one of them replied, 'I hope we know
better—we can work any day, but we cannot any day have such a lady as you under our
roof.' Surely this was not the manners of a cabin, but a court.

Almost suffocated, and not surprised that it was deserted *pro tempo*,* I hastened away, and was attracted towards a ruinous barn by a full chorus of females—where a group of young females were seated round an old hag who formed the centre of the circle; they were all busily employed at their *wheels*, which I observed went merrily round in exact time with their song, and so intently were they engaged by both, that my proximity was unperceived. At last the song ceased—the wheel stood still—every eye was fixed on the old *primum mobile** of the circle, who, after a short pause, began a *solo* that gave much satisfaction to her young auditors, and taking up the strain, they again turned their wheels round in unison.—The whole was sung in Irish, and as soon as I was observed, suddenly ceased; the girls looked down and tittered—and the old woman addressed me *sans ceremonie*,* and in a language I now heard for the first time.[1]

Supposing that some one among the number must understand English, I explained with all possible politeness the cause of my intrusion on this little harmonic society. The old woman looked up in my face and shook her head; *I* thought contemptuously—while the young ones, stifling their smiles, exchanged looks of compassion, doubtlessly at my ignorance of their language.

'So many languages a man knows,' said Charles V 'so many times is he a man,' and its certain *I* never felt myself less invested with the dignity of one, than while I stood twirling my stick, and 'biding the encounter of the eyes,' and smiles of these 'spinners in the sun.' Here, you will say, was prejudice opposed to prejudice with a vengeance; but I comforted myself with the idea that the natives of Greenland, the most gross and savage of mortals, compliment a stranger by saying, 'he is as well bred as a Greenlander.'

While thus situated, a sturdy looking young fellow, with that

[1] These *conventions* of female industry, so frequent in many parts of Ireland, especially in the west and north, are called *Ouris*, and are thus ingeniously traced to their origin by General Vallancey:—Speaking of the Scythian religion, he observes, that the ceremonies pertaining to their worship were comprehended in the word '*Haman*,' or '*Mann*.' From this *Mann* many of our mountains receive their names. 'Take an old Irish fable still in every one's mouth, of *Shliabh na Mann Mountain*; they say it was first inhabited by foreigners, who came from very distant countries; that they were of both sexes, and taught the Irish the art of *Oshiris*, or *Ouris*; that is, the management of flax or hemp, etc. etc. The word *Ouris*, now means a meeting of women or girls at one house or barn, to card a quantity of flax, and sometimes there are a hundred together. Wherever there is an *Ouris* the *Mann* comes invisibly and assists.'—*Collectanea de Rebus Hibernica*, vol. iv. Preface, p. 8.

boldness of figure and openness of countenance so peculiar to the young Irish peasants, and with his hose and brogues suspended from a stick over his shoulder, approached, and hailed the party in Irish: the girls instantly pointed his attention towards me; he courteously accosted me in English, and having learnt the nature of my dilemma, offered to be my guide—'it will not take me above a mile out of my way, and if it did *two*, it would make no *odds*,' said he. I accepted his offer, and we proceeded together over the summit of the mountain.

In the course of our conversation (which was very fluently supported on his side), I learnt, that few strangers ever passing through this remote part of the province, and even very many of the gentry here speaking Irish, it was a rare thing to meet with any one wholly unacquainted with the language, which accounted for the surprise, and I believe contempt, my ignorance had excited.

When I inquired into the nature of those choral strains I had heard, he replied—'O! as to that, it is according to the old woman's fancy;' and in fact I learnt that Ireland, like Italy, has its *improvisatorés*, and that those who are gifted with the impromptu talent are highly estimated by their rustic compatriots;[1] and by what he added, I discovered that their inspirations are either drawn from the circumstances of the moment, from some striking excellence or palpable defect in some of the company present, or from some humorous incident or local event generally known.

As soon as we arrived at the little *auberge** of the little village, I ordered my courteous guide his breakfast, and having done all due honour to my own, we parted.

My route from the village to Bally—— lay partly through a desolate bog, whose burning surface, heated by a vertical sun, gave me no inadequate idea of *Arabia Deserta*; and the pangs of an acute head-ach, brought on by exercise more violent than my still delicate constitution was equal to support, determined me to defer my journey until the meridian ardors were abated; and taking your Horace* from my pocket, I wandered into a shady path, 'impervious to the noon tide ray.' Throwing my 'listless length' at the foot of a

---

[1] In the romantic story of the beautiful *Deirdre*, as related in Keating's History of Ireland (page 176), it is mentioned, that Conor, King of Ulster, gave his ward a governess celebrated for her poetic talents, named *Leal harchan*, 'as she could deliver *extempore* verses on any subject, and was consequently much respected by the nobility.'—This was A.M. 3940.

spreading beech, I had already got to that sweet ode to Lydia, which Scaliger* in his enthusiasm, declares he would rather have written than to have possessed the monarchy of Naples, when somebody accosted me in Irish, and then with a 'God save you, Sir!' I raised my eyes, and beheld a poor peasant driving, or rather soliciting, a sorry lame cow to proceed.

'May be,' said he, taking off his hat, 'your Honour would be after telling me what's the hour?' 'Later than I supposed, my good friend,' replied I, rising; 'it is past two.' He bowed low, and stroking the face of his companion, added, 'well, the day is yet young, but you and I have a long journey before us, my poor Driminduath.'

'And how far are you going, friend?'

'Please your Honour, two miles beyond Bally——.'

'It is my road exactly, and you, Driminduath, and I, may perform the journey together.' The poor fellow seemed touched and surprized by my condescension, and profoundly bowed his sense of it, while the curious *triumviri** set off on their pedestrian tour together.

I now cast an eye over the person of my *compagnon de voyage.** It was a tall, thin, athletic figure, 'bony and gaunt,' with an expressive countenance, marked features, a livid complexion, and a quantity of coarse black hair hanging about the face; the drapery was perfectly appropriate to the wearer—an under garment composed of '*shreds and patches*,' was partially covered with an old great coat of coarse frize,* fastened on the breast with a large wooden skewer, the sleeves hanging down on either side unoccupied,[1] and a pair of yarn hose which scarcely reached *mid-leg*, left the ancle and foot naked.[2]

Driminduath seemed to share in the obvious poverty of her master—she was almost an anatomy, and scarcely able to crawl. 'Poor beast!' said he, observing I looked at her, 'Poor beast! little she dreamed of coming back the road she went, and little able she is to go it, poor soul; not that I am *overly* sorry I could not get nobody to take her off my hands at all at all; though to be sure 'tis better loose one's cow nor one's wife, any day in the year.'

'And had you no alternative?' I asked.

---

[1] This manner of wearing the coat, so general among the peasantry, is deemed by the natives of the county of Galway a remnant of the Spanish modes.

[2] They are called '*triathians*.'—Thus in a curious dissertation on an ancient marble statue, of a bag-piper, by Signor Canonico Orazio Maccari, of Cortona, he notices, '*Nudi sono i piedi ma due rozze calighe pastorali cuoprone le gambe.*'*

'Anan!' exclaimed he, staring.

'Were you obliged to part with one or the other?' Sorrow is garrulous, and in the natural selfishness of its suffering, seeks to lessen the weight of its woe by participation. In a few minutes I was master of Murtoch O'Shaughnassey's story:[1] he was the husband of a sick wife; the father of six children, and a labourer, or *cotter*, who worked daily throughout the year for the hut that sheltered the heads, and the little potatoe rick which was the sole subsistence, of his family. He had taken a few acres of ground, he said, from his employer's steward, to set grass potatoes in, by which he hoped to make something handsome; that to enable himself to pay for them, he had gone to work in Leinster during the last harvest, 'where, please your Honour,' he added, 'a poor man gets more for his labour than in Connaught;[2] but here it was my luck (and bad luck it was), to get the shaking fever upon me, so that I returned sick and sore to my poor people, without a cross to bless myself with, and then there was an end of my fine grass potatoes, for devil receive the sort they'd let me dig till I paid for the ground; and what was worse, the steward was going to turn us out of our cabin, because I had not worked out the rent with him as usual, and not a potatoe had I for the children, besides finding my wife and two boys in a fever: the boys got well, but my poor wife has been decaying away ever since; so I was fain to sell my poor Driminduath here, which was left me by my gossip,* in

---

[1] Neither the rencontre with, nor the character or story of Murtoch, partakes in the least degree of fiction.

[2] This is a very general practice, and though attended frequently with fatal consequences, still pursued; for by over labour, over heatings, fatigue and colds (caught by lying in numbers together on the earth, and only covered with a blanket), these poor adventurers return home to their expecting families with fevers lurking in their veins, or suffering under violent ague fits, which they call shaking fevers.

It is well known that within these thirty years the Connaught peasant laboured for *three-pence* a day and two meals of potatoes and milk, and four-pence when he maintained himself; while in Leinster the harvest hire rose from eight-pence to a shilling. Riding out one day near the village of Castletown Delvin, in Westmeath, in company with the younger branches of the respectable family of the F——ns, of that country, we observed two young men lying at a little distance from each other in a dry ditch, with some lighted turf burning near them; they both seemed on the verge of eternity, and we learned from a peasant who was passing, that they were Connaught men who had come to Leinster to work; that they had been disappointed, and owing to want and fatigue, had been first seized with agues and then with fevers of so fatal a nature, that no one would suffer them to remain in their cabins; owing to the benevolent exertions of my young friends we, however, found an asylum for these unfortunates, and had the happiness of seeing them return comparatively well and happy to their native province.

order to pay my rent and get some nourishment for my poor woman, who I believe was just weak at heart for the want of it; and so, as I was after telling your Honour, I left home yesterday for a *fair* twenty-five good miles off, but my poor Driminduath has got such bad usage of late, and was in such bad plight, that nobody would bid nothing for her, and so we are both returning home as we went, with full hearts and empty stomachs.'

This was uttered with an air of despondency that touched my very soul, and I involuntarily presented him some sea biscuit I had in my pocket. He thanked me, and carelessly added, 'that it was the first morsel he had tasted for twenty-four hours;[1] not,' said he, 'but I can fast with any one, and well it is for me I can.' He continued brushing an intrusive tear from his eye; and the next moment whistling a lively air, he advanced to his cow, talked to her in Irish, in a soothing tone, and presenting her such wild flowers and blades of grass as the scanty vegetation of the bog afforded, turned round to me with a smile of self satisfaction and said, 'One can better suffer themselves a thousand times over than see one's poor dumb beast want: it is next, please your Honour, to seeing one's child in want—God help him who has witnessed both!'

'And art thou then (I mentally exclaimed) that intemperate, cruel, idle savage, an Irish peasant? with an heart thus tenderly alive to the finest feelings of humanity; patiently labouring with daily exertion for what can scarce afford thee a bare subsistence; sustaining the unsatisfied wants of nature without a murmur; nurtured in the hope (the *disappointed hope*) of procuring nourishment for *her* dearer to thee than thyself, tender of thy animal as thy child, and suffering the consciousness of *their* wants to absorb all consideration of thy own; and yet resignation smooths the furrow which affliction has traced upon thy brow, and the national exility of thy character cheers and supports the natural susceptibility of thy heart.' In fact, he was at that moment humming an Irish song by my side.

I need not tell you that the first village we arrived at I furnished him with means of procuring a comfortable dinner for himself and

---

[1] The temperance of an Irish peasant in this respect is almost incredible; many of them are satisfied with one meal a day—none of them exceed two—breakfast and supper; which invariably consists of potatoes, sometimes with, sometimes without milk. One of the rules observed by the *Finian land*, or ancient militia of Ireland, was to eat but once in the twenty-four hours.—See *Keating's History of Ireland*.

Driminduath, and advice and medicine from the village apothecary
for his wife. Poor fellow! his surprise and gratitude was expressed in
the true hyperbola of Irish emotion.

Meantime I walked on to examine the ruins of an abbey, where in
about half an hour I was joined by Murtoch and his patient companion, whom he assured me he had regaled with some hay, as he
had himself with a glass of whiskey.—What a breakfast for a famish-
ing man!

'It is a dreadful habit, Murtoch,' said I.

'It is so, please your Honour,' replied he, 'but then it is meat,
drink, and clothes to us, for we forget we have but little of one and
less of the other, when we get *the drop* within us;[1] Och, long life to
them that lightened the tax on the whiskey, for by my safe conscience, if they had left it on another year we should have forgotten
how to drink it.'

I shall make no comment on Murtoch's unconscious philippic*
against the legislature, but surely a government has but little right to
complain of those popular disorders to which in a certain degree it
may be deemed accessary, by removing the strongest barrier that
confines within moral bounds the turbulent passions of the lower
orders of society.

To my astonishment, I found that Murtoch had only purchased
for his sick wife a little wine and a small piece of bacon:[2] both, he
assured me, were universal and sovereign remedies, and better than
any thing the *physicianers* could prescribe, to keep the disorder *from
the heart*.[3] The spirits of Murtoch were now quite afloat, and during
the rest of our journey the vehemence, pliancy, and ardour of the
Irish character strongly betrayed itself in the manners of this poor
unmodified Irishman; while the natural facetiousness of a temperament 'complexionally pleasant,' was frequently succeeded by such
heart-rending accounts of poverty and distress, as shed involuntary

---

[1] 'J'ai souvent entendu reprocher la paresse et l'ivrogné au paysan. Mais lorsque on
est reduit a mourir de faim, n'est-ce pas preferable de ne rien faire, puisque le travail le
plus assidus ne sauroit-en empecher; dans cette situation n'est il pas fort simple de boire
quand on le peut une goutte de fleuve de Lethe pour oublier sa misere.'—*La Tocknay.**

[2] It is common to see them come to gentlemen's houses with a little vial bottle to beg
a table spoonful of wine (for a sick relative), which they esteem the elixir of life.

[3] To be able to keep any disorder from the heart, is supposed (by the lower orders of
the Irish) to be the secret of longevity.

tears on those cheeks which but a moment before were distended by the exertions of a boisterous laugh.

Nothing could be more wildly sweet than the whistle or song of the ploughman or labourer as we passed along; it was of so singular a nature, that I frequently paused to catch it; it is a species of voluntary recitative, and so melancholy, that every plaintive note breathes on the heart of the auditor a tale of hopeless despondency or incurable woe. By heavens! I could have wept as I listened, and found a luxury in tears.[1]

The evening was closing in fast, and we were within a mile of Bally——, when to a day singularly fine, succeeded one of the most violent storms of rain and wind I had ever witnessed. Murtoch, who seemed only to regard it on my account, insisted on throwing his great coat over me, and pointed to a cabin at a little distance, where, he said, 'if my Honour would demean myself so far, I could get good shelter for the night.'

'Are you sure of that, Murtoch?' said I.

Murtoch shook his head, and looking full in my face, said something in Irish; which at my request he translated—the words were—'Happy are *they* whose roof shelters the head of the traveller.'

'And is it indeed a source of happiness to you, Murtoch?'

Murtoch endeavoured to convince me it *was*, even upon a *selfish* principle: 'For (said he) it is thought right lucky to have a stranger sleep beneath one's roof.'

If superstition was ever thus on the side of benevolence, even reason herself would hesitate to depose her.—We had now reached the door of the cabin, which Murtoch opened without ceremony, saying as he entered—'May God and the Virgin Mary pour a blessing on this house!'[2] The family, who were all circled round a fine turf fire that blazed on the earthen hearth, replied, 'Come in, and a thousand welcomes'—for Murtoch served interpreter, and translated as they were spoken these warm effusions of Irish cordiality. The master of the house, a venerable old man, perceiving me, made a

---

[1] Mr Walker, in his Historical Memoir of the Irish Bards, has given a specimen of the Irish plough-tune; and adds, 'While the Irish ploughman drives his team, and the female peasant milks her cow, they warble a succession of wild notes which bid defiance to the rules of composition, yet are inexpressibly sweet.'—Page 132.

[2] A *salutation* and a *benediction* are synonymous, among the lower orders of the Irish.

low bow, and added, 'You are welcome, and ten thousand welcomes, *gentleman*.'[1]

So you see I hold my letter patent of nobility in my countenance, for I had not yet divested myself of Murtoch's costume—while in the act, the best stool was wiped for me, the best seat at the fire forced on me, and on being admitted into the social circle, I found its central point was a round oaken stool heaped with smoking potatoes thrown promiscuously over it.

To partake of this national diet I was strongly and courteously solicited, while as an incentive to an appetite that needed none, the old dame produced what she called a *madder** of sweet milk, in contradistinction to the sour milk of which the rest partook; while the cow which supplied the luxury[2] slumbered most amicably with a large pig at no great distance from where I sat; and Murtoch glancing an eye at *both*, and then looking at me, seemed to say, 'You see into what snug quarters we have got.' While I (as I sat with my damp clothes smoking by the turf fire, my madder of milk in one hand, and hot potatoe in the other), assured him by a responsive glance, that I was fully sensible of the comforts of our situation.

As soon as supper was finished the old man said grace, the family piously blessed themselves, and the stool being removed, the hearth swept, and the fire replenished from the bog, Murtoch threw himself on his back along a bench,[3] and unasked began a song, the wild and plaintive melody of which went at once to the soul.

When he had concluded, I was told it was the lamentation of the poor Irish for the loss of their *glibbs*, or long tresses, of which they were deprived by the arbitrary will of Henry VIII.—The song (com-

---

[1] '*Fáilte augus cead ro ag, duine uasal.*' The term *gentleman*, however, is a very inadequate version of the Irish *uasal*, which is an epithet of superiority that indicates more than mere gentility of birth can bestow, although that requisite is also included. In a curious dialogue between Ossian and St Patrick, in an old Irish poem, in which the former relates the combat between Oscar and Illan, St Patrick solicits him to the detail, addressing him as, '*Ossian uasal, a mhic Fionne.*' '*Ossian the Noble*—the son of Fingal.'

[2] To supply the want of this (by them) highly esteemed luxury, they cut an onion into a bowl of water, into which they dip their potatoes.—This they call a *scadan caoch*, or blind herring.

[3] This curious vocal position is of very ancient origin in Connaught, though now by no means prevalent. Formerly the songster not only lay on his back, but had a weight pressed on his chest. The author's father recollects to have seen a man in the county of Mayo, of the name of O'Melvill, who sung for him in this position some years back.

posed in his reign), is called the *Cualin*,[1] which I am told is literally, the fair ringlet.

When the English had drawn a pale* round their conquests in this country, such of the inhabitants as were compelled to drag on their existence beyond the barrier, could no longer afford to cover their heads with metal, and were necessitated to rely on the resistance of their matted locks. At length this necessity became 'the fashion of their choice.'

The partiality of the ancient Irish to long hair is still to be traced in their descendants of both sexes, the women in particular; for I observed that the young *ones* only wore their 'native ornament of *hair*,' which sometimes flows over their shoulders, sometimes is fastened up in tresses, with a pin or bodkin. A fashion more in unison with grace and nature, though less in point with formal neatness, than the round-eared caps and large hats of our rustic fair in England.

Almost every word of Murtoch's lamentation was accompanied by the sighs and mournful lamentations of his auditors, who seemed to sympathize as tenderly in the sufferings of their progenitors, as though they had themselves been victims to the tyranny which had caused them. The arch-policy of the 'ruthless king,' who destroyed at once the records of a nation's woes, by extirpating 'the tuneful race,' whose art would have perpetuated them to posterity, never appeared to me in greater force than at that moment.

In the midst, however, of the melancholy which involved the mourning auditors of Murtoch, a piper entered, and seating himself by the fire, *sans façon*,* drew his pipes from under his coat, and struck up an Irish lilt of such inspiring animation, as might have served St Basil of Limoges, the merry patron of dancing, for a jubilate.*

In a moment, in the true pliability of Irish temperament, the whole pensive group cheered up, flung away their stools, and as if bit to merry madness by a tarantula, set to dancing jigs with all their hearts, and all their *strength* into the bargain. Murtoch appeared not less skilled in the dance than song; and every one (according to the just description of Goldsmith,* who was a native of this province), seemed

---

[1] The Cualin is one of the most popular and beautiful Irish airs extant.

'To seek renown,
By holding out to tire each other down.'

Although much amused by this novel style of devotion at the shrine of Terpsichore,* yet as the night was now calm, and an unclouded moon dispersed the gloom of twilight obscurity, I arose to pursue my journey. Murtoch would accompany me, though our hospitable friends did their utmost to prevail on both to remain for the night.

When I insisted on my host receiving a trifle, I observed poverty struggling with pride, and gratitude superior to both: he at last reluctantly consented to be prevailed on, by my assurance of forgetting to call on them again when I passed that way, if I were now denied. I was followed for several paces by the whole family, who parted *with*, as they *received* me, with blessings;—for their courtesy upon all occasions, seems interwoven with their religion, and not to be pious in their forms of etiquette, is not to be polite.

Benevolent and generous beings whose hard labour

'Just gives what life requires, but gives no more;'

yet who, with the ever ready smile of heart-felt welcome, are willing to share that hard-earned little with the weary traveller whom chance conducts to your threshold, or the solitary wanderer whom necessity throws upon your bounty. How did my heart smite me, while I received the cordial rites of hospitality from your hands, for the prejudices I had hitherto nurtured against your characters. But your smiling welcome, and parting benediction, retributed my error—in the feeling of remorse they awakened.

It was late when I reached Bally——, a large, ugly, irregular town, near the sea coast; but fortunately meeting with a chaise, I threw myself into it, gave Murtoch my address, (who was all amazement at discovering I was son to the Lord of the Manor), and arrived without further adventure at this antique *chateau*, more gratified by the result of my little pedestrian tour, than if (at least in the present state of my feelings), I had performed it Sesostris-like,* in a triumphal chariot drawn by kings; for 'so weary, stale, flat, and unprofitable,' appear to me the tasteless pleasures of the world I have left, that every sense, every feeling, is in a state of revolt against its sickening joys, and their concommitant sufferings.

Adieu! I am sending this off by a courier extraordinary, to the next post-town, in the hope of receiving one from you by the same hand.

H.M.

LETTER III

TO J.D. ESQ. M.P.

I perceive my father emulates the policy of the British Legislature, and delegates English ministers to govern his Irish domains. Who, do you think, is his *fac-totum** here? The rascally son of his cunning Leicestershire steward who unites all his father's artifice to a proportionable share of roguery of his own. I have had some reason to know the fellow; but his servility of manner, and apparent rigid discharge of his duties, has imposed on my father; who, with all his superior mind, is to be imposed on, by those who know how to find the clue to his point of fallibility: his noble soul can never stoop to dive into the minute vices of a rascal of this description.

Mr Clendinning was absent from M—— house when I arrived, but attended me the next morning at breakfast, with that fawning civility of manner I abhor, and which, contrasted with the manly courteousness of my late companion, never appeared more grossly obvious. He endeavoured to amuse me with a detail of the ferocity, cruelty, and uncivilized state of those among whom (as he hinted), I was banished for my sins. He had now, he said, been near five years among them, and had never met an individual of the lower order who did not deserve an halter at least: for his part, he kept a tight hand over them, and he was justified in so doing, or his Lord would be the sufferer; for few of them would pay their rents till their cattle were driven, or some such measure was taken with them. And as for the labourers and workmen, a slave-driver was the only man fit to deal with them: they were all rebellious, idle, cruel, and treacherous; and for his part, he never expected to leave the country with his life.

It is not possible a better defence for the imputed turbulence of the Irish peasantry could be made, than that which lurked in the unprovoked accusations of this narrow-minded sordid steward, who, it is evident, wished to forestall the complaints of those on whom he had exercised the native tyranny of his disposition (even according to his own account), by every species of harassing oppression within the compass of his ability. For if power is a dangerous gift even in the regulated mind of elevated rank, what does it become in the delegated authority of ignorance, meanness and illiberality?[1]

My father, however, by frequent visitations to his Irish estates (within these few years at least), must afford to his suffering tenantry an opportunity of redress; for who that ever approached him with a *tear* of suffering, left his presence with a tear of gratitude! But many, very many of the English nobility who hold immense tracts of land in this country, and draw from hence in part the suppliance of their luxuries, have never visited their estates, since conquest first put them in the possession of their ancestors. Ours, you know, fell to us in the Cromwellian wars,* but since the time of General M——, who earned them by the sword, my father, his lineal descendant, is the first of the family who ever visited them. And certainly a wish to conciliate the affections of his tenantry, could alone induce him to spend so much of his time here as he has done; for the situation of this place is bleak and solitary, and the old mansion, like the old manor houses of England, has neither the architectural character of an antique structure, nor the accommodation of a modern one.

> *'Ayant l'air delabri, sans l'air antique.'**

On inquiring for the key of the library, Mr Clendinning informed me his Lord always took it with him, but that a box of books had come from England a few days before my arrival.

As I suspected, they were all law books—well, be it so; there are few sufferings more acute than those which forbid complaint, because they are self-created.

Four days have elapsed since I began this letter, and I have been prevented from continuing it merely for want of something to say.

I cannot now sit down, as I once did, and give you a history of my ideas or sensation, in the deficiency of fact or incident; for I have survived my sensations, and my ideas are dry and exhausted.

I cannot now trace my joys to their source, or my sorrows to their

---

[1] 'A horde of tyrants exist in Ireland, in a class of men that are unknown in England, in the multitude of *agents of absentees*, small proprietors, who are the pure Irish squires, middle men who take large farms, and squeeze out a forced kind of profit by letting them in small parcels; lastly, the little farmers themselves, who exercise the same insolence they receive from their superiors, on those unfortunate beings who are placed at the extremity of the scale of degradation—the Irish Peasantry!'—*An Enquiry into the Causes of Popular Discontents in Ireland, etc. etc.*

spring, for I am destitute of their present, and insensible to their former existence. The energy of youthful feeling is subdued, and the vivacity of warm emotion worn out by its own violence. I have lived too fast in a moral as well as a physical sense, and the principles of my intellectual, as well as my natural constitution are, I fear, fast hastening to decay. I live the tomb of my expiring mind, and preserve only the consciousness of my wretched state, without the power, and almost without the wish to be otherwise than what I am. And yet, God knows I am nothing less than contented.

Would you hear my journal? I rise late to my solitary breakfast, because it is solitary; then to study, or rather to yawn over *Giles* versus *Haystack*, until (to check the creeping effects of lethargy), I rise from my reading desk, and lounge to a window, which commands a boundless view of a boundless bog; then 'with what appetite I may,' sit down to a joyless dinner. Sometimes, when seduced by the blandishments of an evening singularly beautiful, I quit my *den*, and *prowl* down to the sea-shore, where, throwing myself at the foot of some cliff that 'battles o'er the deep,' I fix my vacant eye on the stealing waves that

> 'Idly swell against the rocky coast,
> And break—as break those glittering shadows,
> Human joys.'

Then wet with the ocean spray and evening dew, return to bed, merely to avoid the intrusive civilities of Mr Clendinning. 'Thus wear the hours away.'

I had heard that the neighbourhood about M—— house was good: I can answer for its being populous. Although I took every precaution to prevent my arrival being known, yet the natives have come down on me in hordes, and this in all the form of *haut ton*,* as the innumerable cards of the clans of Os and Macs evince. I have, however, neither been visible to the visitants, nor accepted their invitations; for 'man delights me not, nor woman either.' Nor woman either! Oh! uncertainty of all human propensities! Yet so it is, that every letter that composes the word *woman*! seems cabilistical,* and rouses every principle of aversion and disgust within me; while I often ask myself with Tasso,

> 'Se pur ve nelle amor alcun diletto.'*

It is certain, that the diminutive body of our worthy steward, is the abode of the transmigrated soul of some *West Indian* planter.* I have been engaged these two days in listening to, and retributing those injuries his tyranny has inflicted, in spite of his rage, eloquence, and threats, none of which have been spared. The victims of his oppression haunt me in walks, fearful lest their complaints should come to the knowledge of this puissant *major domo*.*

'But why,' said I to one of the sufferers, after a detail of seized geese, pounded cows, extra-labour, cruelty extorted, ejectments, etc. etc. given in all the tedious circumlocution of Irish oratory,—'why not complain to my father when he comes among you?'

'Becaise, please your Honour, my Lord stays but a few days at a time here together, nor that same neither: besides, we be loath to trouble his Lordship, for feard it would be after coming to measter Clendinnin's ears, which would be the ruination of us all; and then when my Lord is at the Lodge, which he mostly is, he is always out amongst the quality, so he is.'

'What Lodge?' said I.

'Why, please your Honour, where my Lord mostly takes up when he comes here, the place that belonged to measter Clendinnin, who called it the *Lodge*; becaise the good old Irish name that was upon it happened not to hit his fancy.'

In the evening I asked Clendinning if my father did not sometimes reside at the Lodge? He seemed surprised at my information, and said, that was the name he had given to a ruinous old place which, with a few acres of indifferent land, he had purchased out of his hard labour, and which his Lord having taken an unaccountable liking to, rented from him, and was actually the tenant of his own steward.

O! what arms of recrimination I should be furnished with against my rigidly moral father, should I discover this remote *Cassino** (for remote I understand it is), to be the *harem* of some wild Irish *Sultana*; for I strongly suspect 'that metal more attractive' than the cause he assigns, induces him to pay an annual visit to a country to which, till within these few years, he nurtured the strongest prejudices. You know there are but 19 years between him and my brother; and his feelings are so unblunted by vicious pursuits, his life has been guided by such epicurean principles of enjoyment, that he still retains much of the first warm flush of juvenile existence, and has only sacrificed to time, its follies and its ignorance. I swear, at this moment he is a younger man than either of his sons; the one chilled by the coldness of an icy temperament into premature old age, and the other!!!

* * * * * * * * * * * *

Murtoch has been to see me. I have procured him a little farm, and am answerable for the rent. I sent his wife some rich wine; she is recovering very fast. Murtoch is all gratitude for the wine, but I perceive his faith still lies in the *bacon*!

LETTER IV

TO J.D. ESQ. M.P.

I can support this wretched state of non-existence, this *articula mortis*,* no longer. I cannot read—I cannot think—nothing touches, nothing interests me; neither is it permitted me to indulge my sufferings in solitude. These hospitable people still weary me with their attentions, though they must consider me as a sullen misanthropist, for I persist in my invisibility. I can escape them no longer but by flight—professional study is out of the question, for a time at least. I mean, therefore, to 'take the wings of' some fine morning and seek a change of being in a change of place; for a perpetual state of evagation alone, keeps up the flow and ebb of existence in my languid frame. My father's last letter informs me he is obliged by business to postpone his journey for a month; this leaves me so much the longer master of myself. By the time we meet, my mind may have regained its native tone. *Laval* too, writes for a longer leave of absence, which I most willingly grant. It is a weight removed off my shoulders; I would be savagely free.

I thank you for your welcome letters, and will do what I can to satisfy your antiquarian taste; and I would take your advice, and study the Irish language, were my powers of comprehension equal to the least of the philological excellencies of *Tom Thumb*, or *Goody Two Shoes*;—but alas!

> 'Se perchetto a me Stesso quale acquisto,
> Faro mai che me piaccia.'[1]*

---

[1] Torquatto Tasso.

Villa di Marino, Atlantic Ocean

Having told Mr Clendinning that I should spend a few days in wandering about the country, I mounted my horse. So I determined to roam free and unrestrained by the presence of a servant, to Mr Clendinning's utter amazement, I ordered a few changes of linen, my drawing-book and pocket escritoire,* to be put in a small valise, which, with all due humility, I had strapped on the back of my steed, whom, by the bye, I expect will be as celebrated as the *Rozinante* of Don Quixote, or the *Beltenebros L'Amadis de Gaul*; and thus accoutred, set off on my peregrination, the most listless knight that ever entered on the lists of errantry.

You will smile, when I tell you my first point of attraction was the *Lodge*; to which (though with some difficulty) I found my way; for it lies in a most wild and unfrequented direction, but so infinitely superior in situation to M—— house, that I no longer wonder at my father's preference. Every feature that constitutes either the beauty or sublime of landscape, is here finely combined. Groves druidically venerable—mountains of Alpine elevation—expansive lakes, and the boldest and most romantic sea coast I ever beheld, alternately diversify and enrich its scenery; while a number of young and flourishing plantations evince the exertion of a taste in my father, he certainly has not betrayed in the disposition of his hereditary domains. I found this *Tusculum** inhabited only by a decent old man and his superannuated wife. Without informing them who I was, I made a feigned wish to make the place a pretext for visiting it. The old man smiled at the idea, and shook his head, presuming that I must be indeed a stranger in the country, as my accent denoted, for that this spot belonged to a great *English Lord*, whom he verily believed would not resign it for his own fine place some miles off; but when, with some jesuitical artifice, I endeavoured to trace the cause of this attachment, he said it was his Lordship's fancy, and that there was no accounting for people's fancies.

'That is all very true,' said I; 'but is it the house only that seized on your Lord's fancy?'

'Nay, for the matter of that,' said he, 'the lands are far more finer; the house, though large, being no great things.' I begged in this instance to judge for myself, and a few shillings procured me not only free egress, but the confidence of the ancient *Cicerone*.*

This fancied *harem*, however, I found not only divested of its expected fair inhabitant, but wholly destitute of furniture, except what filled a bed-room occupied by my father, and an apartment which was *locked*. The old man with some tardiness produced the key, and I found this mysterious chamber was only a study; but closer inspection discovered, that almost all the books related to the language, history, and antiquities of Ireland.

So you see, in fact, my father's *Sultana* is no other than the *Irish Muse*; and never was son so tempted to become the rival of his father, since the days of Antiochus and Stratonice.* For, at a moment when my taste, like my senses, is flat and palled, nothing can operate so strongly as an incentive, as novelty. I strongly suspect that my father was aware of this, and that he had despoiled the temple, to prevent me becoming a worshipper at the same shrine. For the old man said he had received a letter from his Lord, ordering away all the furniture (except that of his own bed-room and study) to the manor house; the study and bed room however, will suffice me, and here I shall certainly pitch my head-quarters until my father's arrival.

I have already had some occasions to remark, that the warm susceptible character of the Irish is open to the least indication of courtesy and kindness.

My *politesse* to this old man, opened every sluice of confidence in his breast, and, as we walked down the avenue together, having thrown the bridle over my horse's neck, and offered him my arm, for he was lame, I inquired how this beautiful farm fell into the hands of Lord M——; still concealing from him that it was his son who demanded the question.

'Why, your Honour,' said he, 'the farm, though beautiful, is small; however, it made the best part of what remained of the patrimony of the Prince, when—'

'What Prince?' interrupted I, amazed.

'Why, the Prince of Inismore, to be sure, jewel, whose great forefathers once owned the half of the barony, from the Red Bog to the sea coast. Och! it is a long story, but I have heard my grand-father tell it a thousand times, how a great Prince of Inismore, in the wars of Queen Elizabeth, here had a castle and a great tract of land on the *borders*, of which he was deprived, as the story runs, becaise he would neither cut his *glibbs*, shave his upper lip, nor shorten his shirt:[1] and so he was driven with the rest of us beyond the *pale*. The family, however, after a while, flourished greater nor ever. Och, and its themselves that might; for they were true Milesians* bred and born, every mother's soul of them. O! not a drop of *Strongbonean** flowed in their Irish veins agrah! Well, as I was after telling your Honour, the family flourished, and beat all before them, for they had an army of *galloglasses** at their back,[2] until the Cromwellian wars broke out, and those same cold-hearted Presbyterians battered the fine *old ancient* castle of Inismore, and left it in the condition it now stands; and what was worse nor that, the poor old Prince was put to death in the arms of his fine young son, who tried to save him, and that by one of Cromwell's English Generals, who received the townlands of Inismore, which lie near Bally——, as his reward. Now this English General who murdered the Prince, was no other than the ancestor of my Lord, to whom these estates descended from father to son. Aye, you may well start, Sir, it was a woeful piece of business; for of all their fine estates, nothing was left to the Princes of Inismore, but the ruins of their old castle, and the rocks that surround it; except this tight little bit of an estate here, on which the father of the present Prince built this house; becaise his Lady, with whom he got a handsome fortune, and who was descended from the Kings of Connaught, took a dislike to the castle; the story going that it was haunted by the murdered Prince; and what with building this house, and living like an Irish Prince, as he was every inch of him, and spending 3000l. a-year out of 300l., when he died (and the sun never shone upon such a funeral; the whiskey ran about like *ditch water*, and the country was stocked with pipes and tobacco for many a long year after. For the present Prince his son, would not be a bit behind with his father in any thing, and so signs on him, for he is not worth one guinea this blessed day, Christ save him);—well, as I was saying, when he died, he left things in a sad way, which his son has not the man to mind, for he was the spirit of a King, and lives in as much state as one to this day.'

---

[1] From the earliest settlement of the English in this country, an inquisitorial persecution had been carried on against the national costume. In the reign of Henry V, there was an act passed against even the English colonists wearing a whisker on the upper lip, like the Irish; and in 1616, the Lord Deputy, in his instructions to the Lord President and Council, directed, that such as appeared in Irish robes or mantles, should be punished by fine and imprisonment.

[2] The second order of military in Ireland.

'But where, where does he live?' interrupted I, with breathless impatience.

'Why,' continued this living Chronicle, in the true spirit of Irish replication, 'he did live there in that Lodge, as they call it now, and in that room where my Lord keeps his books, was our young Princess born; her father never had but her, and loves her better than his own heart's blood, as well he may, the blessing of the Virgin Mary and the Twelve Apostles light on her sweet head. Well, the Prince would never let it come near him, that things were not going on well, and continued to take at great rents, farms that brought him in little; for being a Prince and a Milesian, it did not become him to look after such matters, and every thing was left to stewards and the like, until things coming to the worst, a rich English gentleman, as it was said, came over here, and offered the Prince, through his steward, a good round sum of money on this place, which the Prince, being harassed by his *spalpeen** creditors, and wanting a little ready money more than any other earthly thing, consented to receive the gentleman; sending him word he should have his own time; but scarcely was the mortgage a year old, when this same Englishman, (Oh, my curse lie about him, Christ pardon me), foreclosed it, and the fine old Prince not having as much as a shed to shelter his grey hairs under, was forced to fit up part of the old ruined castle, and open those rooms which it has been said were haunted. Discharging many of his old servants, he was accompanied to the castle by the family steward, the *fosterers*, the *nurse*,[1] the harper, and Father John, the chaplain.

'Och, it was a piteous sight the day he left this: he was leaning on the Lady Glorvina's arm, as he walked out to the chaise. "James Tyral," says he to me in Irish, for I caught his eye; "James Tyral," but he could say no more, for the old tenants kept crying about him, and he put his mantle to his eyes and hurried into the chaise; the

[1] The custom of retaining the nurse who reared the children, has ever been, and is still in force among the most respectable families in Ireland, as it is still in modern, and was formerly in ancient *Greece*, and they are probably both derived from the same origin. We read, that when Rebecca left her father's house to marry Isaac at Beersheba, the nurse was sent to accompany her. But in Ireland, not only the nurse herself, but her husband and children, are objects of peculiar regard and attention, and are called *fosterers*; the claims of these fosterers frequently descend from generation to generation, and the tie which unites them is indissoluble. Sometimes, however, it is cemented by a less disinterested sentiment than affection; and the claims of the fosterers become an hereditary tax on the bounty of the fostered.

Lady Glorvina kissing her hand to us all, and crying bitterly till she was out of sight. But then, Sir, what would you have of it: the Prince shortly after found out that this same Mr *Mortgagee*, was no other than a spalpeen steward of Lord M——'s. It was thought he would have at first run mad, when he found that almost the last acre of his hereditary lands was in the possession of the servant of his hereditary enemy; for so deadly is the hatred he bears my Lord, that upon my conscience, I believe the young Prince who held the bleeding body of his murdered father in his arms, felt not greater for the murdered, than our Prince does for that murderer's descendant.

'Now, my Lord is just such a man as God never made better, and wishing with all the veins in his heart to serve the old Prince, and do away all difference between them, what does he do jewel? but writes him a mighty pretty letter, offering this house and part of the land as a present. O! divil a word a lie I'm after telling you; but what would you have of it, but this offer sets the Prince madder than all; for you know that this was an insult on his honour, which warmed every drop of Milesian blood in his body, for he would rather starve to death all his life, than have it thought he would be obligated to any body at all at all for wherewithal to support him; so with that the Prince writes him a letter: it was brought by the old steward, who knew every line of the contents of it, though divil a line in it but two, and that same was but one and half, as one may say, and this it was, as the old steward told me:

"The son of the son of the son's son of Bryan Prince of Inismore, can receive no favour from the descendant of his ancestor's murderer."

'Now it was plain enough to be seen, that my Lord took this to heart, as well he might faith; however, he considered that it came from a misfortunate Prince, he let it drop, and so this was all ever passed between them; however, he was angry enough with his steward, but measter Clendinnin put his *comehither* on him, and convinced him that the biggest rogue alive was an honest man.'

'And the Prince!' I interrupted eagerly.

'Och, jewel, the Prince lives away in the old Irish fashion, only he has not a Christian soul now at all at all, most of the old Milesian gentry having quit the country; besides, the Prince being in a bad state of health, and having nearly lost the use of his limbs, and his heart being heavy, and his purse light; for all that he keeps up the old Irish customs and dress, letting nobody eat at the same table but his daughter,[1] not even his Lady, when she was alive.'

'And do you think the son of Lord M—— would have no chance of obtaining an audience from the Prince?'

'What, the young gentleman that they say is come to M—— house? why about as much chance as his father; but by my conscience that's a bad one.'

'And your young Princess, is she as implacable as her father?'

'Why faith! I cannot well tell you what the Lady Glorvina is, for she is like nothing upon the face of God's creation but herself. I do not know how it comes to pass, that every mother's soul of us love her better nor the Prince; aye, by my conscience, and fear her too; for well may they fear her, on the score of her great learning, being brought up by Father John, the chaplain, and spouting Latin faster nor the priest of the parish: and we may well love her, for she is a saint upon earth, and a great *physicianer* to boot; curing all the sick and maimed for twenty miles round. Then she is so proud, that divil a one soul of the quality will she visit in the whole barony, though she will sit in a smoky cabin for hours together, to talk to the poor: besides all this, she will sit for hours at her Latin and Greek, after the family are gone to bed, and yet you will see her up with the dawn, running like a doe about the rocks; her fine yellow hair streaming in the wind, for all the world like a mermaid. Och! my blessing light on her every day she sees the light, for she is the jewel of a child.'

'A child! say you?'

'Why, to be sure I think her one; for many a time I carried her in these arms, and taught her to bless herself in Irish; but she is no child either, for as one of our old Irish songs says, "Upon her cheek

---

[1] M'Dermot, Prince of Coolavin, never suffered his wife to sit at table with him; although his daughter-in-law was permitted to that honour, as she was descended from the royal family of the *O'Conor*.

When the Earl of K——, Mr O'H——, member for Sligo, and Mr S——, a gentleman of fortune, waited on the Prince, he received them in the following manner:—'K—— you are welcome; O'H——, you may sit down; but for you,' (turning to Mr S——, who was unfortunately of English extraction), 'I know nothing of you.' The compliment paid to Mr O'H——, arose from his mother being the descendant of Milesian ancestry.

we see love's letter sealed with a damask rose."[1] But if your Honour has any curiosity you may judge for yourself; for matins and vespers are celebrated every day in the year, in the old chapel belonging to the castle, and the whole family attend.'

'And are strangers also permitted?'

'Faith and its themselves that are; but few indeed trouble them, though none are denied. I used to get mass myself sometimes, but it is now too far to walk for me.'

This was sufficient, I waited to hear no more, but repaid my communicative companion for his information, and rode off, having inquired the road to Inismore from the first man I met.

It would be vain, it would be impossible, to describe the emotion which the simple tale of this old man awakened. The descendant of a murderer! The very scoundrel steward of my father revelling in the property of a man, who shelters his aged head beneath the ruins of those walls where his ancestors bled under the uplifted sword of mine.

Why this, you will say, is the romance of a novel-read school boy. Are we not all, the little and the great, descended from assassins; was not the first born man a fratricide? and still, on the field of unappeased contention, does not 'man the murderer, meet the murderer, man?'

Yes, yes, 'tis all true; humanity acknowledges it and shudders. But still I wish *my* family had never possessed an acre of ground in this country, or possessed it on other terms. I always knew the estate fell into our family in the civil wars of Cromwell, and in the world's language, was the well-earned meed of my progenitors' valour; but I seemed to hear it now for the first time.

I am glad, however, that this old Irish chieftain is such a ferocious savage; that one pity his fate awakens, is qualified by aversion for his implacable, irascible disposition. I am glad his daughter is *red-headed*, a pedant, and a romp; that she spouts Latin like the priest of the parish, and cures sore fingers; that she avoids genteel society, where her ideal rank would procure her no respect, and her

---

[1] This is a line in a song of one Dignum, who composed in his native language, but could neither read or write, nor spoke any language but his own.

'I have seen,' said the celebrated Edmund Burke (who in his boyish days had known him), 'some of his effusions translated into English, but was assured by judges, that they fell far short of the originals; yet they contained some graces "snatched beyond the reach of art".'—Vide *Life of Burke*.

unpolished ignorance, by force of contrast, make her feel her real inferiority; that she gossips among the poor peasants, over whom she can reign liege Lady; and, that she has been brought up by a Jesuitical priest, who has doubtlessly rendered her as bigotted and illiberal as himself. All this soothes my conscientious throes of feeling and compassion; for Oh! if this savage chief was generous and benevolent, as he is independent and spirited; if this daughter was amiable and intelligent, as she must be simple and unvitiated! But I dare not pursue the supposition. It is better as it is.

You would certainly never guess that the *Villa di Marino*, from whence I date the continuation of my letter, was simply a *fisherman's hut* on the sea coast, half way between the Lodge and Castle of Inismore, that is, seven miles distant from each. Determined on attending vespers at Inismore, I was puzzling my brain to think where or how I should pass the night, when this hut caught my eye, and I rode up to it to inquire if there was any inn in the neighbourhood, where a *Chevalier Errant** could shelter his adventurous head for a night; but I was informed the nearest inn was fifteen miles distant, so I bespoke a little fresh straw, and a clean blanket, which hung airing on some fishing tackle outside the door of this *marine hotel*, in preference to riding so far for a bed, at so late an hour as that in which the vespers would be concluded.

This, mine host of the Atlantic promised me, pointing to a little board suspended over the door, on which was written

'Good Dry Lodging.'

My landlord, however, convinced me his hotel afforded something better than good dry lodging; for entreating I would alight, till a shower passed over which was beginning to fall, I entered the hut, and found his wife, a sturdy lad their eldest son, and two naked little ones, seated at their dinner, and enjoying such a feast, as Apicius,* who sailed to Africa from Rome to eat good oysters, would gladly have voyaged from Rome to Ireland, to have partaken of; for they were absolutely dining on an immense turbot* (whose fellow-sufferers were floundering in a boat that lay anchored near the door). A most cordial invitation on their part, and a most willing compliance on mine, was the ceremony of a moment; and never did an English alderman on turtle day, or Roman Emperor on lampreys* and peacocks' livers, make a more delicious repast, than the chance guest

of these good people, on their boiled turbot and roasted potatoes,
which was quaffed down with the pure phalernian* of a neighbouring
spring.

Having learnt that the son was going with the compeers of the
demolished turbot to Bally——, I took out my little escritoire to
write you an account of the first adventure of my chivalrous tour;
while one of spring's most grateful sunny showers, is pattering on
the leaves of the only tree that shades this simple dwelling, and my
Rosinante is nibbling a scanty dinner from the patches of vegetation
that sprinkle the surrounding cliffs. Adieu! the vesper hour arrives.
In all 'my orisons thy sins shall be remembered.' The spirit of adventure wholly possesses me, and on the dusky horizon of life, some
little glimmering of light begins to dawn.

Encore adieu,

H.M.

LETTER V

TO J.D. ESQ. M.P.

Castle of Inismore, Barony of ——

Aye, 'tis even so—point your glass, and rub your eyes, 'tis all
one; here I am, and here I am likely to remain for some time. But
whether a prisoner of war, or taken up on a suspicion of espionage,
or to be offered as an appeasing sacrifice to the *manes** of the old
Prince of Inismore, you must for a while suspend your patience to
learn.

According to the *carte du pays* laid out for me by the fisherman, I
left the shore and crossed the summit of a mountain that 'battled o'er
the deep,' and which after an hour's ascension, I found sloped almost
perpendicularly down to a bold and rocky coast, its base terminating
in a peninsula, that advanced for near half a mile into the ocean.
Towards the extreme western point of this peninsula, which was
wildly romantic beyond all description, arose a vast and grotesque
pile of rocks, which at once formed the scite and fortifications of the
noblest mass of ruins on which my eye ever rested. Grand even in
desolation, and magnificent in decay—it was the Castle of Inismore.
The setting sun shone brightly on its mouldering turrets, and the

waves which bathed its rocky basis, reflected on their swelling bosoms the dark outlines of its awful ruins.[1]

As I descended the mountain's brow, I observed that the little isthmus which joined the peninsula to the mainland, had been cut away, and a curious danger-threatening bridge was rudely thrown across the intervening gulf, flung from the rocks on one side to an angle of the mountain on the other, leaving a yawning chasm of some fathoms deep beneath the foot of the wary passenger. This must have been a very perilous pass in days of civil warfare; and in the intrepidity of my daring ancestor, I almost forgot his crime. Amidst the interstices of the rocks which skirted the shores of this interesting peninsula, patches of the richest vegetation were to be seen, and the trees, which sprung wildly among its venerable ruins, were bursting into all the vernal luxuriancy of spring. In the course of my descent, several cabins of a better description than I had yet seen, appeared scattered beneath the shelter of the mountain's innumerable projections; while in the air and dress of their inhabitants (which the sound of my horse's feet brought to their respective doors), I evidently perceived a something original and primitive, I had never noticed before in this class of persons here.

They appeared to me, I know not why, to be in their holiday garb, and their dress, though grotesque and coarse, was cleanly and characteristic. I observed that round the heads of the elderly dames were folded several wreaths of white or coloured linen,[2] that others had handkerchiefs[3] lightly folded round their brows, and curiously fastened under the chin; while the young wore their hair fastened up with wooden bodkins. They were all enveloped in large shapeless mantles* of blue frize, and most of them had a rosary hanging on their arm, from whence I inferred they were on the point of attending vespers at the chapel of Inismore. I alighted at the door of a cabin a few paces distant from the Alpine bridge, and entreated a shed for

[1] Those who have visited the Castle of Dunluce, near the Giants' Causeway, may, perhaps, have some of its striking features in this rude draught of the Castle of Inismore.

[2] 'The women's ancient head-dress so perfectly resembles that of the Egyptian Isis, that it cannot be doubted but that the modes of Egypt were preserved among the Irish.'—*Walker on the Ancient Irish Dress*, page 62.

The Author's father, who lived in the early part of his life in a remote skirt of the Province of Connaught, remembers to have seen the heads of the female peasantry encircled with folds of linen in form of a turban.

[3] These handkerchiefs they call *Binnogues*: it is a remnant of a very ancient mode.

my horse, while I performed my devotions. The man to whom I addressed myself, seemed the only one of several who surrounded me, that understood English, and appeared much edified by my pious intention, saying, 'that God would prosper my Honour's journey, and that I was welcome to a shed for my horse, and a night's lodging for myself into the bargain.' He then offered to be my guide, and as we crossed the draw-bridge, he told me I was out of luck by not coming earlier, for that high mass had been celebrated that morning for the repose of the soul of a Prince of Inismore, who had been murdered on this very day of the month. 'And when this day comes round,' he added, 'we all attend dressed in our best; for my part, I never wear my poor old grandfather's *berrad* but on the like occasion,' taking off a curious cap of a conical form, which he twirled round his hand, and regarded with much satisfaction.[1]

By heavens! as I breathed this region of superstition, so strongly was I infected, that my usual scepticism was scarcely proof against my inclination to mount my horse and gallop off, as I shudderingly pronounced,

'I am then entering the Castle of Inismore, on the anniversary of that day on which my ancestors took the life of its venerable Prince!'

You see, my good friend, how much we are the creatures of situation and circumstance, and with what pliant servility the mind resigns itself to the impressions of the senses, or the illusions of the imagination.

We had now reached the ruined cloisters of the chapel; I paused to examine their curious but delapidated architecture when my guide, hurrying me on said, 'if I did not quicken my pace, I should miss getting a good view of the Prince,' who was just entering by a door opposite to that we had passed through. Behold me then mingling among a group of peasantry, and, like them, straining my eyes to that magnet which fascinated every glance.

And sure, Fancy, in her boldest flight, never gave to the fairy vision of poetic dreams, a combination of images more poetically fine, more strikingly picturesque, or more impressively touching. Nearly one half of the chapel of Inismore has fallen into decay, and the ocean breeze, as it rushed through the fractured roof, wafted the

---

[1] A few years back, Hugh Dugan, a peasant of the County of Kilkenny, who affected the ancient Irish dress, seldom appeared without his *berrad*.

torn banners of the family which hung along its dismantled walls. The red beams of the sinking sun shone on the glittering tabernacle which stood on the altar, and touched with their golden light the sacerdotal vestments of the two officiating priests, who ascended its broken steps at the moment that the Prince and his family entered.

The first of this most singular and interesting group, was the venerable Father John, the chaplain. Religious enthusiasm never gave to the fancied form of the first of the Patriarchs, a countenance of more holy expression, or divine resignation; a figure more touching by its dignified simplicity, or an air more beneficently mild— more meekly good. He was dressed in his pontificals, and with his eyes bent to earth, his hands spread upon his breast, he joined his coadjutors.

What a contrast to this saintly being now struck my view; a form almost gigantic in stature, yet gently thrown forward by evident infirmity; limbs of Herculean mould, and a countenance rather furrowed by the inroads of vehement passions, than the deep trace of years. Eyes still emanating the ferocity of an unsubdued spirit, yet tempered by a strong trait of benevolence; which, like a glory,* irradiated a broad expansive brow, a mouth on which even yet the spirit of convivial enjoyment seemed to hover, though shaded by two large whiskers on the upper lip,[1] which still preserved their ebon hue; while time or grief had bleached the scattered hairs, which hung their snows upon the manly temple. The drapery which covered this striking figure was singularly appropriate, and, as I have since been told, strictly conformable to the ancient costume of the Irish nobles.[2]

The only part of the under garment visible, was the ancient Irish *truis*, which closely adhering to the limbs from the waist to the ancle, includes the pantaloon and hose, and terminates in a kind of buskin, not dissimilar to the Roman *perones*. A triangular mantle of bright *scarlet* cloth, embroidered and fringed round the edges, fell from his shoulders to the ground, and was fastened at the breast with a large

---

[1] 'I have been confidently assured, that the grandfather of the present Rt. Hon. John O'Neil, (great grandfather to the present Lord O'Neil), the elegant and accomplished owner of Shanes Castle, wore his beard after the *prohibited* Irish mode.'—*Walker*, p. 62.

[2] The Irish mantle, with the fringed or shagged borders sewed down the edges of it, was not always made of frize and such coarse materials, which was the dress of the lower sort of people, but, according to the rank and quality of the wearer, was sometimes made of the finest cloth, bordered with silken fringe of scarlet, and various colours—*Ware*, vol. ii. p. 75.

circular golden broach,[1] of a workmanship most curiously beautiful; round his neck hung a golden collar, which seemed to denote the wearer of some order of knighthood, probably hereditary in his family; a dagger, called a *skiene* (for my guide explained every article of the dress to me), was sheathed in his girdle, and was discerned by the sunbeam that played on its brilliant haft. And as he entered the chapel, he removed from his venerable head a cap, or berrad, of the same form as that I had noticed with my guide, but made of velvet, richly embroidered.

The chieftain moved with dignity—yet with difficulty—and his colossal, but infirm frame, seemed to claim support from a form so almost impalpably delicate, that as it floated on the gaze, it seemed like the incarnation of some pure etherial spirit, which a sigh too roughly breathed would dissolve into its kindred air; yet to this sylphid elegance of spheral beauty was united all that symmetrical *contour* which constitutes the luxury of human loveliness. This scarcely 'mortal mixture of earth's mould,' was vested in a robe of vestal white, which was enfolded beneath the bosom with a narrow girdle embossed with precious stones.

From the shoulder fell a mantle of scarlet silk, fastened at the neck with a silver bodkin, while the fine turned head was enveloped in a veil of point lace, bound round the brow with a band, or diadem, ornamented with the same description of jewels as encircled her arms.[2]

Such was the *figure* of the Princess of Inismore!—But Oh! not once was the face turned round towards that side where I stood. And when I shifted my position, the envious veil intercepted the ardent

---

[1] Several of these useful ornaments (in Irish, *dealg fallain*), some gold, some silver, have been found in various parts of the kingdom, and are to be seen in the cabinets of our national *virtuosi*. Joseph Cooper Walker, Esq. to whose genius, learning, and exertions, Ireland stands so deeply indebted, speaking of a broach he had seen in the possession of R. Ousley, Esq. says—'Neither my pen or pencil can give an adequate idea of the elegant gold filligree work with which it is composed.'

[2] This was, with little variation, the general costume of the female *noblesse* of Ireland from a very early period. In the 15th century the veil was very prevalent, and was termed fillag, or scarf; the Irish ladies, like those of ancient and modern Greece, seldom appearing unveiled. As the veil made no part of the Celtic costume, its origin was probably merely oriental.

The great love of ornaments betrayed by the Irish ladies of other times, 'the beauties of the heroes of old,' are thus described by a quaint and ancient author:—'Their necks are hung with chains and carkanets—their arms wreathed with many bracelets.'

glance which eagerly sought the fancied charms it concealed: for was it possible to doubt the face would not 'keep the promise which the form had made.'

The group that followed was grotesque beyond all powers of description. The ancient bard, whose long white beard

'Descending, swept his aged breast,'

the incongruous costume—half modern, half antique—of the barefooted domestics; the ostensible air of the steward, who closed the procession—and above all, the dignified importance of the *nurse*, who took the lead in it immediately after her young lady: her air, form, countenance, and dress, were indeed so singularly fantastic and *outré*,* that the genius of masquerade might have adopted her figure as the finest model of grotesque caricature.

Conceive for a moment a form whose longitude bore no degree of proportion to her latitude; dressed in a short jacket of brown cloth, with loose sleeves from the elbow to the wrist, made of red camblet, striped with green, and turned up with a broad cuff—a petticoat of scarlet frize, covered by an apron of green serge, longitudinally striped with scarlet tape, and sufficiently short to betray an ancle that sanctioned all the libels ever uttered against the ancles of the Irish fair—true national brogues set off her blue worsted stockings, and her yellow hair, dragged over an high roll, was covered on the summit with a little coiff, over which was flung a scarlet handkerchief, which fastened in a large bow under her rubicund chin.[1]

As this singular and interesting group advanced up the centre aisle of the chapel, reverence and affection were evidently blended in the looks of the multitude, which hung upon their steps; and though the Prince and his daughter seemed to lose in the meekness of true religion all sense of temporal inequality, and promiscuously mingled with the congregation, yet *that* distinction they humbly avoided, was reverentially forced on them by the affectionate crowd, which drew back on either side as they advanced—until the chieftain and his child stood alone, in the centre of the ruined choir—the winds of

[1] Such was the dress of Mary Morgan, a poor peasant, in the neighbourhood of Drogheda, in 1786.—'In the close of the last century Mrs Power, of Waterford, vulgarly called the *Queen of Credan*, appeared constantly in this dress, with the exception of ornaments being gold, silver and fine Brussels lace.'—See *Walker's Essay on Ancient Irish Dress*, p. 73.

Heaven playing freely amidst their garments—the sun's setting beam enriching their beautiful figures with its orient tints, while he, like Milton's ruined angel,

> 'Above the rest,
> In shape and feature proudly eminent,
> Stood like a tower;'

and she, like the personified spirit of Mercy, hovered round him, or supported more by her tenderness than her strength, him from whom she could no longer claim support.

Those grey-headed domestics too—those faithful though but nominal vassals, who offered that voluntary reverence with their looks, which his repaid with fatherly affection, while the anguish of a suffering heart hung on his pensive smile, sustained by the firmness of that indignant pride which lowered on his ample brow!

What a picture!

As soon as the first flush of interest, curiosity, and amazement, had subsided, my attention was carried towards the altar; and then I thought, as I watched the impressive avocation of Father John, that had I been the Prince, I would have been the *Caiphas** too.

What a religion is this! How finely does it harmonize with the weakness of our nature; how seducingly it speaks to the senses; how forcibly it works on the passions; how strongly it seizes on the imagination; how interesting its forms; how graceful its ceremonies; how awful its rites.—What a captivating, what a *picturesque* faith! Who would not become its proselyte, were it not for the stern opposition of reason—the cold suggestions of philosophy!

The last strain of the vesper hymn died on the air as the sun's last beam faded on the casements of the chapel; and the Prince and his daughter, to avoid the intrusion of the crowd, withdrew through a private door, which communicated by a ruinous arcade with the castle.

I was the first to leave the chapel, and followed them at a distance as they moved slowly along. Their fine figures sometimes concealed behind a pillar, and again emerging from the transient shade, flushed with the deep suffusion of the crimsoned firmament.

Once they paused, as if to admire the beautiful effect of the retreating light, as it faded on the ocean's swelling bosom; and once the Princess raised her hand and pointed to the evening star, which rose brilliantly on the deep cerulean blue of a cloudless atmosphere, and shed its fairy beam on the mossy summit of a mouldering turret.

Such were the sublime objects which seemed to engage their attention, and added their *sensible* inspiration to the fervour of those more abstracted devotions in which they were so recently engaged. At last they reached the portals of the castle, and I lost sight of them. Yet still spell-bound, I stood transfixed to the spot from whence I had caught a last view of their receding figures.

While I felt like the victim of superstitious terror when the spectre of its distempered fancy vanishes from its strained and eager gaze, all I had lately seen revolved in my mind like some pictured story of romantic fiction. I cast round my eyes; all still seemed the vision of awakened imagination—Surrounded by a scenery grand even to the boldest majesty of nature, and wild even to desolation—the day's dying splendours awfully involving in the gloomy haze of deepening twilight—the grey mists of stealing night gathering on the still faintly illumined surface of the ocean, which awfully spreading to infinitude, seemed to the limited gaze of human vision to incorporate with the heaven whose last glow it reflected—the rocks, which on every side rose to Alpine elevation, exhibiting, amidst the soft obscurity, forms savagely bold or grotesquely wild; and those finely interesting ruins which spread grandly desolate in the rear, and added a moral interest to the emotions excited by this view of nature in her most awful, most touching aspect.

Thus suddenly withdrawn from the world's busiest haunts, its hackneyed modes, its vicious pursuits, and unimportant avocations—dropt as it were amidst scenes of mysterious sublimity—alone—on the wildest shores of the greatest ocean of the universe; immersed amidst the decaying monuments of past ages; still viewing in recollection such forms, such manners, such habits (as I had lately beheld), which to the worldly mind may be well supposed to belong to a race long passed beyond the barrier of existence, with 'the years beyond the flood,' I felt like the being of some other sphere newly alighted on a distant orb. While the novel train of thought which stole on my mind seemed to seize its tone from the awful tranquillity by which I was surrounded, and I remained leaning on the fragment of a rock, as the waves dashed idly against its base, until their dark heads were silvered by the rising moon, and while my eyes dwelt on her silent progress, the castle clock struck nine. Thus warned, I arose to depart, yet not without reluctance. My soul, for the first

time, had here held commune with herself; the 'lying vanities' of life
no longer intoxicating my senses, appeared to me for the first time in
their genuine aspect, and my heart still fondly loitered over those
scenes of solemn interest, where some of its best feelings had been
called into existence.

Slowly departing, I raised my eyes to the Castle of Inismore,
and sighed, and almost wished I had been born the Lord of these
beautiful ruins, the Prince of this isolated little territory, the adored
Chieftain of these affectionate and natural people. At that moment a
strain of music stole by me, as if the breeze of midnight stillness had
expired in a manner on the Eolian lyre. Emotion, undefinable emotion, thrilled on every nerve. I listened. I trembled. A breathless
silence gave me every note. Was it the illusion of my now all
awakened fancy, or the professional exertions of the bard of
Inismore? Oh, no! for the voice it symphonized; the low wild tremu-
lous voice, which sweetly sighed its soul of melody o'er the harp's
responsive chords, was the voice of a *woman*!

Directed by the witching strain, I approached an angle of the
building from whence it seemed to proceed; and perceiving a light
which streamed through an open casement, I climbed, with some
difficulty, the ruins of a parapet wall, which encircled this wing of
the castle, and which rose so immediately under the casement as to
give me, when I stood on it, a perfect view of the interior of that
apartment to which it belonged.

Two tapers which burned on a marble slab, at the remotest
extremity of this vast and gloomy chamber, shed their dim blue light
on the saintly countenance of Father John; who, with a large folio
open before him, seemed wholly wrapt in studious meditation; while
the Prince, reclined on an immense gothic couch, with his robe
thrown over the arm that supported his head, betrayed by the
expression of his countenance, those emotions which agitated his
soul, while he listened to those strains which spoke once to the heart
of the father, the patriot, and the man—breathed from the chords of
his country's emblem—breathed in the pathos of his country's
music—breathed from the lips of his apparently inspired daughter!
The 'white rising of her hands upon the harp;' the half-drawn veil,
that imperfectly discovered the countenance of a seraph; the moon-
light that played round her fine form, and partially touched her
drapery with its silver beam—her attitude! her air! But how cold—

how inanimate—how imperfect this description! Oh! could I but seize the touching features—could I but realize the vivid tints of this enchanting picture, as they then glowed on my fancy! By heavens! you would think the mimic copy fabulous; the 'celestial visitant' of an over-heated imagination. Yet as if the independent witchery of the lovely minstrel was not in itself all, all-sufficient, at the back of her chair stood the grotesque figure of her antiquated nurse. O! the precious contrast. And yet it heightened, it finished the picture.

While thus entranced in breathless observation, endeavouring to support my precarious tenement, and to prolong this rich feast of the senses and the soul, the loose stones on which I tottered gave way under my feet, and impulsively clinging to the wood-work of the casement, it mouldered in my grasp. I fell—but before I reached the earth I was bereft of sense. With its return I found myself in a large apartment, stretched on a bed, and supported in the arms of the Prince of Inismore! His hand was pressed to my bleeding temple; while the priest applied a styptic to the wound it had received; and the nurse was engaged in binding up my arm, which had been dreadfully bruised and fractured a little above the wrist. Some domestics, with an air of mingled concern and curiosity, surrounded my couch; and at her father's side stood the Lady Glorvina, her looks pale and disordered—her trembling hands busily employed in preparing bandages, for which my skilful doctress impatiently called.

While my mind almost doubted the evidence of my senses, and a physical conviction alone *painfully* proved to me the reality of all I beheld, my wandering, wondering eyes met those of the Prince of Inismore! A volume of pity and benevolence was registered in their glance; nor were mine, I suppose, inexpressive of my feelings, for he thus replied to them:—

'Be of good cheer, young stranger; you are in no danger; be composed; be confident; conceive yourself in the midst of friends; for you are surrounded by those who would wish to be considered as such.'

I attempted to speak, but my voice faultered; my tongue was nerveless; my mouth dry and parched. A trembling hand presented a cordial to my lip. I quaffed the philtre, and fixed my eyes on the face of my ministering angel.—That angel was Glorvina!—I closed them, and sunk on the bosom of her father.

'Oh, he faints again!' cried a sweet and plaintive voice.

'On the contrary,' replied the priest, 'the weariness of acute pain something subsided, is lulling him into a soft repose; for see, the colour re-animates his cheek, and his pulse quickens.'

'It indeed beats most wildly;' returned the sweet physician—for the pulse which responded to her finger's thrilling pressure, moved with no languid throb.

'Let us retire,' added the priest, 'all danger is now, thank heaven, over; and repose and quiet the most salutary requisites for our patient.'

At these words he arose from my bed-side; and the Prince gently withdrawing his supporting arms, laid my head upon the pillow. In a moment all was death-like stillness, and stealing a glance from under my half-closed eyes, I found myself alone with my skilful doctress, the nurse; who, shading the taper's light from the bed, had taken her distaff and seated herself on a little stool at some distance.

This was a golden respite to feelings wound up to that vehement excess which forbade all expression, which left my tongue powerless, while my heart overflowed with emotion the most powerful.

Good God! I, the son of Lord M——, the hereditary object of hereditary detestation, beneath the roof of my implacable enemy! Supported in his arms; relieved from anguish by his charitable attention; honored by the solicitude of his lovely daughter; overwhelmed by the charitable exertions of his whole family; and reduced to that bodily infirmity that would of necessity oblige me to continue for some time the object of their beneficent attentions.

What a series of emotions did this conviction awaken in my heart! Emotions of a character, an energy, long unknown to my apathized feelings; while gratitude to those who had drawn them into existence, combined with the interest, the curiosity, the admiration, they had awakened, tended to confirm my irresistible desire of perpetuating the immunities I enjoyed, as the guest and patient of the Prince and his daughter. And while the touch of this Wild Irish Girl's hand thrilled on every sense—while her voice of tenderest pity murmured on my ear, and I secretly triumphed over the prejudices of her father, I would not have exchanged my broken arm and wounded temple for the strongest limb and soundest head in the kingdom; but the same chance which threw me in the supporting arms of the irasible Prince, might betray to him in the person of his patient, the son of his hereditary enemy: it was at least probable he would make some inquiries relative to the object of his benevolence, and the singular cause which rendered him such; it was therefore a necessary policy in me to be provided against this scrutiny.

Already deep in adventure, a thousand seducing reasons were suggested by my newly awakened heart, to go on with the romance, and to secure for my future residence in the castle, that interest, which, if known to be the son of Lord M——, I must eventually have forfeited, for the cold aversion of irreclaimable prejudice. The imposition was at least innocent, and might tend to future and mutual advantage; and after the ideal assumption of a thousand fictitious characters, I at last fixed on that of an itinerant artist, as consonant to my most cultivated talent, and to the testimony of those witnesses which I had fortunately brought with me, namely, my drawing book, pencils, etc. etc.—self-nominated *Henry Mortimer*, to answer the initials on my linen, the only proofs against me, for I had not even a letter with me.

I was now armed at all points for inspection; and as the Prince lived in a perfect state of isolation, and I was unknown in the country, I entertained no apprehensions of discovery during the time I should remain at the castle; and full of hope, strong in confidence, but wearied by incessant cogitation, and something exhausted by pain, I fell into that profound slumber I did before but feign.

The mid-day beam shone brightly through the faded tints of my bed curtains before I awakened the following morning, after a night of such fairy charms as only float round the couch of

> 'Fancy trained in bliss.'

The nurse, and the two other domestics, relieved the watch at my bed-side during the night; and when I drew back the curtain, the former complimented me on my somniferous powers, and in the usual mode of inquiry, but in a very unusual accent and dialect, addressed me with much kindness and good-natured solicitude. While I was endeavouring to express my gratitude for her attentions, and what seemed most acceptable to her, my high opinion of her skill, the Father Director entered.

To the benevolent mind, distress or misfortune is ever a sufficient claim on all the privileges of intimacy; and, when Father John seated himself by my bed-side, affectionately took my hand, lamented my accident, and assured me of my improved looks, it was with an air so kindly familiar, so tenderly intimate, that it was impossible to suspect the sound of his voice was yet a stranger to my ear.

Prepared and collected, as soon as I had expressed my sense of his and the Prince's benevolence, I briefly related my feigned story; and in a few minutes I was a young Englishman, by birth a gentleman, by inevitable misfortunes reduced to a dependence on my talents for a livelihood, and by profession an artist. I added, that I came to Ireland to take views, and seize some of the finest features of its landscapes; that having heard much of the wildly picturesque charms of the north-west coasts, I had penetrated thus far into this remote corner of the province of Connaught; that the uncommon beauty of the views surrounding the castle, and the awful magnificence of its ruins, had arrested my wanderings, and determined me to spend some days in its vicinity: that having attended divine service the preceding evening in the chapel, I continued to wander along the romantic shores of Inismore, and in the adventuring spirit of my art, had climbed part of the mouldering ruins of the castle, to catch a fine effect of light and shade, produced by the partially-veiled beams of the moon, and had then met with the accident which now threw me on the benevolence of the Prince of Inismore; an unknown in a strange country, with a fractured limb, a wounded head, and an heart oppressed with the sense of gratitude under which it laboured.

'That you were a stranger and a traveller, who had been led by curiosity or devotion to visit the chapel of Inismore,' said the priest, 'we were already apprised of, by the peasant who brought to the castle last night the horse and valise left at his cabin, and who feared, from the length of your absence, some accident had befallen you. What you have yourself been kind enough to detail, is precisely what will prove your best letter of recommendation to the Prince. Trust me, young gentleman, that your standing in need of his attention, is the best claim you could make on it; and your admiration of his native scenes, of that ancient edifice, the monument of that decayed ancestral splendour still dear to his pride; and your having so severely suffered through an anxiety by which he must be flattered, will induce him to consider himself as even *bound* to administer every attention that can meliorate the unpleasantness of your present situation.'

What an idea did this give me of the character of him whose heart I once believed divested of all the tender feelings of humanity. Every thing that mine could dictate on the subject, I endeavoured to express, and borne away by the vehemence of my feelings, did it in a manner that more than once fastened the eyes of Father John on my face, with that look of surprise and admiration which, to a delicate mind, is more gratifying than the most finished verbal eulogium.

Stimulated by this silent approbation, I insensibly stole the conversation from myself to a more general theme; one thought was the link to another—the chain of discussion gradually extended, and before the nurse brought up my late breakfast, we had ranged through the whole circle of *sciences*. I found that this intelligent and amiable being, had trifled a good deal in his young days with chemistry, which he still spoke like a lover who, in mature life fondly dwells on the charms of that object who first awakened the youthful raptures of his heart. He is even still an enthusiast in botany, and as free from monastic pedantry as he is rich in the treasures of classical literature, and the elegancies of belles lettres. His feelings even yet preserve something of the ardour of youth, and in his mild character, evidently appears blended, a philosophical knowledge of human nature, with the most perfect worldly inexperience, and the manly intelligence of an highly-gifted mind, with the sentiments of a recluse, and the simplicity of a child. His still ardent mind seemed to dilate to the correspondence of a kindred intellect, and two hours bed-side chit chat, with all the unrestrained freedom such a situation sanctions, produced a more perfect intimacy, than an age would probably have effected under different circumstances.

After having examined and dressed the wounded temple, which he declared to be a mere scratch, and congratulated me on the apparent convalescence of my looks, he withdrew, politely excusing the length of his visit, by pleading the charms of my conversation as the cause of his detention. There is, indeed, an evident vein of French suavity flowing through his manners, that convinced me he had spent some years of his life in that region of the graces. I have since learned that he was partly educated in France; so that, to my astonishment, I have discovered the manners of a gentleman, the conversation of a scholar, and sentiments of a philanthropist, united in the character of an Irish priest.*

While my heart throbbed with the natural satisfaction arising from the consciousness of having awakened an interest in those whom it was my ambition to interest, my female Esculapius* came and seated herself by me; and while she talked of fevers, inflammations, and the Lord knows what, insisted on my not speaking another word for the rest of the day. Though by no means appearing to labour under the same Pythagorean* restraint she had imposed on me; and after having extolled her own surgical powers, her celebrity as the best bone-setter in the barony, and communicated the long list of patients her skill had saved, her tongue at last rested on the only theme I was inclined to hear.

'Arrah! now jewel,' she continued, 'there is our Lady Glorvina now, who with all her skill, and knowing every leaf that grows, why she could no more set your arm than she could break it. Och! it was herself that turned white, when she saw the blood upon your face, for she was the first to hear you fall, and hasten down to have you picked up; at first, faith, we thought you were a robber; but it was all one to her; into the castle you must be brought, and when she saw the blood spout from your temple—Holy Virgin! she looked for all the world as if she was kilt dead herself.'

'And is she,' said I, in the selfishness of my heart, 'is she always thus humanely interested for the unfortunate?'

'Och! it is she that is tender-hearted for man or beast,' replied my companion. 'I shall never forge till the day of my death, *nor then* either, faith, the day that Kitty Mulrooney's cow was bogged: you must know, honey, that a bogged cow   *   *   *   *   *

Unfortunately, however, the episode of Kitty Mulrooney's cow was cut short, for the Prince now entered, leaning on the arm of the priest.

Dull indeed must be every feeling, and blunted every recollective faculty, when the look, the air, the smile, with which this venerable and benevolent Chieftain, approaching my bed, and kindly taking me by the hand, addressed me in the singular idiom of his expressive language.

'Young man,' said he, 'the stranger's best gift is upon you, for the eye that sees you for the first time, wishes it may not be the last; and the ear that drinks your words, grows thirsty as it quaffs them. So says our good Father John here; for you have made him your friend ere you are his acquaintance; and as the *friend of my friend*, my heart opens to you—you are welcome to my house, as long as it is pleasant to you; when it ceases to be so, we will part with you with regret, and speed your journey with our wishes and our prayers.'

Could my heart have lent its eloquence to my lip—but that was impossible; very imperfect indeed was the justice I did to my feelings; but as my peroration was an eulogium on these romantic scenes and interesting ruins, the contemplation of which I had nearly purchased with my life, the Prince seemed as much pleased as if my gratitude had poured forth with *Ciceronian** eloquence, and he replied,

'When your health will permit, you can pursue here uninterrupted your charming art. Once, the domains of Inismore could have supplied the painter's pencil with scenes of smiling felicity, and the song of the bard—with many a theme of joy and triumph; but the harp can now only mourn over the fallen greatness of its sons; and the pencil has nothing left to delineate, but the ruins which shelter the grey head of the last of their descendants.'

These words were pronounced with an emotion that shook the debilitated frame of the Prince, and the tear which dimmed the spirit of his eye, formed an associate in that of his auditor. He gazed on me for a moment with a look that seemed to say, 'you feel for me then—yet you are an Englishman;' and taking the arm of Father John, he walked towards a window which commanded a view of the ocean, whose troubled bosom beat wildly against the castle cliffs.

'The day is sad,' said he, 'and makes the soul gloomy: we will summons O'Gallagher to the hall, and drive away sorrow with music.'

Then turning to me, he added, with a faint smile, 'the tones of an Irish harp have still the power to breathe a spirit over the drooping soul of an Irishman; but if its strains disturb your repose, command its silence: the pleasure of the host always rests in that of his guest.'

With these words, and leaning on the arm of his chaplain, he retired; while the nurse, looking affectionately after him, raised her hands, and exclaimed,

'Och! there you go, and may the blessing of the Holy Virgin go with you, for it's yourself that's the jewel of a Prince!'

The impression made on me by this brief but interesting interview, is not to be expressed. You should see the figure, the countenance, the dress of the Prince; the appropriate scenery of the old Gothic chamber, the characteristic appearance of the priest and the nurse, to understand the combined and forcible effect the whole produced.

Yet, though experiencing a pleasurable emotion, strong as it was novel there was still one little wakeful wish throbbing vaguely at my heart.

Was it possible that my chilled, my sated misanthropic feelings, still sent forth one sigh of wishful solicitude for woman's dangerous presence! No, the sentiment the daughter of the Prince inspired, only made a *part* in that general feeling of curiosity, which every thing in this new region of wonders continued to nourish into existence. What had I to expect from the unpolished manners, the confined ideas of this Wild Irish Girl? Deprived of all those touching allurements which society only gives; reared in wilds and solitudes, with no other associates than her nurse, her confessor, and her father; endowed indeed by nature with some personal gifts, set off by the advantage of a singular and characteristic dress, for which she is indebted to whim and natural prejudice, rather than native taste:—I, who had fled in disgust even from those to whose natural attraction the bewitching blandishments of education, the brilliant polish of fashion, and the dazzling splendour of *real* rank, contributed their potent spells.

And yet, the roses of Florida, though the fairest in the universe, and springing from the richest soil, emit no fragrance; while the mountain violet, rearing its timid form from a steril bed, flings on the morning breeze the most delicious perfume.

While given up to such reflections as these—while the sound of the Irish harp arose from the hall below, and the nurse muttered her prayers in Irish over her beads by my side, I fell into a gentle slumber, in which I dreamed that the Princess of Inismore approached my bed, drew aside the curtains, and raising her veil, discovered a face I had hitherto rather guessed at, than seen. Imagine my horror—it was the face, the head, of a *Gorgon*!*

Awakened by the sudden and terrific motion it excited, though still almost motionless, as if from the effects of a night-mare (which in fact, from the position I lay in, had oppressed me in the form of the Princess), I cast my eyes through a fracture in the old damask drapery of my bed, and beheld—not the horrid spectre of my recent dream, but the form of a cherub hovering near my pillow—it was the Lady Glorvina herself! Oh! how I trembled lest the fair image should only be the vision of my slumber: I scarcely dared to breathe, lest it should dissolve.

She was seated on the nurse's little stool. Her elbow resting on her knee, her cheek reclined upon her hand; for once the wish of Romeo appeared no hyperbola.

Some snow-drops lay scattered in her lap, on which her downcast eyes shed their beams; as though she moralized over the modest blossoms, which, in fate and delicacy, resembled herself. Changing her pensive attitude, she collected them into a bunch, and sighed, and waved her head as she gazed on them. The dew that trembled on their leaves seemed to have flowed from a richer source than the exhalation of the morning's vapour—for the flowers were faded—but the drops that gem'd them were fresh.

At that moment the possession of a little kingdom would have been less desirable to me, than the knowledge of that association of ideas and feelings which the contemplation of these honoured flowers awakened. At last, with a tender smile, she raised them to her lip, and sighed; and placed them in her bosom; then softly drew aside my curtain. I feigned the stillness of death—yet the curtain remained unclosed—many minutes elapsed—I ventured to unseal my eyes, and met the soul dissolving glance of my sweet attendant spirit, who seemed to gaze intently on her charge. Emotion on my part the most delicious, on hers the most modestly confused, for a moment prevented all presence of mind; the beautiful arm still supported the curtain—my ardent gaze was still rivetted on a face alternately suffused with the electric flashes of red and white. At last the curtain fell, the priest entered, and the vision, the sweetest, brightest, vision of my life, dissolved!

Glorvina sprung towards her tutor, and told him aloud, that the nurse had entreated her to take her place, while she descended to dinner.

'And no place can become thee better, my child,' said the priest, 'than that which fixes thee by the couch of suffering and sickness.'

'However,' said Glorvina, smiling, 'I will gratify you by resigning for the present in your favour;' and away she flew, speaking in Irish to the nurse, who passed her at the door.

The benevolent confessor then approached, and seated himself beside my bed, with that premeditated air of chit-chat sociality, that it went to my soul to disappoint him. But the thing was impossible. To have tamely conversed in mortal language on mortal subjects, after having held 'high communion' with an ethereal spirit; when a sigh, a tear, a glance, were the delicious vehicles of our souls' secret intercourse—to stoop from this 'coloquy sublime!' I could as soon have delivered a logical essay on identity and diversity, or any other subject equally interesting to the heart and imagination.

I therefore closed my eyes, and breathed most sonorously; the good priest drew the curtain and retired on tip-toe, and the nurse once more took her distaff, and for her sins was silent.

These good people must certainly think me a second Epimenides,* for I have done nothing but sleep, or feign to sleep, since I have been thrown amongst them.

LETTER VI

TO J.D. ESQ. M.P.

I have already passed four days beneath this hospitable roof. On the third, a slight fever with which I had been threatened passed off, my head was disencumbered, and on the fourth I was able to leave my bed, and to scribble thus far of my journal. Yet these kind solicitous beings will not suffer me to leave my room, and still the nurse at intervals gives me the pleasure of her society, and hums old *cronans*, or amuses me with what she calls a little *shanaos*,[1] as she plies her distaff; while the priest frequently indulges me with his interesting and intelligent conversation. The good man is a great logician, and fond of displaying his metaphysical prowess, where he feels that he is understood, and we diurnally go over *infinity*, *space*, and *duration*, with innate, simple, and complex ideas, until our own are exhausted in the discussion; and then we generally relax with Ovid, or trifle with Horace and Tibullus, for nothing can be less austerely pious than this cheerful and gentle being: nothing can be more innocent than his life; nothing more liberal than his sentiments.

The Prince, too, has thrice honoured me with a visit. Although he possesses nothing of the erudition which distinguishes his all-intelligent chaplain, yet there is a peculiar charm, a spell in his

---

[1] *Shanaos* pronounced, but properly spelt *Sheanachus*, is a term in very general use in Ireland, and is applied to a kind of genealogical chit-chat, or talking over family antiquity, family anecdotes, descent, alliances, etc. etc. to which the lower, as well as the higher order of Irish in the provincial parts are much addicted. I have myself conversed with several old ladies in Connaught and Munster, who were living chronicles of transactions in their families of the most distant date and complicated nature. *Senachy*, was the name of the antiquary retained in every noble family to preserve its exploits, etc. etc.

conversation, that is irresistibly fascinating; and chiefly arising, I believe, from the curious felicity of his expressions, the originality of the ideas they clothe, the strength and energy of his delivery, and the enthusiasm and simplicity of his manners.

He seems not so much to speak the English language, as literally to translate the Irish; and he borrows so much and so happily, from the peculiar idiom of his vernacular tongue, that though his conversation were deficient in matter, it would still possess a singular interest from its manner. But it is far otherwise; there is indeed in the uncultivated mind of this man, much of the *vivida vis anima** of native genius, which neither time or misfortune has wholly damped, and which frequently flings the brightest corruscations of thought over the generally pensive tone that pervades his conversation. The extent of his knowledge on subjects of national interest is indeed wonderful; his memory is rich in oral tradition, and most happily faithful to the history and antiquities of his country, which, notwithstanding peevish complaints of its degeneracy, he still loves with idolatrous fondness. On these subjects he is always borne away, but upon no subject whatever does he speak with coolness or moderation; he is always in extremes, and the vehemence of his gestures and looks ever corresponds to the energy of his expressions or sentiments. Yet he possesses an infinite deal of that *suaviter in modo*,* so prevailing and insinuating, even among the lower classes of this country; and his natural, or, I should rather say, his national politeness, frequently induces him to make the art in which he supposes me to excel, the topic of our conversation. While he speaks in rapture of the many fine views this country affords to the genius of the painter, he dwells with melancholy pleasure on the innumerable ruined palaces and abbeys which lie scattered amidst the richest scenes of this romantic province: he generally thus concludes with a melancholy apostrophe:

'But the splendid dwelling of princely grandeur, the awful asylum of monastic piety, are just mouldering into oblivion with the memory of those they once sheltered. The sons of little men triumph over those whose arm was strong in war, and whose voice breathed no impotent command; and the descendant of the mighty chieftain has nothing left to distinguish him from the son of the peasant, but the decaying ruins of his ancestors' castle; while the blasts of a few storms, and the pressure of a few years, shall even of them leave scarce a wreck to tell the traveller the mournful tale of fallen greatness.'

When I shewed him a sketch I had made of the Castle of Inismore, on the evening I had first seen it from the mountain's summit, he seemed much gratified, and warmly commended its fidelity, shaking his head as he contemplated it, and impressively exclaiming,

'Many a morning's sun has seen me climb that mountain in my boyish days, to contemplate these ruins, accompanied by an old follower of the family, who possessed many strange stories of the feats of my ancestors, with which I was then greatly delighted. And then I dreamed of my arm wielding the spear in war, and my hall resounding to the song of the bard, and the mirth of the feast; but it was only a dream!'

As the injury sustained by my left arm (which is in a state of rapid convalescence) is no impediment to the exertions of my right, we have already talked over the various views I am to take; and he enters into every little plan with that enthusiasm, which childhood betrays in the pursuit of some novel object, and seems wonderfully gratified in the idea of thus perpetuating the fast decaying features of this 'time honoured' edifice.

The priest assures me, I am distinguished in a particular manner by the partiality and condescension of the Prince.

'As a man of genius,' said he this morning, 'you have awakened a stronger interest in his breast, than if you had presented him with letters patent of your nobility, except, indeed, you had derived them from *Milesius* himself.

'An enthusiastic love of talents is one of the distinguishing features of the true ancient Irish character; and, independent of your general acquirements, your professional abilities coinciding with his ruling passion, secures you a larger portion of his esteem and regard than he generally lavishes upon any stranger, and almost incredible, considering you are an Englishman. But national prejudice ceases to operate when individual worth calls for approbation; and an Irishman seldom asks or considers the country of him whose sufferings appeal to his humanity, whose genius makes a claim on his applause.'

But, my good friend, while I am thus ingratiating myself with the father, the daughter (either self-wrapt in proud reserve, or determined to do away that temerity she may have falsely supposed her condescension and pity awakened) has not appeared even at the door of my chamber, with a charitable inquiry for my health, since our last silent, but eloquent, interview; and I have lived for these three days on the recollection of those precious moments which gave her to my view, as I last beheld her, like the angel of pity hovering round the pillow of mortal suffering.

Ah! you will say, this is not the language of an apathist, of one 'whom man delighteth not, nor *woman* either.' But let not your vivid imagination thus hurry over at once the scale of my feelings from one extreme to the other, forgetting the many intermediate degrees that lie between the deadly chill of the coldest, and the burning ardor of the most vehement of all human sentiments.

If I am less an apathist, which I am willing to confess, trust me, I am not a whit more the lover.—Lover!—Preposterous!—I am merely interested for this girl on a philosophical principle. I long to study the purely national, natural character of an Irishwoman: in fine, I long to behold any woman in such lights and shades of mind, temper, and disposition, as Nature has originally formed her in. Hitherto I have only met servile copies, sketched by the finger of art, and finished off by the polished touch of fashion.

I fear, however, that this girl is already spoiled by the species of education she has received. The priest has more than once spoke of her erudition! *Erudition*! the pedantry of a schoolboy of the third class, I suppose. How much must a woman lose, and how little can she gain, by that commutation which gives her our acquirements for her own graces! For my part, you know I have always kept clear of the *bas-bleus;** and would prefer one playful charm of a *Ninon*, to all the classic lore of a *Dacier*.*

But you will say, I could scarcely come off worse with the pedants than I did with the dunces; and you will say right. And, to confess the truth, I believe I should have been easily led to desert the standard of the pretty *fools*, had female pedantry ever stole on my heart under such a form as the little *soi-disant** Princess of Inismore. 'Tis, indeed, impossible to look *less* like one who spouts Latin with the priest of the parish, than this same Glorvina. There is something beautifully wild about her air and look, that is indescribable; and, without a very perfect regularity of feature, she possesses that effulgency of countenance, that bright *lumine purpureo*,* which poetry assigns to the dazzling emanations of divine beauty. In short, there are a thousand little fugitive graces playing around her, which are not beauty, but the cause of it; and were I to personify the word *spell*, she should sit for the picture... A thousand times she swims before my sight, as I last beheld her; her locks of living gold parting on her brow of snow, yet seeming to separate with reluctance, as they were lightly shaken off with that motion of the head, at once so infantine and graceful; a motion twice put into play, as her recumbent attitude poured the luxuriancy of her tresses over her face and neck, for she was unveiled, and a small gold bodkin was unequal to support the redundancy of that beautiful hair, which I more than once apostrophized in the words of Petrarch:

> 'Onde tolse amor l'oro e di qual vena
> Per far due treccie biondê,' etc.*

I understand a servant is dispatched once a week to the next post-town, with and for letters; and this intelligence absolutely amazed me; for I am astonished that these beings, who

> 'Look not like the inhabitants of the earth,
> And yet are on it,'

should hold any intercourse with the world.

This is post-day, and this packet is at last destined to be finished and dispatched. On looking it over, the titles of prince and princess so often occur, that I could almost fancy myself at the court of some foreign potentate, basking in the warm sunshine of regal favour, instead of being the chance guest of a poor Irish gentleman, who lives on the produce of a few rented farms, and, infected with a species of pleasant mania, believes himself as much a prince as the heir apparent of boundless empire and exhaustless treasures.

Adieu! Direct as usual: for though I certainly mean to accept the invitation of the Prince, yet I intend, in a few days, to return home, to obviate suspicion, and to have my books and wardrobe removed to the Lodge, which now possesses a stronger magnet of attraction than when I first fixed on it as my head-quarters.

LETTER VII

TO J.D. ESQ. M.P.

This is the sixth day of my convalescence, and the first of my descent from my western tower; for I find it is literally in a tower, or turret, which terminates a wing of these ruins, I have been lodged. These good people, however, would have persuaded me into the possession of a slow fever, and confined me to my room another day, had not the harp of Glorvina, with 'supernatural solicitings,' spoken more irresistibly to my heart than all their eloquence.

I had just made my *toilette*, for the first time since my arrival at the castle; and with a black ribbon of the nurse's across my forehead, and silk handkerchief of the priest's supporting my arm, with my own 'customary suit of solemn black,' tintless cheek, languid eye, and pensive air, I looked indeed as though 'melancholy had marked me for her own;' or an excellent personification of 'pining atrophy' in its last stage of decline.

While I contemplated my *memento mori** of a figure in the glass, I heard a harp tuning in an underneath apartment. The Prince, I knew, had not yet left his bed, for his infirmities seldom permit him to rise early; the priest had rode out; and the venerable figure of the old harper at that moment gave a fine effect to a ruined arch under which he was passing, led by a boy, just opposite my window. 'It is Glorvina then,' said I, 'and alone!' and down I sallied; but not with half the intrepidity that Sir Bertram followed the mysterious blue flame along the coridors of the enchanted castle.

A thousand times since my arrival in this trans-mundane region, I have had reason to feel how much we are the creatures of situation; how insensibly our minds and our feelings take their tone from the influence of existing circumstances. You have seen me frequently the very prototype of *nonchalance*, in the midst of a circle of birth-day beauties, that might have put the fabled charms of the *Mount Ida triumviri** to the blush of inferiority. Yet here I am, groping my way down the dismantled stone stairs of a ruined castle in the wilds of Connaught, with my heart fluttering like the pulse of green eighteen in the presence of its first love, merely because on the point of appearing before a simple rusticated girl, whose father calls himself a *prince*, with a *potatoe ridge* for his *dominions*! O! with what indifference I should have met her in the drawing-room, or at the Opera!—

there she would have been merely a woman!—here, she is the fairy vision of my heated fancy.

Well, having finished the same circuitous journey that a squirrel diurnally performs in his cage, I found myself landed in a dark stone passage, which was terminated by the identical chamber of fatal memory already mentioned, and the vista of a huge folding door, partly thrown back, beheld the form of Glorvina! She was alone, and bending over her harp; one arm was gracefully thrown over the instrument, which she was tuning; with the other she was lightly modulating on its chords.

Too timid to proceed, yet unwilling to retreat, I was still hovering near the door, when, turning round, she observed me, and I advanced. She blushed to the eyes, and returned my profound bow with a slight inclination of the head, as if I were unworthy a more marked obeisance.

Nothing in the theory of sentiment could be more diametrically opposite, than the bashful indication of that crimson blush, and the haughty spirit of that graceful bow. What a logical analysis would it have afforded to Father John, on innate and acquired ideas! Her blush was the effusion of nature; her bow the result of inculcation— the one spoke the native woman; the other the *ideal* princess.

I endeavoured to apologize for my intrusion; and she, in a manner that amazed me, congratulated me on my recovery; then drawing her harp towards her, she seated herself on the great Gothic couch, with a motion of the hand, and a look, that seemed to say, 'there is room for you too.' I bowed my acceptance of the silent welcome invitation.

Behold me then seated *tête-à-tête* with this Irish Princess!—my right arm thrown over her harp, and her eyes rivetted on my left.

'Do you still feel any pain from it?' said she so naturally, as though we had actually been discussing the accident it had sustained.

Would you believe it! I never thought of making her an answer; but fastened my eyes on her face. For a moment she raised her glance to mine, and we both coloured, as if she read there—I know not what!

'I beg your pardon,' said I, recovering from the spell of this magic glance—'you made some observation, Madam?'

'Not that I recollect,' she replied, with a slight confusion of manner, and running her finger carelessly over the chords of the harp, till it came in contact with my own, which hung over it. The touch circulated like electricity through every vein. I impulsively arose, and walked to the window from whence I had first heard the tones of that instrument which had been the innocent accessary to my present unaccountable emotion. As if I were measuring the altitude of my fall, I hung half my body out of the window, thinking, Heaven knows, of nothing less than *that* fall, of nothing more than its fair cause, until abruptly drawing in my dizzy head, I perceived her's (such a cherub head you never beheld!) leaning against her harp, and her eye directed towards me. I know not why, yet I felt at once confused and gratified by this observation.

'My fall,' said I, glad of something to say, to relieve my school-boy bashfulness, 'was greater than I suspected.'

'It was dreadful!' she replied shuddering. 'What could have led you to so perilous a situation?'

'That,' I returned, 'which has led to more certain destruction, senses more strongly fortified than mine—the voice of a syren!'

I then briefly related to her the rise, decline, and fall, of my physical empire; obliged, however, to qualify the gallantry of my *debut* by the subsequent plainness of my narration, for the delicate reserve of her air made me tremble, lest I had gone too far.

By Heavens! I cannot divest myself of a feeling of inferiority in her presence, as though I were actually that poor, wandering, unconnected being I have feigned myself.

My compliment was received with a smile and a blush; and to the eulogium which rounded my detail on the benevolence and hospitality of the family of Inismore, she replied, that 'had the accident been of less material consequence to myself, the family of Inismore must have rejoiced at any event which enriched its social circle with so desirable an acquisition.'

The *matter* of this little *politesse* was nothing; but the *manner*, the air, with which it was delivered! Where can she have acquired this elegance of manner!—reared amidst rocks, and woods, and mountains! deprived of all those graceful advantages which society confers—a manner too that is at perpetual variance with her looks, which are so *naif*—I had almost said so wildly simple—that while she speaks in the language of a court, she looks like the artless inhabitant of a cottage:—a smile, and a blush, rushing to her cheek, and her lip, as the impulse of fancy or feeling directs, even when smiles and blushes are irrelevant to the etiquette of the moment.

This elegance of manner, then, must be the pure result of elegance of soul; and if there is a charm in woman, I have hitherto vainly sought, and prized beyond all I have discovered, it is this refined, celestial, native elegance of soul, which effusing its spell through every thought, word, and motion, of its enviable possessor, resembles the peculiar property of gold, which subtilely insinuates itself through the most minute and various particles, without losing any thing of its own intrinsic nature by the amalgamation.

In answer to the flattering observation which had elicited this digression, I replied:

That far from regretting the consequences, I was enamoured of an accident that had procured me such happiness as I now enjoyed (even with the risk of life itself); and that I believed there were few who, like me, would not prefer peril to security, were the former always the purchase of such felicity as the latter, at least on me, had never bestowed.

Whether this reply savoured too much of the world's common-place gallantry, or that she thought there was more of the head than the heart in it, I know not; but, by my soul, in spite of a certain haughty motion of the head not unfrequent with her, I thought she looked wonderfully inclined to laugh in my face, though she primed up her pretty mouth, and fancied she looked like a nun, when her lip pouted with the smiling archness of an Hebe.*

In short, I never felt more in all its luxury the comfort of looking like a fool; and to do away the no very agreeable sensation which the conviction of being laughed at awakens, as a *pis-aller,** I began to examine the harp, and expressed the surprise I felt at its singular construction.

'Are you fond of music?' she asked with *naiveté.*

'Sufficiently so,' said I, 'to risk my life for it.'

She smiled, and cast a look at the window, as much as to say, 'I understand you.'

As I now was engaged in examining her harp, I observed that it resembled less any instrument of that kind I had seen, than the drawings of the Davidic lyre in Montfaucon.

'Then,' said she with animation, 'this is another collateral proof of the antiquity of its origin, which I never before heard adduced, and which sanctions that universally received tradition among us, by which we learn, that we are indebted to the first Milesian colony that settled here, for this charming instrument, although some modern historians suppose that we obtained it from Scandinavia.'[1]

'And is this, Madam?' said I, 'the original ancient Irish harp?'

'Not exactly, for I have strung it with gut instead of wire, merely for the gratification of my own ear;[2] but it is, however, precisely the

[1] The supposition is advanced by Dr Ledwich; but neither among the 'Sons of Song,' or by those of the interior part of the island, who are guided in their faith by 'tradition's volubly transmitting tongue,' could I ever find *one* to agree in the supposition. 'That the harp was the common musical instrument of the Anglo-Saxons, might be inferred from the very word itself, which is not derived from the British, or any other Celtic language, but of genuine Gothic original, and current among every branch of that people, viz. Angl-Sax. Hearpe, Hearpa. Iceland. Haurpa. Dan. and Bel. Harpe. Ger. Harpffa. Gal. Harpe. Span. Harpa. Ital. Arpa, etc. etc.'—Vide *Essay on Ancient Minstrels in England, by Dr Percy. Reliques of Ancient English Poetry.*

It is reserved then for the national *Lyre* of *Erin* only, to claim a title independent of a Gothic origin. For *clarseach*, is the only Irish epithet for the harp†, a name more in unison with the cithera of the Greeks, and even the *chinor* of the Hebrew, than the Anglo-Saxon harp. 'I cannot but think the *clarseach*, or Irish harp, one of the most ancient instruments we have among us, and had perhaps its origin in remote periods of antiquity.'—*Essay on the Construction, etc. etc. of the Irish Harp, by Dr Beauford.*

† A few months back the Author having played the Spanish guitar in the hearing of some Connaught peasants, they called it a *clarseach beg*, or little harp.

[2] As the modern Irish harp is described in a letter I have just received from a very eminent modern Irish bard, Mr O'Neil, I beg leave to quote the passage which relates to it.

'My harp has thirty-six strings' (the harp of *Brian Boiromh* had but 28 strings), 'of four kinds of wire, increasing in strength from treble to bass; your method of tuning yours (by octaves and fifths) is perfectly correct; but a change of keys or half tones, can only be effected by the tuning hammer. As to my mode of travelling, the privation of sight has long obliged me to require a servant who carries the harp for me. I remember in this neighbourhood, fifteen ladies proficients on the Irish harp, two in particular excelled, a Mrs Bailly, and a Mrs Hermar; but all are now dead; so is Rose Moony (a professional bardess), who was likewise celebrated. Fanning I knew, and thought well of his performance.'

Fanning was an eminent professional harper, and, like O'Neil, and some others of the Bardic order, rode about the country attended by a servant who carried his harp. It was thus, in ancient times, the 'light of song' was effused over Europe. 'The Minstrel,' says Dr Percy, 'had sometimes his servant to carry his harp, and even to sing his music.' Thus in the old romantic legend of 'King Estmere,' we find the younger Prince proposing to accompany his brother in the disguise of a minstrel, and carry his harp.

> And you shall be a harper's brother,
> Out of the north countrye,
> And I'll be your boy so fine of sighte,
> And bear your harp by your knee.
> And thus they renesht them to ryde
> On two good Renish steedes,
> And when they came to King Adland's hall
> Of red gold shone their weedes.

Vide *Percy's Reliques*, page 62

[*cont. on p. 72*]

same form as that preserved in the Irish university, which belonged to one of the most celebrated of our heroes, Brian Boru;* for the warrior and the bard often united in the character of our kings, and they sung the triumphs of those departed chiefs whose feats they emulated.

'You see,' she added, with a smile, while my eager glance pursued the kindling animation of her countenance as she spoke,—'you see, that in all which concerns my national music, I speak with national enthusiasm; and much indeed do we stand indebted to the most charming of all the sciences for the eminence it has obtained us; for in *music only*, do *you* English allow us poor Irish any superiority; and therefore your King, who made the *harp* the armorial bearing of Ireland, perpetuated our former musical celebrity beyond the power of time or prejudice to destroy it.'

Not for the world would I have annihilated the triumph which this fancied superiority seemed to give to this patriotic little being, by telling her, that we thought as little of the music of her country, as of every thing else that related to it; and that all we knew of the style of its melodies, reached us through the false medium of comic airs, sung by some popular actor, who, in coincidence with his author, caricatures those national traits he attempts to delineate.

I therefore simply told her, that though I doubted not the former musical celebrity of her country, yet that I perceived the *Bardic* order in Wales seemed to have survived the tuneful race of *Erin*; for that though every little Cambrian village had its harper, I had not yet met one of the profession in Ireland.

She waved her head with a melancholy air, and replied—'The rapid decline of the Sons of Song, once the pride of our country, is indeed very evident; and the tones of that tender and expressive instrument which gave birth to those which now survive them in happier countries, no longer vibrates in our own; for of course you are not ignorant that the importation of Irish bards and Irish

---

Dr Percy justly observes, that in this ballad, the character of the old minstrels (those successors to the bards) is placed in a very respectable light; for that 'here we see one of them represented mounted on a *fine horse*, accompanied with an attendant to bear his harp, etc. etc.' And I believe in Ireland only, is the minstrel of remote antiquity justly represented in the itinerant bard of modern days.

instruments into Wales,[1] by *Griffith ap Conan*, formed an epocha in Welsh music, and awakened there a genius of style in composition, which still breathes a kindred spirit to that from whence it derived its being, and that even the invention of Scottish music is given to Ireland.'[2]

'Indeed,' said I, 'I must plead ignorance to this singular fact, and almost to every other connected with this *now* to me, most interesting country.'

'Then suffer me,' said she, with a most insinuating smile, 'to indulge another national little triumph over you, by informing you, that we learn from musical record, that the first piece of music ever seen in *score*, in Great Britain, is an air sung time immemorial in this country on the opening of summer—an air which, though animated in its measure, yet still, like all the Irish melodies, breathes the very soul of melancholy.'[3]

'And do your melodies then, Madam, breathe the soul of melancholy?' said I.

'Our national music,' she returned, 'like our national character, admits of no medium in sentiment: it either sinks our spirit to despondency, by its heart-breaking pathos, or elevates it to wildness by its exhilarating animation.

'For my own part, I confess myself the victim of its magic—an Irish planxty* cheers me into maddening vivacity; an Irish lamentation depresses me into a sadness of melancholy emotion, to which the energy of despair might be deemed comparative felicity.'

Imagine how I felt while she spoke—but you cannot conceive the feelings, unless you beheld and heard the object who inspired them—unless you watched the kindling lumination of her countenance, and the varying hue of that mutable complexion, which seemed to ebb and flow to the impulse of every sentiment she expressed; while her round and sighing voice modulated in unison with each expression it harmonized.

---

[1] Cardoc (of Lhancarvan), without any of that illiberal partiality so common with national writers, assures that the Irish devised all the instruments, tunes, and measures, in use among the Welsh. *Cambrensis* is even more copious in its praise, when he peremptorily declares that the Irish, above any other nation, is incomparably skilled in symphonal music.—See *Walker's Hist. Mem. of the Irish Bards.*

[2] See Doctor Campbell, Phil. Surv. Letter 44; and Walker's Hist. of Irish Bards, page 131–2.

[3] Called in Irish, '*To an Samradth teacht*,' or, '*We brought Summer along with us.*'

After a moment's pause, she continued:

'This susceptibility to the influence of my country's music, discovered itself in a period of existence, when no associating sentiment of the heart could have called it into being; for I have often wept in convulsive emotion at an air, before the sad story it accompanied was understood: but now—now—that feeling is matured, and understanding awakened. Oh! you cannot judge—cannot feel—for you have no national music; and your country is the happiest under heaven!'

Her voice faultered as she spoke—her fingers seemed impulsively to thrill on the chords of the harp—her eyes, her tear-swollen beautiful eyes, were thrown up to heaven, and her voice, 'low and mournful as the song of the tomb,' sighed over the chords of her national lyre, as she faintly murmured Campbell's beautiful poem to the ancient Irish air of *Erin go Brack*!

Oh! is there on earth a being so cold, so icy, so insensible, as to have made a comment, even an *encomiastic** one, when this song of the soul ceased to breathe! God knows how little I was inclined or empowerd to make the faintest eulogium, or disturb the sacred silence which succeeded to her music's dying murmur. On the contrary, I sat silent and motionless, with my head unconsciously leaning on my broken arm, and my handkerchief to my eyes: when at last I withdrew it, I found her hurried glance fixed on me with a smile of such expression! Oh! I could weep my heart's most vital drop for such another glance—such another smile!—they seemed to say, but who dares to translate the language of the soul, which the eye only can express?

In (I believe) equal emotion, we both arose at the same moment, and walked to the window. Beyond the mass of ruins which spread in desolate confusion below, the ocean, calm and unruffled, expanded its awful bosom almost to infinitude; while a body of dark sullen clouds, tinged with the partial beam of a meridian sun, floated above the summits of those savage cliffs which skirt this bold and rocky coast; and the tall spectral figure of Father John, leaning on a broken pediment, appeared like the embodied spirit of philosophy moralizing amidst the ruins of empires, on the instability of all human greatness.

What a sublime assemblage of images!

'How consonant,' thought I, gazing at Glorvina, 'to the sublimated tone of our present feelings.' Glorvina waved her head in accedence to the idea, as though my lips had given it birth.

How think you I felt, on this sweet involuntary acknowledgment of a mutual intelligence?

Be that as it may, my eyes, too faithful I fear to my feelings, covered the face on which they were passionately rivetted, with blushes.

At that moment Glorvina was summoned to dinner by a servant, for she only is permitted to dine with the Prince, as being of royal descent. The vision dissolved—she was again the proud Milesian Princess, and I, the poor wandering *artist*—the eleemosynary* guest of her hospitable mansion.

The priest and I dined *tête-à-tête*; and, for the first time, he had all the conversation to himself; and got deep in Locke and Malbranche,* in solving quidities,* and starting hypotheses, to which I assented with great gravity, and thought only of Glorvina.

I again beheld her gracefully drooping over her harp—I again caught the melody of her song, and the sentiment it conveyed to the soul; and I entered fully into the idea of the Greek painter, who drew *Love*, not with a bow and arrow, but a lyre.

I could not avoid mentioning with admiration her great musical powers.

'Yes,' said he, 'she inherits them from her mother, who obtained the appellation of *Glorvina*, from the sweetness of her voice, by which name our little friend was baptized at her mother's request.'[1]

Adieu! Glorvina has been confined in her father's room during the whole of the evening—to this circumstance you are indebted for this long letter.

Adieu!

H.M.

---

[1] To derive an appellation from some eminent quality or talent, is still very common in the interior parts of Ireland. The Author's grandmother was known in the neighbourhood where she resided (in the County of Mayo), by the appellative of *Clarseach na Vallagh*, or, the *Village Harp*; for the superiority of her musical abilities. *Glor-bhin* (pronounced *vin*), is literally 'sweet voice.'

LETTER VIII

TO J.D. ESQ. M.P.

The invitation I received from the hospitable Lord of these ruins, was so unequivocal, so cordial, that it would have been folly, not delicacy, to think of turning out of his house the moment my health was re-established. But then, I scarcely felt it warranted that length of residence here, which, for a thousand reasons, I am now anxious to make.

To prolong my visit till the arrival of my father in this country was my object; and how to effect the desired purpose, the theme of cogitation during the whole of the restless night which succeeded my interview with Glorvina; and to confess the truth, I believe this interview was not the least potent spell which fascinated me to Inismore.

Wearied by my restlessness, rather than refreshed by my transient slumbers, I arose with the dawn, and carrying my *port-feuille*** and pencils with me, descended from my tower, and continued to wander for some time among the wild and romantic scenes which surround these interesting ruins, while

> 'La sainte recueilment le paisible innocence
> Sembler de ces lieus habiter le silence;'*

until, almost wearied in the contemplation of the varying sublimities which the changes of the morning's seasons shed over the ocean's boundless expanse, from the first grey vapour that arose from its swelling wave, to that splendid refulgence with which the risen sun crimsoned its bosom, I turned away my dazzled eye, and fixed it on the ruins of Inismore. Never did it appear in an aspect so picturesquely felicitous: it was a golden period for the poet's fancy or the painter's art; and in a moment of propitious genius, I made one of the most interesting sketches my pencil ever produced. I had just finished my successful *ebauche*,* when Father John, returning from matins, observed, and instantly joined me. When he had looked over, and commended the result of my morning's avocation, he gave my port-folio to a servant who passed us, and taking my arm, we walked down together to the sea shore.

'This happy specimen of your talent,' said he, as we proceeded, 'will be very grateful to the Prince. In him, who has no others left, it is a very innocent pride, to wish to perpetuate the fading honours of his family—for as such the good Prince considers these *ruins*. But, my young friend, there is another and a surer path to the Prince's heart, to which I should be most happy to lead you.'

He paused for a moment, and then added:

'You will, I hope, pardon the liberty I am going to take; but as I boast the merit of having first made your merit known to your worthy host, I hold myself in some degree (smiling, and pressing my hand) accountable for your confirming the partiality I have awakened in your favour.

'The daughter of the Prince, and my pupil, of whom you can have yet formed no opinion, is a creature of such rare endowments, that it should seem Nature, as if foreseeing her isolated destiny, had opposed her own liberality to the chariness of fortune: and lavished on her such intuitive talents, that she almost sets the necessity of education at defiance. To all that is most excellent in the circle of human intellect, or human science, her versatile genius is constantly directed; and it is my real opinion, that nothing more is requisite to perfect her in any liberal or elegant pursuit, but that method or system which even the strongest native talent, unassisted, can seldom attain (without a long series of practical experience), and which is unhappily denied her; while her doating father incessantly mourns over that poverty, which withholds from him the power of cultivating those shining abilities that would equally enrich the solitude of their possessor, or render her an ornament to that society she may yet be destined to grace. Yet the occasional visits of a strolling dancing-master, and a few musical lessons received in her early childhood from the family bard, are all the advantages these native talents have received.

'But who that ever beheld her motions in the dance, or listened to the exquisite sensibility of her song, but would exclaim—"here is a creature for whom Art can do nothing—Nature has done all!"

'To these elegant acquirements, she unites a decided talent for drawing, arising from powers naturally imitative, and a taste, early imbibed (from the contemplation of her native scenes), for all that is most sublime and beautiful in Nature. But this, of all her talents, has been the least assisted, and yet is the most prized by her father, who, I believe, laments his inability to detain you here as her preceptor; or rather, to make it worth your while to forego your professional pursuits, for such a period as would be necessary to invest her with such rudiments in the art, as would form a basis for her future improvement. In a word, can you, consistently with your present plans, make the Castle of Inismore your head-quarters for two or three months, from whence you can take frequent excursions amidst the neighbouring scenery, which will afford to your pencil subjects rich and various as almost any other part of the country?'

Now, in the course of my life, I have had more than one occasion to remark certain desirable events, brought about by means diametrically opposite to the supposition of all human probability;— but that this worthy man should (as if infected with the intriguing spirit of a French Abbé reared in the purlieus of the *Louvre*)— should thus forward my views, and effect the realization of my wishes, excited so strong an emotion of pleasurable surprise, that I with difficulty repressed my smiles, or concealed my triumph.

After, however, a short pause, I replied with great gravity, that I always conceived with Pliny,* that the dignity we possess by the good offices of a friend, is a kind of sacred trust, wherein we have his judgment as well as our own character to maintain, and therefore to be guarded with peculiar attention; that consequently, on his account, I was as anxious as on my own, to confirm the good opinion conceived in my favour through the medium of his partiality; and with very great sincerity I assured him, that I knew of no one event so coincident to my present views of happiness, as the power of making the Prince some return for his benevolent attentions, and of becoming his (the priest's) coadjutor in the tuition of his highly-gifted pupil.

'Add then, my dear Sir,' said I, 'to all the obligations you have forced on me, by presenting my respectful compliments to the Prince, with the offer of my little services, and an earnest request that he will condescend to accept of them; and if you think it will add to the delicacy of the offer, let him suppose that it voluntarily comes from a heart deeply impressed with a sense of his kindness.'

'That is precisely what I was going to propose,' returned this excellent and unsuspecting being. 'I would even wish him to think you conceive the obligation all on your own side; for the pride of fallen greatness is of all others the most sensitive.'

'And God knows so I do,' said I, fervently;—then carelessly added, 'do you think your pupil has a decided talent for the art?'

'It may be partiality,' he replied; 'but I think she has a decided talent for every elegant acquirement. If I recollect right, somebody has defined *genius* to be "the various powers of a strong mind directed to one point:" making it the *result* of combined force, not the vital source whence all intellectual powers flow; in which light, the genius of Glorvina has ever appeared to me as a beam from heaven, an emanation of divine intelligence, whose nutritive warmth cherishes into existence that richness and variety of talent which wants only a little care to rear it to perfection.

'When I first offered to become the preceptor to this charming child, her father, I believe, never formed an idea that my tuition would have extended beyond a little reading and writing; but I soon found that my interesting pupil possessed a genius that bore all before it—that almost anticipated instruction by force of its intuitive powers, and prized each task assigned it, only in proportion to the difficulty by which it was to be accomplished.

'Her young ambitious mind even emulated rivalry with mine, and that study in which she beheld me engaged, seldom failed to become the object of her desires and her assiduity. Availing myself, therefore, of this innate spirit of emulation—this boundless thirst of knowledge, I left her mind free in the election of its studies, while I only threw within its power of acquisition, that which could tend to render her a rational, and consequently a benevolent being; for I have always conceived an informed, intelligent, and enlightened mind, to be the best security for a good heart; although the many who mistake talent for intellect, and unfortunately too often find the former united to vice, are led to suppose that the heart loses in goodness what the mind acquires in strength, as if (as a certain paradoxical writer has asserted), there was something in the natural mechanism of the human frame necessary to constitute a fine genius, that is not altogether favourable to the heart.

'But here comes the unconscious theme of our conversation.'

And at that moment Glorvina appeared, springing lightly forward, like Gresset's beautiful personification of Health:

> 'As Hebe swift, as Venus fair,
> Youthful, lovely, light as air.'

As soon as she perceived me she stopt abruptly, blushed, and returning my salutation, advanced to the priest, and twining her arm familiarly in his, said with an air of playful tenderness,

'O! I have brought you something you will be glad to see—here is the spring's first violet, which the unusual chillness of the season has suffered to steal into existence: this morning as I gathered herbs at the foot of the mountain, I inhaled its odour ere I discovered its purple head, as solitary and unassociated it drooped beneath the heavy foliage of a neighbouring plant.

'It is but just you should have the first violet, as my father has already had the first snow-drop. Receive, then, my offering,' she added with a smile; and while she fondly placed it in his breast, with an air of exquisite *naiveté*, to my astonishment she repeated from B. Tasso, those lines so consonant to the tender simplicity of the act in which she was engaged:

> 'Poiche d'altro honorarte
> Non posso, prendi lieta
> Queste negre viole
> Dall umor rugiadose.'*

The priest gazed at her with looks of parental affection, and said, 'Your offering, my dear, is indeed the

> "Incense of the heart;"

'and more precious to the receiver, than the richest donation that ever decked the shrine of Loretto. How fragrant it is!' he added, presenting it to me.

I took it in silence, but raised it no higher than my lip—the eye of Glorvina met mine, as my kiss breathed upon her flower: Good God! what an undefinable, what a delicious emotion thrilled through my heart at that moment! and the next—yet I know not how it was, or whether the motion was made by her, or by me, or by the priest—but somehow, Glorvina had got between us, and while I gazed at her beautiful flower, I personified the blossom, and addressed to her the happiest lines that form '*La Guirlande de Julie*,' while, as I repeated

> 'Mais si sur votre front je peux briller un jour,
> La plus humble des fleurs sera la plus superbe;'*

I reposed it for a moment on her brow in passing it over to the priest.

'Oh!' said she with an arch smile, 'I perceive you too . . . expect a tributary flower for these charming lines; and the summer's first rose'—she paused abruptly; but her eloquent eye continued, 'should be thine, but that thou may'st be far from hence when the summer's first rose appears.' I thought too—but it might be only the fancy of my wishes, that a sigh floated on the lip, when recollection checked the effusion of the heart.

'The *rose*,' (said the priest with simplicity, and more engaged with the classicality of the idea, than the inference to be drawn from it), 'the rose is the flower of Love.'

I stole a look at Glorvina, whose cheek now emulated the tint of the theme of our conversation; and plucking a thistle that sprung from a broken pediment, she blew away its down with her balmy breath, merely to hide her confusion.

Surely she is the most sensient of all created beings!

'I remember,' continued the priest, 'being severely censured by a rigid old priest, at my college at St Omers, who found me reading the Idylium of Ausonius,* in which he so beautifully celebrates the rose, when the good father believed me deep in St Augustus.'*

'The rose,' said I, 'has always been the poet's darling theme. The impassioned Lyre of Sappho* has breathed upon its leaves. Anacreon* has wooed it in the happiest effusions of his genius; and poesy seems to have exhausted her powers in celebrating the charms of the most beautiful and transient of flowers.

'Among its modern panegyrists, few have been more happily successful than Monsieur de Bernard, in that charming little ode beginning—

> "Tendre fruits des pleurs d'aurore,
> Objets des baisers du zephyrs,
> Reine de l'empire de Flore,
> Hâte toi d'epanouir." "*

'O! I beseech you go on,' exclaimed Glorvina; and at her request, I finished the poem.

'Beautiful, beautiful!' said she, with enthusiasm. 'O! there is a certain delicacy of genius in elegant trifles of this description, which I think the French possess almost exclusively; it is a language formed almost by its very construction *d'éterniser la bagatelle*,* and to clothe the fairy effusions of fancy in the most appropriate drapery.

'I thank you for this beautiful ode; the rose was always my idol flower; in all its different stages of existence, it speaks a language my heart understands; from its young bud's first crimson glow, to the last silky blush of its faded bosom. It is the flower of sentiment in all its sweet transitions; it breathes a moral, and seems to preserve an undecaying soul in that fragrant essence which still survives the bloom and symmetry of the fragile form which every beam too ardent, every gale too chill, injures and destroys.'

'And is there,' said I, 'no parallel in the moral world for this lovely offspring of the natural?'—

Glorvina raised her humid eyes to mine, and I read the parallel there.

'I vow,' said the priest with affected pettishness, 'I am half tempted to fling away my violet, since this *idol* flower has been decreed to Mr Mortimer; and to revenge myself, I will shew him your ode on the rose.'

At these words, he took out his pocket-book, laughing at his gratified vengeance, while Glorvina coaxed, blushed, and threatened; until snatching the book out of his hand, as he was endeavouring to put it into mine, away she flew like lightning, laughing heartily at her triumph, in all the elixity and playfulness of a youthful spirit.

'What a *Hebe*!' said I, as she kissed her hand to us in her airy flight.

'Yes,' said he, 'she at least illustrates the possibility of a woman uniting in her character, the extremes of intelligence and simplicity: you see, with all her information and talent, she is a mere child.'

When we reached the castle, we found her waiting for us at the breakfast table, flushed with her race—all animation, all spirits! her reserve seemed gradually to vanish, and nothing could be more interesting, yet more *enjoueé*,* than her manner and conversation. While the fertility of her imagination supplied incessant topic of conversation, always new, always original, I could not help reverting in idea to those languid *tête-à-têtes*, even in the hey-day of our inter-course, when Lady C—— and I have sat yawning at each other, or biting our fingers, merely for want of something to say, in those intervals of passion, which every connexion even of the tenderest nature, must sustain—she in the native dearth of her mind, and I, in the habitual apathy of mine.

But here is a creature who talks of a violet or a rose with the artless air of infancy, and yet fascinates you in the simple discussion, as though the whole force of intellect was roused to support it.

By Heaven! if I know my own heart, I would not love this being for a thousand worlds; at least as I have hitherto loved. As it is, I feel a certain commerce of the soul—a mutual intelligence of mind and feeling with her, which a look, a sigh, a word is sufficient to betray— a sacred communion of spirit, which raises me in the scale of existence almost above mortality; and though we had been known to each other by looks only, still would this amalgamation of soul (if I may use the expression), have existed.

What a nausea of every sense does the turbulent agitation of gross common-place passion bring with it. But the sentiment which this seraph awakens, 'brings with it no satiety.' There is something so pure, so refreshing about her, that in the present state of my heart, feelings, and constitution, she produces the same effect on me as does the health-giving breeze of returning spring to the drooping spirit of slow convalescence!

After breakfast she left us, and I was permitted to kiss his Highness's hand, on my instalment in my new and enviable office. He did not speak much on the subject, but with his usual energy. However, I understood I was not to waste my time, as he termed it, for nothing.

When I endeavoured to argue the point (as if the whole business was not a *farce*), the Prince would not hear me; so behold me to all intents and purposes an hireling tutor. Faith, to confess the truth, I know not whether to be pleased or angry with this wild romance: this too, in a man whose whole life has been a laugh at romancers of every description.

What, if my father learns the extent of my folly, in the first era too of my probation! Oh! what a spirit of *bizarté* ever drives me from the central point of common sense, and common prudence! With what tyranny does impulse rule my wayward fate? and how imperiously my heart still takes the lead of my head! yet if I could ever consider the 'meteor ray' that has hitherto misled my wanderings, as a 'light from heaven,' it is now, when virtue leads me to the shrine of innocent pleasure; and the mind becomes the better for the wanderings of the heart.

'But what,' you will say with your usual foreseeing prudence— 'what is the aim, the object of your present romantic pursuit?'

Faith, none; save the simple enjoyment of present felicity, after an age of cold, morbid apathy; and a self-resignation to an agreeable illusion, after having recently sustained the actual burthen of real sufferings (sufferings the more acute, as they were self-created), succeeded by that dearth of feeling and sensation which, in permitting my heart to lie *fallow* for an interval, only rendered it the more genial to those exotic seeds of happiness which the vagrant gale of chance has flung on its surface. But whether they will take deep root, or only wear 'the perfume and suppliance of a moment,' is an unthought of 'circumstance still hanging in the stars;' to whose decision I commit it.

Would you know my plans of meditated operation, they run thus:—In a few days I shall avail myself of my professional vocation, and fly home, merely to obviate suspicion in Mr Clendinning, receive and answer letters, and get my books and wardrobe sent to the Lodge, previous to my own removal there, which I shall effect under the plausible plea of the dissipated neighbourhood of M—— house being equally inimical to the present state of my constitution and my studious pursuits; and in fact, I must either associate with, or offend these hospitable Milesians—an alternative by no means consonant to my inclinations.

From Inismore to the Lodge, I can make constant sallies, and be in the way to receive my father, whose arrival I think I may still date at some weeks' distance; besides, should it be necessary, I think I should find no difficulty in bribing the old steward of the Lodge to my interest. His evident aversion to Clendinning, and attachment to the Prince, renders him ripe for any scheme by which the latter could be served, or the former outwitted; and I hope in the end to effect both: for, to unite this old Chieftain in bonds of amity with my father, and to punish the rascality of the worthy Mr Clendinning, is a double 'consummation devoutly to be wished.' In short, when the heart is interested in a project, the stratagems of the imagination to forward it are inexhaustible.

It should seem that the name of M. is interdicted at Inismore: I have more than once endeavoured (though remotely) to make the residence of our family in this country a topic of conversation; but every one seemed to shrink from the subject, as though some fatality was connected with its discussion. To avoid speaking ill of those of whom we have but little reason to speak well, is the temperance of aversion, and seldom found but in great minds.

I must mention to you another instance of liberality in the sentiments of these isolated beings:—I have only once attended the celebration of divine service here since my arrival; but my absence seemed not to be observed, or my attendance noticed; and though, as an Englishman, I may be naturally supposed to be of the most popular faith, yet for all they know to the contrary, I may be Jew, Mussulman or Infidel; for, before me at least, religion is a topic never discussed.

Adieu!

H.M.

END OF VOL. I

LETTER IX

TO J.D. ESQ. M.P.

I have already given two lessons to my pupil, in an art in which, with all due deference to the judgment of her quondam* tutor, she was never destined to excel.

Not, however, that she is deficient in talent—very far from it; but it is too progressive, too tame a pursuit for the vivacity of her genius. It is not sufficiently connected with those lively and vehement emotions of the soul she is so calculated to feel and to awaken. She was created for a musician—there she is borne away by the magic of the art in which she excels, and the natural enthusiasm of her impassioned character: she can sigh, she can weep, she can smile, over her harp. The sensibility of her soul trembles in her song, and the expression of her rapt countenance harmonizes with her voice. But at her drawing-desk, her features lose their animated character—the smile of rapture ceases to play, and the glance of inspiration to beam. And with the transient extinction of those feelings from which each touching charm is derived, fades that all-pervading interest, that energy of admiration which she usually excites.

Notwithstanding, however, the pencil is never out of her hand; her harp lies silent, and her drawing-book is scarcely ever closed. Yet she limits my attendance to the first hour after breakfast, and then I generally lose sight of her the whole day, until we all meet *en-famille** in the evening. Her improvement is rapid—her father delighted, and she quite fascinated by the novelty of her avocation; the priest congratulates me, and I alone am dissatisfied.

But, from the natural impatience and volatility of her character (both very obvious), this, thank heaven! will soon be over. Besides, even in the hour of tuition, from which I promised myself so much, I do not enjoy her society—the priest always devotes that time to reading out to her; and this too at her own request:—not that I think her innocent and unsuspicious nature cherishes the least reserve at her being left *tête-à-tête* with her less venerable preceptor; but that her ever active mind requires incessant exercise; and in fact, while I am hanging over her in uncontrouled emotion, she is drawing as if her livelihood depended on the exertions of her pencil, or commenting on the subject of the priest's perusal, with as much ease as judgment; while she minds me no more than if I was a well-organized piece of mechanism, by whose motions her pencil was to be guided.

What if, with all her mind, all her genius, this creature had no heart! And what were it to me, though she had? * * *

The Prince fancies his domestic government to be purely patriarchal, and that he is at once the 'Law and the Prophet' to his family; never suspecting that he is all the time governed by a girl of nineteen, whose soul, notwithstanding the playful softness of her manner, contains a latent ambition, which sometimes breathing in the grandeur of her sentiments, and sometimes sparkling in the haughtiness of her eye, seems to say, 'I was born for empire!'

It is evident that the tone of her mind is naturally stronger than her father's, though to a common observer, *he* would appear a man of nervous and masculine understanding; but the difference between them is this—his energies are the energies of the passions—hers of the mind!

Like most other Princes, *mine* is governed much by *favouritism*; and it is evident that I already rank high on the list of partiality.

I perceive, however, that much of his predilection in my favour, arises from the coincidence of my present curiosity and taste with his favourite pursuits and national prejudices. Newly awakened (perhaps by mere force of novelty) to a lively interest for every thing that concerns a country I once thought so little worthy of consideration; in short, convinced by the analogy of existing habits, with recorded customs, of the truth of those circumstances so generally ranked in the apocryphal tales of the history of this vilified country; I have determined to resort to the witness of time, the light of truth, and the corroboration of living testimony, in the study of a country which I am beginning to think, would afford to the mind of philosophy a rich subject of analysis, and to the powers of poetic fancy a splendid series of romantic detail.

'Sir William Temple,'* says Dr Johnson,* 'complains that Ireland is less known than any other country, as to its ancient state, because the natives have little leisure, and less encouragement for inquiry; and that a stranger, not knowing its language, has no ability.'

This impediment, however, shall not stand in the way of *one* stranger, who is willing to offer up his national prejudices at the Altar of Truth, and expiate the crime of an unfounded but habitual antipathy, by an impartial examination, and an unbiassed inquiry. In short, I have actually began to study the Irish language; and though I recollect to have read the opinion of Temple, 'that the Celtic dialect used by the native Irish is the purest and most original language that yet remains;' yet I never suspected that a language spoken *par routine*,* and chiefly by the lower classes of society, could be acquired upon *principle*, until the other day, when I observed in the Prince's truly national library some philological works, which were shewn me by Father John, who has offered to be my preceptor in this wreck of ancient dialect, and who assures me he will render me master of it in a short time—provided I study *con amore*.*

'And I will assist you,' said Glorvina.

'We will *all* assist him,' said the Prince.

'Then I shall study *con amore!* indeed,' returned I.

Behold me then, buried amidst the monuments of past ages!—deep in the study of the language, history, and antiquities of this ancient nation—talking of the invasion of Henry II as a recent circumstance—of the Phœnician migration hither from Spain, as though my grandfather had been delegated by Firbalgs to receive the Milesians on their landing—and of those transactions passed through

> 'The dark posterns of time long elapsed,'

as though their existence was but freshly registered in the annals of recollection.

In short, infected by my antiquarian* conversation with the Prince, and having fallen in with some of those monkish histories which, on the strength of Druidical tradition, trace a series of wise and learned Irish monarchs before the Flood, I am beginning to have as much faith in antediluvian* records as Dr Parsons himself, who accuses *Adam* of authorship, or Thomas Banguis, who almost gives *fac-similies* of the hand-writing of Noah's progenitors.

Seriously, however, I enter on my new studies with avidity, and read from the morning's first dawn till the usual hour of breakfast, which is become to me as much the banquet of the heart, as the Roman supper was to the Augustan wits 'the feast of reason and the flow of soul,'—for it is the only meal at which Glorvina presides.

Two hours each day does the kind priest devote to my philological pursuits, while Glorvina, who is frequently present on these occasions, makes me repeat some short poem or song after her, that I may catch the pronunciation (which is almost unattainable), then translates them into English, which I word for word write down. Here then is a specimen of Irish poetry, which is almost always the effusion of some blind itinerant bard, or some rustic minstrel, into whose breast the genius of his country has breathed inspiration, as he patiently drove the plough, or laboriously worked in the bog.[1]

'CATHBEIN NOLAN

I

'My love, when she floats on the mountain's brow, is like the dewy cloud of the summer's loveliest evening. Her forehead is as a pearl; her spiral locks are of gold; and I grieve that I cannot banish her from my memory.

II

'When she enters the forest like the bounding doe, dispersing the dew with her airy steps, her mantle on her arm, the axe in hand, to cut the branches of flame; I know not which is the most noble—the King of the Saxons,[2] or Cathbein Nolan.'

This little song is of so ancient a date, that Glorvina assures me, neither the name of the composer (for the melody is exquisitely beautiful) nor the poet, have escaped the oblivion of time. But if we may judge of the rank of the poet by that of his mistress, it must have been of a very humble degree; for it is evident that the fair Cathbein, whose form is compared, in splendour, to that of the Saxon Monarch, is represented as cutting wood for the fire.

The following songs, however, are by the most celebrated of all the modern Irish bards, Turloch Carolan,[3] and the airs to which he has

---

[1] Miss Brooks,* in her elegant version of the works of some of the Irish Bards, says, ''Tis scarcely possible that any language can be more adapted to lyric poetry than the Irish; so great is the smoothness and harmony of its numbers: it is also possessed of a refined delicacy, a descriptive power, and an exquisite tender simplicity of expression: two or three little artless words, or perhaps a single epithet, will sometimes convey such an image of sentiment or suffering, to the mind, that one lays down the book to look at the picture.'

[2] The King of England is still called by the common Irish, *Riagh Sasseanach*.

[3] He was born in the village of Nobber, county Westmeath, in 1670, and died in 1739. He never regretted the loss of sight, but used gayly to say, 'my eyes are only transplanted into my ears.' Of his poetry, the reader may form some judgment from these examples: of his music, it has been said by O'Connor, the celebrated historian (who knew him intimately), 'so happy, so elevated was he in some of his compositions, that he excited

composed them, possess the *arioso* elegance of Italian music, united
to the heart-felt pathos of Irish melody.

I

'I must sing of the youthful plant of gentlest mien—Fanny, the beautiful
and warm-soul'd—the maid of the amber-twisted ringlets; the air-lifted
and light-footed virgin—the elegant pearl and heart's treasure of Erin;
then waste not the fleeting hour—let us enjoy it in drinking to the health
of Fanny, the daughter of David.

II

'It is the maid of the magic lock I sing, the fair swan of the shore—for
whose love a multitude expires: Fanny, the beautiful, whose tresses are like
the evening sun-beam; whose voice is like the black-bird's morning song:
O, may I never leave the world until dancing *in the air* (this expression in
the Irish is beyond the power of translation) at her wedding, I shall send
away the hours in drinking to Fanny, the daughter of David.'[1]

the wonder, and obtained the approbation, of a great master who never saw him, I mean
Geminiani.' And his execution on the harp was rapid and impressive—far beyond that
of all the professional competitors of the age in which he lived. The charms of women,
the pleasures of conviviality, and the power of poesy and music, were at once his theme
and inspiration; and his life was an illustration of his theory: for until its last ardour was
chilled by death, he loved, drank, and sung. He was the welcome guest of every house,
from the peasant to the prince; but, in the true wandering spirit of his profession, he
never stayed to exhaust that welcome. He lived and died poor. While in the fervor of
composition, he was constantly heard to pass sentence on his own effusions, as they
arose from his harp, or breathed on his lips; blaming and praising with equal vehemence,
the unsuccessful effort and felicitous attempt.

[1] She was daughter to David Power, Esq. of the county of Galway, and mother to the
late Lord Cloncarty. The epithet bestowed on her, of *swan of the shore*, arose from her
father's mansion being situated on the edge of *Lough Leah, or the grey lake*, of which
many curious legends are told. When Carolan, alone, and in the act of composing the
music and words of the above song, hung over his harp, wrapt in the golden visions of
his art, the theme of his effusions suddenly entered the room where he sat, and, by the
noise which the rustling of her silks made, disturbed the poetic reveries of the bard,
who, enraged at the interruption, which probably put to flight some happy inspiration
of genius, flung at the unknown intruder a large sapling stick which he always carried
with him. Miss Power, however, fortunately escaped the frenzied intention of the passionate minstrel, which, had it been realized, would have turned his panegyric strains to
elegies of woe. This anecdote the Author had from her father, who had the honour of
hearing it from the lips of the lady herself, and who, though at that period in an
advanced era of life, retained strong traces of that exquisite beauty for which she was so
justly celebrated in the strains of her native bard.

'GRACY NUGENT

I

'I delight to talk of thee! blossom of fairness! Gracy, the most frolic of the young and lovely—who from the fairest of the province bore away the palm of excellence—happy is he who is near her, for morning nor evening grief, nor fatigue, cannot come near him: her mien is like the mildness of a beautiful dawn; and her tresses flow in twisted folds—she is the daughter of the branches.—Her neck has the whiteness of alabaster—the softness of the cygnet's bosom is hers; and the glow of the summer's sun-beam is on her countenance. Oh! blessed is he who shall obtain thee, fair daughter of the blossoms—maid of the spiry locks!

II

'Sweet is the word of her lip, and sparkling the beam of her blue rolling eye; and close round her neck cling the golden tresses of her head; and her teeth are arranged in beautiful order.—I say to the maid of youthful mildness, thy voice is sweeter than the song of birds; every grace, every charm play round thee; and though my soul delights to sing thy praise, yet I must quit the theme—to drink with a sincere heart to thy health, Gracy of the soft waving ringlets.'[1]

Does not this poetical effusion awakened by the charms of the fair Gracy, recall to your memory the description of Helen by Theocritus,* in his beautiful epithalamium* on her marriage?—

'She is like the rising of the golden morning, when the night departeth, and when the winter is over and gone—she resembleth the cypress in the garden, the horse in the chariot of Thessaly.'

While the invocation to the enjoyment of convivial pleasure which breathes over the termination of every verse, glows with the festive spirit of the Tean bard.

When I remarked the coincidence of style which existed between the early Greek writers and the bards of Erin,* Glorvina replied, with a smile,

'In drawing this analogy, you think, perhaps, to flatter my national vanity; but the truth is, we trace the spirit of Milesian poetry to a higher source than the spring of Grecian genius; for many figures in Irish song are of oriental origin; and the bards who ennobled the

[1] She was the daughter of John Nugent, Esq. of Castle Nugent, Culambre, at whose hospitable mansion the bard was frequently entertained. In the summer of 1797, the Author conversed with an old peasant in Westmeath, who had frequently listened to the tones of Carolan's harp in his boyish days.

train of our Milesian founders, and who awakened the soul of song here, seem, in common with the Greek poets, "to have kindled their poetic fires at those unextinguished lamps which burn within the tomb of oriental genius." Let me, however, assure you, that no adequate version of an Irish poem can be given; for the peculiar construction of the Irish language, the felicity of its epithets, and force of its expressions, bid defiance to all translation.'

'But while your days and nights are thus devoted to Milesian literature,' you will say, 'what becomes of Blackstone and Coke?'*

Faith, e'en what may for me—the mind, the mind, like the heart, is not to be forced in its pursuits; and, I believe, in an intellectual as in a physical sense, there are certain antipathies which reason may condemn, but cannot vanquish. Coke is to me a dose of ipecacuhana;* and my present studies, like those poignant incentives which stimulate the appetite without causing repletion. It is in vain to force me to a profession, against which my taste, my habits, my very nature, revolts; and if my father persists in his determination, why, as a *dernier resort*,* I must turn *historiographer** to the Prince of Inismore.

*   *   *   *   *

Like the spirit of Milton,* I feel myself, in this new world, 'vital in every part:'

> 'All heart I live, all head, all eye, all ear,
> All intellect, all sense.'

LETTER X

TO J.D. ESQ. M.P.

The more I know of this singular girl, the more the happy *discordia concors** of her character awakens my curiosity and surprise. I never beheld such an union of intelligence and simplicity, infantine playfulness and profound reflexion, as her character exhibits. Sometimes when I think I am trifling with a child, I find I am conversing with a philosopher; and sometimes in the midst of the most serious and interesting conversation, some impulse of the moment seizes on her imagination, and a vein of frolic humour and playful sarcasm is indulged at the expence of my most sagacious arguments or philosophic gravity. Her reserve (unknown to herself) is gradually giving way to the most bewitching familiarity.

When the priest is engaged, I am suffered to tread with her the 'pathless grass,' climb the mountain's steep, or ramble along the sea-beat coast, sometimes followed by her nurse, and sometimes by a favourite little dog only.

Of nothing which concerns her country is she ignorant; and when a more interesting, a more soul-felt conversation, cannot be obtained, I love to draw her into a little national chit-chat.

Yesterday, as we were walking along the base of that mountain from which I first beheld her dear residence (and sure I may say with Petrarch, 'Benedetto sia il giorno e'l Mese e'lanno'*), several groups of peasants (mostly females) passed us, with their usual courteous salutations, and apparently dressed in their holiday garbs.

'Poor souls!' said Glorvina—'this is a day of jubilee to them, for a great annual fair is held in the neighbourhood.'

'But from whence,' said I, 'do they draw the brightness of those tints which adorn their coarse garments; those gowns and ribbons, that rival the gay colouring of that heath hedge; those bright blue and scarlet mantles? Are they, too, vestiges of ancient modes and ancient taste?'

'Certainly they are,' she replied, 'and the colours which the Irish were celebrated for wearing and dying a thousand years back, are now most prevalent. In short, the ancient Irish, like the Israelites, were so attached to this many-coloured *costume*, that it became the mark by which the different classes of the people were distinguished. Kings were limited to seven colours in their roal robes; and six were allowed the bards. What an idea does this give of the reverence paid to superior talent in other times by our forefathers! But that bright yellow you now behold so universally worn, has been in all ages their favourite hue. Spenser* think this custom came from the East; and Lord Bacon* accounts for the propensity of the Irish to it, by supposing it contributes to longevity.'

'But where,' said I, 'do these poor people procure so expensive an article as saffron, to gratify their prevailing taste?'[1]

'I have heard Father John say,' she returned, 'that saffron, as an

---

[1] 'A Portuguese physician attempts to account for their use of this yellow dye, by alledging that it was worn as a vermifuge. He should first demonstrate that all the people were infected with worms.'—*Dr Patterson's Observations on the Climate of Ireland.*

article of importation, could never have been at any time cheap enough for general use. And I believe formerly, as *now*, they communicated this bright yellow tinge with indigenous plants, with which this country abounds.

'See,' she added, springing lightly forward, and culling a plant which grew from the mountain's side—'see this little blossom, which they call here, "yellow lady's bed-straw," and which you, as a botanist, will better recognize as the *Galicens borum*; it communicates a beautiful yellow; as does the *Lichen juniperinus*, or "cypress moss," which you brought me yesterday; and I think the *resida Luteola*, or "yellow weed," surpasses them all.[1]

'In short, the botanical treasures of our country, though I dare say little known, are inexhaustible.

'Nay,' she continued, observing, I believe, the admiration that sparkled in my eyes, 'give me no credit, I beseech you, for this local information, for there is not a peasant girl in the neighbourhood, but will tell you more on the subject.'

While she was thus dispensing knowledge with the most unaffected simplicity of look and manner, a group of boys advanced towards us, with a car laden with stones, and fastened to the back of an unfortunate dog, which they were endeavouring to train to this new species of canine avocation, by such unmerciful treatment as must have procured the wretched animal a speedy release from all his sufferings.

Glorvina no sooner perceived this, than she flew to the dog, and while the boys looked all amaze, effected his liberation, and by her caresses endeavoured to soothe him into forgetfulness of his late sufferings; then turning to the ringleader, she said:

'Dermot, I have so often heard you praised for your humanity to animals, that I can scarcely believe it possible that you have been accessary to the sufferings of this useful and affectionate animal; he is just as serviceable to society in his way, as you are in your's, and you are just as well able to drag a loaded cart as he is to draw that little car. Come now, I am not so heavy as the load you have destined him to bear, and you are much stronger than your dog, and now you shall

---

[1] Purple, blue, and green dyes, were introduced by *Tighumas* the Great, in the year of the world 2815. The Irish also possessed the art of dyeing a fine scarlet; so early as the day of St Bennia, a disciple of St Patrick, scarlet clothes and robes highly embroidered, are mentioned in the book of *Glandelogh*.

draw me home to the castle; and then give me your opinion on the subject.'

In one moment his companions, laughing vociferously at the idea, had the stones flung out of the little vehicle, and fastened its harness on the broad shoulders of the half-pouting, half-smiling Dermot; and the next moment this little agile sylph was seated in the car.

Away went Dermot, dragged on by the rest of the boys, while Glorvina, delighted as a child, with her new mode of conveyance, laughed with all her heart, and kissed her hand to me as she flew along; while I, trembling for her safety, endeavoured to keep pace with her triumphal chariot, till her wearied, breathless Phaeton,* unable to run any further with his lovely, laughing burthen, begged a respite.

'How!' said she, 'weary of this amusement, and yet you have not at every step been cruelly lashed, like your poor dog.'

The panting Dermot hung his head, and said in Irish, 'the like should not happen again.'

'It is enough,' said Glorvina, in the same language—'we are all liable to commit a fault, but let us never forget it is in our power to correct it. And now go to the castle, where you shall have a good dinner, in return for the good and pleasant exercise you have procured me.'

The boys were as happy as kings. Dermot was unyoked, and the poor dog, wagging his tail in token of his felicity, accompanied the gratified group to the castle.

When Glorvina had translated to me the subject of her short dialogue with Dermot, she added, laughing,

'Oh! how I should like to be dragged about this way for two or three hours every day: never do I enter into any little folly of this kind, that I do not sigh for those sweet hours of my childhood when I could play the fool with impunity.'

'Play the fool!' said I—'and do you call this playing the fool?—this dispensation of humanity,—this culture of benevolence in the youthful mind, these lessons of truth and goodness, so sweetly, simply given.'

'Nay,' she returned, 'you always seem inclined to flatter me into approbation of myself! but the truth is, I was glad to seize on the opportunity of lecturing that urchin Dermot, who, though I praised his humanity, is the very beadle to all the unfortunate animals in the neighbourhood. But I have often had occasion to remark, that by giving a virtue to those neglected children, which they do not possess, I have awakened their emulation to attain it.'

'To say that you are an angel,' said I, 'is to say a very commonplace thing, which every man says to the woman he either does, or affects to admire; and yet'—

'Nay,'—interrupted she, laying her hand on my arm, and looking up full in my face with that arch glance I have so often caught revelling in her eloquent eye—'I am not emulous of a place in the angelic choir; canonization is more consonant to my *papistical* ambition; then let me be your saint—your tutelar saint, and'—

'And let me,' interrupted I, impassionately—'let me, like the members of the Greek church, adore my saint, not by prostration, but by a kiss;'—and, for the first time in my life, I pressed my lips to the beautiful hand which still rested on my arm, and from which I first drew a glove that has not since left my bosom, nor been redemanded by its charming owner.

This little freedom (which, to another, would have appeared nothing), was received with a degree of blushing confusion, that assured me it was the first of the kind ever offered; even the fair hand blushed its sense of my boldness, and enhanced the pleasure of the theft by the difficulty it promised of again obtaining a similar favour.

By Heaven there is an infection in the sensitive delicacy of this creature, which even my hardened confidence cannot resist!

No *prieux Chevalier*,* on being permitted to kiss the tip of his liege lady's finger, after a seven years' siege, could feel more pleasantly embarrassed than I did, as we walked on in silence, until we were happily relieved by the presence of the old garrulous nurse, who came out in search of her young lady—for, like the princesses in the Greek tragedies, *my* Princess seldom appears without the attendance of this faithful representative of fond maternity.

For the rest of the walk she talked mostly to the nurse in Irish, and at the castle-gate we parted—she to attend a patient, and I to retire to my own apartment, to ruminate on my morning's ramble with this fascinating *lusus naturæ*.*

Adieu!

H.M.

LETTER XI

TO J.D. ESQ. M.P.

The drawing which I made of the castle is finished—the Prince is charmed with it, and Glorvina insisted on copying it. This was as I expected—as I wished; and I took care to finish it so minutely, that her patience (of which she has no great store), should soon be exhausted in the imitation, and I should have something more of her attention than she generally affords me at the drawing-desk.

Yesterday, in the absence of the priest, I read to her as she drew. After a thousand little symptoms of impatience and weariness—'here,' said she, yawning—'here is a straight line I can make nothing of—do you know, Mr Mortimer, I never could draw a perpendicular line in my life. See now my pencil *will* go into a curve or an angle; so you must guide my hand, or I shall draw it all zig-zag.'

(I 'guide her hand to draw a straight line!')

'Nay then,' said I, with the ostentatious gravity of a pedagogue master, 'I may as well do the drawing myself.'

'Well then,' said she playfully, '*do* it yourself.'

Away she flew to her harp; while I, half lamenting, half triumphing, in my forbearance, took her pencil and her seat. I perceived, however, that she had not even drawn a single line of the picture, and yet her paper was not a mere *carte-blanche*—for close to the margin was written in a fairy hand, '*Henry Mortimer*, April 2d, 10 o'clock,'—the very day and hour of my entrance into the castle; and in several places, the half-defaced features of a face evidently a copy my own, were still visible.

If any thing could have rendered this little circumstance more deliciously gratifying to my heart, it was, that I had been just reading to her the anecdote of 'the *Maid of Corinth*.'

I raised my eyes from the paper to her with a look that must have spoken my feelings; but she, unconscious of my observation, began a favourite air of her favourite Carolan's, and supposed me to be busy at the *perpendicular line*.

Wrapt in her charming avocation, she seemed borne away by the magic of her own numbers, and thus inspired and inspiring as she appeared, faithful, as the picture it formed was interesting, I took her likeness. Conceive for a moment a form full of character, and full of grace, bending over an instrument singularly picturesque—a profusion of auburn hair fastened up to the top of the finest formed head I ever beheld, with a golden bodkin—an armlet of curious workmanship glittering above a finely turned elbow, and the loose sleeves of a flowing robe drawn up unusually high, to prevent this drapery from sweeping the chords of the instrument. The expression of the divinely touching countenance breathed all the fervour of genius under the influence of inspiration, and the contours of the face, from the peculiar uplifted position of the head, were precisely such, as lends to painting the happiest line of feature, and shade of colouring. Before I had near finished the lovely picture, her song ceased; and turning towards me, who sat opposite her, she blushed to observe how intensely my eyes were fixed on *her*.

'I am admiring,' said I, carelessly, 'the singular elegance of your costume: it is indeed to me a never-failing source of wonder and admiration.'

'I am not sorry,' she replied, 'to avail myself of my father's prejudices in favour of our ancient national costume, which, with the exception of the drapery being made of modern materials (on the antique model), is absolutely drawn from the wardrobes of my great grandames. This armlet, I have heard my father say, is near four hundred years old, and many of the ornaments and jewels you have seen me wear, are of a date no less ancient.'

'But how,' said I, while she continued to tune her harp, and I to ply the pencil, 'how comes it that in so remote a period, we find the riches of Peru and Golconda* contributing their splendour to the magnificence of Irish dress?'

'O!' she replied, smiling, 'we too had our Peru and Golconda in the bosom of our country—for it was once thought rich not only in gold and silver mines, but abounded in pearls,[1] amethysts, and other precious stones: even a few years back, Father John saw some fine pearl taken out of the river Ban;[2] and Mr O'Halloran, the celebrated

---

[1] 'It should seem,' says Mr Walker, in his ingenious and elegant essay on Ancient Irish Dress—'that Ireland teemed with gold and silver, for as well as in the laws recited, we find an act ordained 35th Henry VIII that merchant strangers should pay 40 pence custom for every pound of silver they carried out of Ireland; and Lord Stafford, in one of his letters from Dublin, to his royal master, says, "with this I land you an ingot of silver of 300 oz."'

[2] Pearls abounded, and still are found in this country; and were in such repute in the 11th century, that a present of them was sent to the famous Bishop Anselm, by a Bishop of Limerick.

Irish historian, declares that within his memory, amethysts of immense value were found in Ireland.[1]

'I remember reading in the life of St Bridget,* that the King of Leinster presented to her father, a sword set with precious stones, which the pious saint, more charitable than honest, devoutly stole, and sold for the benefit of the poor; but it should seem that the sources of our national treasures are now shut up, like the gold mines of La Valais, for the public weal, I suppose; for we now hear not of amethysts found, pearls discovered, or gold mines worked; and it is to the caskets of my female ancestors that I stand indebted that my dress or hair is not fastened or adorned like those of my humbler countrywomen, with a wooden bodkin.'

'That, indeed,' said I, 'is a species of ornament I have observed very prevalent with your fair *paysannes*;* and of whatever materials it is made, when employed in such an happy service as I *now* behold it, has an air of simple useful elegance, which in my opinion constitutes the great art of female dress.'

'It is at least,' replied she, 'the most ancient ornament we know here—for we are told that the celebrated palace of Emania,[2] erected previous to the Christian era, was sketched by the famous Irish Empress Macha, with her bodkin.*

'I remember a passage from a curious and ancient romance in the Irish language, that fastened wonderfully upon my imagination when I read it to my father in my childhood, and which gives to the bodkin a very early origin:—it ran thus, and is called the "*Interview between Fionn M'Cumhal and Cannan.*"

'"Cannan, when he said this, was seated at table; on his right hand was seated his wife, and upon his left his beautiful daughter, so exceedingly fair, that the snow driven by the winter storms surpassed not her in fairness, and her cheeks wore the blood of a young calf; her hair hung in curling ringlets, and her teeth were like pearl—a spacious veil hung from her lovely head down her delicate form, and the veil was fastened by a golden bodkin."

'The bodkin, you know, is also an ancient Greek ornament, and

[1] The Author is indebted to — Knox, Esq. barister at law, Dublin, for the sight of some beautiful amethysts, which belonged to his female ancestors, and which many of the lapidaries of London, after a diligent search, found it impossible to match.

[2] The resident palace of the Kings of Ulster, of which Colgan speaks as '*redolens splendorem.*'

mentioned by Vulcan, as among the trinkets he was obliged to forge.'[1]

By the time she had finished this curious quotation in favour of the antiquity of her dress, her harp was tuned, and she began another exquisite old Irish air, called the 'Dream of the Young Man,' which she accompanied rather by a plaintive *murmur*, than with her voice's full melodious powers. It is thus this creature winds round the heart, while she enlightens the mind, and entrances the senses.

I had finished the sketch in the meantime, and just beneath the figure, and above her flattering inscription of my name, I wrote with my pencil,

> ' 'Twas thus Apelles bask'd in beauty's blaze,
>   Nor felt the danger of the stedfast gaze;'

while she, a few minutes after, with that restlessness that seemed to govern all her actions to–day, arose, put her harp aside, and approached me with

'Well, Mr Mortimer, you are very indulgent to my insufferable indolence—let me see what you have done for me;' and looking over my shoulder, she beheld not the ruins of her castle, but a striking likeness of her blooming self; and bending her head close to the paper, read the lines, and that name honoured by the inscription of her own fair hand.

For the world I would not have looked her full in the face; but from beneath my downcast eye I stole a transient glance: the colour did not rush to her cheek (as it usually does under the influence of any powerful emotion), but rather deserted its beautiful standard, and she stood with her eyes rivetted on the picture, as though she dreaded by their removal she should encounter those of the artist.

After about three minutes endurance of this mutual confusion, (could you believe me such a blockhead!)—the priest, to our great relief, entered the room.

Glorvina ran and shook hands with him, as though she had not seen him for an age, and flew out of the room; while I, effacing the quotation, but not the honoured inscription, asked Father John's

---

[1] See *Iliad*, 13, 17.

opinion of my effort at portrait painting. He acknowledged it was a most striking resemblance, and added,

'Now you will indeed give a *coup de grace** to the partiality of the Prince in your favour, and you will rank so much the higher in his estimation, in proportion as his daughter is dearer to him than his *ruins*.'

Thus encouraged, I devoted the rest of the day to copying out this sketch; and I have finished the picture in that light tinting, so effective in these kind of characteristic drawings. That beautifully pensive expression which touches the countenance of Glorvina, when breathing her native strains, I have most happily caught; and her costume, attitude, and harp, form as happy a combination of traits, as a single portrait perhaps ever presented.

When it was shewn to the Prince, he gazed on it in silence, till tears obscured his glance; then laying it down, he embraced me, but said nothing. Had he detailed the merits and demerits of the picture in all the technical farrago* of *cognoscenti** phrase, his comments would not have been half so eloquent as this simple action, and the silence which accompanied it.

Adieu!

H.M.

LETTER XII

TO J.D. ESQ. M.P.

Here is a *bonne bouche** for your antiquarian taste, and *Ossianic** palate! Almost every evening after vespers, we all assemble in a spacious hall,[1] which had been shut up for near a century, and first opened by the present prince when he was driven for shelter to his paternal ruins.

This *Vengolf*, this *Valk-halla*, where the very spirit of Woden*

---

[1] 'Amidst the ruins of Buan Ratha, near Limerick, is a princely hall and spacious chambers; the fine stucco in many of which is yet visible, though uninhabitable for near a century.'—*O'Halloran's Introduction to the Study of the Hist. and Antiq. of Ireland*, p. 8.

There are very few, if any, of those venerable mansion houses, such as in England bear the stamp of that style of architecture so prevalent about two hundred years back, to be found in Ireland. But in town, every village, every considerable tract of land, the spacious ruins of princely residence or religious edifices, the palace, the castle, or the abbey, are to be seen.

seems to preside, runs the full length of the castle as it now stands (for the centre of the building only, has escaped the dilapidations of time), and its beautifully arched roof is enriched with numerous devices, which mark the spirit of that day in which it was erected. This very curious roof is supported by two rows of pillars of that elegant spiral lightness which characterizes the Gothic order in a certain stage of its progress. The floor is a finely tesselated* pavement; and the ample but ungrated hearths which terminate it at either extremity, blaze every evening with the cheering contributions of a neighbouring bog. The windows, which are high, narrow, and arched, command on one side a noble view of the ocean, on the other they are closed up.

When I inquired of Father John the cause of this singular exclusion of a very beautiful land view, he replied, 'that from those windows were to be seen the greater part of that rich tract of land which once formed the territory of the Princes of Inismore;[1] and since,' said he, 'the possessions of the present Prince are limited to a few hereditary acres, and a few rented farms, he cannot bear to look on the domains of his ancestors, nor ever goes beyond the confines of this little peninsula.'

This very curious apartment is still called the banquetting-hall—where

> 'Stately the feast and high the cheer,
> Girt with many a valiant Peer,'

was once celebrated in all the boundless extravagance and convivial spirit of ancient Irish hospitality. But it now serves as an armory, a museum, a cabinet of national antiquities, and national curiosities. In short, it is the receptacle of all those precious relics, which the Prince has been able to rescue from the wreck of his family splendour.

Here, when he is seated by a blazing hearth in an immense arm-chair, made, as he assured me, of the famous wood of *Shilelah*, his daughter by his side, his harper behind him, and his *domestic altar* not destitute of that national libation which is no disparagement

---

[1] I understand that it is only a few years back, since the present respectable representative of the M'Dermot family opened these windows, which the Prince of Coolavin closed up, upon a principle similar to that by which the Prince of Inismore was actuated.

to princely taste, since it has received the sanction of imperial approbation;[1] his gratified eye wandering over the scattered insignia of the former prowess of his family; his gratified heart expanding to the reception of life's sweetest ties—domestic joys and social endearments;—he forgets the derangement of his circumstances— he forgets that he is the ruined possessor of a visionary title; he feels only that he is a man—and an Irishman! While the transient happiness that lights up the vehement feelings of his benevolent breast, effuses its warmth o'er all who come within its sphere.

Nothing can be more delightful than the evenings passed in this *vengolf*—this hall of Woden; where my sweet Glorvina hovers round us, like one of the beautiful *valkyries** of the Gothic paradise, who bestow on the spirit of the departed warrior that heaven he eagerly rushes on death to obtain. Sometimes she accompanies the old bard on her harp, or with her voice; and frequently as she sits at her wheel (for she is often engaged in this simple and primitive avocation), endeavours to lure her father to speak on those subjects most interesting to him or to me; or, joining the general conversation, by the playfulness of her humour, or the original whimsicality of her sallies, materially contributes to the '*molle atque facetum*'* of the moment.

On the evening of the day of the picture scene, the absence of Glorvina (for she was attending a sick servant) threw a gloom over our little circle. The Prince, for the first time, dismissed the harper, and, taking me by the arm, walked up and down the hall in silence, while the priest yawned over a book.

I have already told you, that this curious hall is the *emporium* of the antiquities of Inismore, which are arranged along its walls, and suspended from its pillars.—As much to draw the Prince from the gloomy reverie into which he seemed plunged, as to satisfy my own curiosity and yours, I requested his Highness to explain some characters on a collar which hung from a pillar, and appeared to be plated with gold.

Having explained the motto, he told me that this collar had belonged to an order of knighthood hereditary in his family—of an institution more ancient than any in England, by some centuries.

'How!' said I, 'was chivalry so early known in Ireland? and rather, did it ever exist here?'

---

[1] Peter the Great of Russia, was remarkably fond of whiskey, and used to say, 'Of all wine, Irish wine is the best.'

'Did it!' said the Prince, impatiently, 'I believe, young gentleman, the origin of knighthood may be traced in Ireland upon surer ground than in any other country whatever.[1] Long before the birth of Christ, we had an hereditary order of knighthood in Ulster, called the Knights of the *Red Branch*. They possessed, near the royal palace of Ulster, a seat, called the *Academy of the Red Branch*; and an adjoining hospital, expressively termed the *House of the Sorrowful Soldier*.

'There was also an order of chivalry hereditary in the royal families of Munster, named the *Sons of Deagha*, from a celebrated hero of that name, probably their founder. The Connaught Knights were called the *Guardians of Jorus*, and those of Leinster, *the Clan of Boisgna*. So famous, indeed, were the knights of Ireland, for the elegance, strength, and beauty of their forms, that they were distinguished, by way of pre-eminence, by the name of *the Heroes of the Western Isles*.

'Our annals teem with instances of this romantic bravery and scrupulous honour. My memory, though much impaired, is still faithful to some anecdotes of both. During a war between the Connaught and Munster Monarchs, in 192, both parties met in the plains of Lena, in this province; and it was proposed to Goll M'Morni, chief of the Connaught Knights, to attack the Munster army at midnight, which would have secured him victory. He nobly and indignantly replied: "On the day the arms of a knight were put into my hands, I swore never to attack my enemy at night, by surprize, or under *any kind of disadvantage*; nor shall that vow now be broken."

'Besides those orders of knighthood which I have already named, there are several others[2] still hereditary in noble families, and the honourable titles of which are still preserved: such as the *White Knights of Kerry*, and the *Knights of Glynn*: that hereditary in my

---

[1] Mr O'Halloran, with a great deal of spirit and ingenuity, endeavours to prove, that the German knighthood (the earliest we read of in chivalry) was of Irish origin: with what success, we leave it to the impartial reader to judge. It is, however, certain, that the German *Ritter*, or knight, bears a very close analogy to the Irish *riddaire*. In 1395, Richard II in his tour through Ireland, offered to knight the four provincial Kings who came to receive him in Dublin. But they excused themselves, as having received that honour from their parents at seven years old—that being the age in which the Kings of Ireland knighted their eldest sons.—See *Froissart*.*

[2] The respectable families of the Fitzgeralds still bear the title of their ancestors, and are never named but as the Knights of Kerry, and of Glynn.

family was the *Knights of the Valley*; and this collar,[1] an ornament never dispensed with, was found about fifty years back in a neighbouring bog, and worn by my father till his death.

'This gorget,' he continued, taking down one which hung on the wall, and apparently gratified by the obvious pleasure evinced in the countenance of his auditor,—'This gorget* was found some years after in the same bog.'[2]

'And this helmet?' said I—

'It is called in Irish,' he replied, '*salet*, and belonged, with this coat of mail, to my ancestor who was murdered in this castle.'

I coloured at this observation, as though I had been myself the murderer.

'As you refer, Sir,' said the priest, who had flung by his book and joined us, 'to the ancient Irish for the origin of knighthood,[3] you will perhaps send us to the Irish *Mala*, for the derivation of the word mail.'

'Undoubtedly,' said the national Prince, 'I should; but pray, Mr Mortimer, observe this shield. It is of great antiquity. You perceive it is made of wicker, as were the Irish shields in general; although I have also heard they were formed of silver, and one was found near Slimore, in the county of Cork, plated with gold, which sold for seventy guineas.'

'But here,' said I, 'is a sword of curious workmanship, the hilt of which seems of gold.'

'It is in fact so,' said the priest—'Golden hilted swords have been in great abundance through Ireland; and it is a circumstance singularly curious, that a sword found in the Bog of Cullen should be of

[1] One of these collars was in the possession of Mr O'Halloran.

[2] In the Bog of Cullen, in the county of Tipperary, some golden gorgets were discovered, as were also some corselets of pure gold in the lands of Clonties, county of Kerry.—See *Smith's History of Kerry*.

[3] At a time when the footstep of an English invader had not been impressed upon the Irish coast, the celebrity of the Irish Knights was sung by the British minstrels. Thus in the old romantic tale of Sir Cauline:

> In Ireland, *ferr* over the sea,
> There dwelleth a bonnye kinge,
> And with him a yong and comlye knight,
> Men call him Syr Cauline.

Sir Cauline's antagonist, the Eldridge knight, is described as being '*a foul paynim*,'* which places the events the romantic tale delineates, in the earliest æra of Christianity in Ireland.

the exact construction and form of those found upon the plains of Canae. You may suppose that the advocates for our Milesian origin gladly seize on this circumstance, as affording new arms against the sceptics to the antiquity of our nation.'

'Here too is a very curious hauberjeon,* once perhaps impregnable! And this curious battle-axe,' said I—

'Was originally called,' returned the Prince, '*Tuath Catha*, or axe of war, and was put into the hands of our Galloglasses, or second rank of military.'

'But how much more elegant,' I continued, 'the form of this beautiful spear; it is of course of a more modern date.'

'On the contrary,' said the Prince, 'this is the exact form of the cranuil or lance, with which Oscar is described to have struck Art to the earth.'

'Oscar!' I repeated, almost starting—but added—'O, true, Mr Macpherson tells us the Irish have some wild improbable tales of Fingal's heroes* among them, on which they found some claim to their being natives of this country.'

'Some claims!' repeated the Prince, and by one of those motions which speak more than volumes, he let go my arm, and took his usual station by the fire-side, repeating *some claims*!

While I was thinking how I should repair my involuntary fault, the good-natured priest said with a smile,

'You know, my dear Sir, that by one half of his English readers, Ossian is supposed to be a Scottish bard of ancient days; by the other he is esteemed the legitimate offspring of Macpherson's own muse.* But here,' he added, turning to me, 'We are certain of his Irish origin, from the testimony of tradition, from proofs of historic fact, and above all, from the internal evidences of the poems themselves, even as they are given us by Mr Macpherson.

'We who are from our infancy taught to recite them,[1] who bear the appellations of their heroes to this day, and who reside amidst those very scenes of which the poems, even according to their *ingenious*,

---

[1] The Irish, like the Greeks, are passionately fond of traditional fictions, fables and romances. Nothing can be more relevant to this asserted analogy, than a passage translated from the works of Monsieur de Guys. Speaking of fables and romances, he says, 'The modern Greeks are excessively attached to them, and much delighted with those received from the Arabians, and other eastern nations; they are particularly pleased with the marvellous, and have, like the Greeks, their Milesian fables.'—*Lettres sur la Grece.*

but not always *ingenuous* translator, are descriptive—we know, believe, and assert them to be translated from the fragments of the Irish bards, or seanachies, whose surviving works were almost equally diffused through the Highlands as through this country. Mr Macpherson combined them in such forms as his judgment (too classically correct in this instance) most approved; retaining the old names and events, and altering the dates of his originals as well as their matter and form, in order to give them an higher antiquity than they really possess; suppressing many proofs which they contain of their Irish origin, and studiously avoiding all mention of St Patrick, whose name frequently occurs in the original poems; only occasionally alluding to him under the character of a *Culdee*; conscious that any mention of the *Saint* would introduce a suspicion that these poems were not the true compositions of Ossian, but of those *Fileas* who, in an after day, committed to verse the traditional details of one equally renowned in song and arms.'[1]

Here, you will allow, was a blow furiously aimed at all my opinions respecting these poems, so long the objects of my enthusiastic admiration: you may well suppose I was for a moment quite stunned. However, when I had a little recovered, I went over the arguments used by Macpherson, Blair, etc. etc. etc. to prove that Ossian was an Highland bard, whose works were handed down to us by *oral* tradition, through a lapse of fifteen hundred years.

'And yet,' said the priest, having patiently heard me out—'Mr Macpherson confesses that the ancient language and traditional history of the Scottish nation became confined to the natives of the Highlands, who falling, from several concurring circumstances, into the last degree of ignorance and barbarism, left the Scots so destitute of historic facts, that they were reduced to the necessity of sending John Fordun* to Ireland for their history, from whence he took the entire first part of his book. For Ireland, owing to its being colonized from Phœnicia,* and consequent early introduction of letters there, was at that period esteemed the most enlightened country in Europe: and indeed Mr Macpherson himself avers, that the Irish, for ages antecedent to the Conquest,* possessed a competent share of that

---

[1] *Samuir*, daughter of Fingal, having married Cormac Cas, their son (says Keating) *Modh Corb*, retained as his friend and confident his uncle, Ossian, contrary to the orders of Cairbre Liffeachair, the then monarch, against whom the Irish militia had taken up arms. Ossian was consequently among the number of rebellious chiefs.

kind of learning which prevailed in Europe; and from their superiority over the Scots, found no difficulty in imposing on the ignorant Highland seanachies, and established that historic system which afterwards, for want of any other, was universally received.

'Now, my dear friend, if historic fact and tradition did not attest the poems of Ossian to be Irish, probability would establish it. For if the Scotch were obliged to Ireland, according to Mr Macpherson's own account, not only for their history, but their tradition, so remote a one as Ossian must have come from the Irish; for Scotland, as Dr Johnson asserts, when he called on Mr Macpherson to shew his originals, had not an Erse* manuscript two hundred years old. And Sir George M'Kenzie, though himself a Scotchman, declares, 'that he had in his possession, an Irish manuscript written by Cairbre Liffeachair,[1] monarch of Ireland, who flourished before St Patrick's mission.'

'But,' said I, 'even granting these beautiful poems to be effusions of Irish genius, it is strange that the feats of your own heroes could not supply your bards with subjects for their epic verse.'

'Strange indeed it would have been,' said the priest, 'and therefore they have chosen the most renowned chiefs in their annals of national heroism, as their Achilleses, their Hectors, and Agamemnons.'

'How!' exclaimed I, 'is not Fingal a Caledonian chief? Is he not expressly called King of Morven?'

'Allowing he were, in the originals, which he is not,' returned the priest, 'give me leave to ask you where Morven lies?'

'Why, I suppose of course in Scotland,' said I, a little unprepared for the question.

'Mr Macpherson supposes so too,' replied he, smiling, 'though he certainly is at no little pains to discover where in Scotland. The fact is, however, that the epithet of *Riagh Môr Fhionne*, which Mr Macpherson translates King of Morven, is literally King or Chief of the Fhians, or Fians, a body of men of whom Mr Macpherson makes no mention, and which, indeed, either in the annals of Scottish history or Scottish poetry, would be vainly sought. Take then their

---

[1] Mr O'Halloran, in his introduction to the study of Irish History etc. quotes some lines from a poem still extant, composed by Torna Ligis, chief poet to Nial the Great, who flourished in the fourth century.

history, as extracted from the book of Howth into the Transactions of the Royal Irish Academy in 1786.[1]

'"In Ireland there were soldiers called *Fynne Erin*, appointed to keep the sea coast, fearing foreign invasion, or foreign princes to enter the realm; the names of these soldiers were, Fin M'Cuil, Coloilon, Keilt, Oscar, M'Ossyn, Dermot, O Doyne, Collemagh, Morna, and divers others. These soldiers waxed bold, as shall appear hereafter, and so strong, that they did contrary to the orders and institutions of the kings of Ireland, their chiefs and governors, and became very strong, and stout, and at length would do things without licence of the King of Ireland, etc. etc." It is added, that one of these heroes was alive till the coming of St Patrick, who recited the actions of his compeers to the Saint. This hero was Ossian, or, as we pronounce it, *Ossyn*; whose dialogues with the Christian missionary is in the mouth of every peasant, and several of them preserved in old Irish manuscripts. Now the Fingal of Mr Macpherson (for it is thus he translates *Fin M'Cuil*, sometimes pronounced and spelled Fionne M'Cumhal, or *Fionn* the son of Cumhal) and his followers, appear like the earth-born myrmidons of Deucalion,* for they certainly have no human origin; bear no connexion with the history of their country; are neither to be found in the poetic legend or historic record[2] of Scotland, and are even furnished with appellations which the Caledonians neither previously possessed nor have since adopted. They are therefore abruptly introduced to our knowledge,

---

[1] *Fionn*, the son of Cumhal (from whom, says Keating, the established militia of the kingdom were called *Fion Erinne*), was first married to Graine, daughter to Cormac, King of Ireland, and afterwards to her sister, and descended in a sixth degree from Nuagadh Neacht, King of Leinster. The history, laws, requisites, etc. etc. of the Fion-na-Erin, are to be found in Keating's History of Ireland, page 269:

Cormac, at the head of the Fion, and attended by Fingal, sailed to that part of Scotland opposite Ireland, where he planted a colony as an establishment for Carbry Riada, his cousin-german. This colony was often protected from the power of the Romans by the Fion, under the command of Fingal, occasionally stationed in the circumjacent country. 'Hence,' says Mr Walker, 'the claim of the Scots to Fin.' In process of time this colony gave monarchs to Scotland, and their posterity at this day reign over the British empire. Fingal fell in an engagement at Rathbree, on the banks of the Boyne, A.D. 294; from whence the name of Rathbree was changed into that of Killeen, or Cill-Fhin, the tomb of Fin.

[2] I know but of one instance that contradicts the assertion of Father John, and that I borrow from the allegorical *Palace of Honour* of Gawin Douglas, Bishop of Dunkeld, who places Gaul, son of Morni and Fingal, among the distinguished characters in the annals of legendary romance; yet even *he* mentions them not as the heroes of Scottish celebrity, but as the almost fabled demi-gods of Ireland.

[*cont. on p. 110*]

as living in a barbarous age, yet endowed with every perfection that renders them the most refined, heroic, and virtuous of men. So that while we grant to the interesting poet and his heroes our boundless admiration, we cannot help considering them as solecisms* in the theory of human nature.

'But with *us*, Fingal and his chiefs are beings of real existence, their names, professions, rank, characters, and feats, attested by historic fact as well as by poetic eulogium. Fingal is indeed romantically brave; benevolent and generous; but he is turbulent, restless, and ambitious: he is a man as well as a hero; and both his virtues and his vices bear the stamp of the age and country in which he lived. His name and feats, as well as those of his chief officers, bear an intimate connexion with our national history.

'Fionne, or Finnius, was the grandsire of Milesius; and it is not only a name to be met with through every period of our history, but there are few old families even at this day in Ireland, who have not the appellative of Finnius in some one or other of its branches; and a large tract of the province of Leinster is called *Fingal*: a title in possession of one of our most noble and ancient families.

'Nay, if you please, you shall hear our old nurse run through the whole genealogy of Macpherson's hero, which is frequently given as a theme to exercise the memory of the peasant children.'[1]

'Nay,' said I, nearly overpowered, 'Macpherson assures us the Highlanders also repeat many of Ossian's poems in the original Erse:

> 'And now the wran cam out of Ailsay,
> And Piers Plowman, that made his workmen few,
> Great Gow MacMorne and Fyn M'Cowl, and how
> They suld be goddis in Ireland, as they say.'

It is remarkable, that the genius of the Ossianic style still prevails over the wild effusions of the modern and unlettered bards of Ireland; while even the remotest lay of Scottish minstrelsy respires nothing of that soul which breathes in 'the voice of Cona;' and the metrical flippancy which betrays its existence, seems neither to rival, or cope with that touching sublimity of measure through whose impressive medium the genius of Ossian effuses its inspiration, and which, had it been known to the early bards of Scotland, had probably been imitated and adopted. In Ireland, it has ever been and is still the measure in which the Sons of Song breathe 'their wood-notes wild.'

[1] They run it over thus: 'Oscar Mac Ossyn, Mac Fionn, Mac Cuil, Mac Cormic, Mac Arte, Mac Fiervin, etc. etc.' That is, Oscar the son of Ossian, the son of Fionn, etc. etc.

nay, that even in the Isle of Sky, they still shew a stone which bears the form and name of Cuchullin's dog.'[1]

'This is the most flagrant error of all,' exclaimed the Prince, abruptly breaking his sullen silence—'for he had synchronized heroes who flourished in two distant periods; both Cuchullin and Conal Cearneath are historical characters with us; they were Knights of the *Red Branch*, and flourished about the birth of Christ. Whereas Fingal, with whom he has united them, did not flourish till near three centuries after. It is indeed Macpherson's pleasure to inform us, that by the Isle of Mist is meant the Isle of Sky, and on that circumstance alone to rest his claim on *Cuchullin*'s being a Caledonian; although, through the whole poems of Fingal and Temora, he is not once mentioned as such: it is by the translator's notes only we are informed of it.'

'It is certain,' said the priest—'that in the first mention made of *Cuchullin* in the poem of Fingal, he is simply denominated "the Son of Semo," "the Ruler of High Temora," "Mossy Tura's Chief."[2] So called, says Macpherson, from his castle on the coast of Ulster, where he dwelt before he took the management of the affairs of Ireland into his hands, though the singular cause which could induce the lord of the Isle of Sky to reside in Ireland previous to his political engagements in the Irish state, he does not mention.

'In the same manner we are told, that his three nephews came from Streamy Etha, one of whom married an Irish lady; but there is

---

[1] There is an old tradition current in Connaught, of which *Bran*, the favourite dog of Ossian, is the hero. In a war between the King of Lochlin and the Fians, a battle continued to be fought on equal terms for so long a period, that it was at last mutually agreed that it should be decided in a combat between Ossian's *Bran* and the famous *Cu dubh*, or dark greyhound, of the Danish Monarch. This greyhound had already performed incredible feats, and was never to be conquered until his name was found out. The warrior dogs fought in a space between the two armies, and with such fury, says the legend, in a language absolutely untranslatable, that they tore up the stony bosom of the earth, until they rendered it perfectly soft, and again trampled on it with such force, that they made it of a rocky substance. The *Cu dubh* had nearly gained the victory, when the *bald-headed Conal*, turning his face to the east, and *biting his thumb*, a ceremony difficult to induce him to perform, and which always endowed him with the gift of divination, made a sudden exclamation of encouragement to *Bran*, the first word of which found the name of the greyhound, who lost at once his prowess and the victory. The chief Order of Denmark was instituted in memory of the fidelity of a dog, 'though it is injuriously called the Order of the Elephant,' says Pope.

[2] The groves of Tura, or Tuar, are often noticed in Irish song. *Emunh Acnuic*, or Ned of the Hill, has mentioned it in one of his happiest and most popular poems. It was supposed to be in the county of Armagh, province of Ulster.

no mention made of the real name of the place of their nativity, although the translator assures us, in another note, that they also were Caledonians. But in fact, it is from the internal evidences of the poems themselves, not from the notes of Mr Macpherson, nor indeed altogether from his beautiful but unfaithful translation, that we are to decide on the nation to which these poems belong. In Fingal, the first and most perfect of the collection, that hero is first mentioned by Cuchullin as Fingal, *King of Desarts*—in the original—*Inis na bfhiodhuide*, or *Woody Island*; without any allusion whatever to his being a Caledonian. And afterwards he is called King of Selma, by Swaran, a name, with little variation, given to several castles in Ireland. Darthulla's castle is named Selma; and another, whose owner I do not remember, is termed Selemath. *Slimora*, to whose fir the spear of Foldath is compared, is a mountain in the province of Munster, and throughout the whole even of Mr Macpherson's translation, the characters, names, allusions, incidents, and scenery are all Irish. And in fact, our *Irish spurious ballads*, as Mr Macpherson calls them, are the very originals out of which he has spun the materials for his version of Ossian.[1]

'Dr Johnson, who strenuously opposed the idea of *Ossian* being the work of a Scotch bard of the third century, asserts that the "Erse never was a written language, and that there is not in the world a written Erse manuscript an hundred years old." He adds, "The Welsh and Irish are cultivated tongues, and two hundred years back insulted their English neighbours for the instability of their orthography. Even the ancient Irish *letter* was unknown in the Highlands in 1690, for an Irish version of the Bible being given there by Mr Kirk, was printed in the Roman character."

'When Dr Young,[2] led by tasteful enterprize, visited the Highlands

---

[1] 'Some of the remaining footsteps of these old warriors are known by their first names at this time (says Keating), as for instance, *Suidhe Finn*, or the Palace of Fin, at *Sliabh na Mann*, etc. etc. etc.' There is a mountain in Donegal still called *Alt Ossoin*, surrounded by all that wild sublimity of scenery so exquisitely delineated through the elegant medium of Mr Macpherson's translation of Ossian; and in its environs many Ossianic tales are still extant.

In an extract given by Camden from an account of the manners of the native Irish in the sixteenth century—'they think (says the author) the souls of the deceased are in communion with the famous men of those places, of whom they retain many stories and sonnets—as of the giants Fin, Mac Huyle, Osker, Mac Osshin, etc. etc. and they say, through illusion, they often see them.'

[2] Dr Young, late Bishop of Clonfert, who united in his character the extremes of human perfection—the most unblemished virtue to the most exalted genius.

(on an Ossianic research) in 1784, he collected a number of Gaelic poems respecting the race of the Fiens, so renowned in the annals of Irish heroism,[1] and found, that the orthography was less pure than that among us; for he says, "the Erse being only a written language within these few years, no means were yet afforded of forming a decided orthographic standard." But he augurs, from the improvement which had lately taken place, that we soon may expect to see the Erse restored to the original purity which it possesses in the *mother* country. And those very poems, whence Mr Macpherson has chiefly constructed his Ossian, bear such strong internal proof of their Irish origin, as to contain in themselves the best arguments that can be adduced against the Scottish claimants on the poems of the bard. But in their translation,[2] many passages are perverted, in order to deprive Ireland of being the residence of Fingal's heroes.'

'I remember,' said the Prince, 'when you read to me a description of a sea-fight between Fingal and Swaran, in Macpherson's translation, that I repeated to you, in Irish, the very poem whence it was taken, and which is still very current here, under the title of *Laoid Mhanuis M'hoir*.'

'True,' returned the priest, 'a copy of which is deposited in the University of Dublin, with another Irish MS entitled, "*Oran eadas Ailte agus do Maronnan*," whence the Battle of Lora is taken.'

The Prince then, desiring Father John to give him down a bundle of old manuscripts which lay on a shelf in the hall, dedicated to national tracts, after some trouble, produced a copy of a poem, called 'The Conversation of Ossian and St Patrick,' the original of which, Father John assured me, was deposited in the library of the Irish University.

It is to this poem that Mr Macpherson alludes, when he speaks of

---

[1] See Transactions of the Royal Irish Academy, 1786.

[2] 'From the remotest antiquity we have seen the military order distinguished in Ireland, codes of military laws and discipline established, and their dress, and rank in the state, ascertained. The learned Keating, and others, tell us, that these *militia* were called *Fine*, from *Fion Mac Cumhal*; but it is certainly a great error; the word *Fine* strictly implying a *military corps*. Many places in the island retain, to this day, the names of some of the leaders of this famous body of men, and whole volumes of poetical fictions have been grafted upon their exploits. The manuscript which I have, after giving a particular account of *Finn*'s descent, his inheritance, his acquisitions from the King of Leinster, and his great military command, immediately adds—"but the reader must not expect to meet here with such stories of him and his heroes *as the vulgar Irish have*."'—*Dr Warner*.

the dispute reported to have taken place between Ossian and a Culdee.

At my request, he translated this curious controversial tract.[1] The dispute was managed on both sides with a great deal of polemic ardour. St Patrick, with apostolic zeal, shuts the gates of Mercy on all whose faith differs from his own, and, with an unsaintly vehemence, extends the exclusion, in a pointed manner, to the ancestors of Ossian, who, he declares, are suffering in the *limbo* of tortured spirits.

The bard tenderly replies, 'It is hard to believe thy tale, O man of the white book! that Fian, *or one so generous*, should be in captivity with God or man.'

When, however, the Saint persists in the assurance, that not even the generosity of the departed hero could save him from the house of torture, the failing spirit of 'the King of Harps' suddenly sends forth a lingering flash of its wonted fire; and he indignantly declares, 'that if the Clan of Boisgna were still in being, they would liberate their beloved general from this threatened hell.'

The Saint, however, growing warm in the argument, expatiates on the great difficulty of *any* soul entering the court of God: to which the infidel bard beautifully replies:— 'Then he is not like *Fionn M'Cuil*, our chief of the Fians; for every man upon the face of the earth might enter *his* court, without asking his permission.'

Thus, as you perceive, fairly routed, I however artfully proposed terms of capitulation, as though my defeat was yet dubious.

'Were I a Scotchman,' said I, 'I should be furnished with more effectual arms against you; but as an Englishman, I claim an armed neutrality, which I shall endeavour to preserve between the two nations. At the same time that I feel the highest satisfaction in witnessing the just pretensions of that country (which now ranks in my estimation next to my own) to a work which would do honour to *any* country so fortunate as to claim its author as her son.'

The Prince, who seemed highly gratified by this avowal, shook me heartily by the hand, apparently flattered by his triumph; and at that moment Glorvina entered.

---

[1] Notwithstanding the sceptical obstinacy that Ossian here displays, there is a current tradition of his having been present at a baptismal ceremony performed by the Saint, who accidentally struck the sharp point of his crozier through the bard's foot, who, supposing it part of the ceremony, remained transfixed to the earth without a murmur.

'O, my dear!' said the Prince, 'you are just come in time to witness an amnesty between Mr Mortimer and me.'

'I should much rather witness the amnesty than the breach,' returned she, smiling.

'We have been battling about the country of Ossian,' said the priest, 'with as much vehemence as the claimants on the birth-place of Homer.'

'O! I know of old,' cried Glorvina, 'that you and my father are natural allies on that point of contention; and I must confess, it was ungenerous in both, to oppose your united strength against Mr Mortimer's single force.'

'What, then,' said the Prince, good humouredly, 'I suppose you would have deserted your national standard, and have joined Mr Mortimer, merely from motives of compassion.'

'Not so, my dear Sir,' said Glorvina, faintly blushing, 'but I should have endeavoured to have compromised between you. To you I would have accorded that Ossian was an Irishman, of which I am as well convinced as of any other self-evident truth whatever, and to Mr Mortimer I would have acknowledged the superior merits of Mr Macpherson's poems, as compositions, over those wild effusions of our Irish bards whence he compiled them.

'Long before I could read, I learned on the bosom of my nurse, and in my father's arms, to recite the songs of our national bards, and almost since I could read, the Ossian of Macpherson has been the object of my enthusiastic admiration.

'In the original Irish poems, if my fancy is sometimes dazzled by the brilliant flashes of native genius, if my heart is touched by strokes of nature, or my soul elevated by sublimity of sentiment, yet my interest is often destroyed, and my admiration often checked, by relations so wildly improbable, by details so ridiculously grotesque, that though these stand forth as the most undeniable proofs of their authenticity and the remoteness of the day in which they were composed, yet I reluctantly suffer my mind to be convinced at the expence of my feeling and my taste. But in the soul-stealing strains of "the Voice of Cona," as breathed through the refined medium of Macpherson's genius, no incongruity of style, character, or manner, disturbs the profound interest they awaken. For my own part, when my heart is coldly void, when my spirits are sunk and drooping, I fly to my English Ossian, and then my sufferings are soothed, and every

desponding spirit softens into a sweet melancholy, more delicious
than joy itself; while I experience in its perusal a similar sensation as
when, in the stillness of an autumnal evening, I expose my harp to
the influence of the passing breeze, which faintly breathing on the
chords, seems to call forth its own requiem as it expires.'

'Oh, Macpherson!' I exclaimed, 'be thy spirit appeased, for thou
hast received that apotheosis thy talents have nearly deserved, in the
eulogium of beauty and genius, and from the lip of an Irishwoman.'

This involuntary and impassioned exclamation extorted from the
Prince a smile of gratified parental pride, and overwhelmed Glorvina
with confusion. She could, I believe, have spared it before her father,
and received it with a bow and a blush. Shortly after she left the
room.

Adieu! I thought to have returned to M—— house, but I know
not how it is——

> 'Mais un invincible contraint
> Malgrè moi fixe ici mes pas,
> Et tu sais que pour aller à Corinth,
> Le desir seul ne suffit pas.'*

Adieu!

H.M.

LETTER XIII

TO J.D. ESQ. M.P.

The conduct of this girl is inexplicable. Since the unfortunate picture scene three days back, she has excused herself twice from the
drawing-desk; and to-day appeared at it with the priest by her side.
Her playful familiarity is vanished, and a chill reserve, uncongenial
to the native ardour of her manner, has succeeded. Surely she cannot
be so vain, so weak, as to mistake my attentions to her as a young and
lovely woman; my admiration of her talents, and my surprize at the
originality of her character, for a serious passion. And supposing me
to be a wanderer and an hireling, affect to reprove my temerity by
haughtiness and disdain.

Would you credit it! By Heavens, I am sometimes weak enough to
be on the very point of telling her who and what I am, when she

plays off her little airs of Milesian pride and female superciliousness. You perceive, therefore, by the conduct of this little Irish recluse, that on the subject of love and vanity, woman is every where, and in all situations, the same. For what coquet reared in the purlieus of St James,* could be more *a portée** to those effects which denote the passion, or more apt to suspect she had awakened it into existence, than this inexperienced, unsophisticated being? who I suppose never spoke to ten men in her life, save the superannuated inhabitants of her paternal ruins. Perhaps, however, she only means to check the growing familiarity of my manner, and to teach me the disparity of rank which exists between us; for, with all her native strength of mind, the influence of invariable example and frequent precept has been too strong for her, and she has unconsciously imbibed many of her father's prejudices respecting antiquity of descent and nobility of birth. She will frequently say, 'O! such a one is a true Milesian!'— or, 'he is a descendant of the *English* Irish;'—or, 'they are new people—we hear nothing of them till the wars of Cromwell,' and so on. Yet at other times, when reason lords it over prejudice, she will laugh at that weakness in others, she sometimes betrays in herself.

The other day, as we stood chatting at a window together, pointing to an elderly man who passed by, she said, 'there goes a poor Connaught gentleman, who would rather starve than work—he is a *follower* of the family, and has been just entertaining my father with an account of our ancient splendour. We have too many instances of this species of *mania* among us.

'The celebrated Bishop of Cloyne relates an anecdote of a kitchen-maid, who refused to carry out cinders, because she was of Milesian descent. And Father John tells a story of a young gentleman in Limerick, who being received under the patronage of a nobleman going out as Governor-General of India, sacrificed his interest to his *national pride*; for having accompanied his Lordship on board the vessel which was to convey them to the East, and finding himself placed at the foot of the dining-table, he instantly arose, and went on shore, declaring that "as a *true Milesian*," he would not submit to any indignity, to purchase the riches of the East India Company.[1]

---

[1] Not long since, the Author met a person in the capacity of a writing-master in a gentleman's family, who assured her that he was a *Prince* by lineal descent, and that the name of his Principality was *Sliabh-Ban*. This Principality of *Sliabh-Ban*, however, is simply a small and rugged mountain, whose rigid soil bids defiance to culture.

'All this,' continued Glorvina, 'is ridiculous, nay it is worse, for it is highly dangerous and fatal to the community at large. It is the source of innumerable disorders, by promoting idleness, and consequently vice. It frequently checks the industry of the poor, and limits the exertions of the rich, and perhaps is not among the least of those sources whence our national miseries flow. At the same time I must own, I have a very high idea of the virtues which exalted birth does or ought to bring with it. Marmontel* elegantly observes, "nobility of birth is a letter of credit given us on our country, upon the security of our ancestors, in the conviction that at a proper period of life we shall acquit ourselves with honour to those who stand engaged for us."'

Observe, that this passage was quoted in the first person, and not, as in the original, in the second, and with an air of dignity that elevated her pretty little head some inches.

'Since,' she continued, 'we are all the beings of education, and that its most material branch, example, lies vested in our parents, it is natural to suppose that those superior talents or virtues which in early stages of society are the purchase of worldly elevation, become hereditary, and that the noble principles of our ancestors should descend to us with their titles and estates.'

'Ah,' said I, smiling, 'these are the ideas of an Irish Princess, reared in the palace of her ancestors on the shores of the Atlantic Ocean.'

'They may be,' she returned, 'the ideas of an inexperienced recluse, but I think they are not less the result of rational supposition, strengthened by the evidence of internal feeling; for though I possessed not that innate dignity of mind which instinctively spurned at the low suggestion of vicious dictates, yet the consciousness of the virtues of those from whom I am descended, would prevent me from sullying by an unworthy action of mine, the unpolluted name I had the honour to bear.'

She then repeated several anecdotes of the heroism, rectitude, and virtue of her ancestors of both sexes, adding 'this was once the business of our Bards, Fileas, and Seanachies;* but we are now obliged to have recourse to our own memories, in order to support our own dignity.

'But do not suppose I am so weak as to be dazzled by a *sound*, or to consider mere title in any other light than as a golden toy judiciously worn to secure the respect of the vulgar, who are incapable of appreciating that "which passeth show,"[1] which, as my father says, is sometimes given to him who saves, and sometimes bestowed on him who betrays, his country. O! no; for I would rather possess *one* beam of that genius which elevates *your* mind above all worldly distinction, and those principles of integrity which breathe in your sentiments and ennoble your soul, than'—

Thus hurried away by the usual impetuosity of her feelings, she abruptly stopped, fearful, perhaps, that she had gone too far. And then, after a moment added—'but who will dare to bring the souls of nobility in competition with the short-lived elevation which man bestows on man!'

This was the first direct compliment she ever paid me; and I received it with a silent bow, a throbbing heart, and a colouring cheek.

Is she not an extraordinary creature! I meant to have given you an unfavourable opinion of her prejudices; and in transcribing my documents of accusation, I have actually confirmed myself in a better opinion of her heart and understanding than I ever before indulged in. For to think well of *her*, is a positive indulgence to my philanthropy, after having thought so ill of all her sex.

But her virtues and her genius have nothing to do with the ice which crystallizes round her heart; and which renders her as coldly indifferent to the talents and virtues with which her fancy has invested me, as though they were in possession of an hermit of four score. Yet God knows, nothing less than cold does her character appear. That mutability of complexion which seems to flow perpetually to the influence of her evident feelings and vivid imagination, that ethereal warmth which animates her manners; the force and energy of her expressions, the enthusiasm of her disposition, the uncontroulable smile, the involuntary tear, the spontaneous sigh!— Are these indications of an icy heart? And yet, shut up as we are together, thus closely associated, the sympathy of our tastes, our pursuits! But the fact is, I begin to fear that I have imported into the shades of Inismore some of my London presumption; and that after all, I know as little of this charming *sport of Nature*, as when I first

---

[1] 'He feels no ennobling principles in his own heart, who wishes to level all the artificial institutes which have been adopted for giving body to opinion, and permanence to future esteem.'—*Burke.*

beheld her—possibly my perceptions have become as sophisticated as the objects to whom they have hitherto been directed; and want refinement and subtilty to enter into all the delicate *minutiæ* of her superior and original character, which is at once both *natural* and *national*.

Adieu!

H.M.

LETTER XIV

TO J.D. ESQ. M.P.

To day I was presented at an interview granted by the Prince to two contending parties, who came to *ask law of him*, as they term it. This, I am told, the Irish peasantry are ready to do upon every slight difference; so that they are the most litigious, or have the nicest sense of *right* and *justice*, of any people in the world.

Although the language held by this little judicial meeting was Irish, it was by no means necessary it should be understood, to comprehend, in some degree, the subject of discussion; for the gestures and countenances both of the judge and the clients, were expressive beyond all conception; and I plainly understood, that almost every other word on both sides was accompanied by a species of *local oath*, sworn on the first object that presented itself to their hands, and strongly marked the vehemence of the national character.

When I took notice of this to Father John, he replied,

'It is certain, that the habit of confirming every assertion with an oath, is as prevalent among the Irish as it *was* among the ancient, and *is* among the modern, Greeks. And it is remarkable, that even at this day, in both countries, the nature and form of their adjurations and oaths are perfectly similar: a Greek will still swear by his parents, or his children; an Irishman frequently swears "by my father, who is no more!" "by my mother in the grave!" Virgil makes his pious Æneas swear by his head. The Irish constantly swear, "by my hand,"—"by this hand,"—or, "by the hand of my gossip!" [1] There is one who has

---

[1] The mention of this oath recalls to my mind an anecdote of the bard Carolan,* as related by Mr Walker, in his inimitable Memoir of the Irish Bards. 'He (Carolan) went once on a pilgrimage to *St Patrick's Purgatory*, a cave in an island in Lough Dergh (county of Donegal), of which more wonders are told than even of the Cave of

just sworn by *the Cross*; another, by the blessed stick he holds in his hand. In short, no intercourse passes between them where confidence is required, in which oaths are not called in to confirm the transaction.'

I am this moment returned from my *Vengolf*, after having declared the necessity of my absence for some time, leaving the term, however, indefinite; so that in this instance, I can be governed by my inclination and convenience, without any violation of promise. The good old Prince looked as much amazed at my determination, as though he expected I were never to depart; and I really believe, in the old-fashioned hospitality of his Irish heart, he would be better satisfied I never should. He said many kind and cordial things in his own curious way; and concluded by pressing my speedy return, and declaring that my presence had created a little jubilee among them.

The priest was absent; and Glorvina, who sat at her little wheel by her father's side, snapped her thread, and drooped her head close to her work, until I casually observed, that I had already passed above three weeks at the castle—then she shook back the golden tresses from her brow, and raised her eyes to mine with a look that seemed to say, 'can that be possible!' Not even by a glance did I reply to the flattering question; but I felt it not the less.

When we arose to retire to our respective apartments, and I mentioned that I should be off at dawn, the Prince shook me cordially by the hand, and bid me farewell with an almost paternal kindness.

Glorvina, on whose arm he was leaning, did not follow his example—she simply wished me 'a pleasant journey.'

'But where,' said the Prince, 'do you sojourn to?'

'To the town of Bally——,' said I, 'which has been hitherto my head-quarters, and where I have left my clothes, books, and drawing utensils. I have also some friends in the neighbourhood, procured me by letters of introduction with which I was furnished in England.'

Triphonius. On his return to shore, he found several pilgrims waiting the arrival of the boat which had conveyed him to the object of his devotion. In assisting some of those devout travellers to get on board, he chanced to take a lady's hand, and instantly exclaimed, "*dar lamh mo Chairdais Criost* (*i.e.* by the hand of my gossip) this is the hand of Bridget Cruise" His sense of feeling did not deceive him—it *was* the hand of her whom he once adored.'

You know that a great part of this neighbourhood is now my father's property, and once belonged to the ancestors of the Prince. He changed colour as I spoke, and hurried on in silence.

Adieu! the castle clock strikes twelve! What creatures we are! when the tinkling of a bit of metal can affect our spirits. Mine, however (though why, I know not), were prepared for the reception of sombre images. This night may be, in all human probability, the last I shall sleep in the castle of Inismore; and what then—it were perhaps as well I had never entered it. A generous mind can never reconcile itself to the practices of deception; yet to prejudices so inveterate, I had nothing but deception to oppose. And yet, when in some happy moment of parental favour, when all my past sins are forgotten, and my present state of regeneration only remembered—I shall find courage to disclose my romantic adventure to my father, and through the medium of that strong partiality the son has awakened in the heart of the Prince, unite in bonds of friendship these two worthy men, but *unknown* enemies—then I shall triumph in my impositions, and, for the first time, adopt the maxim, that good consequences may be effected by means not strictly conformable to the rigid laws of truth.

I have just been at my window, and never beheld so gloomy a night—not a star twinkles through the massy clouds that are driven impetuously along by the sudden gusts of a rising storm—not a ray of light partially dissipates the profound obscurity, save what falls on a fragment of an opposite tower, and seems to issue from the window of a closet which joins the apartment of Glorvina. She has not yet then retired to rest, and yet 'tis unusual for her to sit up so late. For I have often watched that little casement—its position exactly corresponds with the angle of the castle where I am lodged.

If I should have any share in the vigils of Glorvina!!!

I know not whether to be most gratified or hurt at the manner in which she took leave of me. Was it indifference, or resentment, that marked her manner? She certainly was surprised, and her surprise was not of the most pleasing nature—for where was the magic smile, the sensient blush, that ever ushers in and betray every emotion of her ardent soul? Sweet being! whatever may be the sentiments which the departure of the supposed unfortunate wanderer awakens in thy bosom, may that bosom still continue the hallowed asylum of the dove of peace! May the pure heart it enshrines still throb to the best impulses of the happiest nature, and beat with the soft palpitation of innocent pleasure and guileless transport, veiled from the rude intercourse of that world to which thy elevated and sublime nature is so eminently superior: long amidst the shade of the venerable ruins of thy forefathers mayest thou bloom and flourish in undisturbed felicity! the ministering angel of thy poor compatriots, who look up to thee for example and support—thy country's muse, and the bright model of the genuine character of her daughters, when unvitiated by erroneous education, and by those fatal prejudices which lead them to seek in foreign refinement for those talents, those graces, those virtues, which are no where to be found more flourishing, more attractive, than in their native land.

H.M.

LETTER XV

TO J.D. ESQ. M.P.

M—— House

It certainly requires less nicety of perception to distinguish differences in kind than differences in degree; but though my present, like my past situation, is solitudinous in the extreme, it demands no very great discernment to discover, that my late life was a life of solitude—my present, of desolation.

In the castle of Inismore I was estranged from the world: here I am estranged from myself. Yet so much more sequestered did that sweet interesting spot appear to me, that I felt, on arriving at this vast and solitary place (after having passed by a few gentlemen's seats, and caught a distant view of the little town of Bally——), as though I were returning to the world—but felt as if that world had no longer any attraction for me.

What a dream was the last three weeks of my life! But it was a dream from which I wished not to be awakened. It seemed to me as if I had lived in an age of primeval simplicity and primeval virtue. My senses at rest, my passions soothed to philosophic repose, my prejudices vanquished, all the powers of my mind gently breathed into motion, yet calm and unagitated—all the faculties of my taste called into exertion, yet unsated even by boundless gratification. My fancy restored to its pristine warmth, my heart to its native sensibility. The past given to oblivion, the future unanticipated, and the present enjoyed, with the full consciousness of its pleasurable existence. Wearied, exhausted, satiated by a boundless indulgence of hackneyed pleasures, hackneyed occupations, hackneyed pursuits, at a moment when I was sinking beneath the lethargic influence of apathy, or hovering on the brink of despair, a new light broke upon my clouded mind, and discovered to my inquiring heart, something yet worth living for. What that mystic something is, I can scarcely yet define myself; but a magic spell now irresistibly binds me to that life which but lately,

> 'Like a foul and ugly witch, did limp
> So tediously away.'

The reserved tints of a grey dawn had not yet received the illuminating beams of the east, when I departed from the castle of Inismore. None of the family were risen, but the hind* who prepared my *rosinante*,* and the nurse, who made my breakfast.

I rode twice round that wing of the castle where Glorvina sleeps: the curtain of her bed-room casement was closely drawn; but as I passed by it the second time, I thought I perceived a shadowy form at the window of the adjoining casement. As I approached it seemed to retreat; the whole, however, might have only been the vision of my wishes—my *wishes!!!* But this girl piques me into something of interest for her.

About three miles from the castle, on the summit of a wild and desolate heath, I met the good Father Director of Inismore. He appeared quite amazed at the rencontre.* He expressed great regret at my absence from the castle, insisting that he should accompany me a mile or two of my journey, though he was only then returning after having passed the night in ministering temporal as well as spiritual comfort to an unfortunate family at some miles distance.

'These poor people,' said he, 'were tenants on the skirts of Lord M.'s estate, who, though by all accounts a most excellent and benevolent man, employs a steward of a very opposite character. This unworthy delegate having considerably raised the rent on a little farm held by these unfortunate people, they soon became deeply in arrears, were ejected, and obliged to take shelter in an almost roofless hut, where the inclemency of the season, and the hardships they endured, brought on disorders by which the mother and two children are now nearly reduced to the point of death;[1] and yesterday, in their last extremity, they sent for me.'

While I commiserated the sufferings of these unfortunates (and cursed the villain Clendinning in my heart), I could not avoid adverting to the humanity of this benevolent priest.

'These offices of true charity, which you so frequently perform,' said I, 'are purely the result of your benevolence, rather than a mere observance of your duty.'

'It is true,' he replied, 'I have no parish; but the incumbent of that in which these poor people reside is so old and infirm, as to be totally incapacitated from performing such duties of his calling as require the least exertion. The duty of one who professes himself the minister of religion, whose essence is charity, should not be confined within the narrow limitation of prescribed rules; and I should consider myself as unworthy of the sacred habit I wear, should my exertions be confined to the suggestions of my interest and my duty only.'

'The faith of the lower order of Catholics here in their priest,' he continued, 'is astonishing: even his presence they conceive an antidote to every evil. When he appears at the door of their huts, and blends his cordial salutation with a blessing, the spirit of consolation seems to hover at its threshold—pain is alleviated, sorrow soothed, and hope, rising from the bosom of strengthening faith, triumphs over the ruins of despair. To the wicked he prescribes penitence and confession, and the sinner is forgiven; to the wretched he asserts, that suffering here, is the purchase of felicity hereafter, and he is resigned; and to the sick he gives a consecrated charm, and by the force of faith and imagination he is made well. Guess then the influence which this order of men hold over the aggregate of the people; for while the Irish peasant, degraded, neglected, and despised,[2] vainly seeks one beam of conciliation in the eye of overbearing superiority; condescension, familiarity and kindness win his gratitude to him whose spiritual elevation is in his mind above all temporal rank.'

'You shed,' said I, 'a patriarchal interest over the character of priesthood among you here; which gives that order to my view in a

[1] The lower orders of Irish are very subject to dreadful fevers, which are generally the result of colds caught by the exposed state of their damp and roofless hovels.
[2] 'The common people of Ireland have no rank in society—they *may* be treated with contempt, and consequently are with inhumanity.'—'*An Inquiry into the Causes,*' etc. etc.

very different aspect from that in which I have hitherto considered it. To what an excellent purpose might this boundless influence be turned!'

'If,' interrupted he, 'priests *were not men*—men too, generally speaking, without education (which is in fact character, principle, every thing), except such as tends rather to narrow than enlarge the mind—men in a certain degree shut out from society, except of the lower class; and men who, from their very mode of existence (which forces them to depend on the eleemosynary contributions of their flock), must eventually in many instances imbibe a degradation of spirit which is certainly not the parent of the liberal virtues.'

'Good God!' said I, surprised, 'and this from one of their own order!'

'These are sentiments I should never have hazarded,' returned the priest, 'could I not have opposed to those natural conclusions, drawn from well known facts, innumerable instances of benevolence, piety, and learning, among the order. While to the whole body let it be allowed as *priests*, whatever may be their failings as *men*, that the activity of their lives,[1] the punctilious discharge of their duty, and their ever ready attention to their flock, under every moral and even under every physical suffering, renders them deserving of that reverence and affection which, above the ministers of any other religion, they receive from those over whom they are placed.'

'And which,' said I, 'if opposed to the languid performance of periodical duties, neglect of the moral functions of their calling, and the habitual indolence of the ministers of other sects, they may certainly be deemed zealots in the cause of the faith they profess, and the charity they inculcate!'

While I spoke, a young lad, almost in a state of nudity, approached us, yet in the crown of his leafless hat were stuck a few pens, and over his shoulder hung a leathern satchel full of books.

'This is an apposite rencontre,' said the priest—'behold the first stage of *one* class of Catholic priesthood among us; a class however no longer very prevalent.'

---

[1] 'A Roman Catholic clergyman is the minister of a very *ritual* religion; and by his profession, subject to many restraints; his life is full of strict observances, and his duties are of a laborious nature towards himself, and of the highest possible trust towards others.'—*Letter on the Penal Laws against the Irish Catholics, by the Right Honourable Edmund Burke.*

The boy approached, and, to my amazement, addressed us in Latin, begging with all the vehement eloquence of an Irish mendicant, for some money to buy ink and paper. We gave him a trifle, and the priest desired him to go on to the castle, where he would get his breakfast, and that on his return he would give him some books into the bargain.

The boy, who had solicited in Latin, expressed his gratitude in Irish; and we trotted on.

'Such,' said Father John, 'formerly was the frequent origin of our Roman Catholic priests. This is a character unknown to you in England, and is called here, "*a poor scholar*." If a boy is too indolent to work, and his parents too poor to support him, or, which is more frequently the case, if he discovers some natural talents, or, as they call it *takes to his learning*, and that they have not the means to forward his improvement, he then becomes by profession a *poor scholar*, and continues to receive both his mental and bodily food at the expence of the community at large.

'With a leathern satchel on his back, containing his portable library, he sometimes travels not only through his own province, but frequently over the greater part of the kingdom.[1] No door is shut against the poor scholar, who, it is supposed, at a future day may be invested with the apostolic key of Heaven. The priest or schoolmaster of every parish through which he passes, receives him for a few days into his bare-footed seminary, and teaches him bad Latin and worse English; while the most opulent of his school-fellows eagerly seize on the young peripatetic philosopher, and provide him with maintenance and lodging; and if he is a boy of talent or *humour* (a gift always prized by the naturally laughter-loving Milesians), they will struggle for the pleasure of his society.

[1] It has been justly said, that 'Nature is invariable in her operations; and that the principles of a polished people will influence even their latest posterity.' And the ancient state of letters in Ireland, may be traced in the love of learning and talent even still existing among the inferior class of the Irish to this day. On this point it is observed by Mr Smith, in his *History of Kerry*, 'that it is well known that classical reading extends itself even to a fault, among the lower and poorer kind of people in this country (Munster), many of whom have greater knowledge in this way than some of the better sort in other places.' He elsewhere observes, that Greek is taught in the mountainous parts of the province. And Mr O'Halloran asserts, that classical reading has most adherents in those retired parts of the kingdom where strangers had least access, and that as good classical scholars were found in most parts of Connaught, as in any part of Europe.

'Having thus had the seeds of dependence sown *irradically* in his mind, and finished his peripatetic studies, he returns to his native home, and with an empty satchel on his back, goes about raising contributions on the pious charity of his poor compatriots: each contributes some necessary article of dress, and assists to fill a little purse, until completely equipped; and for the first time in his life, covered from head to foot, the divine in embryo sets out for some sea-port, where he embarks for the colleges of Douay or St Omers; and having begged himself, *in forma pauperis*, through all the necessary rules and discipline of the seminary, he returns to his own country, and becomes the minister of salvation to those whose generous contributions enabled him to assume the sacred profession.[1]

'Such is the man by whom the minds, opinions, and even actions of the people are often influenced; and if man is but the creature of education and habit, I leave you to draw the inference. But this is but *one* class of priesthood, and its description rather applicable to twenty or thirty years back than to the present day. The other two may be divided into the sons of tradesmen and farmers, and the younger sons of Catholic gentry.

'Of the latter order am I; and the interest of my friends on my return from the Continent procured me what was deemed the best parish in the diocese. But the good and the evil attendant on every situation in life, is rather to be estimated by the feelings and sensibility of the objects whom they affect, than by their own intrinsic nature. It was in vain I endeavoured to accommodate my mind to the mode of life into which I had been forced by my friends. It was in vain I endeavoured to assimilate my spirit to that species of exertion necessary to be made for my livelihood.

'To owe my subsistence to the precarious generosity of those wretches, whose every gift to me must be the result of a sensible deprivation to themselves; to be obliged to extort (even from the alter where I presided as the minister of the Most High) the trivial contributions for my support, in a language which, however appropriate to the understandings of my auditors, sunk me in my own esteem to the last degree of self-degradation; or to receive from the religious affection of my flock such voluntary benefactions as,

---

[1] The French Revolution, and the foundation of the Catholic college at Maynooth, in Leinster, has put a stop to these pious emigrations.

under all the pressure of scarcity and want, their rigid economy to themselves enabled them to make to the pastor whom they revered.[1] In a word, after three years miserable dependence on those for whose poverty and wretchedness my heart bled, I threw up my situation, and became chaplain to the Prince of Inismore, on a stipend sufficient for my little wants, and have lived with him for thirty years, on such terms as you have witnessed for these three weeks back.

'While my heart-felt compassion, my tenderest sympathy, is given to those of my brethren who are by birth and education divested of that low scale of thought, and obtuseness of feeling, which distinguish those of the order, who, reared from the lowest origin upon principles the most servilising, are callous to the innumerable humiliations of their dependent state—'

Here an old man mounted on a mule, rode up to the priest, and with tears in his eyes informed him that he was just going to the castle to humbly entreat his Reverence would visit a poor child of his, who had been looked on with '*an evil eye*' a few days back,[2] and who had ever since been pining away.

'It was our misfortune,' said he, 'never to have tied a gospel about her neck, as we did round the other children's, or this heavy sorrow would never have befallen us. But we know if your Reverence would only be pleased to say a prayer over her, all would go well enough!'

The priest gave me a significant look, and shaking me cordially by the hand, and pressing my speedy return to Inismore, rode off with the suppliant.

Thus, in his duty, 'prompt at every call,' after having passed the night in acts of religious benevolence, his humanity willingly obeyed

---

[1] 'Are these men supposed to have no sense of justice, that, in addition to the burthen of supporting their own establishment exclusively, they should be called on to pay ours; that, where they pay sixpence to their own priest, they should pay a pound to our clergyman; that, while they can scarce afford their own horse, they should place ours in his carriage; and that when they cannot build a mass-house to cover their multitudes, they should be forced to contribute to build sumptuous churches for half a dozen Protestants to pray under a shed!'—*Inquiry into the Causes of Popular Discontents, etc. etc.* page 27.

[2] It is supposed among the lower order of Irish, as among the Greeks, that some people are born with *an evil eye*, which injures every object on which it falls, and they will frequently go many miles out of their direct road, rather than pass by the house of one who has *an evil eye*. To frustrate its effects, the priest hangs a consecrated charm around the necks of their children, called *a gospel*; and the fears of the parents are quieted by their faith.

the voice of superstitious prejudice which endowed him with the fancied power of alleviating fancied evils.

As I rode along reflecting on the wondrous influence of superstition, and the nature of its effects, I could not help dwelling on the strong analogy which in so many instances appears between the vulgar errors of this country and that of the ancient as well as modern Greeks.

St Crysostom[1]* relating the bigotry of his own times, particularly mentions the superstitious horror which the Greeks entertained against '*the evil eye*.' And an elegant modern traveller assures us, that even in the present day they 'combine cloves of garlic, talismans, and other charms, which they hang about the neck of their infants, with the same intention of keeping away *the evil eye*.'

Adieu!

H.M.

LETTER XVI

TO J.D. ESQ. M.P.

I wish you were to have seen the look with which the worthy Mr Clendinning met me, as I rode up the avenue to M—— House.

To put an end at once to his impertinent surmises, curiosity, and suspicion, which I evidently saw lurking in his keen eye, I made a display of my fractured arm, which I still wore in a sling; and naturally enough accounted for my absence, by alleging that a fall from my horse, and a fractured limb, had obliged me to accept the humane attentions of a gentleman, near whose house the accident had happened, and whose guest and patient I had since been. Mr Clendinning affected the tone of regret and condolence, with some appropriate suppositions of what his Lord would feel when he learnt the unfortunate circumstance.

'In a word, Mr Clendinning,' said I, 'I do not choose my father's feelings should be called in question on a matter which is now of no ill consequence; and as there is not the least occasion to render him unhappy to no purpose, I must insist that you neither write or mention the circumstance to him on any account.'

---

[1] 'Some write on the hand the names of several rivers; while others make use of ashes, tallow, and salt, for the like purpose—all this being to divert the *evil eye*.'

Mr Clendinning bowed obedience, and I contrived to ratify his promise by certain inuendoes; for as he is well aware many of his villanies have reached my ear, he hates and fears me with all his soul.

My first inquiry was for letters. I found two from my father, and one, only one, from you.

My father writes in his usual style. His first is merely an epistle admonitory; full of prudent axioms, and fatherly solicitudes. The second informs me, that his journey to Ireland is deferred for a month or six weeks, on account of my brother's marriage with the heiress of the richest banker in the city. It is written in his best style, and a brilliant flow of spirit pervades every line. In the plenitude of his joy, all *my* sins are forgiven: he even talks of terminating my exile sooner than I had any reason to expect: and he playfully adds, 'of changing my banishment into slavery'—'knowing, from experience, that provided my shackles are woven by the rosy fingers of beauty, I can wear them patiently and pleasurably enough. In short,' he adds, 'I have a connexion in my eye for you, not less brilliant in point of fortune than that your brother has made; and which will enable you to forswear your Coke, and burn your Blackstone.'

In fact, the spirit of matrimonial establishment seems to have taken such complete possession of my good speculating *dad*, that it would by no means surprise me though he were on the point of sacrificing at the Hymeneal altar* himself. You know he has more than once, in a frolic, passed for my elder brother; and certainly has more sensibility than should belong to *forty-five*. Nor should I at all wonder if some insinuating coquette should one day or other *sentimental-ize* him into a Platonic passion, which would terminate *in the old way*. I have, however, indulged in a little triumph at his expence; and have answered him in a strain of apathetic content—that habit and reason have perfectly reconciled me to my present mode of life, which leaves me without a wish to change it.

Now for your letter. With respect to the advice you demand, I have only to repeat the opinion already advanced, that   *   *   *

*   *   *   *   *   *   *   *   *   *   *

But with respect to that you give me—

> 'Go bid physicians preach our veins to health,
> And with an argument new set a pulse.'

And as for your prediction—of this be certain, that I am too hackneyed in *les affaires du cœur*,* ever to fall in love beyond all redemption with any woman in existence. And even this little Irish girl, with all her witcheries, is to me a subject of philosophical analysis, rather than amatory discussion.

You ask me if I am not disgusted with her brogue? If she had one, I doubt not but I should; but the accent to which we English apply that term, is here generally confined to the lower orders of society; and I certainly believe, that purer and more grammatical English is spoken generally through Ireland, than in any part of England whatever; for here you are never shocked by the barbarous and unintelligible dialect peculiar to each shire in England. As to Glorvina, an aptitude to learn languages is, you know, peculiar to her country; but in her it is a decided and striking talent: even her Italian is, '*la langua Toscana, nel' bocca Romana*;'* and her English, grammatically correct, and elegantly pure, is spoken with an accent that could never denote her country. But it is certain that in *that* accent there is a species of languor very distinct from the brevity of ours. Yet (to me at least) it only renders the lovely speaker more interesting. A simple question from her lip seems rather tenderly to solicit, than abruptly to demand. Her every request is a soft supplication; and when she stoops to entreaty, there is in her voice and manner such an energy of supplication, that while she places *your* power to grant in the most ostensible light to yourself, you are insensibly vanquished by that soft persuasion whose melting meekness bestows your fancied exaltation. Her sweet-toned mellifluous voice, is always sighed forth rather below than above its natural pitch, and her mellowed softened mode of articulation is but imperfectly expressed by the *susaro susingando*, or *coaxy murmurs*, of Italian persuasion.

To Father John, who is the first and most general linguist I ever met, she stands highly indebted; but to Nature, and her own ambition to excell, still more.

I am now but six hours in this solitary and deserted mansion, where I feel as though I reigned the very king of desolation. Let me hear from you by return.

Adieu!

H.M.

LETTER XVII

TO J.D. ESQ. M.P.

I forgot to mention to you in my last, that to my utter joy and surprise, our *premier* here has been recalled. On the day of my return, he received a letter from his Lord, desiring his immediate attendance in London, with all the rents he could collect; for I suppose the necessary expenditures requisite for my brother's matrimonial establishment, will draw pretty largely on our family treasury.

This change of things in our domestic politics has changed all my plans of operation. This arch spy being removed, obviates the necessity of my retreat to the Lodge. My establishment here consists only of two females, who scarcely speak a word of English; an old gardener, who possesses not one *entire sense*; and a groom, who, having nothing to do, I shall discharge: so that if I should find it my pleasure to return, and remain any time at the castle of Inismore, I shall have no one here to watch my actions, or report them to my father.

There is something Bœotian* in this air. I can neither read, write, or think. Does not Locke assert, that the soul sometimes dozes? I frequently think I have been bit by a torpedo,* or that I partake in some degree of the nature of the seven sleepers, and suffer a transient suspension of existence. What if this Glorvina has an *evil eye*, and has overlooked me? The witch haunts me, not only in my dreams, but when *I fancy myself*, at least, awake. A thousand times I think I hear the tones of her voice and harp. Does she feel my absence at the accustomed hour of tuition, the fire-side circle in the *Vengolf*, the twilight conversation, the noon-tide ramble?—Has my presence become a want to her? Am I missed, and missed with regret? It is scarcely vanity to say, *I am—I must be*. In a life of so much sameness, the most trivial incident, the most inconsequent character, obtains an interest in a certain degree.

One day I caught her weeping over a pet robin, which died on her bosom. She smiled, and endeavoured to hide her tears. 'This is very silly, I know,' said she, 'but one must feel even the loss of *a bird*, that has been the *companion of one's solitude*!'

To day I flung by my book, in down-right deficiency of comprehension to understand a word in it, though it was a simple case in the Reports of —— ——; and so in the most *nonchalante* mood possible, I mounted my *rosinante*, and throwing the bridle over her neck, said 'please thyself;' and it was her pious pleasure to tread on consecrated ground: in short, after a ride of half an hour, I found myself within a few paces of the parish mass-house, and recollected that it was the Sabbath day; so that you see my mare reproved me, though in an oblique manner, with little less gravity than the ass of Balaam* did his obstinate rider.

The mass-house was of the same order of architecture as the generality of Irish cabins; with no other visible mark to ascertain its sacred designation than a stone cross, roughly hewn, over its entrance. I will not say that it was merely a sentiment of piety which induced me to enter it; but it certainly required, at first, an effort of energy to obtain admittance, as for several yards round this simple tabernacle, a crowd of *devotees* were prostrated on the earth, praying over their beads with as much fervour as though they were offering up their orisons in the golden-roofed temple of Solyman.*

When I had fastened my horse's bridle to a branch of an hawthorn, I endeavoured to make my way through the pious crowd, who all arose the moment I appeared—for the *last mass*, I learnt, was over; and those who had prayed *par hazard*,* without hearing a word the priest said within, departed. While I pressed my way into the body of the chapel, it was so crowded that with great difficulty I found means to fix myself by a large triangular stone vessel filled with holy water, where I fortunately remained (during the sermon) unnoticed.

This sermon was delivered by a little old mendicant, in the Irish language. Beside him stood the parish priest in pontificalibus, and with as much self-invested dignity as the *dalai lama* of Little Thibet could assume before his votarists. When the shrivelled little mendicant had harangued them some time on the subject of Christian charity, for so his countenance and action indicated, a general *secula seculorum* concluded his discourse; and while he meekly retreated a few paces, the priest mounted the steps of the little altar, and after preparing his lungs, he delivered an oration, to which it would be impossible to do any justice. It was partly in Irish, partly in English; and intended to inculcate the necessity of contributing to the relief of the mendicant preacher, if they hoped to have the benefit of his prayers; addressing each of his flock by their name and profession, and exposing their faults and extolling their virtues, according to the nature of their contributions. While the friar, who stood with his face to the wall, was with all human diligence piously turning his beads to two accounts—with one half he was making intercession for the souls of his good subscribers, and with the other diligently keeping count of the sum total of their benefactions. As soon as I had sent in mind, almost stifled with heat, I effected my escape.

In contrasting this parish priest with the chaplain of Inismore, I could not help exclaiming with Epaminondas*—'It is the *man* who must give dignity to the situation—not the situation to the man.'

Adieu!

M.H.

LETTER XVIII

TO J.D. ESQ. M.P.

'La solitude est certainement une belle chose, mais il-y-a plaisir d'avoir quelqu'une qui en sache repondre, a qui on puis dire, la solitude est une belle chose.'*

So says Monsieur de Balsac,* and so repeats my heart a thousand times a day. In short, I am devoured by *ennui*, by apathy, by discontent! What should I do here? Nothing. I have spent but four days here, and all the symptoms of my old disease begin to re-appear; in short, like other impatient invalids, I believed my cure was effected when my disease was only on the decline. I must again fly to sip from the fountain of intellectual health at Inismore, and receive the vivifying drops from the hand of the presiding priestess, or stay here, and fall into an incurable atrophy of the heart and mind!

Having packed up a part of my wardrobe, and a few books, I sent them by a young rustic to the little *Villa di Marino*, and in about an hour after I followed myself. The old fisherman and his dame seemed absolutely rejoiced to see me, and having my valise laid in their cabin, and dismissed my attendant, I requested they would permit their son to carry my luggage as far as the next *cabaret*,* where I expected a man and horse to meet me. They cheerfully complied, and I proceeded with my *compagnon de voyage* to a hut which lies half way between the fisherman's and the castle. This hut they call a *Sheebeen House*, and is something inferior to a certain description of a Spanish inn. Although a little board informs the weary traveller he is only to expect 'good dry lodgings,' yet the landlord contrives to let you know in an *entre nous** manner, that he keeps some real *Inishone* (or spirits, smuggled from a tract of country so called) for his particular friends. So having dismissed my second courier, and paid for the whiskey I did not taste, and the potatoes I did not eat, I sent my host forward, mounted on a sorry mule, with my travelling equipage, to the cabin at the foot of the draw-bridge; and by these precautions obviated all possibility of discovery.

As I now proceeded on my route, every progressive step awakened some new emotion; while my heart was agitated by those unspeakable little flutterings which are alternately excited and governed by the ardour of hope, or the timidity of fear. 'And shall I, or shall I not be welcome?' was the problem which engaged my thoughts during the rest of my little journey.

As I descended the mountain at whose base the peninsula of Inismore reposes, I perceived a form at some distance, whose drapery ('*nebulam lineam*') seemed light as the breeze on which it floated. It is impossible to mistake the figure of Glorvina, when its graces are called forth by motion. I instantly alighted, and flew to meet her. She too sprang eagerly forward. We were almost within a few paces of each other, when she suddenly turned back, and flew down the hill with the bounding step of a fawn. This would have mortified another—I was charmed. And the bashful consciousness which repelled her advances, was almost as grateful to my heart as the warm impulse which had nearly hurried her into my arms. How freshly does she still wear the first gloss of nature!

In a few minutes, however, I perceived her return, leaning on the arm of the Father Director. You cannot conceive what a festival of the feelings my few days absence had purchased for me. Oh! he knows nothing of the doctrine of enjoyment, who does not purchase his pleasures at the expence of temporary restraint. The good priest, who still retains something of the etiquette of his foreign education, embraced me *à la Française*.* Glorvina, however, who *malhereuse-*

ment,* was not reared in France, only offered me her *hand*, which I had not the courage to raise to my unworthy lip, although the cordial *cead mille a falta** of her country revelled in her shining eyes, and her effulgent countenance was lit up with an unusual blaze of animation.

When we reached the castle the Prince sent for me to his room, and told me, as he pressed my hand, that 'his heart warmed at my sight.' In short, my return seems to have produced a carnival in the whole family.

You who know, that notwithstanding my late vitiated life, the simple pleasures of the heart were always dead to mine, may guess how highly gratifying to my feelings is this interest which, independent of all adventitious circumstances of rank and fortune, I have awakened in the bosoms of these cordial, ingenuous beings.

The late insufferable reserve of Glorvina has given way to the most bewitching (I had almost said *tender*) softness of manner.

As I descended from paying my visit to the Prince, I found her and the priest in the hall.

'We are waiting for you,' said she—'there is no resisting the fineness of this evening.'

And as we left the door, she pointed towards the west, and added—

'See—

> 'The weary sun hath made a golden set,
> And by yon ruddy brightness of the clouds,
> Gives tokens of a goodly day to-morrow.'

'O! *a-propos*, Mr Mortimer, you are returned in most excellent time—for to-morrow is the *first of May*.'

'And is the arrival of a guest,' said I, 'on the *eve* of that day, a favourable omen?'

'The arrival of such a guest,' said she, 'must be at least ominous of happiness. But the first of May is our great national festival; and you who love to trace modern customs to ancient origins, will perhaps feel some curiosity and interest to behold some of the rites of our heathen superstitions still lingering among our present ceremonies.'

'What then,' said I, 'have you, like the Greeks, the festivals of the spring among you?'

'It is certain,' said the priest, 'that the ancient Irish sacrificed on the *first of May* to *Beal*, or the *Sun*; and that day, even at this period, is called *Beal*.'

'By this idolatry to the God of Light and Song,' said I, 'one would almost suppose that Apollo was the tutelar deity of your Island.'

'Why,' returned he, 'Hecatæus tells us that the Hyperborean Island* was dedicated to Apollo, and that most of its inhabitants were either priests or bards, and I suppose you are not ignorant that we claim the honour of being those happy Hyperboreans, which were believed by many to be a fabulous nation.

'And if the peculiar favour of the God of Poetry and Song may be esteemed a sufficient proof, it is certain that our claims are not weak. For surely no nation under Heaven was ever more enthusiastically attached to poetry and music than the Irish. Formerly every family had its poet or bard, called Filea and Crotarie; and indeed the very language itself seems most felicitously adapted to be the vehicle of poetic images; for its energy, strength, expression, and luxuriancy, never leave the bard at a loss for apposite terms to realize "the thick coming fancies" of his genius.'[1]

'But,' said Glorvina, 'the first of May was not the only festival held sacred by the Irish to their tutelar deity: on the 24th of June they sacrificed to the Sun, to propitiate his influence in bringing the fruit to perfection; and to this day those lingering remains of heathen rites are performed with something of their ancient forms. "*Midsummer's Night*," as it is called, is with us a night of universal lumination—the whole country blazes: from the summit of every mountain, every hill, ascends the flame of the bonfire, while the unconscious perpetuators of the heathen ceremony dance round the fire in circles, or, holding torches to it made of straw, run with the burning brands wildly through the country with all the gay frenzy of so many Bacchantes.* But though I adore our inspiring *Beal* with all my soul, I worship our popular deity *Samhuin* with all my heart—he is the god of the heart's close-knitting socialities, for the domesticating month of November is sacred to him.'

'And on its eve,' said the priest, 'the great fire of *Samhuin* was illuminated, all the culinary fires in the kingdom being first extin-

[1] Mr O'Halloran informs us, that in a work entitled '*Uiraceacht na Neaigios*,' or Poetic Tales, above an hundred different species of Irish verse is exhibited. O'Molloy, in his Irish and Latin Grammar, has also given rules and specimens of our modes of versification, which may be seen in Dr Lhuid's *Achaeologia*.

guished, as it was deemed sacrilege to awaken the winter's social flame, except by a spark snatched from this sacred fire,[1] and so deep rooted are the customs of our forefathers among us, that the present Irish have no other name for the month of November than *Samhuin*.

'Over our mythological accounts of this *winter* god, an almost impenetrable obscurity seems to hover; but if *Samhuin* is derived from *Samh-fhuin*, as it is generally supposed, the term literally means the gathering or closing of summer; and in fact, on the eve of the first of November we make our offerings round the domestic altar (the fireside), of such fruits as the lingering seasons afford, besides playing a number of curious gambols, and performing many superstitious ceremonies, in which our young folk find great pleasure, and put great faith.'

'For my part,' said Glorvina, 'I love all those old ceremonies which force us to be periodically happy, and look forward with no little impatience to the gay-hearted pleasures which to-morrow will bring in its train.'

The little post-boy has this moment tapped at my door for my letter, for he tells me he sets off before dawn, that he may be back in time for the sport. It is now past eleven o'clock, but I could not resist giving you this little scrap of Irish mythology, before I wished you good night.

H.M.

LETTER XIX

TO J.D. ESQ. M.P.

All the life-giving spirit of spring, mellowed by the genial glow of summer, shed its choicest treasures on the smiling hours which yesterday ushered in the most delightful of all the seasons.

I arose earlier than usual; the elixity of my mind would not suffer me to rest, and the scented air, as it breathed its odours through my open casement, seduced me abroad. I walked as though I scarcely touched the earth, and my spirit seemed to ascend like the lark which soared over my head to hail the splendour of the dewy dawn.

---

[1] To this day, the inferior Irish look upon bonfires as sacred; they say their prayers walking round them; the young dream upon their ashes, and the old steal away the fire, to light up their domestic hearths with it.

There is a fairy vale in the little territories of Inismore, which is almost a miniature *Tempé*,* and which is indeed the only spot on the peninsula where the luxuriant charms of the most bounteous nature are evidently improved by taste and cultivation. In a word, it is a spot sacred to the wanderings of Glorvina. It was there our theological discourse was held on the evening of my return, and thither my steps were now with an irresistible impulse directed.

I had scarcely entered this Eden, when the form of the Eve to whose picturesque fancy it owes so many charms, presented itself. She was standing at a little distance *en profile*—with one hand she supported a part of her drapery filled with wild flowers gathered ere the sun had kissed off the tears which night had shed upon their bosoms: with the other she seemed carefully to remove some branches that entwined themselves through the sprays of a little hawthorn hedge richly embossed with the first-born blossoms of May.

As I stole towards her, I exclaimed, as Adam did when he first saw Eve—

> '—Beheld her,
> Such as I saw her in my dream adorned,
> With all that earth or heaven could bestow.'*

She started and turned round, and in her surprise let fall her flowers, yet she smiled, and seemed confused—but pleasure, pure animated life-breathing pleasure, was the predominant expression of her countenance. The Deity of Health was never personified in more glowing colours—her eye's rich blue, her cheek's crimson blush, her lip's dewy freshness, the wanton wildness of her golden tresses, the delicious languor that mellowed the fire of her beamy glance—I gazed, and worshiped! but neither apologized for my intrusion, nor had the politeness to collect her scattered flowers.

'If Nature,' said I, 'had always such a priestess to preside at her altar, who would worship at the shrine of Art?'

'I am her votarist* only,' she replied, smiling, and, pointing to a wild rose which had just begun to unfold its blushing breast amidst the snowy blossoms of the hedge—added, 'see how beautiful! how orient its hue appears through the pure crystal of the morning dew-drop! It is nearly three weeks since I discovered it in the germ, since when I have screened it from the noon-day ardors, and the evening's frost, and now it is just bursting into perfection to reward my cares.'

At these words, she plucked it from the stem. Its crimson head drooped with the weight of the gems that spangled it. Glorvina did not shake them off, but imbibed the liquid fragrance with her lip; then held the flower to me!

'Am I to pledge you?' said I.

She smiled, and I quaffed off the fairy nectar, which still trembled on the leaves her lip had consecrated.

'We have now,' said I, '*both* drank from the same cup; and if the delicious draught which Nature has prepared for us, circulates with mutual effect through our veins—If'—I paused, and cast down my eyes. The hand which still sustained the rose, and was still clasped in mine, seemed to tremble with an emotion scarcely inferior to that which thrilled through my whole frame.

After a minute's pause—'Take the rose,' said Glorvina, endeavouring to extricate the precious hand which presented it—'Take it; it is the first of the season! My father has had his snow-drop—the confessor his violet—and it is but just you should have your *rose*.'

At that moment the classical remark of the priest rushed, I believe, with mutual influence, to both our hearts. I, at least, was borne away by the rapturous feelings of the moment, and knelt to receive the offering of my lovely votarist.

I kissed the sweet and simple tribute with pious ardor; but with a devotion more fervid, kissed the hand that presented it. I would not have exchanged that moment for the most pleasurable hours of the most pleasurable era of my existence. The blushing radiance that glowed on the cheek, sent its warm suffusion even to the hand I had violated with my unhallowed lip; while the sparkling fluid of her eyes, turned on mine in almost dying softness, beamed on the latent powers of my once-chilled heart, and awakened there a thousand delicious transports, a thousand infant wishes and chaste desires, of which I lately thought its worn-out feelings were no longer susceptible.

As I arose, I plucked off a small branch of that myrtle which here grows wild, and which, like my rose, was dripping in dew, and putting it into the hand I still held, said,

'This offering is indeed less beautiful, less fragrant, than that which you have made; but remember, it is also less *fragile*—for the sentiment of which it is an emblem, carries with it an eternity of duration.'

Glorvina took it in silence, and placed it in her bosom; and in silence we walked together towards the castle; while our eyes, now timidly turned on each other, now suddenly averted (Oh, the insidious danger of the abruptly downcast eye!), met no object but what breathed of love, whose soul seemed

> '—Sent abroad,
> Warm thro' the vital air, and on the heart
> Harmonious seiz'd.'

The morning breeze flushed with ethereal fervour; the luxury of landscape through which we wandered, the sublimity of those stupendous cliffs which seemed to shelter two hearts from the world, to which their profound feelings were unknown, while

> '—Every copse
> Deep tangled, but irregular, and bush,
> Bending with dewy moisture o'er the heads
> Of the coy quiresters that lodg'd within,
> Were prodigal of harmony;'

and crowned imagination's wildest wish, and realized the fancy's warmest vision.

'Oh! my sweet friend!' I exclaimed, 'since now I feel myself entitled thus to call you—well indeed might your nation have held this day sacred; and while the heart which now throbs with an emotion to which it has hitherto been a stranger, beats with the pulse of life, on the return of this day will it make its offering to that glorious orb, to whose genial nutritive beams this precious rose owes its existence.'

As I spoke, Father John suddenly appeared. Vexed as I was at his unseasonable intrusion, yet in such perfect harmony was my spirit with the whole creation, that in the true hyperbola of Irish cordiality, I wished him a thousand happy returns of this season!

'Spoken like a true-born Irishman!' said the priest, laughing, and shaking me heartily by the hand—'While with something of the phlegm of an Englishman, I wish you only as many returns of it as shall bring health and felicity in their train.'

Then looking at the myrtle which reposed on the bosom of

Glorvina, and the rose which I so proudly wore, he added—'So, I perceive you have both been sacrificing to *Beal*; and, like the priests and priestesses of this country in former times, are adorned with the flowers of the season. For you must know, Mr Mortimer, *we* had our Druidesses as well as our Druids; and both, like the ministers of Grecian mythology, were crowned with flowers at the time of sacrifice.'

At this apposite remark of the good priest's, I stole a glance at *my* lovely priestess. Hero, at the altar of the deity she rivalled, never looked more attractive in the eyes of the enamoured Leander.*

We had now come within a few steps of the portals of the castle, and I observed that since I had passed that way, the path and entrance were strewed with green flags, rushes, and wild crocusses;[1] while the heavy framework of the door was hung with garlands, and bunches of flowers tastefully displayed.

'This, Madam,' said I to Glorvina, 'is doubtless the result of your happy taste.'

'By no means,' she replied—'this is a custom prevalent among the peasantry time immemorial.'

'And most probably was brought hither,' said the priest, 'from Greece by our Phœnician progenitors; for we learn from Athenæus, that the young Greeks hung garlands on the doors of their favourite mistresses on the first of May. Nor indeed does the Roman *floralia* differ in any respect from ours.'

'Those, however, which you now admire,' said Glorvina, smiling, 'are no offerings of rustic gallantry; for every hut in the country, on this morning, will bear the same fanciful decorations. The wild crocus, and indeed every flower of that rich tint, is peculiarly sacred to this day.'

And, in fact, when, in the course of the day, I rambled out alone, and looked into the several cabins, I perceived not only their floors covered with flags and rushes, but a 'May-bush,' as they call it, or small tree, planted before all the doors, covered with every flower the season affords.

I saw nothing of Glorvina until evening, except for a moment,

[1] 'Seeing the doors of the Greeks on the first of May, profusely ornamented with flowers, would certainly recall to your mind the many descriptions of that custom which you have met with in the Greek and Latin poets.'—*Letters on Greece, by Monsieur De Guys*, vol. i. p. 153.

when I perceived her lost over a book (as I passed her closet window), which, by the Morocco binding, I knew to be the Letters of the impassioned Heloise. Since her society was denied me, I was best satisfied to resign her to Rousseau. *A-propos!* it was among the books I brought hither; and they were all precisely such books as Glorvina had *not*, yet *should* read, that she may know herself, and the latent sensibility of her soul. They have, of course, all been presented to her, and consist of '*La Nouvelle Heloise*,' de Rousseau—the unrivalled '*Lettres sur la Mythologie*,' de Moustier—the '*Paul et Virginie*' of St Pierre—the *Werter* of Göethe—the *Dolbreuse* of Lousel, and the *Attila* of Chateaubriand.* Let our English novels carry away the prize of morality from the romantic fictions of every other country; but will you find they rarely seize on the imagination through the medium of the heart; and as for their heroines, I confess that though they are the most perfect of beings, they are also the most stupid. Surely virtue would not be the less attractive for being united to genius and the graces.

But to return to the never-to-be-forgotten *first of May*! Early in the evening the Prince, his daughter, the priest, the bard, the old nurse, and indeed all the household of Inismore, adjourned to the vale, which being the only level ground on the peninsula, is always appropriated to the sports of the rustic neighbours. It was impossible I should enter this vale without emotion; and when I beheld it crowded with the vulgar throng, I felt as it were profanation for the

'Sole of unblest feet!'

to tread that ground sacred to the most refined emotions of the heart.

Glorvina, who walked on before the priest and me, supporting her father, as we entered the vale stole a glance at me; and a moment after, as I opened the little wicker through which we passed, I murmured in her ear—*La val di Rosa!*

We found this charming spot crowded with peasantry of both sexes, and all ages.[1] Since morning they had planted a May-bush in the centre, which was hung with flowers, and round the seats appropriated to the Prince and his family, the flag, crocus, and prim-

---

[1] In the summer of 1802 the Author was present at a rural festival at the seat of an highly respected friend in Tipperary, from which this scene is partly copied.

rose, were profusely scattered. Two blind fiddlers, and an excellent piper,[1] were seated under the shelter of the very hedge which had been the nursery of my precious rose; while the old bard, with true druidical dignity, sat under the shade of a venerable oak, near his master.

The sports began with a wrestling-match;[2] and in the gymnastic exertions of the youthful combatants there was something, I thought, of Spartan energy and hardihood.

But, as 'breaking of ribs is no sport for ladies,' Glorvina turned from the spectacle in disgust; which I wished might have been prolonged, as it procured me (who leaned over her seat) her undivided attention; but it was too soon concluded, though without any disagreeable consequences, for neither of the combatants were hurt, though one was laid prostrate. The victorious wrestler was elected King of the May; and, with 'all his blushing honours thick about him,' came timidly forward, and laid his rural crown at the feet of Glorvina. Yet he evidently seemed intoxicated with his happiness, and though he scarcely touched the hand of his blushing charming queen, yet I perceived a thousand saucy triumphs basking in his fine black eyes, as he led her out to dance. The fellow was handsome too. I know not why, but I could have knocked him down with all my heart.

'Every village has its Cæsar,' said the priest, 'and this is ours. He

---

[1] Although the bagpipe is not an instrument indigenous to Ireland, it holds an high antiquity in the country. It was the music of the Kearns, in the reign of Edward the Third[†]. It is still the favourite accompaniment of those mirthful exertions with which laborious poverty crowns the temporary cessation of its weekly toil, and the cares and solicitudes of the Irish peasant ever dissipate to the spell which breathes in the humorous drones of the Irish pipes. To Scotland we are indebted for this ancient instrument, who received it from the Romans; but to the native musical genius of Ireland are we indebted for its present form and improved state. 'That at present in use in Ireland,' says Dr Burney,[*] in a letter to J. C. Walker, Esq. 'is an improved bagpipe, on which I have heard some of the natives play very well in two parts, without the drone, which, I believe, is never attempted in Scotland. The tone of the lower notes resembles that of an hautboy and clarinet, and the high notes, that of a German flute; and the whole scale of one I heard lately was very well in tune, which has never been the case of any Scottish bagpipe that I have yet heard.'

[†] (See Smith's Hist. of Cork, p. 43.)

[2] The young Irish peasantry particularly prize themselves on this species of exertion: they have almost reduced it to a science, by dividing it into two distinct species—the one, called *sparniaght*, engages the arms only; the other, *carriaght*, engages the whole body.

has been elected King of the May for these five years successively. He is second son to our old steward, and a very worthy, as well as very fine young fellow.'

'I do not doubt his worth,' returned I peevishly, 'but it certainly cannot exceed the condescension of his young mistress.'

'There is nothing singular in it, however,' said the priest. 'Among us, over such meetings as these, inequality of rank holds no *obvious* jurisdiction, though in fact it is not the less regarded, and the condescension of the master or mistress on these occasions, lessens nothing of the respect of the servant upon every other; but rather secures it, through the medium of gratitude and affection.'

The piper had now struck up one of those lilts, whose mirth-inspiring influence it is almost impossible to resist.[1] The Irish jig, above every other dance, leaves most to the genius of the dancer; and Glorvina, above all the women I have ever seen, seems most formed by Nature to excell in the art. Her little form, pliant as that of an Egyptian *alma*,* floats before the eye in all the swimming languor of the most graceful motion, or all the gay exility of soul-inspired animation. She even displays an exquisite degree of comic humour in some of the movements of her national dance; and her eyes, countenance, and air, express the wildest exhilaration of pleasure, and glow with all the spirit of health, mirth, and exercise.

I was so struck with the grace and elegance of her movements, the delicacy of her form, and the play of her drapery gently agitated by the air, that I involuntarily gave to my admiration an audible existence.

'Yes,' said the priest, who overheard me, 'she performs her national dance with great grace and spirit. But the Irish are all dancers; and, like the Greeks, we have no idea of any festival here which

---

[1] Besides the Irish jig, tradition has rescued from that oblivion which time has hung over the ancient Irish dance, the *rinceadh-fada*, which answers to the festal dance of the Greeks; and the *rinceadh*, or war dance, 'which seems,' says Mr Walker, 'to have been of the nature of the armed dance, which is so ancient, and with which the Grecian youth amused themselves during the siege of Troy.'

Previous to the adoption of the French style in dancing, Mr O'Halloran asserts, that both our private and public balls always concluded with the *rinceadh-fada*. On the arrival of James the Second at Kinsale, his adherents received the unfortunate Prince on the shore with this dance, with whose taste and execution he was infinitely delighted; and even still, in the county of Limerick, and many other parts of Ireland, the *rinceadh-fada* is danced on the eve of May.

does not conclude with a dance;[1] old and young, rich and poor, all join here in the sprightly dance.'

Glorvina, unwearied, still continued to dance with unabated spirit, and even seemed governed by the general principle which actuates all the Irish dancers—of not giving way to any competitor in the exertion; for she actually outdanced her partner, who had been jigging with all his *strength*, while she had only been dancing with all her *soul*; and when he retreated, she dropped a simple curtsey (according to the laws of jig-dancing here) to another young rustic, whose seven-leagued brogues finally prevailed, and Glorvina at last gave way, while he made a scrape to a rosy-cheeked, bare-footed damsel, who out-jigg'd him and his two successors; and thus the chain went on.

Glorvina, as she came panting and glowing towards me, exclaimed, 'I have done my duty for the evening,' and threw herself on a seat, breathless and smiling.

'Nay,' said I, 'more than your duty; for you even performed a work of supererogation.'* And I cast a pointed look at the young rustic who had been the object of her election.

'O!' she replied eagerly—'it is the custom here, and I should be sorry, for the indulgence of an overstrained delicacy, to violate any of those established rules to which, however trifling, they are devotedly attached. Besides, you perceive,' she added, smiling, 'this condescension on the part of the females who are thus "won unsought," does not render the men more presumptuous. You see what a distance the youth of both sexes preserve—a distance which always exists in these kind of public meetings.'

And in fact, the lads and lasses were ranged opposite to each other, with no other intercourse than what the communion of the eyes afforded, or the transient intimacy of the jig bestowed.[2]

'And will not you dance a jig?' asked Glorvina.

'I seldom dance,' said I—'Ill health has for some time back coincided with my inclination, which seldom led me to try my skill at the *Poetry of Motion*.'

---

[1] 'The passion of the Greeks for dancing is common to both sexes, who neglect every other consideration, when they have an opportunity of indulging that passion.'

[2] This custom, so prevalent in some parts of Ireland, is of a very ancient origin. We read in Keating's History of Ireland, that in the remotest periods, when the Irish brought their children to the fair of Tailtean, in order to dispose of them in marriage, the strictest order was observed: the men and women having distinct places assigned them, at a certain distance from each other.—See *Keating*, page 216.

'*Poetry of Motion!*' repeated Glorvina—'What a beautiful idea!'

'It is so,' said I, 'and if it had been my own, it must have owed its existence to you; for your dancing is certainly the true poetry of motion, and *Epic* poetry too.'

'I love dancing with all my heart,' she replied: 'when I dance I have not a care on earth—every thing swims gayly before me; and I feel as if swiftly borne away in a vortex of pleasurable sensation.'

'Dancing,' said I, 'is the talent of your sex—that pure grace which must result from a symmetrical form, and that elixity of temperament which is the effect of woman's delicate organization, creates you dancers. And while I beheld your performance this evening, I no longer wondered that the gravity of Socrates could not resist the spell which lurked in the graceful motions of Aspasia, but followed her in the mazes of the dance.'

She bowed, and said, 'I flattered too agreeably, not to be listened to with *pleasure*, if not with *faith*.'

In short, I have had a thousand occasions to observe, that while she receives a decided compliment with the ease of almost *bon ton nonchalance*,* a look, a broken sentence, a word, has the power of overwhelming her with confusion, or awakening all the soul of emotion in her bosom. All this I can understand.

As the dew of the evening now began to fall, the invalid Prince and his lovely daughter arose to retire. And those who had been rendered so happy by their condescension, beheld their retreat with regret, and followed them with blessings. Whiskey, milk, and oaten bread, were now distributed in abundance by the old nurse and the steward; and the dancing was recommenced with new ardor.

The priest and I remained behind, conversing with the old and jesting with the young—he in Irish, and I in English, with such as understood it. The girls received my little gallantries with considerable archness, and even with some point of repartee; while the priest rallied them in their own way, for he seems as playful as a child among them, though evidently worshipped as a saint. And the moon rose resplendently over the vale, before it was restored to its wonted solitary silence.

Glorvina has made the plea of a head-ach these two mornings back, for playing the truant at her drawing-desk; but the fact is, her days and nights are devoted to the sentimental sorcery of Rousseau; and the effects of her studies are visible in her eyes. When we meet, their glance sinks beneath the ardor of mine, in soft confusion: her manner is no longer childishly playful, or carelessly indifferent, and sometimes a sigh, scarce breathed, is discovered by the blush which glows on her cheek for the inadvertency of her lip. Does she then begin to feel she has an heart? Does *'Le besoin de l'ame tendre,'** already throb with vague emotion in her bosom? Her abstracted air, her delicious melancholy, her unusual softness, betray the nature of the feelings by which she is overwhelmed—they are new to herself; and sometimes I fancy, when she turns her melting eyes on me, it is to solicit their meaning. O! if I dared become the interpreter between her and her heart—if I dared indulge myself in the hope, the belief that—And what then? 'Tis all folly, 'tis madness, 'tis worse! But who ever yet rejected the blessing for which his soul thirsted?—And in the scale of human felicities, if there is one in which all others are summed up—above all others supremely elevated—It is the consciousness of having awakened the first sentiment of the sweetest, the sublimest of all human passions, in the bosom of youth, genius, and sensibility.

Adieu!

H.M.

LETTER XX

TO J.D. ESQ. M.P.

I had just finished my last by the beams of a gloriously setting sun, when I was startled by a pebble being thrown in at my window. I looked out, and perceived Father John in the act of flinging up another, which the hand of Glorvina (who was leaning on his arm) presented.

'If you are not engaged in writing to your mistress,' said he, 'come down and join us in a ramble.'

'And though I were,' I replied, 'I could not resist your challenge.' And down I flew—Glorvina laughing, sent me back for my hat, and we proceeded on our walk.

'This is an evening,' said I, looking at Glorvina, 'worthy of the

morning of the first of May, and we have seized it in that happy
moment so exquisitely described by Collins:*

> —'While now the bright hair'd sun
> Sits in yon western tent, whose cloudy skirts,
> With brede ethereal wove,
> O'erhang his wavy bed.'

'O! that beautiful Ode!' exclaimed Glorvina, with all her wildest
enthusiasm—'never can I read—never hear it repeated, but with
emotion. The perusal of Ossian's "Song of other Times," the breezy
respiration of my harp at twilight, the last pale rose that outlives its
season, and bears on its faded breast the frozen tears of the wintry
dawn, and Collins's Ode to Evening, awaken in my heart and fancy
the same train of indescribable feeling, of exquisite yet unspeakable
sensation. Alas! the solitary pleasure of feeling thus alone the utter
impossibility of conveying to the bosom of another those ecstatic
emotions by which our own is sublimed.'

While my very soul followed this brilliant comet to her perihelium
of sentiment and imagination, I fixed my eyes on her 'mind-
illumin'd face,' and said,

'And is expression then necessary for the conveyance of such
profound, such exquisite feeling? May not a similarity of refined
organization exist between souls, and produce that mutual intelligence which sets the necessity of cold verbal expression at defiance?
May not the sympathy of a kindred sensibility in the bosom of
another, meet and enjoy those delicious feelings by which yours is
warmed, and, sinking beneath the inadequacy of language to give
them birth, feel like you in silent and sacred emotion?'

'Perhaps,' said the priest, with his usual simplicity, 'this sacred
sympathy between two refined, elevated, and sensible souls, in the
sublime and beautiful of the moral and natural world, approaches
nearest to the rapturous and pure emotions which uncreated spirits
may be supposed to feel in their heavenly communion, than any
other human sentiment with which we are acquainted.'

For all the looks of blandishment which ever flung their spell from
beauty's eye, I would not have exchanged the glance which Glorvina
at that moment cast on me. While the priest, who seemed to have
been following up the train of thought awakened by our preceding
observations, abruptly added, after a silence of some minutes—

'There is a species of metaphorical taste, if I may be allowed the expression, whose admiration for certain objects is not deducible from the established rules of beauty, order, or even truth; which *should* be the basis of our approbation; yet which ever brings with it a sensation of more lively pleasure; as for instance, a chromatic passion in music, will awaken a thrill of delight which a simple chord could never effect.'

'Nor would the most self-evident truth,' said I, 'awaken so vivid a sensation, as when we find some sentiment of the soul illustrated by some law or principle in science. To an axiom we grant our assent, but we lavish our most enthusiastic approbation when Rousseau tells us that, "Les ames humaines veulent être accomplies pour valoir toute leurs prix, et la force unie des ames *comme celles des larmes d'un aimant artificiel*, est incomparablement plus grands que la somme de leurs force particulier."'*

As this quotation was meant *all* for Glorvina, I looked earnestly at her as I repeated it. A crimson torrent rushed to her cheek, and convinced me that she felt the full force of a sentiment so applicable to us both.

'And why,' said I, addressing her in a low voice, 'was Rousseau excluded from the sacred coalition with Ossian, Collins, your twilight harp, and winter rose?'

Glorvina made no reply; but turned full on me her 'eyes of dewy light.' Mine almost sunk beneath the melting ardor of their soul-beaming glance.

Oh! child of Nature! child of genius and of passion! why was I withheld from throwing myself at thy feet; from offering thee the homage of that soul thou hast awakened; from covering thy hands with my kisses, and bathing them with tears of such delicious emotion, as thou only hast power to inspire?

While we thus '*buvames à longs traits le philtre de l'amour*,'* Father John gradually restored us to common-place existence, by a common-place conversation on the fineness of the weather, promising aspect of the season, etc. until the moon, as it rose sublimely above the summit of the mountain, called forth the melting tones of my Glorvina's syren voice.

Casting up her eyes to that Heaven whence they seem to have caught their emanation, she said, 'I do not wonder that unenlightened nations should worship the moon. Our ideas are so intimately connected with our senses, so ductilely transferrable from cause to effect, that the abstract thought may readily subside in the sensible image which awakens it. When, in the awful stillness of a calm night, I fix my eyes on that mild and beautiful orb, the *created* has become the awakening medium of that adoration I offered to the *Creator*.'

'Yes,' said the priest, 'I remember, that even in your childhood, you used to fix your eyes on the moon, and gaze and wonder. I believe it would have been no difficult matter to have plunged you back in the heathenism of your ancestors, and to have made it one of the gods of your idolatry.'

'And was the chaste Luna in the *album sanctorum* of your Druidical mythology?' said I.

'Undoubtedly,' said the priest, 'we read in the life of our celebrated saint, St Columba,* that on the altar-piece of a Druidical temple, the sun, moon, and stars, were curiously depicted; and the form of the ancient Irish oath of allegiance, was to swear by the sun, moon, and stars, and other deities, celestial as well as terrestrial.'

'How,' said I, 'did your mythology touch so closely on that of the Greeks? had you also your Pans and your Daphnes, as well as your Dians and Apollos?'

'Here is a curious anecdote that evinces it,' returned the priest— 'It is many years since I read it in a black-letter memoir of St Patrick. The Saint, says the biographer, attended by three bishops, and some less dignified of his brethren, being in this very province, arose early one morning, and with his pious associates placed himself near a fountain or well, and began to chaunt a hymn. In the neighbourhood of this honoured fountain, stood the palace of *Cruachan*, where the two daughters of the Emperor Laogaire were educating in retirement; and as the saints sung by no means *sotto voce*,[1]* their pious strains caught the attention of the royal fair ones, who were enjoying an early ramble, and who immediately sought the sanctified choristers. Full of that curiosity so natural to the youthful recluses, they were by no means sparing of interrogations to the Saint, and among other questions, demanded "and who is your God? where dwells he,

---

[1] A musical voice was an indispensable quality in an Irish Saint, and *lungs of leather* no trivial requisite towards obtaining canonization. St Columbkill, we are told, sung so loud, that, according to an old Irish poem, called *Amhra Choilluim chille*, or the Vision of *Columbkill*,

'His hallow'd voice beyond a mile was heard.'

in heaven or on earth, or beneath the earth, or in the mountain or the valley; or the sea or the stream?"—And indeed even to this day, we have Irish for a river god, which we call *Divona*. You perceive, therefore, that our ancient religion was by no means an unpoetical one.'

While he spoke, we observed a figure emerging from a coppice, towards a small well, which issued from beneath the roots of a blasted oak. The priest motioned us to stop, and be silent—the figure (which was that of an ancient female wrapt in a long cloak), approached, and having drank of the well out of a little cup, she went three times round it on her knees, praying with great fervency over her beads; then rising after this painful ceremony, she tore a small part of her under garb, and hung it on the branch of the tree which shaded the well.

'This ceremony, I perceive,' said the priest, 'surprises you; but you have now witnessed the remains of one of our most ancient superstitions.—The ancient Irish, like the Greeks, were religiously attached to the consecrated fountain, the *Vel expiatoria*; and our early missionaries discovering the fondness of the natives for these sanctified springs, artfully averted the course of their superstitious faith, and dedicated them to Christian saints.'

'There is really,' said I, 'something truly classic in this spot; and here is this little shrine of Christian superstition hung with the same votive gifts as Pausanius tells us obscured the statue of Hygeia* in Secyonia.'

'This is nothing extraordinary here,' said the priest—'these consecrated wells are to be found in every part of the kingdom. But of all our *Aquæ Sanctificatæ*, Lough Derg is the most celebrated. It is the *Loretto* of Ireland, and votarists from every part of the kingdom resort to it. So great, indeed, is the still-existing veneration among the lower orders for these holy wells, that those who live at too great a distance to make a pilgrimage to one, are content to purchase a species of amulet made of a sliver of the tree which shades the well (and imbued in its waters), which they wear round their necks. These curious amulets are sold at fairs, by a species of sturdy beggar called a *Bacagh*, who stands with a long pole, with a box fixed at the top of it, for the reception of alms; while he alternately extols the miraculous property of the amulet, and details his own miseries; thus at once endeavouring to interest the faith and charity of the always benevolent, always credulous multitude.'

'Strange,' said I, 'that religion in all ages, and in all countries, should depend so much on the impositions of one half of mankind, and the credulity and indolence of the other. Thus the Egyptians (to whom even Greece herself stood indebted for the principles of those arts and sciences by which she became the most illustrious country in the world), resigned themselves so entirely to the impositions of their priests, as to believe that the safety and happiness of life itself depended on the motions of an ox, or the tameness of a crocodile.'

'Stop, stop,' interrupted Father John, smiling—'you forget, that though you wear the *San-Benito*, or robe of heresy yourself, you are in the company of those who—'

'Exactly think on *certain points*,' interrupted I, 'even as my heretical self.'

This observation led to a little controversial dialogue, which, as it would stand a very poor chance of being read by you, will stand none at all of being transcribed by me.

When we returned home we found the Prince impatiently watching for us at his window, fearful lest the dews of heaven should have fallen too heavily on the head of his heart's idol, who finished her walk in silence—either I believe not much pleased with the turn given to the conversation by the priest, or not sufficiently interested to participate in it.

I know not how it is, but since the morning of the first of May, I feel as though my soul had entered into a sacred covenant with hers—as though our very beings were indissolubly interwoven with each other. And yet the freedom which once existed in our intercourse is fled. I approach her trembling; and she repels the most distant advances with such dignified softness, such chastely modest reserve, that the restraint I sometimes labour under in her presence, is almost concomitant to the bliss it bestows.

This morning, when she came to her drawing-desk, she held a volume of *De Moustier* in her hand—'I have brought this,' said she, 'for our *bon Pere Directeur* to read out to us.'

'He has commissioned me,' said I, 'to make his excuses—he is gone to visit a sick man on the other side of the mountain.'

At this intelligence she blushed to the eyes; but suddenly recovering herself, she put the book into my hands, and said with a smile, 'then you must officiate for him.'

As soon as she was seated at the drawing desk I opened the book, and by chance at the beautiful description of the *Boudoir*:

> 'J'aime une boudoir etroite qu'un demi jour eclaire,
> La mon cœur est chez lui, le premier demi jour
> Fuit par la volupte, menagé pour l'amour,
> La discrete amitiè, veut aussi du mystere.
> Quand de nos bons amis dans un lieu limite,
> Le cercle peu nombreux pres de nous le rassemble
> Le sentiment, la paix, la franche liberté
> Preside en commun,' etc. etc.

I wish you could see this creature, when any thing is said or read that comes home to her heart, or strikes in immediate unison with the exquisite tone of her feelings. Never sure was there a finer commentary, than her looks and gestures pass on any work of interest which engages her attention. Before I had finished the perusal of this charming little fragment, the pencil had dropped from her fingers; and often she waved her beautiful head and smiled, and breathed a faint exclamation of delight; and when I laid down the book, she said, while she leaned her face on her clasped hands—

'And I too have a boudoir!—but even a *boudoir* may become a dreary solitude, except'—she paused; and I added, from the poem I had just read, 'except that within its social little limits

> 'La confidence ingenû rapproche deux amis.'*

Her eyes, half raised to mine, suddenly cast down, beamed a tender acquiescence to the sentiment.

'But,' said I, 'if the being worthy of sharing the bliss such an intercourse in such a place must confer, is yet to be found, is its hallowed circle inviolable to the intrusive footstep of an inferior, though perhaps not less ardent votarist?'

'Since you have been here,' said she, 'I have scarcely ever visited this once favourite retreat myself.'

'Am I to take that as a compliment or otherwise?' said I.

'Just as it is meant,' said she—'as a fact;' and she added, with an inadvertent simplicity into which the ardor of her temper often betrays her—'I never can devote myself partially to any thing—I am either all enthusiasm or all indifference.'

Not for the world would I have made her *feel* the full force of this avowal; but requested permission to visit this now deserted boudoir.

'Certainly,' she replied—'it is a little closet in that ruined tower, which terminates the corridor in which your apartment lies.'

'Then I am privileged?' said I.

'Undoubtedly,' she returned; and the Prince, who had risen unusually early, entered the room at that moment, and joined us at the drawing-desk.

The absence of the good priest left me to a solitary dinner. Glorvina (as is usual with her) spent the first part of the evening in her father's room, and thus denied her society, I endeavoured to supply its want—its soul-felt want, by a visit to her boudoir.

There is a certain tone of feeling when fancy is in its acmé, when sentiment holds the senses in subordination, and the visionary joys which float in the imagination shed a livelier bliss on the soul than the best pleasures cold reality ever conferred. Then, even the presence of a beloved object is not more precious to the heart than the spot consecrated to her memory; where we fancy the very air is impregnated with her respiration; every object is hallowed by her recent touch, and that all around breathes of her.

In such a mood of mind, I ascended to Glorvina's boudoir; and I really believe, that had she accompanied me, I should have felt less than when alone and unseen I stole to the asylum of her pensive thoughts. It lay as she had described; and almost as I passed its threshold, I was sensibly struck by the incongruity of its appearance—it seemed to me as though it had been partly furnished in the beginning of one century, and finished in the conclusion of another. The walls were rudely wainscotted with oak, black with age; yet the floor was covered with a Turkey carpet, rich, new, and beautiful—better adapted to cover a Parisian dressing-room than the closet of a ruined tower. The casements were high and narrow, but partly veiled with a rich drapery of scarlet silk: a few old chairs, heavy and cumbrous, were interspersed with stools of an antique form; one of which lay folded up on the ground, so as to be portable in a travelling trunk. On a pondrous Gothic table (which seemed a fixture coeval with the building), was placed a silver *escritoire*, of curious and elegant workmanship, and two small, but beautiful antique vases (filled with flowers) of Etrurian* elegance. Two little book-shelves, elegantly designed, but most clumsily executed (probably by some hedge carpenter), were filled with the best French, English, and Italian poets; and, to my utter astonishment, not only some new publications scarce six months old, but two London newspapers of no distant date, lay scattered on the table, with some MS music, and unfinished drawings.

Having gratified my curiosity, by examining the singular incongruities of this paradoxical boudoir, I leaned for some time against one of the windows, endeavouring to make out some defaced lines cut on its panes with a diamond, when Glorvina herself entered the room.

As I stood concealed by the silken drapery, she did not perceive me. A basket of flowers hung on her arm, from which she replenished the vases, having first flung away their faded treasures. As she stood thus engaged, and cheering her sweet employment with a murmured song, I stole softly behind her, and my breath disturbing the ringlets which had escaped from the bondage of her bodkin, and seemed to cling to her neck for protection, she turned quickly round, and with a start, a blush, and a smile, said, 'Ah! *so soon* here!'

'You perceive,' said I, 'your immunity was not lost on me! I have been here this half hour!'

'Indeed!' she replied, and casting round a quick inquiring glance, hastily collected the scattered papers, and threw them into a drawer; adding, 'I intended to have made some arrangements in this deserted little place, that you might see it in its best garb; but had scarcely began the necessary reform this morning, when I was suddenly called to my father, and could not till this moment find leisure to return hither.'

While she spoke I gazed earnestly at her. It struck me there was a something of mystery over this apartment, yet wherefore should mystery dwell where all breathes the ingenuous simplicity of the golden age. Glorvina moved towards the casement, threw open the sash, and laid her fresh gathered flowers on the seat. Their perfume scented the room; and a new fallen shower still glittered on the honeysuckle which she was endeavouring to entice through the window, round which it crept.

The sun was setting with rather a mild than a dazzling splendour, and the landscape was richly impurpled with his departing beams, which, as they darted through the scarlet drapery of the curtain, shed warmly over the countenance and figure of Glorvina, '*Love's proper hue.*'

We both remained silent, until her eye accidentally meeting mine, a more 'celestial rosy red' invested her cheek. She seated herself in the window, and I drew a chair, and sat near her. All within was the softest gloom—all without the most solemn stillness. The grey vapours of twilight were already stealing amidst the illumined clouds that floated in the atmosphere—the sun's golden beams no longer scattered round their rich suffusion; and the glow of retreating day was fading even from the horizon where its parting glories faintly lingered.

'It is a sweet hour,' said Glorvina, softly sighing.

'It is a *boudoirizing* hour,' said I.

'It is a golden one for a poetic heart,' she added.

'Or an enamoured one,' I returned. 'It is the hour in which the soul best knows herself; when every low-thoughted care is excluded, and the pensive pleasures take possession of the dissolving heart.

> "Ces douces lumieres
> Ces sombre clairtés
> Sont les *jours* de la volupté."*

And what was the *voluptas* of Epicurus,* but those refined and elegant enjoyments which must derive their spirit from virtue and from health; from a vivid fancy, susceptible feelings, and a cultivated mind; and which are never so fully tasted as in this sweet season of the day? then the influence of sentiment is buoyant over passion; the soul, alive to the sublimest impression, expands in the region of pure and elevated meditation: the passions, slumbering in the soft repose of Nature, leave the heart free to the reception of the purest, warmest, tenderest sentiments—when all is delicious melancholy, or pensive softness—when every vulgar wish is hushed, and a rapture, an indefinable rapture, thrills with sweet vibration on every nerve.'

'It is thus *I* have felt,' said the all-impassioned Glorvina, clasping her hands, and fixing her humid eyes on mine—'thus, in the dearth of all *kindred* feeling, have *I* felt. But never, Oh! till *now—never!*'— and she abruptly paused, and drooped her head on the back of my chair, over which my hand rested, and felt the soft pressure of her glowing cheek, while her balmy sigh breathed its odour on my lip.

Oh! had not her celestial confidence, her angelic purity, sublimed every thought, restrained every wish—at that moment—that too fortunate—too dangerous moment!!!—Yet even as it was, in the delicious agony of my soul, I secretly exclaimed, with the legislator of Lesbos*—'*It is too difficult to be always virtuous!*' while I half audibly breathed on the ear of Glorvina—

'Nor I, O first of all created beings! never, never till I beheld thee, did I know the pure rapture which the intercourse of a kindred soul awakens—of that sacred communion with a superior intelligence, which, while it raises me in my own estimation, tempts me to emulate that excellence I adore.'

Glorvina raised her head—her melting eyes met mine, and her cheek rivalled the snow of that hand which was pressed with passionate ardor to my lips. Then her eyes were bashfully withdrawn—she again drooped her head—not on the chair, but on my shoulder. What followed, angels might have attested—but the eloquence of bliss is silence.

Suffice it to say, that I am now certain of at least being understood; and that in awakening her comprehension, I have roused my own. In a word, I *now* feel I love!!—for the first time I feel it. For the first time my heart is alive to the most profound, the most delicate, the most ardent, and most refined of all human passions. I am now conscious that I have hitherto mistaken the senses for the heart, and the blandishments of a vitiated imagination for the pleasures of the soul. In short, I now feel myself in that state of beatitude, when the fruition of all the heart's purest wishes leaves me nothing to desire, and the innocence of those wishes nothing to fear. You know but little of the sentiment which now pervades my whole being, and blends with every atom of my frame, if you suppose I have formerly told Glorvina I loved her, or that I appear even to suspect that I am (rapturous thought!) beloved in return. On the contrary, the same mysterious delicacy, the same delicious reserve still exist. It is a sigh, a glance, a broken sentence, an imperceptible motion (imperceptible to all eyes but our own), that betrays us to each other. Once I used to fall at the feet of the '*Cynthia of the moment*,' avow my passion, and swear eternal truth. Now I make no genuflexion, offer no vows, and swear no oaths; and yet feel more than ever—More!—dare I then place in the scale of comparison what I now feel with what I ever felt before? The thought is sacrilege!

This Child of Nature appears to me each succeeding day, in a *phasis**more bewitchingly attractive than the last. She now feels her power over me (with woman's *intuition*, where the heart is in question!); and this consciousness gives to her manners a certain roguish tyranny, that renders her the most charming tantalizing being in the world. In a thousand little instances she contrives to teaze me; most, when most she delights me! and takes no pains to conceal my simple folly from others, while she triumphs in it herself. In short, she is the last woman in the world who would incur the risk of satiating him who was blest in her love; for the variability of her manner, always governed by her ardent, though volatilized, feelings, keeps suspense on the eternal *qui vive!** and the sweet assurance given by the eyes one moment, is destroyed in the next by some arch sally of the lip.

To day I met her walking with the nurse. The old woman, very properly, made a motion to retire as I approached. Glorvina would not suffer this, and twined her arm round that of her foster-mother. I was half inclined to turn on my heel, when a servant came running to the nurse for the keys. It was impossible to burst them from her side, and away she hobbled after the bare-footed *laquais.** I looked reproachfully at Glorvina, but her eyes were fixed on an arbutus tree rich in blossom.

'I wish I had that high branch,' said she, 'to put in my vase.' In a moment I was climbing up the tree like a great school-boy, while she, standing beneath, received the blossoms in her extended drapery; and I was on the point of descending, when a branch, lovelier than all I had culled, attracted my eye: this I intended to present in *propria persona,** that I might get a kiss of the hand in return. With my own hands sufficiently engaged in effecting my descent, I held my Hesperian branch in my teeth, and had nearly reached the ground, when Glorvina playfully approached her lovely mouth to snatch the prize from mine. We were just in contact—I suddenly let fall the branch—and—Father John appeared walking towards us; while Glorvina, who, it seems, had perceived him before she had placed herself in the way of danger, now ran towards him, covered with blushes and malignant little smiles. In short, she makes me feel in a thousand trivial instances, the truth of Epictetus's maxim, that to *bear* and *forbear*, are the powers that constitute a wise man: to *forbear* alone, would, in my opinion, be a sufficient test.

Adieu!

H.M.

LETTER XXI

TO J.D. ESQ. M.P.

I cannot promise you any more Irish history. I fear my *Hiberniana** is closed, and a volume of more dangerous, more delightful tendency, draws towards its bewitching subject every truant thought. To him who is deep in the *Philosophia Amatoria,** every other science is cold and vapid.

The oral legend of the Prince and the historic lore of the priest, all go for nothing! I shake my head, look very wise, and appear to listen, while my eyes are rivetted on Glorvina—who, not unconscious of the ardent gaze, sweeps with a feathery touch the chords of her harp, or plies her fairy wheel with double vigilance. Meantime, however, I am making a rapid progress in the Irish language, and well I may; for besides that I now listen to the language of Ossian with the same respect a Hindoo would to the Shanscrit of the Bramins,** the Prince, the priest, and even Glorvina, contribute their exertions to my progress. The other evening, as we circled round the evening fire in the great hall, the Prince would put my improvements to the test, and taking down a grammar, he insisted on my conjugating a verb. The verb he chose was '*to love*.'—'Glorvina,' said he, seeing me hesitate, 'go through the verb.'

Glorvina had it at her fingers' ends; and in her eyes swam a thousand delicious comments on the text she was expounding.

The Prince, who is as unsuspicious as an infant, would have us repeat it together, that I might catch the pronunciation from her lip!

'*I love*,' faintly articulated Glorvina.

'*I love*,' I more faintly repeated.

This was not enough—the Prince would have us repeat the plural twice over; and again and again we murmured together—'*we love!*'

Heavens and earth! had you at that moment seen the preceptress and the *pupil*! The attention of the simple Prince was rivetted on

Vallancy's grammar: he grew peevish at what he called our stupidity, and said we knew nothing of the verb to love, while in fact we were running through all its moods and tenses with our eyes and looks.

Good God! to how many delicious sensations is the soul alive, for which there is no possible mode of expression.

Adieu!—The little post-boy is at my elbow. I observe he goes more frequently to post than usual; and one morning I perceived Glorvina eagerly watching his return, from the summit of a rock. Whence can this solicitude arise? Her father may have some correspondence on business—she can have none.

LETTER XXII

TO J.D. ESQ. M.P.

This creature is deep in the metaphysics of love. She is perpetually awakening ardor by restraint, and stealing enjoyment from privation. She still persists in bringing the priest with her to the drawing-desk; but it is evident she does not the less enjoy that casual absence which leaves us sometimes alone; and I am now become such an epicure in sentiment, that I scarcely regret the restraint the presence of the priest imposes; since it gives a keener zest to the transient minutes of felicity his absence bestows—even though they are enjoyed in silent confusion. For nothing can be more seducing than her looks, nothing can be more dignified than her manners. If, when we are alone, I even offer to take her hand, she grows pale, and shrinks from my touch.—Yet I regret not that careless confidence which once prompted the innocent request that I would guide her hand to draw a perpendicular line.

'Solitude (says the Spectator) with the person beloved, even to a woman's mind, has a pleasure beyond all the pomp and splendor in the world.'

O! how my heart subscribes to a sentiment I have so often laughed at, when my ideas of pleasure were very different from what they are at present. I cannot persuade myself that three weeks have elapsed since my return hither; and still less am I willing to believe that it is necessary I should return to M—— House. In short, the rocks which embosom the peninsula of Inismore bound all my hopes, all my wishes; and my desires, like the *radii* of a *circle*, all point towards one and the same centre. This creature grows on me with boundless influence: her originality, her genius, her sensibility, her youth and person! In short, their united charms in this profound solitude thus closely associated, is a species of witchcraft.　　＊　　＊　　＊　　＊

＊　＊　＊　＊　＊　＊　＊　＊　＊　＊　＊

It was indispensably necessary I should return to M—— House, as my father's visit to Ireland is drawing near; and it was requisite I should receive and answer his letters. At last, therefore, I summoned up resolution to plead my former excuses to the Prince for my absence; who insisted on my immediate return—which I promised should be in a day or two; while the eyes of Glorvina echoed her father's commands, and mine looked implicit obedience. With what different emotions I now left Inismore, to those which accompanied my last departure! My feelings were then unknown to myself—now I am perfectly aware of their nature.

I found M—— House, as usual, cold, comfortless, and desolate—with a few wretched looking peasants working languidly about the grounds. In short, every thing breathed the deserted mansion of an *absentee*.

The evening of my arrival I answered my father's letters—one from our pleasant but libertine friend D——n—read over yours three times—went to bed—dreamed of Glorvina—and set off for Inismore the next morning. I rode so hard, that I reached the castle about that hour which we usually devoted to the exertions of the pencil. I flew at once to that vast and gloomy room which her presence alone cheers and illumines. Her drawing-desk lay open; she seemed but just to have risen from the chair placed before it; and her work-basket hung on its back. Even this well known little work-basket is to me an object of interest. I kissed the muslin it contained; and in raising it, perceived a small book splendidly bound and gilt. I took it up, and read on its cover, marked in letters of gold—'*Breviare du Sentiment.*'＊

Impelled by the curiosity which this title excited, I opened it—and found between its first two leaves several faded snow-drops *stained with blood*. Under them was written, in Glorvina's hand,

'Prone to the earth we bowed our pallid flowers—
And caught the drops divine, the purple dyes
Tinging the lustre of our native hues.'[1]

A little lower in the page was traced—'Culled from the spot where he fell—April the 1st, 17—.'

Oh! how quickly my bounding heart told me who was that *he*, whose vital drops had stained these *treasured* blossoms, thus, 'tinging the lustre of their native hues'—While the sweetest association of ideas convinced me that these were the identical flowers which Glorvina had hallowed with a tear, as she watched by the couch of him with whose blood they were polluted.

While I pressed this sweet testimony of a pure and lively tenderness to my lips, she entered. At sight of *me*, pleasurable surprise invested every feature; and the most innocent joy lit up her countenance, as she sprang forward and offered me her hand. While I carried it eagerly to my lips, I pointed to the snow-drops. Glorvina, with the hand which was disengaged, covered her blushing face, and would have fled. But the look which preceded this natural motion discovered the wounded feelings of a tender but proud heart. I felt the indelicacy of my conduct, and still clasping her struggling hand, exclaimed—

'Forgive, forgive, the vain triumph of a being intoxicated by your pity—transported by your condescension.'

'*Triumph*!' repeated Glorvina, in an accent tenderly reproachful, yet accompanied by a look proudly indignant—'*Triumph*!'

How I cursed the coxcomical* expression in my heart, while I fell at her feet, and kissing the hem of her robe, without daring to touch the hand I had relinquished, said,

'Does this look like triumph, Glorvina?'

Glorvina turned towards me a face in which all the witcheries of her sex were blended—playful fondness, affected anger, animated tenderness, and soul-dissolving languishment. Oh! she should not have looked thus, or I should have been more or less than man.

With a glance of undeniable supplication, she released herself from that glowing fold, which could have pressed her for ever to an heart where she must for ever reign unrivalled. I saw she wished I should think her very angry, and another pardon was to be solicited,

---

[1] From the Italian of Lorenzo de Medicis.

for the transient indulgence of that passionate impulse her own seducing looks had called into existence. The pardon, after some little pouting playfulness, *was* granted, and I was suffered to lead her to that Gothic sofa where our first *tête-à-tête* had taken place; and partly by artifice, partly by entreaty, I drew from her the little history of the treasured snow-drops, and read in her eloquent eyes, more than her bashful lips will ever dare to express.

Thus, like the *assymtotes** of an hyperbola, without absolutely rushing into contact, we are, by a sweet impulse, gradually approximating closer and closer towards each other.

Ah! my dear friend, this is the golden age of love; and I sometimes think, with the refined Weiland,* that the passion begins with the first sigh, and ends, in a certain degree, with the first kiss—mine, therefore, is now in its climacteric.*

The impetuosity with which I rush on every subject that touches her, often frustrates the intention with which I sit down to address you. I left his letter behind me unfinished, for the purpose of filling it up on my return, with answers to those I expected to receive from you. The arguments which your friendly foresight and prudent solicitude have furnished you, are precisely such as the understanding cannot refute, nor the heart subscribe to.

You say my *wife* she *cannot* be—and my mistress!—perish the thought! What! I repay the generosity of the father by the destruction of the child! I steal this angelic being from the peaceful security of her native shades, with all her ardent tender feelings thick about her: I

> 'Crop this fair rose, and rifle all its sweetness!'

No; you do me but common justice when you say, that though you have sometimes known me *affect* the character of a libertine, yet never, even for a moment, have you known me forfeit that of a man of honour. I would not be understood to speak in the mere commonplace worldly acceptation of the word, but literally, according to the text of all moral and divine laws.

'Then what,' you ask me, 'is the aim, the object, in pursuing this *ignus fatuus** of the heart and fancy?'

In a word, then, virtue is my object—felicity my aim; or, rather, I am lured towards the former through the medium of the latter. And whether the tye which binds me at once to moral and physical good, is of a fragile texture and transient existence, or whether it will become 'close twisted with the fibres of the heart, and breaking, break it,' time only can determine—to time, therefore, I commit my fate; but while thus led by the hand of virtue, I inebriate at the living spring of bliss,

> 'Wild reeling thro' a wilderness of joy,'

can you wonder that I fling off the goading chain of prudence, and in daring to be *free*, at once be virtuous and be happy?

My father's letter is brief, but pithy. My brother is married, and has sold his name and *title* for a hundred thousand pounds; and *his* brother has a chance of selling his happiness for ever for something about the same sum. And who, think you, is to be the purchaser? Why our old sporting friend D——. In my last grousing visit at his seat, you may remember the pretty *pert* little girl, his only daughter, who, he assured us, was that day *unkennelled* for the first time, in honour of our success, and who rushed upon us from the nursery in all the bloom of fifteen, and all the boldness of a hoyden; whose society was the housekeeper and the chamber-maid, and whose ideas of pleasure extended no further than blind-man's buff in the servant's hall, and a game of hot cockles with the butler and footman in the pantry. I had the good fortune to touch her heart at cross-purposes, and completely vanquished her affections by a romping match in the morning; and so it seems the fair *susceptible* has pined in thought ever since, but not 'let concealment prey on her damask cheek,' for she *told* her love to an old maiden aunt, who told it to another confidential friend, until the whole neighbourhood was full of the tale of the *victim of constancy* and the *cruel deceiver*.

The father, as is usual in such cases, was the last to hear it; and believing me to be an excellent shot, and a keen sportsman, all he requires in a son-in-law, except a good family, he proposed the match to my father, who gladly embraces the offer, and fills his letter with blooms, blushes, and unsophisticated charms; congratulates me on my conquest, and talks either of recalling me shortly to England, or bringing the fair *fifteen* and old *Nimrod** to Ireland on a visit with him. But the former he will not easily effect, and the latter I know business will prevent for some weeks, as he writes that he is still up to his ears in parchment deeds, leases, settlements, and jointures. Mean time,

'Song, beauty, youth, love, virtue, joy, this group
   Of bright ideas, flowers of Paradise as yet unforfeit,'

crown my golden hours of bliss; and whatever may be my future
destiny, I will at least rescue one beam of unalloyed felicity from its
impending clouds—for, oh! my good friend, there is a prophetic
something which incessantly whispers me, that in clouds and storms
will the evening of my existence expire.

Adieu!

H.M.

LETTER XXIII

TO J.D. ESQ. M.P.

It is certain, that you men of the world are nothing less than men of
pleasure:—would you taste it in all its essence, come to Inismore. Ah!
no, pollute not with your presence the sacred *palladium** of all the
primeval virtues; attempt not to participate in those pure joys of the
soul it would be death to me to divide even with you. Here Plato
might enjoy, and Epicurus revel: here we are taught to feel according
to the doctrine of the latter, that the happiness of mankind consists
in *pleasure*, not such as arises from the gratification of the senses,
or the pursuits of vice—but from the enjoyments of the mind, the
pleasures of the imagination, the affections of the heart, and
the sweets of virtue. And here we learn, according to the precepts
of the former, that the summit of human felicity may be attained, by
removing from the material, and approaching nearer to the intellectual world; by curbing and governing the passions, which are so
much oftener inflamed by imaginary than real objects; and by bor-
rowing from temperance, that zest which can alone render pleasure
forever poignant, and forever new. Ah! you will say, like other lovers,
you now see the moral as well as the natural world through a prism;
but would this unity of pleasure and virtue be found in the wilds of
Inismore, if Glorvina was no longer there?

I honestly confess to you, I do not think it would, for where yet
was pleasure ever found where woman was not? and when does the
heart so warmly receive the pure impressions of virtue, as when its
essence is imbibed from woman's lip?

My life passes away here in a species of delectability to which I can give no name; and while, through the veil of delicate reserve which the pure suggestions of the purest nature have flung over the manners of my sweet Glorvina, a thousand little tendernesses unconsciously appear. Her amiable preceptor clings to me with a parent's fondness; and her father's increasing partiality for his hereditary enemy, is visible in a thousand instances; while neither of these excellent, but inexperienced men, suspect the secret intelligence which exists between the younger tutor and his lovely pupil. As yet, indeed, it has assumed no determinate character. With me it is a delightful dream, from which I dread to be awakened, yet feel that it is but a dream; while she, bewildered, amazed, at those vague emotions which throb impetuously in her unpractised heart, resigns herself unconsciously to the sweetest of all deliriums, and makes no effort to dissolve the vision!

If, in the refined epicurism of my heart, I carelessly speak of my departure for England in the decline of summer, Glorvina changes colour; the sainted countenance of Father John loses its wonted smile of placidity; and the Prince replies by some peevish observation on the solitude of their lives, and the want of attraction at Inismore to detain a man of the world in its domestic circle.

But he will say, 'it was not always thus—this hall once echoed to the sound of mirth and the strain of gaiety; for the day was, when none went sad of heart from the castle of Inismore!'

I much fear that the circumstances of this worthy man are greatly deranged, though it is evident his pride would be deeply wounded if it was even suspected. Father John, indeed, hinted to me, that the Prince was a great agricultural speculator some few years back; 'and even still,' said he, 'likes to hold more land in his hands than he is able to manage.'

I have observed too, that the hall is frequently crowded with importunate people, whom the priest seems endeavouring to pacify in Irish; and twice, as I passed the Prince's room last week, an ill-looking fellow appeared at the door, whom Glorvina was shewing out. Her eyes were moist with tears; and at sight of me she deeply coloured, and hastily withdrew. It is impossible to describe my feelings at that moment!

Notwithstanding, however, the Prince affects an air of grandeur, and opulence—he keeps a kind of open table in his servants' hall, where a crowd of labourers, dependents, and mendicants, are daily entertained;[1] and it is evident his pride would receive a mortal stab, if he supposed that his guest, and that guest an Englishman, suspected the impoverished state of his circumstances.

Although not a man of very superior understanding, yet he evidently possesses that innate grandeur of soul, which haughtily struggles with distress, and which will neither yield to, nor make terms with misfortune; and when, in the dignity of that pride which scorns the revelation of its woes, I behold him collecting all the forces of his mind, and asserting a right to a better fate, I feel my own character energize in the contemplation of his, and am almost tempted to envy him those trials which call forth the latent powers of human fortitude and human greatness.

H.M.

END OF VOL. II

[1] The kitchen, or servants' hall, of an Irish country gentleman, is open to all whom distress may lead to its door. Professed and indolent mendicants take advantage of this indiscriminating hospitality, enter without ceremony, seat themselves by the fire, and seldom (indeed never) depart with their demands unsatisfied, by the misapplied benevolence of an old Irish custom, which in many instances would be—'more honoured in the breach than the observance.'

LETTER XXIV

TO J.D. ESQ. M.P.

'Tout s'evanouit sous les cieux,
Chaque instant varie à nos yeux
Le tableau mouvant de la vie.'*

Alas! that even this solitude, where all seems

'The world forgetting, by the world forgot,'

should be subject to that mutability of fate which governs the busiest
haunts of man. Is it possible, that among these dear ruins, where all
the 'life of life' has been restored to me, the worst of human pangs
should assail my full all-confiding heart. And yet I am jealous only
on surmise; but who was ever jealous on conviction; for where is the
heart so weak, so mean, as to cherish the passion when betrayed by
the object. I have already mentioned to you the incongruities which
so forcibly struck me in Glorvina's *boudoir*. Since the evening, the
happy evening in which I first visited it, I have often stolen thither
when I knew her elsewhere engaged, but always found it locked till
this morning, when I perceived the door standing open. It seemed as
though its mistress had but just left it, for a chair was placed near the
window, which was open, and her book and work-basket lay on the
seat. I mechanically took up the book, it was my own *Eloisa*, and
was marked with a slip of paper in that page where the character of
Wolmar* is described; I read through the passage, I was throwing it
by when some writing on the *paper mark* caught my eye; supposing it
to be Glorvina's, I endeavoured to decypher the lines, and read as
follows: 'Professions, my lovely friend, are for the world. But I would
at least have you believe, that *my* friendship, like gold, though not
sonorous, is indestructible.' This was all I could make out—and this I
read a hundred times—the hand writing was a man's—but it was not
the priest's—it could not be her father's. And yet, I thought the
hand was not entirely unknown to me, though it appeared disguised.
I was still engaged in gazing on the *sibyl leaf* when I heard *Glorvina*
approach. I never was mistaken in her little feet's light bound; for
she seldom walks, and hastily replacing the book, I appeared deeply
engaged in looking over a fine *Atlas* that lay open on the table. She
seemed surprised at my appearance, so much so, that I felt the

necessity of apologizing for my intrusion. 'But,' said I, 'an immunity granted by you is too precious to be neglected, and if I have not oftener availed myself of my valued privileges, I assure you the fault was not mine.'

Without noticing my innuendo she only bowed her head, and asked me with a smile, 'what favourite spot on the globe I was tracing with such earnestness when her entrance had interrupted my geographic pursuits.'

I placed my finger on that point of the north-west shores of Ireland, where we then stood, and said in the language of *St Preux*,* 'The world in my imagination is divided into two regions—that where *she is*—and that where she is not.'

With an air of bewitching insinuation she placed her hand on my shoulder, and with a faint blush and a little smile shook her head, and looked up in my face, with a glance half incredulous—half tender. I kissed the hand by whose pressure I was thus honoured, and said, 'professions, my lovely friend, are for the world, but I would at least have you believe that my friendship, like gold, though not sonorous, is indestructible.'

This I said, in the irascibility of my jealous heart, for, though too warm for another, oh! how cold for me! Glorvina started as I spoke, I thought changed colour! while at intervals she repeated, 'strange!— nor is this the only coincidence!' 'Coincidence!' I eagerly repeated, but she affected not to hear me, and appeared busily engaged in selecting for herself a bouquet from the flowers which filled one of those *vases* I before noticed to you. 'And is that beautiful vase,' said I, 'another family antiquity? it looks as though it stole its elegant form from an Etruscan model: is this too an effort of ancient Irish taste?' 'No,' said she, I thought confusedly, 'I believe it came from Italy.'

'Has it been long in the possession of the family?' said I, with persevering impertinence. 'It was a present from a friend of my father's,' she replied, colouring, 'to me!' The bell at that moment rang for breakfast, away she flew, apparently pleased to be released from my importunities.

'A friend of her father's!' and who can this friend be, whose delicacy of judgment so nicely adapts the gifts to the taste of her on whom they are lavished. For undoubtedly the same hand that made the offering of the vases, presented also those other portable elegancies which are so strongly contrasted by the rude original furniture of the *boudoir*. The tasteful *doneur** and the author of that letter whose torn fragment betrayed the sentiment of no common mind, are certainly one and the same person. Yet who visits the castle? scarcely any one; the pride and circumstances of the *Prince* equally forbid it. Sometimes, though rarely, an old Milesian cousin, or poor relation will drop in, but those of them that I have seen, are more common-place people. I have indeed heard the Prince speak of a cousin in the Spanish service, and a nephew in the Irish brigades, now in Germany. But the cousin is an old man, and the nephew he has not seen since he was a child. Yet after all, these presents may have come from one of these relatives; if so, as Glorvina has no recollection of either, how I should curse that jealous temper which has purchased for me some moments of torturing doubts. I remember you used often to say, that any woman could *pique* me into love, by affecting indifference, and that the native jealousy of my disposition, would always render me the slave of any woman who knew how to play upon my dominant passion. The fact is, when my heart erects an idol for its secret homage, it is madness to think that another should even bow at the shrine, much less that his offerings should be propitiously received.

But it is the silence of Glorvina on the subject of this generous friend, that distracts me; if after all—oh! it is impossible—it is sacrilege against heaven to doubt her—she practised in deception! she, whose every look, every motion, betrays a soul that is all truth, innocence, and virtue! I have endeavoured to sound the priest on the subject, and affected to admire the vases; repeating the same questions with which I had teased Glorvina. But he too carelessly replied, 'they were given her by a friend of her father's.'

LETTER XXV

TO J.D. ESQ. M.P.

Just as I had finished my last, the Prince sent for me to his room; I found him alone, and sitting up in his bed! he only complained of the effects of years and sickness, but it was evident some recent cause of uneasiness preyed on his mind. He made me sit by his bed-side, and said, that my good-nature upon every occasion, induced him to prefer a request, he was induced to hope would not meet with a denial. I begged he would change that request to a command, and rely in every instance on my readiness to serve him. He thanked and told me in a few words, that the priest was going on a very particular, but not very pleasing business for him (the Prince) to the *north*; that the journey was long, and would be both solitary and tedious to his good old friend, whose health I might have observed was delicate and precarious, except I had the goodness to cheat the weariness of the journey by giving the priest my company. 'I would not make the request' he added, 'but that I think your compliance will be productive of pleasure and information to yourself; in a journey of an hundred miles, many new sources of observation to your inquiring mind will appear. Besides, you who seem to feel so lively an interest in all which concerns this country, will be glad to have an opportunity of viewing the Irish character in a new aspect; or rather of beholding the Scotch character engrafted upon ours. But,' said the Prince, with his usual nationality, 'that *exotic* branch is not very distinguishable from the old stock.'

I need not tell you that I complied with this request with *seeming* readiness, but with real reluctance.

In the evening, as we circled round the fire in the great hall, I proposed to *Father John* to accompany him on his journey the following day. The poor man was overjoyed at the offer, while Glorvina betrayed neither surprise nor regret at my intention, but looked first at her father, and then at me, with kindness and gratitude.

Were my heart more at ease, were my confidence in the affections of Glorvina something stronger, I should greatly relish this little tour, but as it is, when I found every thing arranged for my departure, without the concurrence of my own wishes, I could not check my pettishness, and for want of some other mode of venting it, I endeavoured to ridicule a work on the subject of *ancient Irish* history which the priest was reading aloud, while Glorvina worked, and I was trifling with my pencil.

'What,' said I, after having interrupted him in many different passages, which I thought savoured of natural Hyperbole, 'what can be more forced than that very supposition of your partial author, that *Albion*, the most ancient name of Britain, was given it as though it

were another, or *second Ireland*, because Banba was one of the ancient
names of your country?'

'It may appear to you a FORGED etymology,' said the priest, 'yet it
has the sanction of *Camden*,* who first risked the supposition. But it
is the fate of our unhappy country to receive as little credit in the
present day, for its former celebrity, as for its great antiquity,[1]
although the former is attested by *Bede*,* and many other early
British writers, and the latter is authenticated by the testimony of
the most ancient Greek authors. For *Jervis* is mentioned in the
Argonautica of *Orpheus*, long before the name of England is any
where to be found in Grecian literature. And surely it had scarcely
been first mentioned, had it not been first known.'

'Then you really suppose,' said I, smiling incredulously, 'we are
indebted to you for the name of our country.' 'I know,' said the
priest, returning my smile, 'the fallacies in general of all etymol-
ogists, but the only part of your island, anciently called by any name
that bore the least affinity to *Albion*, was *Scotland*, then called *Albin*,
a word of *Irish* etymology, *Albin* signifying mountainous, from Alb
a mountain.'

'But, my dear friend,' I replied, 'admitting the great antiquity
of your country, allowing it to be early inhabited by a lettered and
civilized people, and that it was the *Nido paterno** of western literature when the rest of Europe was involved in darkness; how is it that
so few monuments of your ancient learning and genius remain?
Where are your manuscripts, your records, your annals, stamped
with the seal of antiquity, to be found.'

'Manuscripts, annals, and records, are not the treasures of a colonized or a conquered country,' said the priest; 'it is always the policy
of the conqueror, (or the invader) to destroy those mementi of
ancient national splendour which keep alive the spirit of the con-

---

[1] It has been the fashion to throw an odium on the modern Irish, by undermining the
basis of their ancient history, and vilifying their ancient national character. If an historian professes to have acquired his information from the records of the country, whose
history he writes, his accounts are generally admitted as authentic, as the commentaries
of *Garcilorsso de Vega* are considered as the chief pillars of Peruvian history, though
avowed by their author to have been compiled from the old national ballads of the
country; yet the old writers of Ireland, (the psalter of Cashel in particular) though they
refer to those ancient records of *their* country, authenticated by existing manners and
existing habits, are plunged into the oblivion of contemptuous neglect, or read, only to
be discredited.

quered or the invaded;[1] the dispersion at various periods,[2] of many of the most illustrious Irish families into foreign countries, has assisted the depredations of time and policy, in the plunder of her literary treasures; many of them are now mouldering in public and private libraries on the Continent, whither their possessors conveyed them from the destruction which civil war carries with it, and many of them (even so far back as the Elizabeth day) were conveyed to Denmark. The Danish monarch applied to the English court for some learned man to translate them, and one *Donald O'Daly*, a person eminently qualified for the task, was actually engaged to perform it, until the illiberality of the English court prevented the intention, on the poor plea of its prejudicing the English interest. I know myself that many of our finest and most valuable MSS are in libraries in France, and have heard that not a few of them enrich the Vatican at Rome.'[3]

'But,' said I, 'are not many of those MSS supposed to be Monkish impositions?' 'Yes,' replied the Priest, 'by those who *never saw them*, and if *they did* were too ignorant of the Irish language to judge of their authenticity by the internal evidences they contain.'

'And if they were the works of Monks,' said the priest, 'Ireland was always allowed to possess at that era, the most devout and learned ecclesiastics in Europe, from which circumstance it received its title of *Island of Saints*. By them indeed many histories of the ancient Irish were composed in the early ages of christianity, but it was certainly from pagan records and traditions, they received their

[1] Sir George Carew, in the reign of Elizabeth, was accused of bribing the family historian of the M'CARTHIES, to convey to him some curious *MSS*. 'But what,' says the author of the '*Analect*,' 'CAREW did in *one* province (Munster) *Henry Sidney*, and his predecessors, did all over the kingdom, being charged to collect all the MSS they could, that they might effectually destroy every vestige of antiquity and letters throughout the kingdom. And St Patrick, in his apostolic zeal, committed to the flames several hundred druidical volumes.'

[2] Fourteen thousand Irish took advantage of the articles of Limerick, and bade adieu to their native country for ever.

[3] In a conversation which passed in Cork, between the author's father, and the celebrated Dr O'Leary the latter said he had once intended to have written a history of Ireland. And added, 'but in truth I found after various researches, that I could not give such a history as I would wish should come from my pen, without visiting the Continent; more particularly *Rome*, where alone the best documents for the history of Ireland are to be had. But it is now too late in the day for me to think of such a journey, or such exertions as the task would require.' 'Mr O'Hallaran informs me,' (Says Mr Walker, *Mem. of Irish Bards*, p. 141.) 'that he lately got in a collection from Rome, several poems of the most eminent bards of the two last centuries.'

information; besides, I do not think any arguments can be advanced more favourable to the truth of their histories, than that the fiction of those histories simply consists in ascribing natural phenomena to super-natural agency.'

'But,' returned I, 'granting that your island was the *Athens* of a certain age, how is the barbarity of the present to be reconciled with the civilization of the enlightened past?'

'When you talk of our *barbarity*,' said the Priest, 'you do not speak as you *feel*, but as you *hear*.' I blushed at this mild reproof, and said, 'what I *now* feel for this country, it would not be easy to express, but I have always been taught to look upon the *inferior* Irish as beings forming an humbler link than humanity in the chain of nature.'

'Yes,' said the priest, 'in your country it is usual to attach to that class of society in ours, a ferocious disposition amounting to barbarity; but this, with other calumnies, of national indolence, and obstinate ignorance, of want of principle, and want of faith, is unfounded and illiberal;[1] "cruelty" says Lord Sheffield, "is not in the nature of these

---

[1] To endeavour to efface from the Irish character the odium of cruelty, by which the venom of prejudiced aversion has polluted its surface, would be to retrace a series of complicated events from the first period of British invasion to a recent day. And by the *exposition* of CAUSES accomplish the extenuation of EFFECTS. To such a task neither the limits of this little work, nor the abilities of its author are competent; much indeed has been already said, and finely said, on the subject by those whose powers were adequate to the task, and who were induced by the mere principle of national affection, to the noble effort of national defence. But the champions were *Irish men*, and the *motive* of the patriotic exertion became its sole reward.

Had the *Historiographer* of MONTEZUMA or ATALIBA defended the *resistance* of his countrymen, or recorded the woes from whence it sprung, though his QUIPAS was bathed in their blood, or embued with their tears, he would have unavailingly recorded them; for the victorious *Spaniard* was insensible to the woes he had created, and called the resistance it gave birth to CRUELTY. But when *nature* is wounded through all her dearest ties, she must *turn* on the hand that stabs, and endeavour to wrest the poniard from the *grasp* that aims at the life-pulse of *her* heart. And this she will do in obedience to that immutable law, which blends the instinct of self-preservation with every atom of human existence. And for this in *less felicitous* times, when *oppression and sedition* succeeded alternately to each other, was the name, *Irishman*, blended with the horrid epithet of cruel. But when the sword of the *oppressor* was *sheathed*, the spirit of the *oppressed* reposed, and the opprobrium it had drawn down on him was no longer remembered, until the unhappy events of a late anarchical period, revived the faded characters in which that opprobrium had been traced. The events alluded to were the *atrocities* which chiefly occurred in the county of Wexford, and its adjoining, and confederate district. Wexford is an English colony planted by Henry the second, where scarcely any feature of the original Irish character, or any trace of the Irish language is to be found. While in the *Barony of Forth*, not only the customs, manners, habits, and *costume*, of the ancient British settlers still prevail, but the ancient Celtic language has

people, more than of other men, for they have many customs among them which discover uncommon gentleness, kindness, and affection; they are so far from possessing natural indolence, that they are constitutionally of an active nature, and capable of the greatest exertions; and of as good dispositions as any nation in the same state of improvement; their generosity, hospitality, and bravery, are proverbial; intelligence and zeal in whatever they undertake will never be wanting: *but it has been the fashion to judge of them by their outcasts.*"'

'It is strange,' said the prince, 'that the earliest British writers should be as diffuse in the praise, as the moderns are in calumniating our unhappy country. Once we were every where, and by all, justly famed for our patriotism, ardor of affection, love of letters, skill in arms and arts, and refinement of manners; but no sooner did there arise a connexion between us and a sister country, than the reputed virtues and well-earned glory of the Irish sunk at once into oblivion: as if' continued this enthusiastic *Milesian*, rising from his seat with all his native vehemence—'as if the moral world was subject to those convulsions which shake the *natural* to its centre, burying by a single shock the monumental splendors of countless ages. Thus it should

been preserved with infinitely less corruption than in any part of *Britain*, where it has been interwoven with the Saxon, Danish, and French languages. In fact here may be found a remnant of an ancient *British Colony*, more pure and unmixed, than in any other part of the world. And here were committed those barbarities, which have recently attached the epithet of cruel to the name of *Irishman*! Strongly as the ancient British character may be found extant in the natives of *Wexford and its environs*, equally pure will the primitive character of the Irish be met with in the provinces of *Connaught and Munster*; yet if the footstep of resistance was sometimes impressed on that soil, which had been the asylum of *ancient* Irish independence, its *track* was bloodless; if the energy of a *once* oppressed, but ever *unsubdued* spirit, sometimes burst beyond the boundary of prudent restraint and politic submission, mercy still hung upon its perilous enterprise, and the irritated vehemence of that soul which dared to *oppose*, was tempered by the generous feelings of that heart which disdained to oppress!

'In the parliament held by king James, after the abdication, the Irish solemnly complained, that the injustice and misrepresentation of their governors had forced them to those unwilling acts of violence by which the Irish gentry had attempted to maintain their security and honour, in the numerous conflicts which took place before and subsequent to that period; the national character of Ireland never deserved the disgraceful epithets of sanguinary: had we affixed it to the transactions of the civil war, we should only conclude that, roused by a series of wrongs too great for human patience, a desperate and desponding people had submitted, in a wild paroxysm of rage, to the fierce impulse of nature on their untutored minds, and sacrificed to their feelings those men whom they regarded as the authors or the instruments of their misfortunes; even on this hypothesis, which the concurring testimony of history and probability compel us to reject, we might palliate, though we could not justify, the frenzy.'

seem, that when the bosom of national freedom was rent asunder, the national virtues which derived their nutriment from its source sunk into the abyss; while on the barren surface which covers the wreck of Irish greatness, the hand of prejudice and illiberality has sown the seeds of calumny and defamation, to choak up those health-ful plants, indigenous to the soil, which still raise their oft-crushed heads, struggling for existence, and which, like the palm-tree, rise in proportion to those efforts made to suppress them.'

To repeat the words of the prince is to deprive them of half their effect: his great eloquence lies in his air, his gestures, and the forcible expression of his dark rolling eye. He sat down exhausted with the impetuous vehemence with which he had spoken.

'If we are to believe Doctor Warner,* however,' said the priest, 'the modern Irish are a degenerated race, comparatively speaking; for he asserts that, even in the days of Elizabeth, "the old natives had degenerated, and that the *wars of several centuries* had reduced them to a state far inferior to that in which they were found in the days of Henry the Second." But still, like the modern Greeks, we perceive among them strong traces of a free, a great, a polished, and an enlightened people.'

Wearied by a conversation in which my heart now took little inter-est, I made the *palinode** of my *prejudices*, and concluded by saying, 'I perceive that on *this* ground I am always destined to be vanquished, yet always to win by the loss, and gain by the defeat; and therefore I ought not in common policy to cease to *oppose*, until nothing further can be obtained by opposition.'

The prince, who was getting a little testy at my '*heresy* and *schism*,' seemed quite appeased by this avowal; and the priest, who was grati-fied by a compliment I had previously paid to his talents, shook me heartily by the hand, and said, I was the most generous opponent he had ever met with. Then taking up his book, was suffered to proceed in its perusal uninterrupted. During the whole of the evening, Glorvina maintained an uninterrupted silence; she appeared lost in thought, and unmindful of our conversation, while her eyes, some-times turned to me, but oftener on her father, seemed humid with a tear, as she contemplated his lately much altered appearance. Yet when the debility of the man was for a moment lost in the energy of the patriot, I perceived the mind of the daughter kind-ling at the sacred fire which illumined the father's; and through the tear of natural affection sparkled the bright beam of national enthusiasm.

I suspect that the embassy of the good priest is not of the most pleasant nature. To-night, as he left me at the door of my room, he said, that we had a long journey before us; for that the house of the nobleman to whom we were going lay in a remote part of the province of Ulster; that he was a Scotchman, and only occasionally visited this country (where he had an immense property) to receive his rents. 'The prince (said he) holds a large but unprofitable farm from this highland chief, the lease of which he is anxious to throw up: that surly-looking fellow who dined with us the other day is his steward; and if the master is as inexorable as the servant, we shall undertake this journey to very little purpose.'

Adieu—I endeavour to write and think on every subject but that nearest my heart, yet *there* Glorvina and her mysterious friend still awaken the throb of jealous doubt and anxious solicitude. I shall drop this for you in the post-office of the first post-town I pass though; and probably endeavour to forget myself, and my anxiety to return hither, at your expence, by writing to you in the course of my journey.

Adieu,

H.M.

LETTER XXVI

TO J.D. ESQ. M.P.

Can you recollect who was that rational moderate youth who exclaimed in the frenzy of passion, 'O Gods! annihilate both *time* and *space*, and make two lovers happy.'

For my part, I should indeed wish the hours annihilated till I again behold Glorvina; but for the space which divides us, it was requisite I should be fifty miles from her to be more entirely with her; to appreciate the full value of her society; and to learn the nature of those wants my heart must ever feel when separated from her. The priest and I arose this morning with the sun. Our lovely hostess was ready at the breakfast-table to receive us. I was so selfish as to observe without regret the air of languor that invested her whole form, and the heaviness that weighed down her eye-lids, as though the influence of sleep had not renovated the lustre of those downcast eyes they veiled. Ah! if I dared believe that these wakeful hours were given to me. But I fear at that moment her heart was more occupied by her father than her lover: for I have observed, in a thousand instances, the interest she takes in his affairs; and indeed the priest hinted to me, that her good sense has frequently retrieved those circumstances the imprudent speculations of her father have as constantly deranged.

During breakfast she spoke but little, and once I caught her eyes turned full on me, with a glance in which tenderness, regret, and even something of despondency was mingled. Glorvina despond! So young, so lovely, so virtuous, and so highly gifted! Oh! at that moment had I been master of worlds! But, dependent myself on another's will, I could only sympathize in the sufferings while I adored the sufferer.

When we arose to depart, Glorvina said, 'If you will lead your horses I will walk to the draw-bridge with you.'

Delighted at the proposal, we ordered our horses to follow us; and with an arm of Glorvina drawn through either of ours, we left the castle.—'This,' said I, pressing the hand which rested on mine, 'is commencing a journey under favourable auspices.'

'God send it may be so!' said Glorvina fervently.

'Amen!' said the priest.

'Amen!' I repeated; and looking at Glorvina, read all the daughter in her eyes.

'We shall sleep to-night,' said the priest, endeavouring to dissipate the gloom which hung over us by indifferent chit-chat; 'we shall sleep to-night at the hospitable mansion of a true-born *Milesian*, to whom I have the honour to be distantly allied; and where you will find the old *Brehon* law,* which forbids that a sept* should suddenly break up lest the traveller should be disappointed of the expected feast, was no fabrication of national partiality.'

'What, then,' said I, 'we shall not enjoy ourselves in all the comfortable unrestrained freedom of *an inn*?'

'We poor Irish,' said the priest, 'find the unrestrained freedom of an inn not only in the house of every friend, but of every acquaintance however distant; and indeed if you are at all known, you may travel from one end of a province to another without entering a house of public entertainment;[1] the host always considering himself the debtor of the guest, as though the institution of the *Beataghs*[2] were still in being. And besides a cordial welcome from my hospitable kinsman, I promise you an introduction to his three handsome daughters. So fortify your heart, for I warn you it will run some risk before you return.'

'Oh!' said Glorvina archly, 'I dare say that, like St Paul, he will "count it all joy to fall into divers temptations."'

'Or rather,' returned I, 'I shall court them, like the saints of old, merely to prove my powers of resistance; for I bear a charmed spell about me; and *now* "none of *woman born* can harm *Macbeth*."'*

'And of what nature is your spell?' said Glorvina smiling, while the priest remained a little behind us talking to a peasant. 'Has father John given you a gospel? or have you got an amulet, thrice passed through the *thrice blessed* girdle of St Bridget, our great Irish charm?'[3]

'My charm,' returned I, 'in some degree certainly partakes of your religious and national superstitions; for since it was presented me by YOUR hand, I could almost believe that its very *essence* has been changed by a touch!' And I drew from my breast the withered remains of my once blooming rose. At that moment the priest joined us; and though Glorvina was silent, I felt the pressure of her arm more heavily on mine, and saw her pass the draw-bridge without a recollection on her part that it was to have been the boundary of her walk. We had not, however, proceeded many paces, when the most

[1] 'Not only have I been received with the greatest kindness, but I have been provided with every thing which could promote the execution of my plan. In taking the circuit of Ireland I have been employed eight or nine months; during which time I have been every where received with an hospitality which is nothing surprising in Ireland: that in such a length of time I have been but six times at an inn will give a better idea of this hospitality than could be done by the most laboured praise.' *M. de Latocknay.*

[2] In the excellent system of the ancient Milesian government, the people were divided into classes;—the *Literati* holding the next rank to royalty itself, and the *Beataghs* the fourth; so that as in China the state was so well regulated, that every one knew his place from the prince to the peasant. 'These Beataghs,' says M. O'Halleran, 'were keepers of open houses for strangers or poor distressed natives; and as honorable stipends were settled on the Literati, so were particular tracts of land on the Beataghs to support, with proper munificence, their station; and there are lands and villages in many places to this day which declare by their names their original appointment.'

[3] On St Bridget's day it is usual for the young people to make a long girdle or rope of straw, which they carry about to the neighbouring houses, and through which all persons who have faith in the charm pass nine times, uttering at each time a certain form of prayer in Irish, which they thus conclude: 'If I enter this thrice-blessed girdle, well may I come out of it nine times better.'

wildly mournful sounds I ever heard rose on the air and slowly died away.

'Hark!' said Glorvina, 'some one is going to *"that bourne from whence no traveller returns."*' As she spoke an hundred voices seemed to ascend to the skies; and, as they subsided, a fainter strain lingered on the air, as though this truly savage choral symphony was reduced to a recitativo, chanted by female voices. All that I had heard of the *Irish howl*, or funeral song, now rushed to my recollection; and turning at that moment the angle of the mountain of Inismore, I perceived a procession advancing towards a little cemetery, which lay by a narrow path-way to the left of the road.

The body, in a plain deal coffin, covered with a white shirt, was carried by four men, immediately preceded by several old women, covered in their mantles, and who sung at intervals in a wild and rapid tone.[1] Before them walked a number of young persons of both sexes, each couple holding by a white handkerchief, and strewing flowers along the path. An elderly woman, with eyes overflown with tears, disheveled hair, and distracted mien, followed the body, uttering many passionate exclamations in Irish; and the procession was filled up by upwards of three hundred people; the recitative of the female choristers relieved at intervals by the combined howlings of the whole body. In one of the pauses of this dreadful death-chorus, I expressed to Glorvina my surprize at the multitude which attended the funeral of a peasant, while we stood on a bank as they passed us.

'The lower order of Irish,' she returned, 'entertain a kind of post-humous pride respecting their funerals; and from sentiments that I have heard them express, I really believe there are many among them who would prefer living neglected to the idea of dying unmourned, or unattended, by a host to their last home.' To my astonishment she then descended the bank, and, accompanied by the priest, mingled with the crowd.

'This will surprise you,' said Glorvina; 'but it is wise to comply

[1] Speaking of the ancient Irish funeral, Mr Walker observes:—'Women, whose voices recommended them, were taken from the lower classes of life, and instructed in music, and the *cur sios*, or elegiac measure, that they might assist in heightening the melancholy which that ceremony was calculated to inspire. This custom prevailed among the Hebrews, from whom it is not improbable we had it immediately.'

  Dr Campbell is of opinion that the word *Ululate* or *hullalor*, the choral burden of the Caoine, and the Greek word of the same import, have a strong affinity to each other. *Phil. Surv. of South of Ireland*, Letter 2, 3.

with those prejudices which we cannot vanquish. And by those poor people it is not only reckoned a mark of great disrespect not to follow a funeral (met by chance) a few paces, but almost a species of impiety.' 'And mankind, you know,' added the priest, 'are always more punctilious with respect to ceremonials than fundamentals. However *you should* see an Irish Roman Catholic funeral; to a protestant and a stranger it must be a spectacle of some interest.

'With respect to the attendant ceremonies on death,' he continued, 'I know of no country which the Irish at present resemble but the modern Greeks. In both countries when the deceased dies unmarried, the young attendants are chiefly dressed in white, carrying garlands, and strewing flowers as they proceed to the grave. Those old women who sing before the body are professional *improvisatori*; they are called *Caoiners* or *Keeners*, from the *Caoine* or death song, and are *hired* to celebrate the virtues of the deceased. Thus we find St Chrysostom censuring the Greeks of his day, for the purchased lamentations and hireling mourners that attended their funerals. And so far back with us as in the days of druidical influence, we find it was part of the profession of the bards to perform the funeral ceremonies, to sing to their harps the virtues of the dead, and to call on the living to emulate their deeds.[1] This you may remember is a custom frequently alluded to in the poems of Ossian.[2] Pray

---

[1] The *Caoine*, or funeral song, was composed by the *Filea* of the departed, set to music by one of his oirfidegh, and sung over the grave by the racasaide, or rhapsodist, who accompanied his 'song of the tomb' with the mourning murmur of his harp, while the inferior order of minstrels at intervals mingled their deep-toned chorus with the strain of grief, and the sighs of lamenting relatives breathed in unison to the tuneful sorrow. Thus was 'the stones of his fame' raised over the remains of the Irish chief with a ceremony resembling that with which the death of the Trojan hero was lamented:
    'A melancholy choir attend around,
    With plaintive sighs and music's solemn sound.'
But the singular ceremonies of the Irish funeral, which are even still in a certain degree extant, may be traced to a remoter antiquity than Grecian origin; for the pathetic lamentations of David for the friend of his soul, and the *conclamatio* breathed over the Phœnician Dido, has no faint coincidence to the *Caoine* or funeral song of the Irish.

[2] Thus over the tomb of Cucullin vibrated the song of the bard:—'Blest be thy soul, son of Semo! thou wert mighty in battle, thy strength was like the strength of the stream, thy speed like the speed of the eagle's wing, thy path in the battle was terrible, the steps of death were behind thy sword; bless be thy soul, son of Semo! Car-borne chief of Dunscaith. The mighty were dispersed at Temora—there is none in Cormac's hall. The king mourns in his youth, for he does not behold thy coming; the sound of thy shield is ceased, his foes are gathering round. Soft be thy rest in thy cave, chief of Erin's wars.'

observe that frantic woman who tears her hair and beats her bosom:—It is the mother of the deceased. She is following her only child to an early grave; and did you understand the nature of her lamentations you would compare them to the complaints of the mother of Euriales in the Eneid:*—the same passionate expressions of sorrow, and the same wild extravagance of grief. They even still most religiously preserve here that custom never lost among the Greeks, of washing the body before interment, and strewing it with flowers.'

'And have you also,' said I, 'the funeral feast, which among the Greeks composed so material a part of the funeral ceremonies?'

'A *wake*, as it is called among us,' he replied, 'is at once the season of lamentation and sorrow, and of feasting and amusement. The immediate relatives of the deceased sit near the body, devoted to all the luxury of woe, which revives into the most piercing lamentations at the entrance of every stranger, while the friends, acquaintances, and guests give themselves up to a variety of amusements; feats of dexterity, and even some exquisite pantomimes are performed; though in the midst of all their games should any one pronounce an *Ave Maria*, the merry groupe are in a moment on their knees; and the devotional impulse being gratified, they recommence their sports with new vigour. The *wake*, however, is of short duration; for here, as in Greece, it is thought an injustice to the dead to keep them long above ground; so that interment follows death with all possible expedition.'

We had now reached the burial ground; near which the funeral was met by the parish priest, and the procession went three times round the cemetery, preceded by the priest, who repeated the *De profundis*, as did all the congregation.

'This ceremony,' said Father John, 'is performed by us instead of the funeral service, which is denied to the Roman Catholics. For *we* are not permitted, like the protestant ministers, to perform the last solemn office for our departed fellow creatures.'

While he spoke we entered the church yard, and I expressed my surprise to Glorvina, who seemed wrapt in solemn meditation, at the singular appearance of this rustic little cemetery, where instead of the monumental marble,

'The storied urn, or animated bust,'

an osier,* twisted into the form of a cross, wreathed with faded foliage, garlands made of the pliant sally, twined with flowers; alone distinguished the 'narrow house,' where

'The rude forefathers of the hamlet slept.'

Without answering, she led me gently forward towards a garland which seemed newly planted. We paused. A young woman who had attended the funeral, and withdrawn from the crowd, approached the garland at the same moment, and taking some fresh gathered flowers from her apron, strewed them over the new made grave, then kneeling beside it wept, and prayed. 'It is the tomb of her lover,' said I.—'*Of her Father!*' said Glorvina, in a voice whose affecting tone sunk to my heart, while her eyes, raised to heaven, were suffused with tears. The filial mourner now arose and departed, and we approached the simple shrine of her sorrowing devotion. Glorvina took from it a sprig of rosemary—its leaves were humid! 'It is not *all* dew,' said Glorvina with a sad smile, while her own tears fell on it, and she presented it to me.

'Then you think me worthy of sharing in these divine feelings,' I exclaimed as I kissed off the sacred drops; while I was now confirmed in the belief that the tenderness, the sufferings, and declining health of her father rendered him at that moment the sole object of her solicitude and affection. And with him only could I, without madness, share the tender, sensible, angelic heart of this sweet interesting being.

Observing her emotion increase, as she stood near the spot sacred to filial grief, I endeavoured to draw away her attention by remarking, that almost every tomb had now a votarist. 'It is a strong instance,' said Glorvina, 'of the sensibility of the Irish, that they repair at intervals to the tombs of their deceased friends to drop a tender tear, or heave a heart-breathed sigh, to the memory of those so lamented in death, so dear to them in life. For my own part, in the stillness of a fine evening, I often wander towards this solemn spot, where the flowers newly thrown on the tombs, and weeping with the tears of departed day, always speak to my heart a tale of woe it feels and understands. While, as the breeze of evening mourns softly round me, I involuntarily exclaim, "And when *I* shall follow the crowd that presses forward to eternity, what affectionate hand will scatter flowers over *my* solitary tomb; for haply ere that period arrive, *my* trembling hand shall have placed the cypress on the tomb of him who alone loved me living, and would lament me dead."'

'*Alone*!' I repeated, and pressing her hand to my heart, inarticulately added, 'Oh! Glorvina, did the pulses which now throb against each other throb in unison, you would understand, that even *love* is a cold inadequate term for the sentiments you have inspired in a soul, which would claim a closer kindred to yours than even parental affinity can assert; if (though but by a glance) yours would deign to acknowledge the sacred union.'

We were standing in a remote part of the cemetery, under the shade of a drooping cypress—we were alone—we were unobserved. The hand of Glorvina was pressed to my heart, her head almost touched my shoulders, her lips almost effused their balmy sighs on mine. A glance was all I required—a glance was all I received.

In the succeeding moments I know not what passed; for an interval all was delirium. Glorvina was the first to recover presence of mind; she released her hand, which was still pressed to my heart, and covered with blushes advanced to Father John. I followed, and found her with her arm entwined in his, while those eyes from whose glance my soul had lately quaffed the essence of life's richest bliss, were now studiously turned from me in love's own downcast bashfulness.

The good Father Director now took my arm; and we were leaving this (to me), interesting spot, when the filial mourner who had first drawn us from his side, approached the priest, and taking out a few shillings from the corner of her handkerchief, offered them to him, and spoke a few words in Irish; the priest returned her an answer and her money at the same time: she curtseyed low, and departed in silent and tearful emotion. At the same moment another female advanced towards us, and put a piece of silver and a little fresh earth into the hand of Father John; he blessed the earth and returned the little offering with it. The woman knelt and wept, and kissed his garment; then addressing him in Irish, pointed to a poor old man, who, apparently overcome with weakness, was reposing on the grass. Father John followed the woman, and advanced to the old man, while I, turning towards Glorvina, demanded an explanation of this extraordinary scene.

'The first of those poor creatures,' said she, 'was offering the fruits of many an hour's labour to have a mass said for the soul of her departed father, which she firmly believes will shorten his sufferings

in purgatory: the last is another instance of weeping humanity stealing from the rites of superstition a solace for its woes. She brought
that earth to the priest, that he might bless it ere it was flung into the
coffin of a dear friend, who, she says, died this morning; for they
believe that this consecrated earth is a substitute for those religious
rites which are denied them on this awful occasion. And though
these tender cares of mourning affection may originate in error, who
would not pardon the illusion, that soothes the sufferings of a breaking heart? Alas! I could almost envy these ignorant prejudices, which
lead their possessors to believe, that by restraining their own enjoyments in this world, they can alleviate the sufferings, or purchase the
felicity of the other for the objects of their tenderness and regret.
Oh! that I could thus believe!'

'Then you do not,' said I, looking earnestly at her, 'you do not
receive all the doctrines of your church as infallible?'

Glorvina approached something closer towards me, and in a few
words convinced me that on the subject of religion, as upon every
other, her strong mind discovered itself to be an emanation of that
divine intelligence, which her pure soul worships 'in spirit and in
truth,'

> 'The bright effluence of bright essence uncreate.'

When she observed my surprise and delight, she added, 'believe
me, my dear friend, the age in which religious error held her empire
undisputed, is gone by. The human mind, however slow, however
opposed its progress, is still, by a divine and invariable law, propelled
towards truth, and must finally attain that goal which reason has
erected in every breast. Of the many who are the inheritors of *our*
persuasion, *all* are not devoted to its errors, or influenced by its
superstitions. If its professors are coalesced, it is in the sympathy of
their destinies, not in the dogmas of their belief. If they are allied, it
is by the tye of temporal interest, not by the bond of speculative
opinion; they are united as *men*, not as sectaries; and once incorporated in the great mass of general society, their feelings will become
diffusive as their interests; their affections, like their privileges, will
be in common; the limited throb with which their hearts now beat
towards each other, under the influence of a kindred fate, will then
be animated to the nobler pulsation of universal philanthropy; and,
as the acknowledged members of the first of all human communities,

they will forget they had ever been the *individual* adherents of an alienated body.'

The priest now returned to us, and was followed by the multitude, who crowded round this venerable and adored pastor: some to obtain his benediction for themselves, others his prayers for their friends, and all his advice or notice; while Glorvina, whom they had not at first perceived, stood like an idol in the midst of them, receiving that adoration which the admiring gaze of some, and the adulatory exclamations of others, offered to her virtues and her charms. While those personally known to her, she addressed with her usual winning sweetness in their native language, I am sure that there was not an individual among this crowd of ardent and affectionate people that would not risk their lives 'to avenge a look that threatened her with danger.'

Our horses now coming up to the gate of the cemetery, we insisted on walking back as far as the draw-bridge with Glorvina. When we reached it, the priest saluted her cheek with paternal freedom, and gave her his blessing. While I was put off with an offer of the hand; but when, for the first time, I felt its soft clasp return the pressure of mine, I no longer envied the priest his cold salute; for oh! cold is every enjoyment which is unreciprocated. Reverberated bliss alone can touch the heart.

When we had parted with Glorvina, and caught a last view of her receding figure, we mounted our horses and proceeded a considerable way in silence. The morning though fine was gloomy; and though the sun was scarcely an hour high, we were met by innumerable groupes of peasantry of both sexes, laden with their implements of husbandry, and already beginning the labours of the day. I expressed my surprise at observing almost as many women as men working in the fields and bogs. 'Yes,' said the priest, 'toil is here shared in common between the sexes, the women as well as the men cut the turf, sow the potatoes, and even assist to cultivate the land; both rise with the sun to their daily labour; but his repose brings not theirs; for after having worked all day for a very trivial remuneration (as nothing here is rated at a lower price than human labour), they endeavour to snatch a beam from retreating twilight; by which they labour in that little spot of ground, which is probably the sole support of a numerous family.'

'And yet,' said I, 'idleness is the chief vice laid to the account of your peasantry.'

'It is certain,' returned he, 'that there is not, generally speaking, that active spirit of industry among the inferior orders here, which distinguishes the same rank in England. But neither have they the same encouragement to awaken their exertions. "The laziness of the Irish," says Sir William Petty,* "seems rather to proceed from want of employment, and encouragement to work, than the constitution of their bodies." And an intelligent and liberal countryman of yours, Mr Young,* the celebrated traveller, is persuaded that, circumstances considered, the Irish do not in reality deserve the character of indolence; and relates a very extraordinary proof of their great industry and exertion in their method of procuring lime for manure; which the mountaineers bring on the backs of their little horses many miles distance, to the foot of the steepest acclivities; and from thence to the summit on their own shoulders, while they pay a considerable rent for liberty to cultivate a barren, waste, and rigid soil. In short, there is not in the creation a more laborious animal than an Irish peasant, with less stimulus to exertion, or less reward to crown his toil.[1] He is indeed in many instances the creature of the soil, and works independent of that hope, which is the best stimulus to every human effort, the hope of reward. And yet it is not rare to find among these oft misguided beings, some who really believe themselves the hereditary proprietors of the soil they cultivate.'

'But surely,' said I, 'the most ignorant among them must be well aware that all could not have been proprietors?'

'The fact is,' said the priest, 'the followers of many a great family having anciently adopted the name of their chiefs, that name has descended to their progeny, who now associate to the name an erroneous claim on the confiscated property of those to whom their progenitors were but vassals or dependants.[2] And this false but strong

---

[1] 'Si le pauvre voyait clairement que la travail pouvoit ameliorer sa situation, il abandonneroit bientot cette apathie, cette indifference qui au fait n'est que l'habitude du desespoir.'* *M. de la Tocknay.*

[2] Although ignorance and interest may cherish this erroneous opinion, its existence is only to be traced among some of the lower orders of Irish, but its influence seldom extends to a superior rank, among many of whom are to be found the *real* descendants of those whose estates were forfeited shortly after the English invasion, and during the reigns of James the First, Oliver Cromwell and William the Third, *particularly. They* consider that 'The property has now been so long vested in the hands of the present proprietors that the interests of justice and utility would be more offended by dispossessing them than they could be advanced by reinstating the original owners.' And that a 'term of prescription is always paramount to the rights of lineal descent.'

rooted opinion, co-operating with their naturally active and impetuous characters, renders them alive to every enterprize, and open to
the impositions of the artful or ambitious. But a brave, though misguided, people is not to be dragooned out of a train of ancient
prejudices, nurtured by fancied interest and real ambition, and confirmed by ignorance, which those who deride, have made no effort to
dispel. It is not by physical force, but moral influence, the illusion is
to be dissolved. The darkness of ignorance must be dissipated before
the light of truth can be admitted, and though an Irishman may be
argued out of an error, it has been long proved he will never be
forced. His understanding may be convinced, but his spirit will
never be subdued. He may culminate to the meridian of loyalty[1] or
truth by the influence of kindness, or the convictions of reason, but
he will never be forced towards the one, nor oppressed into the other,
by the lash of power, or the "insolence of office."

'This has been strongly evinced by the attachment of the Irish to
the House of Stuart,* by whom they have always been so cruelly, so
ungratefully treated. For what the coercive measures of 400 years
could not effect, the accession of *one* prince to the throne accomplished. Until that period, the unconquered Irish, harassing and
harassed, struggled for that liberty which they at intervals obtained,
but never were permitted to enjoy. Yet the moment a Prince of the
Royal line of Milesius placed the British diadem* on his brow, the
sword of resistance was sheathed, and those principles which force
could not vanquish yielded to the mild empire of national and hereditary affection: the Irish of *English* origin from natural tenderness,
and those of the *true old stock*, from the firm conviction that they
were *then* governed by a *Prince* of their own blood. Nor is it now
unknown to them that in the veins of his present Majesty, and his
ancestors, from James the First, flows the Royal blood of the *three*
kingdoms united.'

'I am delighted to find,' said I, 'the lower ranks of a country, to
which I am now so endeared, thus rescued from the obloquy thrown
on them by prejudiced illiberality; and from what you have said, and

---

[1] Speaking of the people of Ireland, Lord Minto thus expresses himself. 'In these
(the Irish) we have witnessed exertions of courage, activity, perseverance, and spirit, as
well as *fidelity* and *honour* in fulfilling the engagements of their connexion with us, and
the protection and defence of their own country, which challenges the thanks of Great
Britain, and the approbation of the world.'

indeed from what I have myself observed, I am convinced that were endeavours[1] for their improvement more strictly promoted, and their respective duties obviously made clear, their true interests fully represented by reason and common sense, and their unhappy situations ameliorated by justice and humanity, they would be a people as happy, contented, and prosperous, in a political sense, as in a natural and a national one. They are brave, hospitable, liberal, and ingenious.'

We now continued to proceed through a country, rich in all the boundless extravagance of picturesque beauty, where Nature's sublimest features every where present themselves, carelessly disposed in wild magnificence; unimproved, and, indeed, almost unimproveable by art. The far-stretched ocean, mountains of alpine magnitude, heaths of boundless desolation, vales of romantic loveliness, navigable rivers, and extensive lakes, alternately succeeding to each other, while the ruins of an ancient castle, or the mouldering remains of a desolated abbey, gave a moral interest to the pleasure derived from the contemplation of Nature in her happiest and most varied aspect.

'Is it not extraordinary,' said I, as we loitered over the ruins of an abbey, 'that though your country was so long before the introduction of christianity inhabited by a learned and ingenious people, yet that among your gothic ruins, no traces of a more ancient and splendid architecture are to be discovered. From the ideas I have formed of the primeval grandeur of Ireland, I should almost expect to see a Balbec or Palmyra* rising amidst these stupendous mountains, and picturesque scenes.'

'My dear Sir,' he replied, 'a country may be civilized, enlightened, and even learned and ingenious, without attaining to any considerable perfection in those arts, which give to posterity *sensible* memorials of its passed splendour. The ancient Irish, like the modern, had more *soul*, more genius, than worldly prudence, or cautious calculating forethought. The feats of the hero engrossed them more

[1] 'Connomara (says Mr de la Tocknay in his Travels through Ireland,) a district in the county of Galway, sixty miles long, and forty broad, is less known than the islands in the Pacific Ocean; and, consequently, the people remain much in their natural uncultivated state. But it is an error to suppose, that even in this sequestered spot the peasants are either ignorant or stupid. On the contrary, I never saw any class of men better disposed to serve their country; and though their huts are miserable, and their general situation comparatively wretched, they are humane and would be industrious, if they found that labour and industry produced advantage or amelioration.'

than the exertions of the mechanist; works of imagination seduced them from pursuing works of utility. With an enthusiasm, bordering on a species of *mania*, were they devoted to poetry and music; and to "*Wake the soul of song*" was to them an object of more interesting importance, than to raise that edifice which would betray to posterity their ancient grandeur; besides, at that period to which you allude, the Irish were in that era of society, when the iron age was yet distant, and the artist confined his skill to the elegant workmanship of gold and brass, which is ascertained by the number of warlike implements and beautiful ornaments of dress of those metals, exquisitely worked, which are still frequently found in the bogs of Ireland.'

'If, however,' said I, 'there are no remnants of a Laurentinum, or Tusculum,* to be discovered, I perceive that at every ten or twelve miles, in the fattest of the land, the ruins of an abbey and its granaries are discernible.'

'Why,' returned the priest laughing, 'you would not have the good father abbots advise the dying but generous sinner to leave the *worst* of his lands to God! that would be sacrilege—but besides the voluntary donation of *estates* from rich penitents, the regular monks of Ireland had *landed properties* attached to their convents. Sometimes they possessed immense tracts of a country, from which the officiating clergy seldom or ever derived any benefit; and I believe that many, if not *most*, of the bishops' leases now existing are the confiscated revenues of these ruined abbeys.'

'So,' said I, 'after all it is only a transfer of property from one opulent ecclesiastic to another;[1] and the great difference between the luxurious abbot of other times, and the rich church dignitary of the present, lies in a few speculative theories which, whether they are or are not consonant to reason and common sense, have certainly no connexion with *true* religion or *true* morality. While the bishopricks now, like the abbeys of old, are estimated rather by the profit gained to the temporal, than the harvest reaped to the heavenly Lord. However I suppose they borrow a sanction from the perversion of scriptural authority, and quote the Jewish law, not intended for the benefit of *individuals* to the detriment of a whole body, but which extended

---

[1] For instance, the abbey of Raphoe was founded by St Columbkill, who was succeeded in it by St Eanon. The first Bishop of Raphoe having converted the abbey into a cathedral see. It is now a protestant bishoprick.

to the whole tribe of Levi, and doubtlessly strengthen it by a sentiment of St Paul:* "If we sow unto you spiritual things is it not just we reap your carnal, etc." It is, however, lucky for your country that your abbots are not as numerous in the present day as formerly.'

'Numerous, indeed, as you perceive,' said the priest, 'by these ruins; for we are told in the Life of St Rumoloi, that there were a greater number of monks and superb monasteries in Ireland than in any other part of Europe. St Columbkill,* and his cotemporaries, alone erected in this kingdom upwards of 200 abbeys, if their biographers are to be credited; and the luxury of their governors kept pace with their power and number.

'In the abbey of Enis a sanctuary was provided for the cowls of the friars and the veils of the nuns, which were costly and beautifully wrought. We read that, knights excepted, the prelates only were allowed to have gold bridles and harnesses; and that among the rich presents bestowed by Bishop Snell, in 1146, on a cathedral, were gloves, pontificals, sandals, and silken robes, interwoven with golden spots, and adorned with precious stones.

'There is a monument of monkish luxury still remaining among the interesting ruins of Sligo Abbey. This noble edifice stands in the midst of a rich and beautiful scenery, on the banks of a river, near which is a spot still shewn, where (as the tradition runs) a box or weir was placed in which the fish casually entered, and which contained a spring that communicated, by a cord, with a bell hung in the refectory. The weight of the fish pressed down the spring; the cord vibrated; the bell rung; and the unfortunate captive thus taken suffered martyrdom, by being placed on the fire alive.'

'And was served up,' said I, 'I suppose on a fast day, to the *abstemious* monks, who would, however, have looked upon a morsel of flesh meat thrown in this way as a lure to eternal perdition.'

Already weary of a conversation in which my heart took little interest, I now suffered it to die away; and while father John began a parley with a traveller who socially joined us, I gave up my whole soul to love and to Glorvina.

In the course of the evening we arrived at the house of our destined host. Although it was late the family had not yet gone to dinner, as the servant who took our horses informed us that his master had but that moment returned from a fair. We had scarcely reached the hall, when, the report of our arrival having preceded our appearance, the whole family rushed out to receive us. What a group!—the father looking like the very *Genius of Hospitality*, the mother like the personified spirit of a cordial welcome, three laughing *Hebe* daughters, two fine young fellows supporting an aged grandsire (a very *Silenus** in appearance), and a pretty demure little governess with a smile and a hand ready as the others.

The priest, according to the good old Irish fashion, saluted the cheeks of the ladies, and had his hands nearly shaken off by the men; while I was received with all the cordiality that could be lavished on a friend, and all the politeness that could be paid to a stranger. A welcome shone in every eye; ten thousand welcomes echoed from every lip; and the arrival of the unexpected guests seemed a festival of the social feelings to the whole warm-hearted family. If this is a true specimen of the first rites of hospitality among the *independent country gentlemen of Ireland*,[1] it is to me the most captivating of all possible ceremonies.

When the first interchange of courtesies had passed on both sides, we were conducted to the refreshing comforts of a dressing-room; but the domestics were not suffered to interfere, all were in fact our servants.

The plenteous dinner was composed of every luxury the season afforded; though only supplied by the demesne of our host and the neighbouring sea-coast, and though served up in a style of perfect elegance, was yet so abundant, so *over plenteous*, that compared to the compact neatness and simple sufficiency of English fare in the same rank of life, it might have been thought to have been 'more than hospitably good.' But to my surprize, and indeed not much to my satisfaction, during dinner the door was left open for the benefit of receiving the combined efforts of a very indifferent fiddler and a tolerable piper, who, however, seemed to hold the life and spirits of the family in their keeping. The ladies left us early after the cloth was removed; and though besides the family there were three strange gentlemen, and that the table was covered with excellent wines, yet conversation circulated with much greater freedom than the bottle; every one did as he pleased, and the ease of the guest seemed the

---

[1] To those who have witnessed (as I so often have) the celebration of these endearing rites, this picture will appear but a very cold and languid sketch.

pleasure of the host.[1] For my part, I arose in less than an hour after the retreat of the ladies, and followed them to the drawing-room. I found them all employed; one at the piano, another at her work, a third reading; mamma at her knitting, and the pretty little duenna* copying out music.

They received me as an old acquaintance, and complimented me on my temperance in so soon retiring from the gentlemen, for which I assured them they had all the credit. It is certain, that the frank and open ingenuousness of an Irishwoman's manners forms a strong contrast to that placid but distant reserve which character-izes the address of my own charming countrywomen. For my part, since I have known Glorvina, I shall never again endure that per-petuity of air, look, and address, which those who mistake formality for good-breeding are so apt to assume. Manners, like the graduated scale of the thermometer, should betray, by degrees, the expansion or contraction of the feelings, as they are warmed by emotion or chilled by indifference. They should *breathe* the soul in order to *win* it.

Nothing could be more animated yet more modest than the man-ners of these charming girls; nor should I require any stronger proof of that pure and exquisite chastity of character which, from the earliest period, has distinguished the women of this country, than that ingenuous candour and enchanting frankness which accompan-ies their every look and word.

> 'The soul as sure to be admired as seen,
> Boldly steps forth, nor keeps a thought within.'

But although the Miss O'D——s are very charming girls, although their mother seems a very rational and amiable being, and although their governess appears to be a young woman of dis-tinguished education and considerable talent; yet I in vain sought in their conversation for that soul-seizing charm which with a magic undefinable influence breathes round the syren *princess of Inismore.* O! it was requisite I should mingle, converse, with other women to justly appreciate all I possess in the society of Glorvina; for surely she is *more*, or every other woman is *less*, than mortal!

[1] 'Drunkenness ought no longer to be a reproach to them; for any table I was at in Ireland I saw a perfect freedom reign, every person drank as little as they pleased, nor have I ever been asked to drink a single glass more than I had an inclination for. I may go farther, and assert, that hard drinking is very rare among people of fortune; yet it is certain that they sit much longer at table than in England.' *Young's Tour through Ireland, etc.*

Before the men joined us in the drawing-room, I was quite *boudoir-ized* with these unaffected and pleasing girls. One wound her working-silk off my hands, another would try my skill at battledore,* and the youngest, a charming little being of thirteen, told me the history of a pet dove that was dying in her lap; while all intreated I would talk to them of the princess of Inismore.

'For my part,' said the youngest girl, 'I always think of her as of the Sleeping Beauty in the Wood, or some other princess in a fairy tale.'

'We know nothing of her, however,' said Mrs O'D——, 'but by report; we live at too great a distance to keep up any connexion with the Inismore family; besides that it is generally understood to be Mr O'Melville's wish to live in retirement.'

This is the first time I ever heard my soi-disant prince mentioned without his title; but I am sure I should never endure to hear my Glorvina called Miss O'Melville. For to me too does she appear more like the Roganda of a fairy tale than 'any mortal mixture of earth's mould.'

The gentlemen now joined us, and as soon as tea was over the piper struck up in the hall, and in a moment every one was on their feet. My long journey was received as a sufficient plea for my being a spectator only; but the priest refused the immunity, and led out the lady mother; the rest followed, and the idol amusement of the gay-hearted Irish received its usual homage. But though the women danced with considerable grace and spirit, they did not, like Glorvina,

'Send the soul upon a jig to heaven.'

The dance was succeeded by a good supper; the supper by a cheerful song, and every one seemed unwilling to be the first to break up a social compact over which the spirit of harmony presided.

As the priest and I retired to our rooms, 'You have now,' said he, 'had a specimen of the mode of living of the Irish gentry of a certain rank in this country: the day is devoted to agricultural business, the evening to temperate festivity and innocent amusement; but neither the avocations of the morning nor the engagements of the evening suspend the rites of hospitality.'

Thus far I wrote before I retired that night to rest, and the next morning at an early hour we took our leave of these courteous and hospitable Milesians; having faithfully promised on the preceding night to repeat our visit on our return from the north.

We are now at a sorry little inn, within a mile or two of the nobleman's seat to whom the priest is come, and on whom he waits to-morrow, having just learned that his lordship passed by here to-day on his way to a gentleman's house in the neighbourhood, where he dines. The little post-boy at this moment rides up to the door; I shall drop this in his bag, and begin a new journal on a fresh sheet.

Adieu,

H.M.

LETTER XXVII

TO J.D. ESQ. M.P.

The priest is gone on his embassy. The rain which batters against the casement of my little hotel prevents my enjoying a ramble. I have nothing to read, and I must write or yawn myself to death.

Yesterday, as we passed the imaginary line which divides the province of Connaught from that of Ulster, the priest said, 'As we now advance northward, we shall gradually lose sight of the genuine Irish character, and those ancient manners, modes, customs, and language with which it is inseparably connected. Not long after the chiefs of Ireland had declared James the First universal monarch of their country, a sham plot was pretended, consonant to the usual ingratitude of the House of Stuart, by which six entire counties of the north became forfeited, which James with a liberal hand bestowed on his favourites;[1] so that this part of Ireland may in some respects be

---

[1] 'The pretext of rebellion was devised as a specious prelude to predetermined confiscations, and the inhabitants of six counties, whose aversion to the yoke of England the shew of lenity might have disarmed, were compelled to encounter misery in desarts, and, what is perhaps still more mortifying to human pride, to behold the patrimony of their ancestors, which force had wrested from their hands, bestowed the prey of a more favoured people. The substantial view of providing for his indigent countrymen might have gratified the national partiality of James; the favourite passion of the English was gratified by the triumph of protestantism, and the downfal of its antagonists: men who professed to correct a system of peace did not hesitate to pursue their purpose through a scene of iniquity which humanity shudders to relate; and by an action more criminal, because more deliberate, than the massacre of St Bartholomew,* two thirds of an extensive province were offered up in one great hecatomb, on the altar of false policy and theological prejudice. Here let us survey with wonder the mysterious operations of divine wisdom, which, from a measure base in its means, and atrocious in its execution, has derived a source of fame, freedom, and industry to Ireland.'—*Vide A Review of some interesting periods of Irish History.*

considered as a Scottish colony; and in fact, Scotch dialect, Scotch manners, Scotch modes, and the Scotch character almost universally prevail. Here the ardor of the Irish constitution seems abated, if not chilled. Here the *cead-mile falta* of Irish cordiality seldom lends its welcome home to the stranger's heart. The bright beams which illumine the gay images of Milesian fancy are extinguished; the convivial pleasures, dear to the Milesian heart, scared at the prudential maxims of calculating interest, take flight to the warmer regions of the south; and the endearing socialities of the soul, lost and neglected amidst the cold concerns of the counting-house and the *bleach green*, droop and expire in the deficiency of that nutritive warmth on which their tender existence depends. So much for the shades of the picture, which however possesses its lights, and those of no dim lustre. The north of Ireland may be justly esteemed the palladium of Irish industry and trade, where the staple commodity of the kingdom is reared and manufactured; and while the rest of Ireland is devoted to that species of agriculture, which, in lessening the necessity of human labour, deprives man of subsistence; while the wretched native of the Southern provinces (where little labour is required, and consequently little hire given) either famishes in the midst of an helpless family, or begs his way to England, and offers those services *there* in harvest time, which his own country rejects. Here, both the labourer and his hire rise in the scale of political consideration: here more hands are called for than can be procured; and the peasant, stimulated to exertions by the rewards it reaps for him, enjoys the fruits of his industry, and acquires a relish for the comforts and conveniencies of life. Industry, and this taste for comparative luxury, mutually re-act; and the former, while it bestows the *means*, enables them to gratify the suggestions of the latter; while their wants, nurtured by enjoyment, afford fresh allurement to continued exertion. In short, a mind not too deeply fascinated by the florid virtues, the warm overflowings of generous and ardent qualities, will find in the Northerns of this island much to admire and more to esteem; but on the heart they make little claims, and from its affections they receive but little tribute.'[1]

---

[1] Belfast cannot be deemed the *metropolis* of Ulster, but may almost be said to be the *Athens* of Ireland. It is at least the CYNOSURE of the province in which it stands; and those beams of genius which are there concentrated send to the extremest point of the hemisphere in which they shine, no faint ray of lumination.

'Then in the name of all that is warm and cordial,' said I, 'let us hasten back to the province of Connaught.'

'That you may be sure we shall (returned father John): for I know none of these sons of trade; and until we once more find ourselves within the pale of Milesian hospitality, we must set up at a sorry inn, near a tract of the sea coast, called the Magilligans, and where one *solitary fane* is raised to the once tutelar deity of Ireland; in plain English, where one of the last of the race of *Irish bards* shelters his white head beneath the fractured roof of a wretched hut.' Although the evening sun was setting on the western wave when we reached the auberge, yet, while our fried eggs and bacon were preparing, I proposed to the priest that we should visit the old bard before we put up our horses. Father John readily consented, and we enquired his address.

'What the *mon wi the twa heads?*' said our host. I confessed my ignorance of this hydra* epithet, which I learnt was derived from an immense wen* on the back of his head.

'O!' continued our host, 'A wull be telling you weel to gang tull the auld Kearn, and one of our wains wull shew the road. Ye need nae fear trusting yoursels to our wee Willy, for he os an uncommon canie chiel.' Such was the dialect of this Hibernian Scot, who assured me he had never been twenty miles from his 'aine wee hame.'

We however dispensed with the guidance of *wee Wully*, and easily found our way to the hut of the man '*wi the twa heads.*' It stood on the right hand by the road side. We entered it without ceremony, and as it is usual for strangers to visit this last of the 'Sons of Song,' his family betrayed no signs of surprize at our appearance. His ancient dame announced us to her husband. When we entered, he was in bed; and when he arose to receive us (for he was dressed, and appeared only to have lain down from debility), we perceived that his harp had been the companion of his repose, and was actually laid under the bed-clothes with him. We found the venerable bard cheerful[1] and communicative, and he seemed to enter even with an eager readiness on the circumstances of his past life, while his 'soul seemed heightened by the song,' with which at intervals he interrupted his

[1] The following account of the Bard of the Magilligans was taken from his own lips, July 3d, 1805, by the Rev. Mr Sampson, of Magilligan, and forwarded to the author (through the medium of Dr Patterson, of Derry) previous to her visit to that part of the North, which took place a few weeks after.

[*cont. on p. 200*]

Umbræ, July 3d, 1805,
Magilligan.

'I made the survey of the man with two heads, according to your desire; but not till yesterday on account of various *impossibilities*. Here is my report—

'Dennis Hampson, or the man with two heads, is a native of Craigmore, near Garvagh, county Derry; his father, Bryan Darrogher (blackish complexion) Hampson, held the whole town-land of Tyrcrevan; his mother's relations were in possession of the wood-town (both considerable farms in Magilligan). He lost his sight at the age of three years by the small-pox; at twelve years he began to learn the harp under Bridget O'Cahan: "For," as he said, "in those old times, *women* as well as men were taught the Irish harp in the best families; and every old Irish family had harps in plenty." His next master was John C. Garragher, a blind travelling harper, whom he followed to Buncranagh, where his master used to play for Colonel Vaughan: he had afterwards Laughlin Hanning and Pat Connor in succession as masters.

'All these were from Connaught, which was, as he added, "the best part of the kingdom for Irish music and for harpers." At eighteen years of age he began to play for himself, and was taken into the house of counsellor Canning, at Garvagh, for half a year; his host, with Squire Gage and Doctor Bacon, found and bought him an harp. He travelled nine or ten years through Ireland and Scotland, and tells facetious stories of gentlemen in both countries: among others, that in passing near the place of Sir J. Campbell, at Aghanbrack, he learned, that this gentleman had spent a great deal, and was living on so much per week of allowance. Hampson through delicacy would not call, but some of the domestics were sent after him; on coming into the castle, Sir J. asked him why he had not called, adding, "Sir, there was never a harper but yourself that passed the door of my father's house;" to which Hampson answered that, "he had heard in the *neighbourhood* that his honour was not often at home;" with which delicate evasion Sir J. was satisfied. He adds, "that this was the highest bred and stateliest man he ever knew; if he were putting on a new pair of gloves, and one of them dropped on the floor, (though ever so clean), he would order the servant to bring him another pair." He says that, in that time he never met but one laird that had a harp, and that was a very small one, played on formerly by the laird's father; that when he had tuned it with new strings the laird and his lady both were so pleased with his music that they invited him back in these words: "Hampson, as soon as you think this child of ours (a boy of three years of age), is fit to learn on his grandfather's harp, come back to teach him, and you shall not repent it;"—but this he never accomplished.

'He told me a story of the laird of Strone with a great deal of comic relish. When he was playing at the house, a message came that a large party of gentlemen were coming to grouse, and would spend some days with *him* (the laird); the lady being in great distress turned to her husband, saying, "What shall we do, my dear, for so many in the way of beds." "Give yourself no vexation," replied the laird, "give us enough to eat, and I will supply the rest; and as to beds, believe me *every man shall find one for himself*;" (meaning that his guests would fall under the table). In his second trip to Scotland, in the year 1745, being at Edinburgh, when *Charley* the Pretender was there, he was called into the great hall to play; at first he was alone, afterwards four fiddlers joined: the tune called for was, "The king shall enjoy his own again:"—he sung here part of the words following—

"I hope to see the day
When the Whigs shall run away,
And the king shall enjoy his own again."

'I asked him if he heard the Pretender speak; he replied—I only heard him ask, "Is Sylvan there;" on which some one answered, "He is not here please your royal highness, but he shall be sent for." He meant to say *Sullivan*, continued Hampson, but that was the way he called the name. He says that Captain Mc.Donnell, when in Ireland, came to see him, and that he told the captain that Charley's cockade was in his fathers house.

'Hampson was brought into the Pretender's presence by Colonel Kelly, of Roscomon, and Sir Thomas Sheridan, and that he (Hampson) was then above fifty years old. He played in many Irish houses; among others, those of Lord de Courcey, Mr Fortescue, Sir P. Belew, Squire Roche; and in the great towns, Dublin, Cork, etc. etc. Respecting all which he interspersed pleasant anecdotes with surprising gaiety and correctness. As to correctness, he mentioned many anecdotes of my grandfather and grand-aunt, at whose houses he used to be frequently. In fact, in this identical harper, whom you sent me to *survey*, I recognised an acquaintance, who, as soon as he found me out, seemed exhilirated at having an old friend of (what he called) "the old stock," in his poor cabin. He even mentioned many anecdotes of my own boyhood, which, though by me long forgotten, were accurately true. These things shew the surprising power of his recollection at the age of an hundred and eight years. Since I saw him last, which was in 1787, the wen on the back of his head is greatly increased; it is now hanging over his neck and shoulders, nearly as large as his head, from which circumstance he derives his appellative, "the man with two heads." General Hart, who is an admirer of music, sent a limner lately to take a drawing of him, which cannot fail to be interesting, if it were only for the venerable expression of his meagre blind countenance, and the symmetry of his tall, thin, but not debilitated, person. I found him lying on his back in bed near the fire of his cabin; his family employed in the usual way; his harp under the bed clothes, by which his face was covered also. When he heard my name he started up (being already dressed), and seemed rejoiced to hear the sound of my voice, which, he said, he began to recollect. He asked for my children, whom I brought to see him, and he felt them over and over;— then, with tones of great affection, he blessed *God* that he had *seen* four generations of the name, and ended by giving the children his blessing. He then tuned his old time-beaten harp, his solace and bedfellow, and played with astonishing justness and good taste.

'The tunes which he played were his favourites; and he, with an elegance of manner, said at the same time, I remember you have a fondness for music, and the tunes you used to ask for I have not forgotten, which were Cualin, The Dawning of the Day, Elleen-a-roon, Ceandubhdilis, etc. These, except the third, were the first tunes, which, according to regulation, he played at the famous meeting of harpers at Belfast, under the patronage of some amateurs of Irish music. Mr Bunton, the celebrated musician of that town, was here the year before, at Hampson's, noting his tunes and his manner of playing, which is in the best old style. He said, with the honest feeling of self love, "When I played the old tunes, not another of the harpers would play after me." He came to Magilligan many years ago, and at the age of eighty-six, married a woman of Innisowen, whom he found living in the house of a friend. "I can't tell," quoth Hampson, "if it was not the devil buckled us together; she being lame and I blind." By this wife he has one daughter, married to a cooper, who has several children, and maintains them all, though Hampson (in this alone seeming to doat), says, that his son-in-law is a spendthrift and that he maintains them; the family humour his whim, and the old man is quieted. He is pleased when they tell him, as he thinks is the case, that several people of character, for musical taste, send letters to invite him; and he, though incapable now of leaving the house, is planning expeditions never to be attempted, much less realized; these are the only traces of mental debility; as to his body, he has no inconvenience but that arising from a chronic disorder: his habits have ever been sober; his favourite drink, once beer, now milk and water; his diet chiefly *potatoes*. I asked him to teach my daughter, but he declined; adding, however, that it was too hard for a young girl, but that nothing would give him greater pleasure, if he thought it could be done.

'Lord Bristol, when lodging at the bathing house of Mount Salut, near Magilligan, narrative. How strongly did those exquisitely beautiful lines of Ossian rush on my recollection: 'But age is now on my tongue, and my mind has failed me; the sons of song are gone to rest; my voice remains like a blast that roars loudly on a sea-surrounded rock after the winds are laid, and the distant mariner sees the waving trees.'

So great was my veneration for this 'bard of other times,' that I felt as though it would have been an indelicacy to have offered him any pecuniary reward for the exertions of his tuneful talent; I therefore made my little offering to his wife, having previously, while he was reciting his 'unvarnished tale,' taken a sketch of his most singularly interesting and striking figure, as a present for Glorvina on my return to Inismore. While my heart a thousand times called on hers to participate in the sweet but melancholy pleasure it experienced, as I listened to and gazed on this venerable being.

Whenever there is a revel of the feelings, a joy of the imagination,

---

gave three guineas, and ground rent free, to build the house where Hampson now lives. At the house warming his lordship with his lady and family came, and the children danced to his harp; the bishop gave three crowns to the family, and in the *dear* year, his lordship called in his coach and six, stopped at the door, and gave a guinea to buy meal.

'Would it not be well to get a subscription for poor old Hampson? It might be sent to various towns where he is known.

Once more ever yours,

G. V. S.'

ADDENDA

'In the time of Noah I was green,
After his flood I have not been seen,
Until seventeen hundred and two. I was found,
By Cormac Kelly, under ground;
He raised me up to that degree;
Queen of music they call me.'

'The above lines are sculptured on the old harp, which is made, the sides and front of white sally, the back of fir, patched with copper and iron plates. His daughter now attending him is only thirty-three years old.

'I have now given you an account of my visit, and even thank you (though my fingers are tired), for the pleasure you procured to me by this interesting commission.

Ever yours,

G. V. SAMPSON.'

In February 1806 the author, being then but eighteen miles distant from the residence of the Bard, received a message from him, intimating that as he heard she wished to purchase his harp, he would dispose of it on very moderate terms. He was then in good health and spirits, though in his hundredth and ninth year.

or a delicate fruition of a refined and touching sentiment, how my soul misses her! I find it impossible to make even the amiable and intelligent priest enter into the nature of my feelings; but how naturally, in the overflowing of my heart, do I turn towards her, yet turn in vain, or find her image only in my enamoured soul, which is full of her. Oh! how much do I owe her. What a vigorous spring has she opened in the wintry waste of a desolated mind. It seems as though a seal had been fixed upon every bliss of the senses and the heart, which her breath alone could dissolve; that all was gloom and chaos until she said, 'let there be light.'

As we rode back to our auberge by the light of a cloudless but declining moon, after some conversation on the subject of the bard whom we had visited, the priest exclaimed, 'Who would suppose that that wretched hut was the residence of one of that order once so revered among the Irish; whose persons and properties were held sacred and inviolable by the common consent of all parties, as well as by the laws of the nation, even in all the vicissitudes of warfare, and all the anarchy of intestine commotion; an order which held the second rank in the state;[1] and whose members, in addition to the interesting duties of their profession, were the heralds of peace and the donors of immortality? Clothed in white and flowing robes, the bards marched to battle at the head of the troops, and by the side of the chief; and while by their martial strains they awakened courage even to desperation in the heart of the warrior, borne away by the furor of their own enthusiasm, they not unfrequently rushed into

[1] The genuine history and records of Ireland abound with incidents singularly romantic, and of details exquisitely interesting. In the account of the death of the celebrated hero Conrigh, as given by Demetrius O'Connor, the following instance of fidelity and affection of a family bard is given:—When the beautiful, but faithless, Blanaid, whose hand Conrigh had obtained as the reward of his valour, armed a favoured lover against the life of her husband, and fled with the murderer; Feirchiertne, the poet and bard of Conrigh, in the anguish of his heart for the loss of a generous master, resolved on sacrificing the criminal Blanaid to the manes of her murdered lord. He therefore secretly pursued her from her palace in Kerry to the court of Ulster, whither she had fled with her homicide paramour. On his arrival there, the first object that saluted his eyes was the king of that province, walking on the edge of the steep rocks of Rinchin Beara, surrounded by the principal nobility of his court; and in the splendid train he soon perceived the lovely, but guilty, Blanaid and her treacherous lover. The bard concealed himself until he observed his mistress withdraw from the brilliant crowd, and stand at the edge of a steep cliff; then courteously and flatteringly addressing her, as he approached her presence, he at last threw his arms round her, and clasping her firmly to his breast, threw himself headlong with his prey down the precipice. They were both dashed to pieces.

the thick of the fight themselves, and by their maddening inspirations decided the fate of the battle: or when victory descended on the ensanguined plain, hung over the warrior's funeral pile, and chaunted to the strains of the national lyre the deeds of the valiant, and the prowess of the hero; while the brave and listening survivors envied and emulated the glory of the deceased, and believed that this tribute of inspired genius at the funeral rites was necessary to the repose of the departed soul.'

'And from what period,' said I, 'may the decline of these once potent and revered members of the state be dated?'

'I would almost venture to say,' returned the priest, 'so early as in the latter end of the sixth century; for we read in an Irish record, that about *that* period the *Irish monarch* convened the princes, nobles, and clergy, of the kingdom, to the parliament of *Drumceat;** and the chief motive alleged for summoning this vast assembly was to banish the Fileas or bards.'

'Which might be deemed then,' interrupted I, 'a league of the *Dunces* against *Wit* and *Genius.*'

'Not altogether,' returned the priest. 'It was in some respects a necessary policy. For strange to say, nearly the third part of Ireland had adopted a profession at once so revered, and so privileged, so honoured and so caressed by all ranks of the state.—Indeed, about this period, such was the influence they had obtained in the kingdom, that the inhabitants without distinction were obliged to receive and maintain them from November till May, if it were the pleasure of the bard to become their guest; nor were there any object on which their daring wishes rested that was not instantly put into their possession. And such was the ambition of one of their order, that he made a demand on the golden broach or clasp that braced the regal robe on the breast of royalty itself, which was unalienable with the crown, and descended with the empire from generation to generation.'

'Good God!' said I, 'what an idea does this give of the omnipotence of music and poetry among those refined enthusiasts, who have ever borne with such impatience the oppressive chain of power, yet suffer themselves to be soothed into slavery by the melting strains of their national lyre.'

'It is certain,' replied the priest, 'that no nation, not even the Greeks, were ever attached with more passionate enthusiasm to the divine arts of poesy and song, than the ancient Irish, until their fatal and boundless indulgence to their professors became a source of inquietude and oppression to the whole state. The celebrated St Columbkill, who was himself a poet, became a mediator between the monarch already mentioned and the "*tuneful throng*;" and by his intercession, the king changed his first intention of banishing the whole college of bards, to limiting their numbers; for it was an argument of the liberal saint's, that it became a great monarch to patronise the arts; to retain about his person an eminent bard and antiquary; and to allow to his tributary princes or chieftains, a poet capable of singing their exploits, and of registering the genealogy of their illustrious families. This liberal and necessary plan of reformation, suggested by the saint, was adopted by the monarch; and these salutary regulations became the prominent standard for many succeeding ages: and though the severity of those regulations against the bards, enforced in the tyrannic reign of Henry VIII as proposed by Baron Finglas, considerably lessened their power;[1] yet until the reign of Elizabeth their characters were not stript of that sacred *stole*, which the reverential love of their countrymen had flung over them. The high estimation in which the bard was held in the commencement of the empire of Ireland's arch-enemy is thus attested by Sir Philip Sydney:* "In our neighbour country," says he, "where truly learning goes very bare, yet are their poets held in devout reverence." But Elizabeth, jealous of that influence which the bardic order of Ireland held over the most puissant of her chiefs, not only enacted laws against them, but against such as received or entertained them: for Spenser informs us that, even *then*, "their verses were taken up with a general applause, and usually sung at all feasts and meetings." Of the spirited, yet pathetic, manner in which the genius of Irish minstrelsy addressed itself to the soul of the Irish chief, many instances are still preserved in the records of traditional lore. A poem of Fearflatha, family bard to the O'Nials of Clanboy, and beginning thus:—"O the condition of our dear countrymen, how languid their joys, how acute their sorrows, etc. etc." the prince of Inismore takes peculiar delight in repeating. But in the lapse of time, and vicissitude

---

[1] Item—That noe Irish minstralls, rhymers, thanaghs, ne bards, be messengers to desire any goods of any man dwelling within the English pale, upon pain of forfeiture of all their goods, and their bodies to be imprisoned at the king's will. *Harris' Hibernica*, p. 98.

of revolution, this order, once so revered, has finally sunk into the casual retention of an harper, piper, or fiddler, which are generally, but not universally, to be found in the houses of the Irish country gentlemen; as you have yourself witnessed in the castle of Inismore and the hospitable mansion of the O'D——s. One circumstance, however, I must mention to you. Although Ulster was never deemed poetic ground, yet when destruction threatened the bardic order in the southern and western provinces, where their insolence, nurtured by false indulgence, often rendered them an object of popular antipathy, hither they fled for protection, and at different periods found it from the northern princes: and Ulster, you perceive, is now the last resort of the most ancient of the surviving of the Irish bards, who, after having imbibed inspiration in the classic regions of Connaught, and effused his national strains through every province of his country, draws forth the last feeble tones of his almost silenced harp amidst the chilling regions of the north; almost unknown and undistinguished, except by the few strangers who are led by chance or curiosity to his hut, and from whose casual bounties he chiefly derives his subsistence.'

We had now reached the door of our auberge; and the dog of the house jumping on me as I alighted, our hostess exclaimed, 'Ah Sir! our wee doggie kens you uncoo.' Is not this the language of the Isle of Sky? The priest left me early this morning on his evidently unpleasant embassy. On his return we visit the Giants' Causeway,* which I understand is but sixteen miles distant. Of this pilgrimage to the shrine of Nature in her grandest aspect, I shall tell you nothing; but when we meet will put into your hands a work written on the subject, from which you will derive equal pleasure and instruction. At this moment the excellent priest appears on his little nag; the rain no longer beats against my casement; the large drops suspended from the foliage of the trees sparkle with the beams of the meridian sun, which, bursting forth in cloudless radiancy, dispels the misty shower, and brilliantly lights up the arch of heaven's promise. Would you know the images now most buoyant in my cheered bosom; they are Ossian and Glorvina: it is for *him* to describe, for *her* to feel, the renovating charms of this interesting moment. Adieu! I shall grant you a reprieve till we once more reach the dear ruins of Inismore.

H.M.

LETTER XXVIII

TO J.D. ESQ. M.P.

Plato compares the soul to a small republic, of which the reasoning and judging powers are stationed in the head as in a citadel, and of which the senses are the guards or servants.

Alas! my dear friend, this republic is with me all anarchy and confusion, and its guards, disordered and overwhelmed, can no longer afford it protection. I would be calm, and give you a succinct account of my return to Inismore; but impetuous feelings rush over the recollection of trivial circumstances, and all concentrate on that fatal point which transfixes every thought, every emotion of my soul.

Suffice it now to say, that our second reception at the mansion of the O'D's had lost nothing of that cordiality which distinguished our first; but neither the cheerful kindness of the parents, nor the bland-ishments of the charming daughters, could allay that burning impatience, which fired my bosom to return to Glorvina, after the tedious absence of five long days. All night I tossed on my pillow in the restless agitation of expected bliss, and with the dawn of that day on which I hoped once more to taste '*the life of life,*' I arose and flew to the priest's room to chide his tardiness. Early as it was I found he had already left his apartment, and as I turned from the door to seek him, I perceived a written paper lying on the floor. I took it up and, carelessly glancing my eye over it, discovered that it was a receipt from the prince's inexorable creditor, who (as father John informed me) refused to take the farm off his hands: but what was my amaze-ment to find that this receipt was an acknowledgment for those jewels which I had so often seen stealing their lustre from Glorvina's charms; and which were now individually mentioned, and given in lieu of the rent for that very farm, by which the prince was so materially injured. The blood boiled in my veins. I could have annihilated this rascally cold-hearted landlord; I could have wept on the neck of the unfortunate prince; I could have fallen at the feet of Glorvina and worshipped her as the first of the Almighty's works. Never in the midst of all my artificial wants, my boundless and craving extravagance, did I ever feel the want of riches as at this moment, when a small part of what I had so worthlessly flung away, would have saved the pride of a noble, an indignant spirit, from a deep and deadly wound, and spared the heart of filial solicitude and tender sensibility, many a pang of tortured feelings. The rent of the farm was an hundred pounds per annum. The prince, I understood, was three years in arrear; yet, though there were no diamonds, and not many pearls, I should suppose the jewels worth more than the sum for which they were given.[1]

While I stood burning with indignation, the paper still trembling in my hand, I heard the footstep of the priest; I let fall the paper; he advanced, snatched it up, and put it in his pocket book, with an air of self reprehension that determined me to conceal the knowledge so accidentally acquired. Having left our adieux for our courteous hosts with one of the young men, we at last set out for Inismore. The idea of so soon meeting my soul's precious Glorvina banished every idea less delightful.

'Our meeting,' said I, 'will be attended with a new and touching interest, the sweet result of that *perfect* intelligence which now for the first time subsisted between us, and which stole its birth from that tender and delicious glance which love first bestowed on me beneath the cypress tree of the rustic cemetery.'

Already I beheld the 'air-lifted' figure of Glorvina floating towards me. Already I felt her soft hands tremble in mine, and gazed on the deep suffusion of her kindling blushes, the ardent welcome of her bashful eyes, and all that dissolving and impassioned languor, with which she would resign herself to the sweet abandonment of her soul's chastened tenderness, and the fullest confidence in that adoring heart which had now unequivocally assured her of its homage and eternal fealty. In short, I had resolved to confess my name and rank to Glorvina, to offer her my hand, and to trust to the affection of our fond and indulgent fathers for forgiveness.

Thus warmed by the visions of my heated fancy I could no longer stifle my impatience; and when we were within seven miles of the castle, I told the priest, who was ambling slowly on, that I would be his *avant-courier*,* and clapping spurs to my horse soon lost sight of my tardy companion.

At the draw-bridge I met one of the servants to whom I gave the panting animal, and flew, rather than walked, to the castle. At its

---

[1] I have been informed that a descendant of the provincial kings of Connaught parted not many years back with the golden crown which, for so many ages, encircled the royal brows of his ancestors.

portals stood the old nurse, she almost embraced me, and I almost returned the caress; but with a sorrowful countenance she informed me that the prince was dangerously ill, and had not left his bed since our departure; *that things altogether were going on but poorly*; and that she was sure *the sight* of me would do her young lady's heart good, for that she did nothing but weep all day, and sit by her father's bed all night. She then informed me that Glorvina was alone in the boudoir. With a thousand pulses fluttering at my breast, full of the ideal of stealing on the melancholy solitude of my pensive love, with a beating heart and noiseless step I approached the sacred asylum of innocence. The door lay partly open; Glorvina was seated at a table, and apparently engaged in writing a letter. I paused a moment for breath ere I advanced. Glorvina at the same instant raised her head from the paper, read over what she had written, and wept bitterly; then wrote again, and again paused; sighed, and drew a letter from her bosom—(yes, her bosom) which she perused, often waving her head, and sighing deeply, and wiping away the tears that dimmed her eyes, while once a cherub smile stole on her lip (*that smile* I once thought *all* my own); then folding up the letter, she pressed it to her lips, and consigning it to her bosom, exclaimed, 'First and best of men!' What else she murmured I could not distinguish; but as if the perusal of this prized letter had renovated every drooping spirit, she ceased to weep, and wrote with greater earnestness than before.

Motionless, transfixed, I leaned for support against the frame of the door until Glorvina, having finished her letter and sealed it, arose to depart; then I had the presence of mind to steal away and conceal myself in a dark recess of the corridor. Yet though unseen, I saw her wipe away the traces of her tears from her cheek, and pass me with a composed and almost cheerful air. I softly followed, and looking down the dark abyss of the steep well stairs, which she rapidly descended, I perceived her to put the letter in the hands of the little post-boy, who hurried away with it. Impelled by the impetuous feelings of the moment I was—yes, I was so far forgetful of myself, my principles and pride, of every sentiment save love and jealousy, that I was on the point of following the boy, snatching the letter, and learning the address of this mysterious correspondent, this '*First and best of men.*' But the natural dignity of a vehement, yet undebased, mind saved me a meanness I should never have forgiven: for what right had I forcibly to possess myself of another's secret? I turned back to a window in the corridor and beheld Glorvina's little herald mounted on his mule riding off, while she, standing at the gate, pursued him with that impatient look so strongly indicative of her ardent character. When he was out of sight she withdrew, and the next minute I heard her stealing towards her father's room. Unable to bear her presence, I flew to mine; that apartment I had lately occupied with an heart so redolent of bliss—an heart that now sunk beneath the unexpected blow which crushed all its new born hopes, and I feared annihilated for ever its sweet but short-lived felicity. 'And is this then,' I exclaimed, 'the fond re-union my fancy painted in such glowing colours?' God of heaven! at the very moment when my thoughts and affections forced for a tedious interval from the object of their idolatry, like a compressed spring set free, bounded with renewed vigour to their native bias. Yet was not the disappointment of my own individual hopes scarcely more agonizing than the destruction of that consciousness which, in giving one perfect being to my view, redeemed the species in my misanthropic opinion.

'Oh, Glorvina!' I passionately added, 'if even thou, fair being, reared in thy native wilds and native solitudes, art deceptive, artful, imposing, deep, deep, in all the wiles of hypocrisy; then is the original sin of our nature unredeemed; vice the innate principle of our being—and those who preach the existence of virtue but idle dreamers, who fancy that in others to themselves unknown. And yet sweet innocent, if thou "art more sinned against than sinning:" if the phantoms of a jealous brain—oh, 'tis impossible! The ardent kiss impressed upon the senseless paper, which thy breast enshrined!!! was the letter of a friend thus treasured! When was the letter of a friend thus answered with tears, with smiles, with blushes, and with sighs? This, this, is love's own language. Besides, Glorvina is not formed for friendship; the moderate feelings of her burning soul are already divided in affection for her father, and grateful esteem for her tutor; and she who, when loved, must be loved to madness, will scarcely feel less passion than she inspires.'

While thought after thought thus chased each other down, like the mutinous billows of a stormy ocean, I continued pacing my chamber with quick and heavy strides; forgetful that the prince's room lay immediately beneath me. Ere that thought occurred, some one softly opened the door. I turned savagely round—it was Glorvina! Impulsively I rushed to meet her; but not impulsively recoiled: while she, with an exclamation of surprize and pleasure, sprung towards me, and by my sudden retreat would have fallen at my feet, but that my willing arms extended involuntarily to receive her. Yet it was no longer the almost sacred person of the once all-innocent, all-ingenuous Glorvina they encircled; but still they twined round the loveliest form, the most charming, the most dangerous, of all human beings. The enchantress!—With what exquisite modesty she faintly endeavoured to extricate herself from my embrace; yet with what willing weakness, which seemed to triumph in its own debility, she panted on my bosom, wearied by the exertion which vainly sought her release. Oh! at that moment the world was forgotten—the whole universe was Glorvina! My soul's eternal welfare was not more precious at that moment than Glorvina! while my passion seemed now to derive its ardour from the overflowing energy of those bitter sentiments which had preceded its revival. Glorvina, with an effort, flung herself from me. Virtue, indignant yet merciful, forgiving while it arraigned, beamed in her eyes. I fell at her feet; I pressed her hand to my throbbing temples and burning lips. 'Forgive me,' I exclaimed, 'for I know not what I do.' She threw herself on a seat, and covered her face with her hands, while the tears trickled through her fingers. Oh! there was a time when tears from those eyes—but now they only recalled to my recollection the last I had seen her shed. I started from her feet and walked towards the window, near that couch where her watchful and charitable attention first awakened the germ of gratitude and love which has since blown into such full, such fatal existence. I leaned my head against the window-frame for support, its painful throb was so violent; I felt as though it were lacerating in a thousand places; and the sigh which involuntarily breathed from my lips seemed almost to burst the heart from whence it flowed.

Glorvina arose: with an air tenderly compassionate, yet reproachful, she advanced and took one of my hands. 'My dear friend,' she exclaimed, 'what is the matter? has any thing occurred to disturb you, or to awaken this extraordinary emotion? Father John! where is he? why does he not accompany you? Speak!—does any new misfortune threaten us? does it touch my father? Oh! in mercy say *it does not*! but release me from the torture of suspense.'

'No, no,' I peevishly replied; 'set your heart at rest, it is nothing; nothing at least that concerns you; it is me, me only it concerns.'

'And therefore, Mortimer, is it nothing to Glorvina,' she softly replied; and with one of those natural motions so incidental to the simplicity of her manners, she threw her hand on my shoulder, and leaning her head on it, raised her eloquent, her tearful eyes to mine. Oh! while the bright drops hung upon her cheek's faded rose, with what difficulty I restrained the impulse that tempted me to gather them with my lips; while she, like a ministering angel, again took my hand, and applying her fingers to my wrist said with a sad smile, 'You know I am a skilful little doctress.'

The feelings I experienced when those lovely fingers first applied their pressure to my arm rushed on my recollection: her touch had lost nothing of its electric power: my emotions at that moment were indescribable.

'Oh, good God, how ill you are!' she exclaimed. 'How wild your pulse; how feverish your looks! You have over-heated yourself; you were unequal to such a journey in such weather; you who have been so lately an invalid. I beseech you to throw yourself on the bed, and endeavour to take some repose; mean time I will send my nurse with some refreshment to you. How could I be so blind as not to see at once how ill you were!'

Glad, for the present, of any pretext to conceal the nature of my real disorder, I confessed I was indeed ill, (and, in fact, I was *physically* as well as morally so; for my last day's journey brought on that nervous head-ache I have suffered so much from;) while she, all tender solicitude and compassion, flew to prepare me a composing-draught. But I was not now to be deceived: this was pity, mere pity. Thus a thousand times have I seen her act by the wretches who were first introduced to her notice through the medium of that reputation which her distinguished humanity had obtained for her among the diseased and the unfortunate.

I had but just sunk upon the bed, overcome by fatigue and the vehemence of my emotions, when the old nurse entered the room. She said she had brought me a composing-draught from the lady Glorvina, who had kissed the cup, after the old Irish fashion,[1] and bade me drink it for her sake.

'Then I pledge her,' said I, 'with the same truth she did me;' and I

---

[1] To this ancient and general custom Goldsmith alludes in his Deserted Village:—
   'And kissed the cup to pass it to the rest.'

eagerly quaffed off the nectar her hand had prepared. Meantime the nurse took her station by my bed side, with some appropriate references to her former attendance there, and the generosity with which that attendance was rewarded; for I had imprudently apportioned my donation rather to my real than apparent rank.

While I was glad that this talkative old woman had fallen in my way; for though I knew I had nothing to hope from that incorruptible fidelity which was grounded on her attachment to her beloved nursling, and her affection for the family she had so long served, yet I had every thing to expect from the garrulous simplicity of her character, and her love of what she calls *Seanachus*, or telling long stories of the Inismore family; and while I was thinking how I should put my jesuitical scheme into execution, and she was talking as usual I know not what, the beautiful '*Breviare du Sentiment*' caught my eye lying on the ground: Glorvina must have dropped it on her first entrance. I desired the nurse to bring it to me; who blessed her stars, and wondered how her child could be so careless: a thing too she valued so much. At that moment it struck me that this *Breviare*, the furniture of the *boudoir*, the vases, and the fragment of the letter, were all connected with this mysterious friend, this 'first and best of men.' I shuddered as I held it, and forgot the snow-drops it contained; yet assuming a composure as I examined its cover, I asked the nurse if she thought I could procure such another at the next market town.

The old woman held her sides while she laughed at the idea; then folding her arms on her knees with that gossiping air which she always assumed when in a mood peculiarly loquacious, she assured me that such a book could not be got in all Ireland; for that it had come from foreign parts to her young lady.

'And who sent it?' I demanded.

'Why, nobody sent it,' she simply replied; 'he brought it himself.'

'Who?' said I.

She stammered and paused.—

'Then, I suppose,' she added, 'of course you never heard'—

'What?' I eagerly asked with an air of curiosity and amazement. As these are two emotions a common mind is most susceptible of feeling and most anxious to excite, I found little difficulty in artfully leading on the old woman by degrees, till at last I obtained from her, almost unawares to herself, the following particulars:

On a stormy night, in the spring of 17——, during that fatal

period when the scarcely cicatrised* wounds of this unhappy country bled afresh beneath the uplifted sword of civil contention; when the bonds of human amity were rent asunder, and every man regarded his neighbour with suspicion or considered him with fear; a stranger of noble stature, muffled in a long dark cloke, appeared in the great hall of Inismore, and requested an interview with the prince. The prince having retired to rest, and being then in an ill state of health, deputed his daughter to receive the unknown visitant, as the priest was absent. The stranger was shewn into an apartment adjoining the prince's, where Glorvina received him, and having remained for some time with him retired to her father's room; and again, after a conference of some minutes, returned to the stranger, whom she conducted to the prince's bedside. On the same night, and after the stranger had passed two hours in the prince's chamber, the nurse received orders to prepare the bed and apartment which I now occupy for this mysterious guest, who from that time remained near three months at the castle; leaving it only occasionally for a few days, and always departing and returning under the veil of night.

The following summer he repeated his visit; bringing with him those presents which decorate Glorvina's boudoir, except the carpet and vases, which were brought by a person who disappeared as soon as he had left them. During both these visits he gave up his time chiefly to Glorvina; reading to her, listening to her music, and walking with her early and late, but never without the priest or the nurse, and seldom during the day.

In short, in the furor of the old woman's garrulity (who however discovered that her own information had not been acquired by the most justifiable means, having, she said, by chance overheard a conversation which passed between the stranger and the prince), I found that this mysterious visitant was some unfortunate gentleman who had attached himself to the rebellious faction of the day, and who being pursued nearly to the gates of the castle of Inismore, had thrown himself on the mercy of the prince; who, with that romantic sense of honour which distinguishes his chivalrous character, had not violated the trust thus forced on him, but granted an asylum to the unfortunate refugee; who, by the most prepossessing manners and eminent endowments, had dazzled the fancy and won the hearts of this unsuspecting and credulous family; while over the minds of Glorvina and her father he had obtained a boundless influence.

The nurse hinted that she believed it was still unsafe for the stranger to appear in this country, for that he was more cautious of concealing himself in his last visit than his first; that she believed he lived in England; and that he seemed to have money enough, '*for he threw it about like a prince.*' Not a servant in the castle, she added, but knew well enough how it was; but there was not one but would sooner *die* than betray him. His name she did not know; he was only know by the appellation of the GENTLEMAN. He was not young, but tall, and very handsome. He could not speak Irish, and she had reason to think he had lived chiefly in America. She added, that *I* often reminded her of him, especially when I smiled and looked down. She was not certain whether he was expected that summer or not; but she believed the prince frequently received letters from him.

The old woman was by no means aware how deeply she had been betrayed by her insatiate passion of hearing herself speak; while the curious and expressive idiom of her native tongue gave me more insight into the whole business than the most laboured phrase or minute detail could have done. By the time, however, she had finished her narrative, she began to have some 'compunctious visitings of conscience:' she made me pass my honour I would not betray her to her young lady; for, she added, that if it got air it might come to the ears of the Lord M——, who was the prince's bitter enemy; and that it might be the ruin of the prince; with a thousand other wild surmises suggested by her fears. I again repeated my assurances of secresy; and the sound of her young lady's bell summoning to the prince's room, she left me, not forgetting to take with her the '*Breviare du Sentiment.*'

Again abandoned to my wretched self, the succeeding hour was passed in such a state of varied perturbation, that it would be as torturing to retrace my agonizing and successive reflections as it would be impossible to express them. In short, after a thousand vague conjectures, many to the prejudice and a lingering few to the advantage of their object, I was led to believe (fatal conviction!) that the virgin rose of Glorvina's affection had already shed its sweetness on a former, happier lover; that the partiality I had flattered myself in having awakened was either the result of natural intuitive coquetry, or, in the long absence of her heart's first object, a transient beam of that fire which once illumined is so difficult to extinguish, and which was nourished by my resemblance to him who had first fanned it into life.—What! *I* receive to my heart the faded spark, while another has basked in the vital flame? *I* contentedly gather this after-blow of tenderness, when another has inhaled the very essence of the nectarious blossoms? No! like the suffering mother, who wholly resigned her bosom's idol rather than divide it with another, I will, with a single effort, tear this late adored image from my heart, though the heart break with the effort, rather than feed on the remnant of those favours on which another has already feasted. Yet to be thus deceived by a recluse, a child, a novice:—*I* who, turning revoltingly from the hackneyed artifices of female depravity in that world where art for ever reigns, sought in the tenderness of secluded innocence and intelligent simplicity that heaven my soul had so long, so vainly panted to enjoy! Yet, even there—No! I cannot believe it! She! Glorvina, false, deceptive! Oh! were the immaculate spirit of *Truth* embodied in a human form, it could not wear upon its radiant brow a brighter, stronger trace of purity inviolable, and holy innocence, than shines in the seraph countenance of Glorvina! Besides, she never *said* she loved me. *Said*!—God of heavens! were words then necessary for such an *avowal*? Oh, Glorvina! thy melting glances, thy insidious smiles, thy ardent blushes, thy tender sighs, thy touching softness and delicious tears; these, these are the sweet testimonies to which my heart appeals. These at least will speak for me, and say, it was not the breath of vain presumption that nourished those hopes which now, in all their vigour, perish by the chilling blight of well-founded jealousy and mortal disappointment.

Two hours have elapsed since the nurse left me, supposing me to be asleep; no one has intruded, and I have employed the last hour in retracing to you the vicissitudes of this eventful day. You, who warned me of my fate, should learn the truth of your fatal prophecy. My father's too; but he is avenged! and I have already expiated a deception, which, however innocent, was still *deception*.

In continuation

I had written thus far, when some one tapped at my door, and the next moment the priest entered: he was not an hour arrived, and with his usual kindness came to enquire after my health, expressing much surprise at its alteration, which he said was visible in my looks. 'But it is scarcely to be wondered at,' he added: 'a man who complains for two days of a nervous disorder, and yet gallops, as if for life, seven miles in a day more natural to the torrid zone than our polar clime, may have some chance of losing his life, but very little of *losing his disorder.*' He then endeavoured to persuade me to go down with him, and take some refreshment, for I had tasted nothing all day, save Glorvina's draught; but finding me averse to the proposal, he sat with me till he was sent for to the prince's room. As soon as he was gone, with that restlessness of body which ever accompanies a wretched mind, I wandered through the deserted rooms of this vast and ruinous edifice, but saw nothing of Glorvina. The sun had set, all was gloomy and still. I took my hat, and in the melancholy maze of twilight wandered I knew not, cared not, whither. I had not, however, strayed far from the ruins, when I perceived the little post-boy galloping his foaming mule over the draw-bridge, and the next moment saw Glorvina gliding beneath the colonade (that leads to the chapel) to meet him. I retreated behind a fragment of the ruins, and observed her take a letter from his hand with an eager and impatient air: when she had looked at the seal, she pressed it to her lips, then by the faint beams of the retreating light, she opened this welcome packet, and putting an inclosed letter in her bosom, endeavoured to read the envelope; but scarcely had her eye glanced over it, than it fell to the earth, while she, covering her face with her hands, seemed to lean against the broken pillar near which she stood for support. Oh! was this an emotion of overwhelming bliss, or chilling disappointment. She again took the paper, and, still holding it open in her hand, with a slow step and thoughtful air, returned to the castle; while I flew to the stables, under pretence of enquiring from the post-boy if there were any letters for me. The lad said there was but one, and that, the post-master had told him, was an English one for the lady Glorvina. This letter then, though it could not have been an answer to that I had seen her writing, was doubtless from the mysterious friend, whose friendship, '*like gold, though not sonorous, was indestructible.*'

My doubts were now all lost in certain conviction; my trembling heart no longer vibrated between a lingering hope and a dreadful fear. I was *deceived*, and another was *beloved*. That sort of sullen firm composure, which fixes man when he knows the worst that can occur, took possession of every feeling, and steadied that wild throb of insupportable suspense, which had agitated and distracted my veering soul; while the only vacillation of mind to which I was sensible, was the uncertainty of whether I should or should not quit the castle that night. Finally resolved to act with the cool determination of a rational being, not the wild impetuosity of a maniac, I put off my departure till the following morning, when I could formally take leave of the prince, the priest, and even Glorvina herself, in the presence of her father. Thus firm and decided, I returned to the castle, and mechanically walked towards that vast apartment where I had first seen her at her harp, soothing the sorrows of parental affliction; but now it was gloomy and unoccupied; a single taper burnt on a black marble slab before a large folio, in which I suppose the priest had been looking; the silent harp of Glorvina stood in its usual place. I fled to the great hall, once the central point of all our social joys, but it was also dark and empty; the whole edifice seemed a desart. I again rushed from its portals, and wandered along the sea-beat shore, till the dews of night, and the spray of the swelling tide, as it broke against the rocks, had penetrated through my clothes. I saw the light trembling in the casement of Glorvina long after midnight. I heard the castle clock fling its peal o'er every passing hour; and not till the faintly awakening beam of the horizon streamed on the eastern wave, did I return through the castle's ever open portals, and steal to that room I was about to occupy (not to sleep in) for the last time: a light and some refreshment had been left there for me in my absence. The taper was nearly burnt out, but by its expiring flame I perceived a billet lying on the table. I opened it tremblingly. It was from Glorvina, and only a simple enquiry after my health, couched in terms of common-place courtesy. I tore it—it was the first she had ever addressed to me, and yet I tore it in a thousand pieces. I threw myself on the bed, and for some time buried my mind in conjecturing whether her father sanctioned, or her preceptor suspected, her attachment to this fortunate rebel. I was almost convinced they did not. The young, the profound deceiver; she whom I had thought

'So green in this old world.'

Wearied by incessant cogitation, I at last fell into a deep sleep, and arose about two hours back, harassed by dreams, and quite unrefreshed; since when I have written thus far. My last night's resolution remains unchanged. I have sent my compliments to inquire after the prince's health, and to request an interview with him. The servant has this moment returned, and informs me the prince has just fallen asleep, after having had a very bad night, but that when he awakens he shall be told of my request. I dared not mention Glorvina's name, but the man informed me she was then sitting by her father's bed-side, and had not attended matins. At breakfast I mean to acquaint the excellent father John of my intended departure. Oh! how much of the woman at this moment swells in my heart. There is not a being in this family in whom I have not excited, for whom I do not feel, an interest. Poor souls! they have almost all been at my room door this morning to inquire for my health, owing to the nurse's exaggerated account: she too, kind creature, has already been twice with me before I arose, but I affected sleep. Adieu! I shall dispatch this to you from M. House. I shall then have seen the castle of Inismore for the last time—the last time!!

H.M.

LETTER XXIX

TO J.D. ESQ. M.P.

M—— House

It is all over—the spell is dissolved, and the vision for ever vanished: yet my mind is not what it was, ere this transient dream of bliss 'wrapt it in Elysium.'* Then I neither suffered or enjoyed: now—!

When I had folded my letter to you, I descended to breakfast, but the priest did not appear, and the things were removed untouched. I ordered my horse to be got ready, and waited all day in expectation of a message from the prince; loitering, wandering, unsettled, and wretched, the hours dragged on: no message came: I fancied I was impatient to receive it, and to be gone; but the truth is, my dear friend, I was weak enough almost to rejoice at the detention. While I walked from room to room with a book in my hand, I saw no one but the servants, who looked full of mystery; save once, when, as I stood at the top of the corridor, I perceived Glorvina leave her father's room; she held her handkerchief to her eyes, and passed on to her own apartment. Oh! why did I not fly and wipe away those tears, inquire their source, and end at once the torture of suspense; but I had not power to move. The dinner hour arrived: I was summoned to the parlour; the priest met me at table, shook me with unusual cordiality by the hand, and affectionately enquired after my health. He then became silent and thoughtful, and had the air of a man whose heart and office are at variance; who is deputed with a commission his feelings will not suffer him to execute. After a long pause he spoke of the prince's illness, the uneasiness of his mind, the unpleasant state of his affairs, his attachment and partiality to me, and his ardent wish always to have it in his power to retain me with him; then paused again, and sighed, and again endeavoured to speak, but failed in the effort. I now perfectly understood the nature of his incoherent speech; my pride served as an interpreter between his feelings and my own, and I was determined to save his honest heart the pang of saying, 'Go, you are no longer a welcome guest.'

I told him then in a few words, that it was my intention to have left the castle that morning for Bally, on my way to England; but that I waited for an opportunity of bidding farewel to the prince: as that however seemed to be denied me, I begged that he (father John) would have the goodness to say for me all ——. Had my life depended on it, I could not articulate another word. The priest arose in evident emotion. I too not unagitated left my seat: the good man took my hand, and pressed it affectionately to his heart, then turned aside, I believe, to conceal the moisture of his eyes; nor were mine dry, yet they seemed to burn in their sockets. The priest then put a paper in the hand he held, and again pressing it with ardour, hurried away. I trembled as I opened it: it was a letter from the prince, containing a bank-note, a plain gold ring which he constantly wore, and the following lines written with the trembling hand of infirmity or emotion:

'Young and interesting Englishman, farewel! Had I not known thee, I never had lamented that God had not blessed me with a son.

O'MELVILLE,

Prince of Inismore.'

I sunk overcome on a chair. When I could sufficiently command myself, I wrote with my pencil on the cover of the prince's letter the following incoherent lines:

'You owe *me* nothing: to you I stand indebted for life itself, and all that could *once* render life desirable. With existence only will the recollection of your kindness be lost; yet though generously it was unworthily bestowed; for it was lavished on an *Impostor*. I am not what I seem: to become an inmate of your family, to awaken an interest in your estimation, I forfeited the dignity of truth, and stooped for the first time to the meanness of deception. Your money therefore I return, but your ring—that ring so often worn by you—worlds would not tempt me to part with.

'I have a father, sir; this father once so dear, so precious to my heart! but since I have been your guest, *he*, the whole world was forgotten. The first tye of nature was dissolved; and from your hands I seemed to have received a new existence. Best and most generous of men, be this recollection present to your heart! should some incident as yet unforeseen discover to you who, and what I am. Remember this—and then forgive him, who, with the profoundest sense of all your goodness, bids you a last farewell!'

When I had finished these lines, written with an emotion that almost rendered them illegible, I rung the bell and inquired (from the servant who answered) for the priest: he said he was shut up in the prince's room.

'Alone, with the prince!' said I.

'No,' he returned, 'for he had seen the lady Glorvina enter at the same time with Father John.' I did not wish to trust the servant with this open billet, I did not wish the prince to get it till I was gone; in a word, though I was resolved to leave the castle that evening, yet I did not wish to go, till, for the last time, I had seen Glorvina.

I therefore wrote the following lines in French to the priest. 'Suffer me to see you; in a few minutes I shall leave Inismore for ever.' As I was putting the billet into the man's hand, the stable boy passed the window; I threw up the sash and ordered him to lead round my horse. All this was done with the agitation of mind, which a criminal feels who hurries on his execution, to terminate the horrors of suspense.

I continued walking up and down the room in such agony of feeling, that a cold dew, colder than ice, hung upon my aching brow. I heard a footstep approach—I became motionless; the door opened, and the priest appeared leading in Glorvina. God of Heaven! The priest supported her on his arm, her veil was drawn over her eyes; I could not advance to meet them, I stood spell bound,—they both approached; I had not the power even to raise my eyes. 'You sent for me,' said the priest in a faultering accent. I presented him my letter for the prince; suffocation choked my utterance; I could not speak. He put the letter in his bosom, and taking my hand, said, 'You must not think of leaving us this evening; the prince will not hear of it.' While he spoke my horse passed the window; I summoned up those spirits my pride, my wounded pride, retained in its service. 'It is necessary I should depart immediately,' said I, 'and the sultriness of the weather renders the evening preferable.' I abruptly paused—I could not finish the sentence, simple as it was.

'Then,' said the priest, '*any* evening will do as well as this.' But Glorvina spoke not; and I answered with vehemence, that I should have been off long since: and my determination is now fixed.

'If you are thus *positive*,' said the priest, surprised by a manner so unusual, 'your friend, your pupil here, who came to second her father's request, must change her solicitations to a *last* farewell.'

Glorvina's head reposed on his shoulder; her face was enveloped in her veil; he looked on her with tenderness and compassion, and I repeated a 'last farewell!' Glorvina, you will at least then say, '*Farewell.*' The veil fell from her face. God of heaven, what a countenance! In the universe I saw nothing but Glorvina; such as I had once believed her, my own, my loving and beloved Glorvina, my tender friend, and impassioned mistress. I fell at her feet; I seized her hands, and pressed them to my burning lips. I heard her stifled sobs; her tears of soft compassion fell upon my cheek; I thought them tears of love, and drew her to my breast; but the priest held her in one arm, while with the other he endeavoured to raise me, exclaiming in violet emotion, 'Oh God, I should have foreseen this! I, I, alone am to blame. Excellent and unfortunate young man, dearly beloved child!' and at the same moment he pressed us both to his paternal bosom. The heart of Glorvina throbbed to mine, our tears flowed together, our sighs mingled. The priest sobbed over us like a child. It was a blissful agony; but it was insupportable. Then to have died would have been to have died most blest. The priest, the cruel priest, dispelled the transient dream. He forcibly put me from him. He stifled the voice of nature and of pity in his breast. His air was sternly virtuous—'Go,' said he, but he spoke in vain. I still clung to the drapery of Glorvina's robe; he forced me from her, and she sunk on a couch. 'I now,' he added, 'behold the fatal error to which I have been an unconscious accessary. Thank God, it is retrievable; go, amiable, but imprudent young man; it is honour, it is virtue commands your departure.'

While he spoke he had almost dragged me to the hall.

'Stay,' said I, in a faint voice, 'let me but speak to her.'

'It is in vain,' replied the inexorable priest, 'for she can *never* be yours; then spare *her*, spare *yourself*.'

'Never!' I exclaimed.

'Never,' he firmly replied.

I burst from his grasp and flew to Glorvina. I snatched her to my breast, and wildly cried 'Glorvina, is this then a last farewell?' She answered not; but her silence was eloquent. 'Then,' said I, pressing her more closely to my heart, '*farewell for ever.*'

In continuation

I mounted the horse that waited for me at the door, and galloped off; but with the darkness of the night I returned, and all night I wandered about the environs of Inismore; to the last I watched the light of Glorvina's window. When it was extinguished, it seemed as though I parted from her again. A grey dawn was already breaking to the mists of obscurity. Some poor peasants were already going to the labours of the day. It was requisite I should go. Yet when I ascended the mountain of Inismore I involuntarily turned, and beheld those dear ruins which I had first entered under the influence of such powerful, such prophetic emotion. What a train of recollection rushed on my mind! What a climax did they form! I turned away my eyes, sick, *sick* at *heart*, and pursued my solitary journey. Within twelve miles of M. House, as I reached an eminence, I again paused to look back, and caught a last view of the mountain of Inismore. It seemed to float like a vapour on the horizon. I took a last farewell of this almost loved mountain. Once it had risen on my gaze like the pharos* to my haven of enjoyment; for never, until this sad moment, had I beheld it but with transport.

On my arrival here I found a letter from my father, simply stating that by the time it reached me he would probably be on his way to Ireland, accompanied by my intended bride, and her father, concluding thus: 'In beholding you honourably and happily established, thus secure in a liberal, a noble independence, the throb of incessant solicitude you have hitherto awakened will at last be *stilled*, and your prudent compliance in this instance will bury in eternal oblivion the suffering, the anxieties which, with all your native virtue and native talent, your imprudence has hitherto caused to the heart of an affectionate and indulgent father.'

This letter which even a few days back would have driven me to distraction I now read with the apathy of a stoic. It is to me a matter of indifference how I am disposed of. I have no wish, no will of my own.

To the return of that mortal torpor from which a late fatally cherished sentiment had roused me, is now added the pang of my life's severest disappointment, like the dying wretch who is only roused from total insensibility, by the quivering pains which, at intervals of fluttering life, shoot through his languid frame.

In continuation

It is two days since I began this letter, yet I am still here; I have not power to move, though I know not what secret spell detains me. But whither shall I go, and to what purpose? the tye which once bound me to physical and moral good, to virtue, and felicity, is broken, for ever broken. My mind is changed, dreadfully changed within these few days. I am ill too, a burning fever preys upon the very springs of life; all around me is solitary and desolate. Sometimes my brain seems on fire, and hideous phantoms float before my eyes; either my senses are disordered by indisposition, or the hand of heaven presses heavily on me. My blood rolls in torrents through my veins. Sometimes I think it *should*, it *must* have vent. I feel it is in vain to think that I shall ever be fit for the discharge of any duty in this life. I shall hold a place in the creation to which I am a dishonour. I shall become a burthen to the few who are obliged to feel an interest in my welfare.

It is the duty of every one to do that which his situation requires, to act up to the measure of judgment bestowed on him by Providence. Should I continue to drag on this load of life, it would be for its wretched remnant a mere animal existence. A moral death! What! I become again like the plant I tread under my feet; endued with a vegetative existence, but destitute of all sensation, of all feeling. I who have so lately revelled in the purest wildest joys of spiritual felicity. I who have tasted of heaven's own bliss; who have known, oh God! that even the recollection, the simple recollection should diffuse through my chilled heart, through my whole languid frame such vital warmth, such cheering renovating ardour.

I have gone over calmly, deliberately gone over every circumstance connected with the recent dream of my life. It is evident that the object of her heart's first election is that of her father's choice. Her passion for me, for I swear most solemnly she loved me. Oh, in that I could not be deceived; every look, every word betrayed it; her passion for me was a paroxism. Her tender, her impassioned nature required some object to receive the glowing ebullitions of its affectionate feelings; and in the absence of another, in that unrestrained intimacy by which we were so closely associated; in that sympathy of pursuit which existed between us, they were lavished on me. I was the substituted toy of the moment. And shall I then sink beneath a woman's whim, a woman's infidelity, unfaithful to another as to me? I who, from my early days, have suffered by her arts and my own credulity. But what were all my sufferings to this? A drop of water to 'the multitudinous ocean.' Yet in the moment of a last farewell she wept so bitterly! tears of pity! Pitied and deceived!

I am resolved I will offer myself an expiatory sacrifice on the altar of parental wrongs. The father whom I have deceived and injured shall be retributed. This moment I have received a letter from him, the most affectionate and tender; he is arrived in Dublin, and with him Mr D. and his daughter! It is well! If he requires it the moment of our meeting shall be that of my immolation. Some act of desperation would be now most consonant to my soul! Adieu.

H.M.

LETTER XXX

TO J.D. ESQ. M.P.

Dublin

I am writing to you from the back room of a noisy hotel in the centre of a great and bustling city: my only prospect the gloomy walls of the surrounding houses. The contrast!—Where now are those refreshing scenes on which my rapt gaze so lately dwelt; those wild sublimities of nature—the stupendous mountain, the Alpine cliff, the boundless ocean, and the smiling vale? Where are those original and simple characters; those habits, those manners, to me at least so striking and so new? All vanished like a dream!—

'The baseless fabric of a vision!'

I arrived here late in the evening, and found my father waiting to receive me. Happily the rest of the party were gone to the theatre; for his agitation was scarcely less than my own. You know, that owing to our late misunderstandings it is some months since we met. He fell on my neck and wept. I was quite overcome. He was shocked at my altered appearance, and his tenderest solicitudes were awakened for my health. I was so vanquished by his goodness that more than once I was on the point of confessing all to him. It was my good angel checked the imprudent avowal; for what purpose could it now serve, but to render me more contemptible in his eyes, and to heighten his antipathy against those who have been in some degree the unconscious accessaries to my egregious folly and incurable imprudence. But *does* he feel an antipathy against the worthy prince? Can it be otherwise? Have not all his conciliatory offers been rejected with scorn? Yet to me he never mentioned the prince's name; this silence surprises me—long may it continue. I dare not trust myself. In your bosom only is the secret safely reposed.

As I had rode day and night since I left M. House, weariness and indisposition obliged me almost on my arrival to go to bed: my father sat by my side till the return of the party from the theatre. What plans for my future aggrandizement and happiness did his parental solicitude canvas and devise! The prospect of my brilliant establishment in life seems to have given him a new sense of being. On our return to England, I am to set up for the borough of ——. My talents are calculated for the senate: fame, dignity, and emolument,* are to wait upon their successful exertion. I am to become an object of popular favor and royal esteem; and all this time, in the fancied triumph of his parental hopes, he sees not that the heart of their object is breaking.

Were you to hear him! were you to see him! What a father! what a man! Such intelligence—such abilities. A mind so dignified, an heart so tender; and still retaining all the ardour, all the enthusiasm of youth. In what terms he spoke of my elected bride! He indeed dwelt chiefly on her personal charms, and the simplicity of her unmodefied character. Alas! I once found both united to genius and sensibility.

'How delightful,' he exclaimed, 'to form this young and ductile mind, to mould it to your desires, to breathe inspiration into this lovely image of primeval innocence, to give soul to beauty, and intelligence to simplicity, to watch the ripening progress of your grateful efforts, and finally clasp to your heart that perfection you have yourself created.'

And this was spoken with an energy, an enthusiasm, as though he had himself experienced all the pleasure he now painted for me. Happily, however, in the warmth of his own feelings he perceived not the coldness, the torpidity of his son's.

They are fast weaving for me the web of my destiny. I look on and take no part in the work. It is over—I have been presented in form. They say she is beautiful—it may be so;—but the blind man cannot be persuaded of the charms of the rose, when his finger is wounded by its thorns. She met me with some confusion, which was natural, considering she had been 'won unsought.' Yet I thought it was the bashfulness of a *hoyden*,* rather than that soul-born delicate bashfulness, which I have seen accompanied with every grace. How few there are who do or can distinguish this in woman; yet in nature, there is nothing more distinct than the modesty of sentiment and of constitution.

The father was as usual boisterously good-humoured, and vulgarly pleasant; he talked over our sporting adventures last winter, as if the topic was exhaustless. For my part, I was so silent, that my father looked uneasy, and I then made amends for my former taciturnity by talking incessantly, and on every subject with vehemence and rapidity. A woman of common sense or common delicacy would have been disgusted, but she is a child; they would fain drag me after them into public, but my plea of ill health has been received by my indulgent father. My gay young mistress seems already to consider me as her husband, and treats me accordingly with indifference. In short, she finds that love in the solitude of the country, and amidst the pleasures of a town, is a very different sentiment; yet her vanity I believe is piqued by my neglect: for to-day she said, when I excused myself from accompanying her to a morning concert, Oh! I should much rather have your father with me: he is the younger man of the two! I indeed never saw him in such health and spirits; he seems to tread on air. Oh! that he were my rival! my successful rival! In the present morbid state of my feelings I give in to every thing, but when it comes to a crisis, will this stupid acquiescence still befriend their wishes? Impossible!

In continuation

I have had a short but extraordinary conversation with my father. Would you believe it? he has for some time back cherished an attachment of the tenderest nature; but to his heart the interests of his children have ever been an object of the first and dearest concern. Having secured their establishment in life, and, as he hopes and believes, effected their happiness, he now feels himself warranted in consulting his own. In short, he has given me to understand that there is a probability of his marriage with a very amiable and deserving person closely following after my brother's and mine. The lady's name he refused to mention, until every thing was finally arranged; and whoever she is, I suspect her rank is inferior to her merits, for he said, 'the world will call the union disproportioned—disproportioned in every sense; but I must, in this instance, prefer the approval of my own heart to the world's opinion.' He then added (but in an equivocal manner), that had he been able to follow me immediately to Ireland, as he had at first proposed, he would have related to me some circumstances of peculiar interest, but that *I should yet know all*! and seemed, I thought, to lament that disparity of character between my brother and him, which prohibited that flow of confidence his heart seems panting to indulge in. You know Edward takes no pains to conceal that he smiles at those ardent virtues in his father's character, to which the phlegmatic temperament of his own gives the name of *romance*.

The two fathers settle every thing as they please. A property which fell to my father a few weeks back by the death of a rich maiden aunt, with every thing not entailed, he has made over to me even during his life. Expostulation was in vain, he would not hear me: for himself he has retained nothing but his purchased estates in Connaught, which are infinitely more extensive than that he possesses by inheritance. What if he resides at the Lodge, in the very neighbourhood of ——. Oh! my good friend, I fear I am deceiving myself: I fear I am preparing for the heart of the best of fathers a mortal disappointment.—When the throes of wounded pride shall have subsided; when the resentments of a doating, a deceived heart shall have gradually abated, and the recollection of former blisses shall have soothed away the pangs of recent suffering; will I then submit to the dictates of an imperious duty, or resign myself unresisting to the influence of morbid apathy?

Sometimes my father fixes his eyes so tenderly on me, yet with a look as if he would search to the most secret folds of my heart. He has never once asked my opinion of my elected bride, who, gay and happy as the first circles of this dissipated city can make her, cheerfully receives the plea which my ill health affords (attributed to a heavy cold), of not attending her in her pursuit of pleasure. The fact is, I am indeed ill; my mind and body seem declining together, and nothing in this life can give me joy but the prospect of its delivery.

By this I suppose the mysterious friend is arrived. It was expedient, therefore, that I should be dismissed. By this I suppose she is . . . So closely does my former weakness cling round my heart, that I cannot think of it without madness.

After having contemplated for a few minutes the sun's cloudless radiancy, the impression left on the averted gaze is two dark spots, and the dazzled organ becomes darkened by a previous excess of lumination. It is thus with my mind; its present gloom is proportioned to its former light. Oh! it was too, too much! Rescued from that moral death, that sicklied satiety of feeling, that state of chill hopeless existence, in which the torpid faculties were impalpable to every impression, when to breathe, to move, constituted all the powers of being: and then suddenly, as if by an intervention of Providence (and what an agent did it appoint for the execution of its divine will!) raised to the summit of human thought, human feeling, human felicity, only again to be plunged in endless night. It was too much.

*   *   *   *   *   *   *   *   *   *   *   *

Good God! would you believe it! My father is gone to M—— House, to prepare for the reception of the bridal party. We are to follow, and he proposes spending the summer there: there too, he says, my marriage with Miss D—— is to be celebrated; he wishes to conciliate the good will, not only of the neighbouring gentry, but of his tenantry in general, and thinks this will be a fair occasion. Well, be it so; but I shall not hold myself answerable for the consequences: my destiny is in their hands—let them look to the result.

Since my father left us, I am of necessity obliged to pay some attention to *his friends*; but I should be a mere automaton by the side of my gay mistress, did I not court an artificial flow of spirits, by means to me the most detestable. In short, I generally contrive to leave my senses behind me at the drinking table; or rather my reason and my spirits, profiting by its absence, are roused to boisterous anarchy: my bride (*my* bride!) is then quite charmed with my gaiety, and fancies she is receiving the homage of a lover, when she is insulted by the extravagance of a maniac; but she is a simple child, and her father is an insensible fool. God knows how little of my thoughts are devoted to either. Yet the girl is much followed for her beauty, and the splendid figure which the fortune of the father enables them to make has procured them universal attention from persons of the first rank.

*   *   *   *   *   *   *   *   *   *   *   *

A thousand times the dream of short slumbers gives her to my arms as I last beheld her. A thousand times I am awakened from an heavy unrefreshing sleep by the fancied sound of her harp and voice. There was one old Irish air she used to sing like an angel, and in the idiom of her national music sighed out certain passages with an heart-breaking thrill, that used to rend my very soul! Well, this song I cannot send from my memory; it breathes around me, it dies upon my ear, and in the weakness of emotion I weep—weep like a child. Oh! this cannot be much longer endured. I have this moment received your letter; I feel all the kindness of your intention, but I must insist on your not coming over; it would now answer no purpose. Besides, a new plan of conduct has suggested itself. In a word, my father shall know all: my unfortunate adventure may come to his ears: it is best he should know it from myself. I will then resign my fate into his hands: surely he will not forget I am still his son. Adieu.

H.M.

CONCLUSION

A few days after the departure of the Earl of M. from Dublin, the intended father-in-law of his son, weary of a town life, to which he had hitherto been unaccustomed, proposed that they should surprise the earl at M—— House, without waiting for that summons which was to have governed their departure for Connaught.

His young and thoughtless daughter, eager only after novelty, was charmed by a plan which promised a change of scene and variety of life. The unfortunate lover of Glorvina fancied he gave a reluctant compliance to the proposal which coincided but too closely with the secret desires of his soul.

This inconsiderate project was put into execution almost as soon as it was formed. Mr D. and his daughter went in their own carriage; Mr M. followed on horseback. On their arrival, they found M—— House occupied by workmen of every description, and the Earl of M. absent. Mr Clendenning, his lordship's agent, had not returned from England; and the steward, who had been but lately appointed to the office, informed the travellers that Lord M. had only been one day at M—— House, and had removed a few miles up the country to a hunting-lodge, until it should be ready for the reception of the family. Mr D. insisted on going on to the hunting-lodge. Mr M. strenuously opposed the intention, and with difficulty prevailed on the thoughtless father and volatile daughter to stop at M—— House, while he went in search of its absent lord. It was early in the day when they had arrived; and when Mr M. had given orders for their accommodation, he set out for the lodge.

From the time the unhappy M. had come within sight of those scenes which recalled all the recent circumstances of his life to memory, his heart had throbbed with a quickened pulse; even the scenery of M—— House had awakened his emotion; his enforced return thither; his brief and restless residence there; and the eager delight with which he flew from the desolate mansion of his father to the endearing circle of Inismore; all rushed to his memory, and awakened that train of tender recollection he had lately endeavoured to stifle. Happy to seize on an occasion of escaping from the restraint the society of his insensible companions imposed, happier still to have an opportunity afforded him of visiting the neighbourhood of Inismore, every step of his little journey to the lodge was marked by the renewed existence of some powerful and latent emotion; and the agitation of his heart and feelings had reached their *acme* by the time he had arrived at the gate of that avenue from which the mountains of Inismore were discernible.

When he reached the lodge, a young lad, who was working in the grounds, replied to his enquiries, that an old woman was its only resident, that the ancient steward was dead, and that Lord M. had only remained there an hour.

This last intelligence overwhelmed Mr M—— with astonishment. To his further enquiries the boy only said, that, as the report went that M—— house was undergoing some repair, it was probable his lord had gone on a visit to some of the *neighbouring quality*.—He added, that his lordship's own gentleman had accompanied him.

Mr M—— remained for a considerable time lost in thought; then throwing the bridle over his horse's neck, folded his arms, and suffered it to take its own course: it was the same animal which had so often carried him to Inismore. When he had determined on following his father to the lodge he had ordered a fresh horse; that which the groom led out was the same which Mr M—— had left behind him, and which, by becoming the companion of his singular adventure, had obtained a peculiar interest in his affections. When he had passed the avenue of the lodge, the animal instinctively took that path he had been accustomed to go: his instinct was too favourable to the secret wishes of the heart of his unhappy master; he smiled sadly, and suffered him to proceed. The evening was far advanced—the sun had sunk in the horizon, as from an eminence he perceived the castle of Inismore. His heart throbbed with violence—a thousand hopes, a thousand wishes, a thousand fears agitated his breast: he dared not for a moment listen to the suggestions of either. Lost in the musings of his heart and imagination, he was already within a mile of Inismore. The world now disappeared—he descended rapidly to a wild and trackless shore, skreened from the high road by a range of inaccessible cliffs. Twilight faintly lingered on the summit of the mountains only: the tide was out; and, crossing the strand, he found himself beneath those stupendous cliffs which shelter the western part of the peninsula of Inismore from the ocean. The violence of the waves had worn several defiles through the rocks, which commanded a near view of the *ruined castle*: it was involved in gloom and silence—all was dark, still, and solemn! No lights issued from the windows—no noise cheered at intervals the silence of desolation.

A secret impulse still impelled the steps of Mr M——, and the darkness of the night favoured his irresistible desire to satisfy the longings of his enamoured heart, by taking a last look at the shrine of its still worshipped idol. He proceeded cautiously through the rocks, and, alighting, fastened his horse near a patch of herbage; then advanced towards the chapel—its gates were open—the silence of death hung over it. The rising moon, as it shone through the broken casements, flung round a dim religious light, and threw its quivering rays on *that* spot where he had first beheld Glorvina and her father engaged in the interesting ceremonies of their religion. And to think that even at that moment he breathed the air that she respired, and was within a few paces of the spot she inhabited!—Overcome by the conviction, he resigned himself to the delirium which involved his heart and senses; and, governed by the overpowering impulse of the moment, he proceeded along that colonade through which he had distantly followed her and the prince on the night of his first arrival at the castle. It seemed to his heated brain as though he still pursued those fine and striking forms which almost appeared but the phantoms of Fancy's creation.

On every mourning breeze he thought the sound of Glorvina's voice was borne; and starting at the fall of every leaf, he almost expected to meet at each step the form of father John, if not that of his faithless mistress; but the idea of her lover occurred not. The review of scenes so dear awakened only recollection of past enjoyments; and in the fond dream of memory his present sufferings were for an interval suspended.

Scarcely aware of the approximation, he had already reached the lawn which fronted the castle, and which was strewed over with fragments of the mouldering ruins, and leaning behind a broken wall which skreened him from observation, he indulged himself in contemplating that noble but decayed edifice where so many of the happiest and most blameless hours of his life had been enjoyed. His first glance was directed towards the casement of Glorvina's room, but there nor in any other did the least glimmering of light appear. With a faultering step he advanced from his concealment towards the left wing of the castle, and snatched an hasty glance through the window of the banquetting hall. It was the hour in which the family were wont to assemble there. It was now impenetrably dark—he ventured to approach still closer, and fixed his eye to the glass; but nothing met the inquiry of his eager gaze save a piece of armour, on whose polished surface the moon's random beams faintly played. His heart was chilled; yet, encouraged by the silent desolation that surrounded him, he ventured forward. The gates of the castle were partly open: the hall was empty and dark—he paused and listened— all was silent as the grave. His heart sunk within him—he almost wished to behold some human form, to hear some human sound. On either side the doors of two large apartments stood open: he looked into each; all was chill and dark.

Grown desperate by gloomy fears, he proceeded rapidly up the stone stairs which wound through the centre of the building. He paused; and, leaning over the balustrade, listened for a considerable time; but when the echo of his footsteps had died away, all was again still as death. Horror-struck, yet doubting the evidence of his senses, to find himself thus far advanced in the interior of the castle, he remained for some time motionless—a thousand melancholy suggestions struck on his soul. With an impulse almost frantic he rushed to the corridor. The doors of the several rooms on either side lay open, and he thought by the moon's doubtful light they seemed despoiled of their furniture.

While he stood rapt in horror and amazement he heard the sound of Glorvina's harp, borne on the blast which sighed at intervals along the passage. At first he believed it was the illusion of his fancy disordered by the awful singularity of his peculiar situation; to satisfy at once his insupportable doubts he flew to that room where the harp of Glorvina always stood: like the rest it was unoccupied and dimly lit up by the moon beams. The harp of Glorvina, and the couch on which he had first sat by her, were the only articles it contained: the former was still breathing its wild melody when he entered, but he perceived the melancholy vibration was produced by the sea breeze (admitted by the open casement) which swept at intervals along its strings. Wholly overcome, he fell on the couch— his heart seemed scarcely susceptible of pulsation—every nerve of his brain was strained almost to bursting—he gasped for breath. The gale of the ocean continued to sigh on the cords of the harp, and its plaintive tones went to his very soul, and roused those feelings so truly in unison with every sad impression. A few burning tears relieved him from an agony he was no longer able to endure; and he was now competent to draw some inference from the dreadful scene of desolation by which he was surrounded. The good old prince was no more!—or his daughter was married! In either case it was probable the family had deserted the *ruins* of Inismore.

While absorbed in this heart-rending meditation he saw a faint light gleaming on the ceiling of the room, and heard a footstep approaching. Unable to move, he sat breathless with expectation. An ancient female, tottering and feeble, with a lantern in her hand, entered; and having fastened down the window, was creeping slowly along and muttering to herself: when she perceived the pale and ghastly figure of the stranger, she shrieked, let fall the light, and endeavoured to hobble away. Mr M—— followed, and caught her by the arm: she redoubled her cries—it was with difficulty he could pacify her—while, as his heart fluttered on his lips, he could only say 'The lady Glorvina!—the prince!—speak!—where are they?'

The old woman had now recovered her light, and holding it up to the face of Mr M——, she instantly recognized him; he had been a popular favourite with the poor followers of Inismore: she was among the number; and her joy at having her terrors thus terminated was such as for an interval to preclude all hope of obtaining any answer from her. With some difficulty the distracted and impatient M—— at last learnt, from a detail interrupted by all the audible testimonies of vulgar grief, that an execution had been laid upon the prince's property, and another upon his person; that he had been carried away to jail out of a sick bed, accompanied by his daughter, father John, and the old nurse; and that the whole party had set off in the old family coach, which the creditors had not thought worth taking away, in the middle of the night, lest the country people should rise to rescue the prince, which the officers who accompanied him apprehended.

The old woman was proceeding in her narrative, but her auditor heard no more; he flew from the castle, and, mounting his horse, set out for the town where the prince was imprisoned. He reached it early the next morning, and rode at once to the jail. He alighted and enquired for Mr O'Melville, commonly called Prince of Inismore.

The jailor, observing his wild and haggard appearance, kindly asked him into his own room, and then informed him that the prince had been released two days back; but that his weak state of health did not permit him to leave the jail till the preceding evening, when he had set off for Inismore. 'But,' said the jailor, 'he will never reach his old castle alive, poor gentleman! which he suspected himself; for he received the last ceremonies of the church before he departed, thinking, I suppose, that he would die on the way.'

Overcome by fatigue and a variety of overwhelming emotions, Mr M—— sunk motionless on a seat; while the humane jailor, shocked by the wretchedness of his looks, and supposing him to be a near relative, offered some words of consolation, and informed him there was then a female domestic of the prince's in the prison, who was to follow the family in the course of the day, and who could probably give him every information he might require. This was welcome tidings to Mr M——; and he followed the jailor to the room where the prince had been confined, and where the old nurse was engaged in packing up some articles which fell out of her hands, when she perceived her favourite and patient, whom she cordially embraced with the most passionate demonstrations of joy and amazement. The jailor retired; and Mr M——, shuddering as he contemplated the close and gloomy little apartment, its sorry furniture, and grated windows, where the suffering Glorvina had been imprisoned with her father, briefly related to the nurse that, having learnt the misfortunes of the prince, he had followed him to the prison, in the hope of being able to give him some assistance, if not to effect his liberation.

The old woman was as usual garrulous and communicative; she wept alternately the prince's sufferings and tears of joy for his release; talked sometimes of the generosity of the good friend who had she said 'been the saviour of them all,' and sometimes of the christian fortitude of the prince; but still dwelt most on the virtues and afflictions of her young lady, whom she frequently termed *a saint out of heaven*, a suffering angel, and a martyr. She then related the circumstances of the prince's imprisonment in terms so affecting, yet so simple, that her own tears dropt not faster than those of her auditor. She said that she believed they had looked for assistance from the concealed friend until the last moment, when the prince, unable to struggle any longer, left his sick bed for the prison of ——; that Glorvina had supported her father during their melancholy journey in her arms, without suffering even a tear, much less a complaint to escape her; that she had supported his spirits and her own as though she were more than human, until the physician who attended the prince gave him over; that then her distraction (when out of the presence of her father) knew no bounds; and that once they feared her senses were touched. When, at a moment when they were all reduced to despair, the mysterious friend arrived, paid the debt for which the prince was confined, and had carried them off the evening before, by a more tedious but less rugged road than that she supposed Mr M—— had taken, by which means he had probably missed them. 'For all this,' continued the old woman weeping, 'my child will never be happy: she is sacrificing herself for her father, and he will not live to enjoy the benefit of it. The gentleman is indeed good and comely to look at; and his being old enough to be her father matters nothing; but then love is not to be commanded though duty may.'

Mr M. struck by these words fell at her feet, conjured her not to conceal from him the state of her lady's affections, confessed his own secret passion, in terms as ardent as it was felt. His recent sufferings and suspicions, and the present distracted state of his mind, his tears, his intreaties, his wildly energetic supplications, his wretched but interesting appearance, and above all the adoration he professed for the object of her own tenderest affection, finally vanquished the small portion of prudence and reserve interwoven in the unguarded character of the simple and affectionate old Irishwoman, and she at last confessed, that the day after his departure from the castle of Inismore Glorvina was seized with a fever in which, after the first day, she became delirious; that during the night, as the nurse sat by her, she awakened from a deep sleep and began to speak much of Mr Mortimer, whom she frequently called *her friend*, her *preceptor*, and her *lover*; talked wildly of her having been *united to him by God in the vale of Inismore*, and drew from her bosom a sprig of withered myrtle which, she said, had been a bridal gift from her beloved, and that she often pressed it to her lips and smiled, and began to sing an air which, she said, was dear to him; until at last she burst into tears, and wept herself to sleep again. 'When she recovered,' continued the nurse, 'which, owing to her youth and fine constitution, she did in a few days, I mentioned to her some of these sayings, at which she changed colour, and begged that as I valued her happiness I would bury all I had heard in my own breast; and above all bid me not mention your name, as it was now her duty to forget you; and last night I heard her consent to become the wife of the good gentleman; but poor child it is all one, for she will die of a broken heart. I see plainly she will not long survive her father, nor will ever love any but you!' At these words the old woman burst into a passion of tears, while Mr M. catching her in his arms, exclaimed 'I owe you my life, a thousand times more than my life;' and throwing his purse into her lap, flew to the inn, where having obtained an hack horse, given his own in care to the master, and taken a little refreshment which his exhausted frame, long fasting, and extraordinary fatigue required, he again set out for the lodge. His sole object was to obtain an interview with Glorvina, and on the result of that interview to form his future determinations.

To retrace the wild fluctuations of those powerful and poignant feelings which agitated a mind alternately the prey of its wishes and its fears, now governed by the impetuous impulses of unconquerable love, now by the sacred ties of filial affection, now sacrificing every consideration to the dictates of duty, and now forgetting every thing in the fond dreams of passion, would be an endless, an impossible task; when still vibrating between the sweet felicities of new born hope, and the gloomy suggestions of habitual doubt. The weary traveller reached the peninsula of Inismore about the same hour that he had done the preceding day. At the draw-bridge he was met by a peasant whom he had known and to whom he gave his horse. The man, with a countenance full of importance, was going to address him, but he sprung eagerly forward and was in a moment immersed in the ruins of the castle; intending to pass through the chapel as the speediest and most private way, and to make his arrival first known to Father John, to declare to the good priest his real name and rank, his passion for Glorvina, and to receive his destiny from her lips only.

He had scarcely entered the chapel when the private door by which it communicated with the castle flew open. He skreened himself behind a pillar, from whence he beheld father John proceeding with a solemn air towards the altar, followed by the prince, carried by three servants in an arm chair, and apparently in the last stage of mortal existence. Glorvina then appeared wrapt in a long veil and supported on the arm of a stranger, whose figure and air was lofty and noble, but whose face was concealed by the recumbent attitude of his head, which drooped towards that of his apparently feeble companion, as if in the act of addressing her. This singular procession advanced to the altar; the chair of the prince reposed at its feet. The priest stood at the sacred table—Glorvina and her companions knelt at its steps. The last red beams of the evening sun shone through a stormy cloud on the votarists: all was awfully silent; a pause solemn and affecting ensued; then the priest began to celebrate the marriage rites; but the first words had not died on his lips when a figure, pale and ghastly, rushed forward, wildly exclaiming, 'Stop, I charge you, stop! you know not what you do! it is sacrilege!' and breathless and faint the seeming maniac sunk at the feet of the bride.

A convulsive shriek burst from the lips of Glorvina. She raised her eyes to heaven, then fixed them on her unfortunate lover, and dropped lifeless into his arms—a pause of indescribable emotions succeeded. The prince, aghast, gazed on the hapless pair; thus seemingly entwined in the embrace of death. The priest transfixed with pity and amazement let fall the sacred volume from his hands. Emotions of an indescribable nature mingled in the countenance of the bridegroom. The priest was the first to dissolve the spell, and to recover a comparative presence of mind; he descended from the altar and endeavoured to raise and extricate the lifeless Glorvina from the arms of her unhappy lover, but the effort was vain. Clasping her to his heart closer than ever, the almost frantic M. exclaimed, 'She is mine! mine in the eye of heaven! and no human power can part us!'

'Merciful Providence!' exclaimed the bridegroom faintly, and sunk on the shoulder of the priest. The voice pierced to the heart of his rival; he raised his eyes, fell lifeless against the railing of the altar, faintly uttering, 'God of Omnipotence! my father!' Glorvina released from the nerveless clasp of her lover, sunk on her knees between the father and the son, alternately fixing her wild regards on both, then suddenly turning them on the now apparently expiring friend, she sprung forward, and throwing her arms round his neck, frantically cried, 'It is my father they will destroy;' and sobbing convulsively, sunk overcome on his shoulder.

The prince pressed her to his heart, and looked round with a ghastly and enquiring glance for the explanation of that mystery no one had the power to unravel, and by which all seemed overwhelmed. At last, with an effort of expiring strength, he raised himself in his seat, entwined his arm round his child, and intimated by his eloquent looks, that he wished the mysterious father and his rival son to approach. The priest led the former towards him: the latter sprung to his feet, and hid his head in the mantle: all the native dignity of his character now seemed to irradiate the countenance of the prince of Inismore; his eyes sparkled with a transient beam of their former fire; and the retreating powers of life seemed for a moment to rush through his exhausted veins with all their pristine vigour. With a deep and hollow voice he said: 'I find I have been deceived, and my child, I fear, is to become the victim of this deception. Speak, mysterious strangers, who have taught me at once to *love* and to *fear* you—what, and who are you? and to what purpose have you mutually, but apparently unknown to each other, stolen on our seclusion, and thus combined to embitter my last hours, by threatening the destruction of my child?'

A long and solemn pause ensued, which was at last interrupted by the Earl of M. With a firm and collected air he replied: 'That youth, who kneels at your feet, is my son; but till this moment I was ignorant that he was known to you: I was equally unaware of those claims which he has now made on the heart of your daughter. If he has deceived you, he also has deceived his father! For myself, if imposition can be extenuated, mine merits forgiveness, for it was founded on honourable and virtuous motives. To restore you to the blessings of independence; to raise your daughter to that rank in life, her birth, her virtues, and her talents merit; and to obtain your assistance in dissipating the ignorance, improving the state, and ameliorating the situation of those of your poor unhappy compatriots, who, living immediately within your own sphere of action, are influenced by your example, and would best be actuated by your counsel. Such were the wishes of my heart; but *prejudice*, the enemy of all human virtue and human felicity, forbad their execution. My first overtures of amity were treated with scorn; my first offers of service rejected with disdain; and my crime was, that in a distant age an ancestor of mine, by the fortune of war, had possessed himself of those domains, which, in a more distant age, a remoter ancestor of your's won by similar means. Thus denied the open declaration of my good intents, I stooped to the assumption of a fictitious character; and he who as an hereditary enemy was forbid your house, as an unknown and unfortunate stranger, under affected circumstances of peculiar danger, was received to your protection, and soon to your heart as its dearest friend. The influence I obtained over your mind, I used to the salutary purpose of awakening it to a train of ideas more liberal than the prejudices of education had hitherto suffered it to cherish; and the little services I had it in my power to render you, the fervour of your gratitude so far over-rated, as to induce you to repay them by the most precious of all donations—your child. But for the wonderful and most unexpected incident which has now crossed your designs, your daughter had been by this the wife of the Earl of M.!'

With a strong convulsion of expiring nature, the prince started from his chair; gazed for a moment on the earl with a fixed and eager look, and again sunk on his seat; it was the last convulsive throe of life roused into existence by the last violent feeling of mortal emotion. With an indefinable expression, he directed his eyes alternately from the father to the son, then sunk back, and closed them: the younger M. clasped his hand, and bathed it with his tears: his daughter, who hung over him, gazed intently on his face, as though she tremblingly watched the extinction of that life in which her own was wrapped up; her air was wild, her eye beamless, her cheek pale; grief and amazement seemed to have bereft her of her senses, but her feelings had lost nothing of their poignancy: the Earl of M. leaned on the back of the prince's chair, his face covered with his hand: the priest held his right hand, and wept like an infant: among the attendants there was not one appeared with a dry eye.

After a long and affecting pause, the prince heaved a deep sigh, and raised his eyes to the crucifix which hung over the altar: the effusions of a departing and pious soul murmured on his lips, but the powers of utterance were gone; every mortal passion was fled, save that which flutters with the last pulse of life in the heart of a doating father, parental solicitude and parental love. Religion claimed his last sense of duty, nature his last impulse of feeling; he fixed his last gaze on the face of his daughter; he raised himself with a dying effort to receive her last kiss: she fell on his bosom, their arms interlaced. In this attitude he expired.

Glorvina, in the arms of the attendants, was conveyed lifeless to the castle. The body of the prince was carried to the great hall, and there laid on a bier. The Earl of M. walked by the side of the body, and his almost lifeless son, supported by the arm of the priest (who himself stood in need of assistance), slowly followed.

The elder M. had loved the venerable prince as a brother and a friend; the younger as a father. In their common regret for the object of their mutual affection, heightened by that sadly affecting scene they had just witnessed, they lost for an interval a sense of that extraordinary and delicate situation in which they now stood related towards each other; they hung on either side in mournful silence over the deceased object of their friendly affliction; while the concourse of poor peasants, whom the return of the prince brought in joyful emotion to the castle, now crowded into the hall, uttering those vehement exclamations of sorrow and amazement so consonant to the impassioned energy of their national character. To still the violence of their emotions, the priest kneeling at the foot of the bier began a prayer for the soul of the deceased. All who were present knelt around him: all was awful, solemn, and still. At that moment Glorvina appeared; she had rushed from the arms of her attendants; her strength was resistless, for it was the energy of madness; her senses were fled.

A dead silence ensued; for the emotion of the priest would not suffer him to proceed. Regardless of the prostrate throng, she glided up the hall to the bier, and gazing earnestly on her father, smiled sadly, and waved her hand; then kissing his cheek, she threw her veil over his face, and putting her finger on her lip, as if to impose silence, softly exclaimed, 'Hush! he does not suffer now! he sleeps! it was I who lulled him to repose with the song his heart loves!' and then kneeling beside him, in a voice scarcely human, she breathed out a soul-rending air she had been accustomed to sing to her father from her earliest infancy. The silence of compassion, of horror, which breathed around, was alone interrupted by her song of grief, while no eye save her's was dry. Abruptly breaking off her plaintive strain, she drew the veil from her father's face, and suddenly averting her gaze from his livid features, it wandered from the Earl of M. to his son; while with a piercing shriek she exclaimed,—'Which of you murdered my father?' Then looking tenderly on the younger M. (whose eyes not less wild than her own had followed her every motion), she softly added, 'It was not you, my love!' and with a loud convulsive laugh she fell lifeless into the priest's arms, who was the first who had the presence of mind to think of removing the still lovely maniac. The rival father and his unhappy son withdrew at the same moment; and when the priest (having disposed of his unfortunate charge) returned to seek them, he found them both in the same apartment, but at a considerable distance from each other, both buried in silent emotion—both labouring under the violence of their respective feelings. The priest attempted some words expressive of consolation to the younger M. who seemed most the victim of uncontroulable affliction; but with a firm manner the earl interrupted him:—'My good friend,' said he, 'this is no time for words; nature and feeling claim their prerogative, and are not to be denied. Your venerable friend is no more, but he has ceased to suffer: the afflicted and angelic being, whose affecting sorrows so recently wrung our hearts with agony, has still, I trust, many years of felicity and health in store to compensate for her early trials; from henceforth I shall consider her as the child of my adoption. For myself, the motives by which my apparently extraordinary conduct was governed were pure and disinterested; though the means by which I endeavoured to effect my laudable purpose were perhaps not strictly justifiable in the eye of rigid, undeviating integrity. For this young man!' he paused, and fixed his eyes on his son till they filled with tears, the strongest emotions agitating his frame; then extending his arms towards him, Mr M. rushed forward, and fell on his father's breast. The earl pressed him to his heart, and putting his hands in those of father John, he said, 'To your care and tenderness I commend my child; and from you,' he added, addressing his son, 'I shall expect the developement of that mystery, which is as yet to me dark and unfathomable. Remain here till we fully understand each other. I depart to-night for M—— House. It is reserved for you to assist this worthy man in the last solemn office of friendship and humanity. It is reserved for you to watch over and cherish that suffering angel, for whose future happiness we both mutually stand accountable.' With these words Lord M. again embraced his almost lifeless son, and pressing the hand of the priest withdrew.—Father John followed him; but importunities were fruitless; his horses were ordered, and having put a bank-note of considerable amount into his hands to defray the funeral expences, he departed from Inismore.

In the course of four days, the remains of the prince were consigned to the tomb. Glorvina's health and fine constitution were already prevailing over her disorder and acute sensibility; her senses were gradually returning, and only appeared subject to wander, when a sense of her recent sufferings struck on her heart. The old nurse was the first who ventured to mention to her that her unhappy lover was in the house; but though she appeared struck and deeply affected by the intelligence, she never mentioned his name.

Mean time Mr M. owing to his recent sufferings of mind and body, was seized with a slow fever and confined for many days to his bed. A physician of eminence in the country had taken up his residence at Inismore, and a courier daily passed between the castle and M. House, with his reports of the health of the two patients to the Earl. In a fortnight they were both so far recovered, as to remove from their respective bed rooms to an adjoining apartment. The benevolent priest who day and night had watched over them, undertook to prepare Glorvina for the reception of Mr M. whose life seemed to hang upon the restoration of hers. When she heard that he was still in the castle, and had just escaped from the jaws of death, she shuddered and changed colour; and with a faint voice enquired for his father. When she learnt that he had left the castle on the night when she had last seen him, she seemed to feel much satisfaction, and said, 'What an extraordinary circumstance! What a mystery!— the father and the son!' She paused, and a faint hectic coloured her pale cheek; then added, 'unfortunate and imprudent young man! Will his father forgive and receive him?'

'He is dearer than ever to his father's heart:' said the priest, 'the first use he made of his returning health, was to write to his inestimable parent, confessing without the least reservation every incident of his late extraordinary adventure.'

'And when does he leave the castle?' inarticulately demanded Glorvina.

'That rests with you;' replied the priest.

She turned aside her head and sighed heavily; then bursting into tears, flung her arms affectionately round her beloved preceptor, and cried, 'I have now no father but you—act for me as such!'

The priest pressed her to his heart, and drawing a letter from his bosom, said, 'This is from one who pants to become your father in the strictest sense of the word; it is from Lord M. but though addressed to his son, it is equally intended for your perusal. That son, that friend, that lover, whose life and happiness now rests in your hands, in all the powerful emotion of hope, doubt, anxiety, and expectation, now waits to be admitted to your presence.'

Glorvina, gasping for breath, caught hold of the priest's arm, then sunk back upon her seat and covered her face with her hands. The priest withdrew, and in a few minutes returned, leading in the agitated invalid: then placing the hands of the almost lifeless Glorvina in his, retired. He felt the mutual delicacy of their situation and forebore to heighten it by his presence.

Two hours had elapsed before the venerable priest again sought the two objects dearest to his heart; he found Glorvina overwhelmed with soft emotion, her cheek covered with blushes, and her hand clasped in that of the interesting invalid, whose flushing colour and animated eyes spoke the return of health and happiness; not indeed confirmed—but fed by sanguine hope; such hope as the heart of a mourning child could give to the object of her heart's first passion, in that era of filial grief, when sorrow is mellowed by reason, and soothed by religion into a tender and not ungracious melancholy. The good priest embraced and blessed them alternately, then seated between them, read aloud the letter of Lord M.

TO THE HON. HORATIO M.

Since human happiness, like every other feeling of the human heart, loses its poignancy by reiteration, its fragrance with its bloom; let me not (while the first fallen dew of pleasure hangs fresh upon the flower of your existence) seize on those precious moments which *Hope*, rescued from the fangs of despondency; and bliss, succeeding to affliction, claim as their own. Brief be the detail which intrudes on the hour of new-born joy, and short the narrative which holds captive the attention, while the heart, involved in its own enjoyments, denies its interest.

It is now unnecessary for me fully to explain *all* the motives which led me to appear at the castle of Inismore in a fictitious character. Deeply interested for a people whose national character I had hitherto viewed thro' the false medium of prejudice; anxious to make it my study in a situation and under such circumstances which as an English landholder, as the Earl of M——, was denied me, and to turn the stream of my acquired information to that channel which would tend to the promotion of the happiness and welfare of those whose destiny in some measure was consigned to my guidance; solicitous to triumph over the hereditary prejudices of my hereditary enemy; to seduce him into amity, and force him to *esteem* the man he *hated*, while he unconsciously became his accessary in promoting the welfare of those of his humble compatriots who dwelt within the sphere of our mutual observation: such were the *motives* which principally guided my late apparently romantic adventure; would that the *means* had been equally laudable.

Received into the mansion of the generous but incautious prince as a proscribed and unfortunate wanderer, I owed my reception to his humanity rather than his prudence; and when I told him that I threw my life into his power, his *honour* became bound for its security, though his principles condemned the conduct which he believed had effected its just forfeiture.

For some months, in two succeeding summers, I contrived to perpetuate with plausive details the mystery I had forged; and to confirm the interest I had been so fortunate at first to awaken into an ardent friendship, which became as reciprocal as it was disinterested. Yet it was still my destiny to be loved identically as myself; as myself adventitiously to be *hated*. And the name of the Earl of M—— was forbidden to be mentioned in the presence of the prince, while he frequently confessed that the happiest of his hours were passed in Lord M——'s society.

Thus singularly situated, I dared not hazard a revelation of my real character, lest I should lose by the discovery all those precious immunities with which my fictitious one had endowed me.

But while it was my good fortune thus warmly to ingratiate myself with the father, can I pass over in silence my prouder triumph in that filial interest I awakened in the heart of his daughter. Her tender commiseration for my supposed misfortunes; the persevering goodness with which she endeavoured to rescue me from those erroneous principles she believed the efficient cause of my sufferings, and which I appeared to sacrifice to her better reason. The flattering interest she took in my conversation; the eagerness with which she received those instructions it was my supreme pleasure to bestow on her; and the solicitude she incessantly expressed for my fancied doubtful fate; awakened my heart's tenderest regard and liveliest gratitude. But though I admired her genius and adored her virtues, the sentiment she inspired never for a moment lost its character of parental affection; and even when I formed the determination, the accomplishment of which you so unexpectedly, so providentially frustrated, the gratification of any selfish wish, the compliance with any passionate impulse, held no influence over the determination. No, it was only dictated by motives pure as the object that inspired them; it was the wish of snatching this lovely blossom from the desart where she bloomed unseen; of raising her to that circle in society her birth entitled her to and her graces were calculated to adorn; of confirming my amity with her father by the tenderest unity of interests and affections; of giving her a legally sanctioned claim on that part of her hereditary property which the suspected villany of my steward had robbed her of; and of retributing the parent through the medium of the child.

Had I had a son to offer her, I had not offered her myself; but my eldest was already engaged, and for the worldly welfare of my second an alliance at once brilliant and opulent was necessary; for, dazzled by his real or supposed talents, I viewed his future destiny through the medium of my parental ambition, and thought only of those means by which he might become great, without considering the more important necessity of his becoming happy. Yet well aware of the phlegmatic indifference of the one, and the romantic imprudence of the other, I denied them my confidence, until the final issue of my adventure would render its revelation necessary. Nor did I suspect the possibility of their learning it by any other means; for the one never visited Ireland, and the other, as the son of Lord M——, would find no admittance to the castle of Inismore.

When a fixed determination succeeded to some months of wavering indecision, I wrote to Glorvina, with whom I had been in habits of epistolary correspondence, distantly touching on a subject I yet considered with timidity, and faintly demanding her sanction of my wishes before I unfolded them to her father, which I assured her I would not do until I could claim her openly in my own character.

In the interim, however, I received a letter from her, written previous to her receipt of mine.—It began thus: 'In those happy moments of boundless confidence, when the pupil and the child hung upon the instructive accents of the friend and the father, you have often said to me, "I am not altogether what I seem; I am not only *grateful*, but I possess a power stronger than words of convincing those to whom I owe so much of my gratitude; and should the hour of affliction ever reach *thee*, Glorvina, call on me as the friend who would fly from the remotest corner of the earth to serve, to *save* thee."

'*The hour of affliction is arrived—I call upon you!*' She then described the disordered state of her father's affairs, and painted his sufferings with all the eloquence of filial tenderness and filial sorrow, requesting my advice and flatteringly lamenting the destiny which placed us at such a distance from each other.

It is needless to add, that I determined to answer this letter in person, and I only waited to embrace my loved and long estranged son on my arrival in Ireland. When I set out for Inismore I found the castle deserted, and learned (with indescribable emotions of pity and indignation), that the prince and his daughter were the inhabitants of a *prison*. I flew to this sad receptacle of suffering virtue, and effected the liberation of the prince. There *was* a time when the haughty spirit of this proud chieftain would have revolted against the idea of owing a pecuniary obligation to any man; but those only who have laboured under a long and continued series of mental and bodily affliction, can tell how the mind's strength is to be subdued, the energies of pride softened, and the delicacy of refined feelings blunted, by the pressure of reiterated suffering, of harassing and incessant disappointment. While the surprise of the prince equalled his emotion he exclaimed in the vehemence of his gratitude, 'Teach me at least how to thank you, since to repay you is impossible.' Glorvina was at that moment weeping on my shoulder, her hands were clasped in mine, and her humid eyes beamed on me all the grateful feelings of her warm and susceptible soul. I gazed on her for a moment,—she cast down her eyes, and I thought pressed my hand; thus encouraged I ventured to say to the prince, 'You talk in exaggerated terms of the little service I have done you,—would indeed it had been sufficient to embolden me to make that request which now trembles on my lips.'

I paused—the prince eagerly replied, 'There is nothing you can ask I am not anxious and ready to comply with.'

I looked at Glorvina—she blushed and trembled. I felt I was understood, and I added, 'Then give me a legal claim to become the protector of your daughter, and, through her, to restore you to that independence necessary for the repose of a proud and noble spirit. In a few days I shall openly appear to the world with honour and with safety in my own name and character. Take this letter, it is addressed to the Earl of M——, whom I solemnly swear is not more your enemy than mine, and who consequently cannot be biassed by partiality: from him you shall learn who and what I am; and until that period I ask not to receive the hand of your inestimable daughter.'

The prince took the letter and tore it in a thousand pieces; exclaiming, 'I cannot indeed equal, but I will at least endeavour to imitate your generosity. You chose me as your protector in the hour of danger, when confidence was more hazardous to him who reposed than him who received it! You placed your life in my hands with no other bond for its security than my *honour*! In the season of my distress you flew to save me: you lavished your property for my release, not considering the improbability of its remuneration! Take my child; her esteem, her affections, have long been your's; let me die in peace, by seeing her united to a worthy man!—*that* I *know* you are; what else you may be I will only learn from *the lips of a son-in-law*. Confidence at least shall be repaid by confidence.' At these words the always generous, always vehement and inconsiderate prince rose from his pillow and placed the hand of his daughter in mine, confirming the gift with a tear of joy and a tender benediction. Glorvina bowed her head to receive it—her veil fell over her face— the index of her soul was concealed: how then could I know what passed there. She was silent—she was obedient—and I was— deceived.

The prince, on his arrival at the castle of Inismore, felt the hour of dissolution stealing fast on every principle of life. Sensible of his situation, his tenderness, his anxiety for his child survived every other feeling; nor would he suffer himself to be carried to his chamber until he had bestowed her on me from the altar. I knew not then what were the sentiments of Glorvina. Entwined in the arms of her doating, dying father, she seemed insensible to every emotion, to every thought but what his fate excited; but however gratified I might have been at the intentions of the prince, I was decidedly averse to their prompt execution. I endeavoured to remonstrate: a *look* from the prince silenced every objection: and—But here let me drop the veil of oblivion over the past; let me clear from the tablets of memory those records of extraordinary and recent circumstances to which my heart can never revert but with a pang vibrating on its tenderest nerve. It is, however, the true spirit of philosophy to draw from the evil which cannot be remedied all the good of which in its tendency it is susceptible; and since the views of my parental ambition are thus blasted in the bloom, let me at least make him happy whom it was once my only wish to render eminent: know then my imprudent but still dear son, that the bride chosen for you by your father's policy has, by an elopement with a more ardent lover (who followed her hither), left your hand as free as your heart towards her ever was.

Take then to thy bosom *her* whom heaven seems to have chosen as the intimate associate of thy soul, and whom national and hereditary prejudice would in vain withhold from thee.—In this the dearest, most sacred, and most lasting of all human ties, let the names of Inismore and M—— be inseparably blended, and the distinctions of English and Irish, of protestant and catholic, for ever buried. And, while you look forward with hope to this family alliance being prophetically typical of a national unity of interests and affections between those who may be factiously severe, but who are naturally allied, lend your *own individual efforts* towards the consummation of an event so devoutly to be wished by every liberal mind, by every benevolent heart.

During my life, I would have you consider those estates as your's which I possess in this country; and at my death such as are not entailed. But this consideration is to be indulged conditionally, on your spending eight months out of every twelve on that spot from whence the very nutrition of your existence is to be derived; and in the bosom of those from whose labour and exertion your independence and prosperity are to flow. Act not with the vulgar policy of vulgar greatness, by endeavouring to exact respect through the medium of self-wrapt reserve, proudly shut up in its own self-invested grandeur; nor think it can derogate from the dignity of the *English landholder* openly to appear in the midst of his Irish peasantry, with an eye beaming complacency, and a countenance smiling confidence, and inspiring what it expresses. Shew them you do not distrust them, and they will not betray you; give them reason to believe you feel an interest in their welfare, and they will endeavour to promote your's even at the risk of their lives; for the life of an Irishman weighs but light in the scale of consideration with his feelings; it is immolated without a murmur to the affections of his heart; it is sacrificed without a sigh to the suggestions of his honour.

Remember that you are not placed by despotism over a band of slaves, creatures of the soil, and as such to be considered; but by Providence, over a certain portion of men, who, in common with the rest of their nation, are the descendants of a brave, a free, and an

enlightened people. Be more anxious to remove *causes*, than to punish *effects*; for trust me that is only to

'Scotch the snake—not kill it,'

to confine error, and to awaken vengeance.

Be cautious how you condemn; be more cautious how you deride,
but be ever watchful to moderate that ardent impetuosity, which
flows from the natural tone of the national character, which is the
inseparable accompaniment of quick and acute feelings, which is the
invariable concomitant of constitutional sensibility; and remember
that the same ardour of disposition, the same vehemence of soul,
which inflames their errors beyond the line of moderate failing,
nurtures their better qualities beyond the growth of moderate
excellence.

Within the influence then of your own bounded circle pursue
those means of promoting the welfare of the individuals consigned to
your care and protection, which lies within the scope of all those in
whose hands the destinies of their less fortunate brethren are placed.
Cherish by kindness into renovating life those national virtues,
which, though so often blighted in the full luxuriance of their vigorous blow by the fatality of circumstances, have still been ever found
vital at the root, which only want the nutritive beam of encouragement, the genial glow of confiding affection, and the refreshing dew
of tender commiseration, to restore them to their pristine bloom and
vigour: place the standard of support within their sphere; and like
the tender vine, which has been suffered by neglect to waste its
treasures on the sterile earth, you will behold them naturally turning
and gratefully twining round the fostering stem, which rescues them
from a cheerless and groveling destiny; and when by justly and
adequately rewarding the laborious exertions of that life devoted to
your service, the source of their poverty shall be dried up, and the
miseries that flowed from it shall be forgotten: when the warm hand
of benevolence shall have wiped away the cold dew of despondency
from their brow; when reiterated acts of tenderness and humanity
shall have thawed the ice which chills the native flow of their ardent
feelings; and when the light of instruction shall have dispelled the
gloom of ignorance and prejudice from their neglected minds, and
their lightened hearts shall again throb with the cheery pulse of

national exility:—then, *and not till then*, will you behold the day-star of national virtue rising brightly over the horizon of their happy existence; while the felicity, which has awakened to the touch of reason and humanity, shall return back to, and increase the source from which it originally flowed: as the elements, which in gradual progress brighten into flame, terminate in a liquid light, which, reverberating in sympathy to its former kindred, genially warms and gratefully cheers the whole order of universal nature.

EXPLANATORY NOTES

1 [*Epigraph*]: Owenson's novel opens with a quotation from a travel book, one of several genres she draws from to lend authority to the positive view of Ireland she wishes to promote. As J. Leerssen observes, in Owenson's many footnotes to *The Wild Irish Girl* 'names of the most illustrious travel writers are all there, italicized and often extensively quoted— Young, Bush, La Tocnaye, etc.' ('How *The Wild Irish Girl* Made Ireland Romantic', in *The Clash of Ireland* (Amsterdam: Rodopi, 1989), 112). In her footnotes, Owenson also draws on the antiquarian discourse of the late eighteenth-century Celtic Revival, which produced studies of the Celtic language, Irish castles, and ancient dwellings as well as collections of Gaelic ballads and folklore. Indeed, Owenson's biographer, Mary Campbell, describes the sources for the textual apparatus of *The Wild Irish Girl* as diverse, ranging 'from Walker's Essay on Irish Dress to the latest transactions of the Royal Irish Academy, and from regular correspondence with equally doctrinaire scholars' (*Lady Morgan: The Life and Times of Sydney Owenson* (London: Pandora, 1988), 68). Jeanne Moskal has argued that Owenson's many notes to *The Wild Irish Girl* 'shor[e] up the author's status as an authority on Ireland, supporting the text's claims' as well as 'the woman writer's claim to authority . . . Ironically, however, much of this authority is mustered by quotations from male authorities' ('Gender, Nationality, and Textual Authority in Lady Morgan's Travel Books', in Paula R. Feldman and Theresa M. Kelley (eds.), *Romantic Women Writers: Voices and Countervoices* (Hanover, NH: University Press of New England, 1995), 177).

4 *coruscations*: flashes of wit.

6 *Connaught*: a region in the west of Ireland.

Temple: name of the Inns of Court in London, the four sets of buildings belonging to the four legal societies which have the exclusive right of admitting persons to practise at the bar (*OED*). Horatio's father is here arguing that the secluded west coast of Ireland is as good a place to study for the law profession as London.

Lavater: the brothers Lavater were seventeenth- and eighteenth-century Swiss physicians and naturalists.

duodecimo: a size of a book, or of its pages, resulting from folding each sheet into twelve leaves, measuring $5\frac{1}{4} \times 8\frac{1}{8}$ in., as a maximum.

7 *Procrostus* [*sic*]: Procrustes was a legendary robber of ancient Greece noted for stretching or cutting off the legs of his victims to adapt them to the length of his bed.

'*Amandatus est ad disciplinum in Hibernia*': 'He was sent away for instruction to Ireland.'

8 *Druidism*: system of religion, philosophy, and instruction of the ancient Celtic priesthood appearing in Irish and Welsh sagas and Christian legends as magicians and wizards.

ebauche: outline.

mechant par air: wicked-seeming person.

9 *mal voluntaire*: unwilling.

King's Bench: one of the three London courts, usually hearing criminal cases and including places of confinement for prisoners.

10 *Balm of Gilead*: a substance that soothes and heals, produced from the aromatic leaves of a small evergreen which grows in Gilead, a region of ancient Palestine.

11 *tedium vitæ*: ennui or boredom.

pensèe couleur de rose: rose-coloured thought.

Rousseau: Jean-Jacques Rousseau (1712–78), the Swiss-French philosopher who argued that human beings in a state of nature are equal and good, but civilization corrupts them by introducing them to private property and commerce and by promoting inequality and luxury.

high German doctor: possibly Johann Wolfgang von Goethe (1749–1832), the great German poet, dramatist, novelist, and scientist.

the Pleasures of Memory: an extremely popular book published by the English poet and art collector Samuel Rogers (1763–1855) in 1792 recording the author's reflections as he revisits the villages of his childhood.

Madame de Sevigne: Marie de Rabutin-Chantal, marquise de Sévigné (1626–96), French writer and lady of fashion known for the letters she wrote to her daughter recording life in Paris under Louis XIV. These letters were published posthumously in 1725.

13 *Moryson*: Fynes Moryson (1566–1630) was an English travel writer known for his depictions of the Irish during Elizabeth's reign. In his travel memoirs, *An Itinerary* (1617), he finds nothing admirable about the Irish except their whiskey.

15 *Ionic order ... Corinthian pillars*: two of the orders of Grecian architecture, the latter considered the more ornate.

coup-d'œil: glance.

16 *Mr Young*: Arthur Young (1741–1820), English agriculturalist and writer who described the Irish peasantry in his *A Tour in Ireland* (1780).

17 *Restoration*: the re-establishment of the monarchy in England in 1660 under Charles II bringing to a close the Commonwealth. After the Restoration, some Irish Catholics regained the estates taken from them during the Cromwellian land settlements.

Blackstone: Sir William Blackstone (1723–80), British jurist whose work *Commentaries on the Laws of England* (1765–9) ordered and explained

English law and greatly influenced both the profession and the study of law.

post-chaise: a travelling carriage, either hired from stage to stage, or drawn by horses so hired (*OED*).

18 *berlin*: a four-wheeled two-seated covered carriage with a hooded rear seat.

Savoy: kingdom in Italy.

Claude Loraine . . . Salvator Rosa: Horatio here elevates Irish landscapes over English ones by positing painters adequate to paint each. The French painter Claude Lorrain (1600–82) is suited to English landscapes, but the 'superior genius' of the Italian painter Salvator Rosa (1615–73) is required for Ireland. Horatio's tastes reflect those of Sydney Owenson, who documented her admiration for the Italian painter in her biography *The Life and Times of Salvator Rosa* (1824). As Owenson's own biographer, Mary Campbell, observes, Rosa's Romantic Italian scenery 'synthesized with the scenery of the West of Ireland in her landscape of the imagination' (*Lady Morgan: The Life and Times of Sydney Owenson* (London: Pandora Press, 1988), 33).

Ceres: Roman goddess of grain, protector of agriculture.

19 *carte du pays*: map of the country.

20 *scutching*: preparing a fibrous material like flax for fabric by beating with sticks.

21 *pro tempo*: temporarily.

primum mobile: the outermost concentric sphere conceived in medieval astronomy as carrying the spheres of the fixed stars and the planets in its daily revolution.

sans ceremonie: without ceremony.

22 *auberge*: inn or tavern.

Horace: Quintus Horatius Flaccus (65 BC–8 BC), Latin lyric poet.

23 *Scaliger*: Julius Caesar Scaliger (1484–1588), Italian soldier, physician, and scholar who wrote both critical commentaries on classical writers and his own verse in Latin.

triumviri: commissions or ruling bodies of three.

compagnon de voyage: travelling companion.

frize: or frieze, a kind of coarse woollen cloth (especially of Irish make) with a nap, usually on one side only (*OED*).

'*Nudi sono . . . le gambe*': 'The feet are bare, but two rough shepherds' leggings(?) cover the legs.'

24 *gossip*: kinsman or relation.

26 '*J'ai souvent entendu . . . pour oublier sa misere*': 'I have often heard the peasants reproached for sloth and drunkenness. But when one is reduced to starvation, isn't it better to do nothing, since the hardest work won't

prevent death? In this situation, isn't it simplest to take when one can a drop of the waters of Lethe in order to forget the misery?'

26 *philippic*: a bitter invective.

28 *madder*: a square wooden drinking cup.

29 *pale*: a region of English rule around Dublin, fortified against Gaelic Ireland.

sans façon: without ceremony.

jubilate: a call to rejoice.

Goldsmith: Oliver Goldsmith (1728–74), an Irish author who drew on memories of his childhood in Ireland when writing his most famous poem, *The Deserted Village*.

30 *Terpsichore*: one of the nine Greek muses, patroness of choral dance and dramatic chorus.

Sesostris-like: like the mythical Egyptian king based on Ramses II (1292–1225 BC) who led Egypt to unprecedented splendour and a vast empire.

31 *fac-totum*: an employee with various duties.

32 *Cromwellian wars*: between 15 Aug. 1649 and 26 May 1650, Oliver Cromwell campaigned in Ireland with a large army and navy. The period of his rule in England between 1649 and 1658 saw the brutal suppression of Catholics in Ireland and the confiscation of Catholic lands.

'Ayant l'air delabri, sans l'air antique': 'Dilapidated in appearance with no air of antiquity.'

33 *haut ton*: high style.

cabilistical [*sic*]: cabbalistical—having a secret or hidden meaning.

'Se pur ve nelle amor alcun diletto': from the work of the Italian poet Torquato Tasso (1544–95)—'If there is any delight for you in love.'

34 *West Indian planter*: during the eighteenth and nineteenth centuries, Britain held colonies in the Caribbean Sea, the West Indies, where planters were known for their brutal treatment of African slaves on sugar-cane plantations. But middlemen who managed Irish estates for absentee landlords were also notorious for their mistreatment of tenants through rack-renting. The connection made here between the two types of over-seers is thus apt.

major domo: a powerful head steward.

Cassino: Monte Cassino, Benedictine monastery midway between Rome and Naples.

35 *'Se perchetto a me Stesso quale acquisto, | Faro mai che me piaccia'*: 'What-ever I get for myself | it never gives me pleasure.'

articula mortis: moments of death.

36 *escritoire*: a writing table or desk.

Tusculum: where Cicero (see note to p. 59) had a villa; hence, a country retreat.

Cicerone: a guide who shows the antiquities or curiosities of a place to strangers (*OED*).

37 *Antiochus and Stratonice*: Stratonice was the second wife of Seleucus I but was passed by him to his son Antiochus with whom she co-ruled; this later became the basis for a romantic fiction on the supposed passion of the son for his stepmother.

38 *Milesians*: early inhabitants of Ireland. The term comes from Milesius, a Latinization of Míl Espáine, whose sons are said to have led the conquest of Ireland.

Strongbonean: Strongbow or Richard Fitz Gilbert, an Englishman, invaded Ireland in 1170 on behalf of Mac Murchada, an exiled Irish king, and, after that king died, succeeded him and settled Leinster in Ireland with tenants from his English and Welsh estates.

galloglasses: one of a particular class of soldiers maintained by Irish chiefs (*OED*).

39 *spalpeen*: rascal.

43 *Chevalier Errant*: a wandering knight and one of many early allusions in the novel to *Don Quixote*, a satirical romance by Cervantes published in 1605.

Apicius: Roman author of a book on cookery.

turbot: a much valued fish, large and flat and exceedingly fine for eating.

lampreys: a type of fish resembling an eel in shape and having no scales (*OED*).

44 *phalernian*: Falernian is a celebrated Roman wine. Thus, Horatio compares the spring water to fine wine.

manes: the deified souls of departed ancestors (*OED*).

45 *mantles*: the wearing of mantles, a symbol of resistance to English rule in Ireland, was banned in an Act of 1537. Because these garments were worn by women and men of all classes and minimized differences of gender and class, the English regarded them as subversive, representing a 'refusal to adopt English order, English social categories, English style' (Ann Rosalind Jones and Peter Stallybrass, 'Dismantling Irena: The Sexuality of Ireland in Early Modern England', in *Nationalisms and Sexualities* (New York: Routledge, 1992), 166).

47 *glory*: a circle or ring of light (*OED*).

49 *outré*: violating convention or propriety; bizarre.

50 *Caiphas*: Caiaphas, the high priest who interrogates Jesus after his arrest and condemns him for claiming to be the Son of God (Matthew 26: 57). Used here to indicate the narrator's ambivalent attitude toward the Catholic Mass: he is both aware of its great appeal and certain in his censure.

57 *Irish priest*: with the enactment of the Penal Laws in the 1690s which disenfranchised Irish Catholics and discriminated against Catholic clergy, it became common for Irish priests to seek education in France.

57 *Esculapius*: Aesculapius, the Greek god of medicine.

58 *Pythagorean*: referring perhaps to the moral and dietary regime practised by followers of Pythagoras (582–507 BC) in order to purify the soul for passage at death into another body.

59 *Ciceronian*: in the manner of Marcus Tullius Cicero (106–43 BC), Roman orator and writer celebrated for his mastery of Latin prose.

60 *Gorgon*: in Greek mythology one of three monstrous women with snakes for hair who turned anyone who looked at them to stone.

62 *Epimenides*: legendary person of ancient Crete, said to have woken from a boyhood nap to find that fifty-seven years had elapsed.

63 *vivida vis anima*: the living force of the soul.

    suaviter in modo: suave manner.

65 *bas-bleus*: blue stockings, i.e. women having intellectual or literary interests.

    Ninon ... Dacier: Ninon de Lenclos (*c*.1620–1705), renowned intellectual as well as celebrated courtesan; Anne Dacier (*c*.1651–1720), an outstanding scholar.

    soi-disant: so-called, self-styled.

    lumine purpureo: crimson glow.

66 '*Onde tolse amor l'oro e di qual vena* | *Per far due treccie biondé*': 'From what mine did love take the gold to make two blond tresses?'

67 *memento mori*: a reminder of death.

    Mount Ida triumviri: the goddesses Hera, Athena, and Aphrodite, who asked Paris (then a shepherd on Mt. Ida near Troy) to choose which of them was the most beautiful.

70 *Hebe*: the Greek goddess of youth.

    pis-aller: a last resource or device.

72 *Brian Boru*: high king of Ireland from 1002 until his death in 1014. Brian Boru's defeat of the Vikings on Good Friday, 1014, marked their final overthrow in Ireland.

73 *Irish planxty*: an animated harp tune.

74 *encomiastic*: characterized by glowing praise.

75 *eleemosynary*: charitable.

    Locke and Malbranche: John Locke (1632–1704), English philosopher and founder of British empiricism; Nicolas de Malebranche (1638–1715), French philosopher.

    quidities: quiddities—alluding to scholastic arguments on the real nature or essence of things (*OED*).

76 *port-feuille*: portfolio.

    '*La sainte recueilment le paisible innocence* | *Sembler de ces lieus habiter le silence*': 'The holy meditation, the calm innocence, | To seem to live in the silence of these places.'

ebauche: rough draft or outline.

78 *Pliny*: probably Pliny the Younger (62–113), Roman statesman and orator known for his letters depicting Roman life.

80 *Poiche d'altro . . . umor rugiadose*: from the work of the Italian poet Bernardo Tasso (1493–1569): 'As I cannot honour thee in any other way, take these dark violas damp with dew.'

'Mais si sur votre . . . sera la plus superbe': 'But if I can shine for one day on your brow | The humblest of flowers will be the proudest.'

81 *Ausonius*: Decimus Magnus Ausonius (310–95), Latin poet known for his travel verses and family sketches.

St Augustus: perhaps St Augustine of Hippo (354–430), whose *City of God* is a defence of Christianity against paganism.

Sappho: great Greek lyric poet who lived in the seventh century BC; her principal subject is love.

Anacreon: sixth-century BC Greek lyric poet who also celebrates love and wine in his work.

'Tendre fruits des pleurs d'aurore . . . Hâte toi d'epanouir': 'Tender fruits of the tears of daybreak | Objects of the kisses of the winds | Queen of the empire of the Flowers | Hasten to blossom.' A poem by Pierre-Joseph Bernard (1710–75).

d'éterniser la bagatelle: to immortalize trifles.

82 *enjouée*: playful, sprightly.

86 *quondam*: former.

en-famille: as a family.

87 *Sir William Temple*: (1628–99) English diplomat, statesman, and author whose many published works include the essay *The Advancement of Trade in Ireland* (1673).

Dr Johnson: Samuel Johnson (1709–84), English author and lexicographer.

88 *par routine*: as a matter of course.

con amore: with love.

antiquarian: a term originating in the latter part of the eighteenth century for the study of antiquities; antiquarians of the Celtic Revival undertook the study of the Irish language and folklore.

antediluvian: relating to the period preceding the flood described in the Bible, the term often used as here in a disparaging sense.

89 *Miss Brooks*: Charlotte Brooke, whose *Reliques of Irish Poetry* (1789) aimed to introduce English readers to 'the productions of our Irish Bards'.

91 *Theocritus*: third-century BC Greek poet remembered primarily as a pastoral poet.

epithalamium: a song or poem in honour of a bride and bridegroom.

Erin: the old Irish name for Ireland.

92 *Coke*: Sir Edward Coke (1552–1634), along with Blackstone (see note to p. 17), was an English jurist. His writings include his *Reports* on common law.

ipecacuhana [*sic*]: ipecacuanha, an agent that induces vomiting.

dernier resort [*sic*]: *dernier ressort*, a last resource.

historiographer: an official historian appointed in connection with a court (*OED*).

Milton: John Milton (1608–74), English poet best known for his epic poem, *Paradise Lost* (1667).

discordia concors: harmonious discord, the artistic device whereby harmony is achieved through the juxtaposition of apparently incompatible elements.

93 *'Benedetto sia il giorno e'l Mese e'lanno'*: 'Blessed be the day and the month and the year.'

Spenser: Edmund Spenser (1552–99), English poet and author of the *Faerie Queene* (1590–6) who went to Ireland in 1580 as secretary to Sir Arthur Gray and later obtained an estate in Kilcolman, Co. Cork, during the establishment of the English plantations in Munster. His attitudes towards the Irish, expressed in *A View of the Present State of Ireland*, were much like those of Horatio early in this narrative.

Lord Bacon: Francis Bacon (1561–1626), English philosopher, essayist, and statesman.

95 *Phaeton*: Phaethon, in Greek mythology, the son of the sun god Apollo, who borrowed his father's chariot and would have set the world on fire if Zeus had not stopped him with a thunderbolt.

96 *prieux Chevalier*: *preux chevalier*, gallant knight.

lusus naturæ: amorously playful character.

98 *Golconda*: an ancient city in India known for diamond-cutting.

99 *St Bridget*: Anglicized form of Brighid (d. 524), Leinster saint and founder of a celebrated convent at Kildare. She shares her name with the Celtic goddess of protecting care.

paysannes: countrywomen.

Irish Empress Macha, with her bodkin: in the Ulster Cycle, Macha is a land goddess said to have captured the sons of the Irish King Dithorba. She set them to building an earthen ring fort whose perimeter she marked out with the clasp she wore at her neck.

101 *coup de grace*: a finishing stroke.

farrago: mixture.

cognoscenti: connoisseur.

bonne bouche: tit-bit.

Ossianic: relating to the legendary Irish bard Ossian, the poems ascribed to him, or the rhythmic prose style used by James Macpherson in his alleged translations.

Valk-halla . . . Woden: Woden or Odin is the supreme Scandinavian deity whose court is at Valhalla, where he is surrounded by warriors who have fallen in battle.

102 *tesselated*: formed with a mosaic pattern (*OED*).

103 *valkyries*: in Scandinavian mythology, war maidens who hover over battlefields and conduct fallen warriors to Valhalla (*OED*).

'molle atque facetum': 'tenderness and wit'.

104 *Froissart*: Jean Froissart (1337–1410), French traveller, chronicler, and poet who recorded the exploits of French and English nobles from 1325 to 1400 in his *Chroniques*, translated into English by J. Bouchier in 1523.

105 *gorget*: the part of a knight's armour that defends the throat.

foul paynim: profane pagan.

106 *hauberjeon*: haubergeon, a sleeveless coat or jacket of mail armour (*OED*).

Fingal's heroes: cf. pp. 109–10.

Ossian . . . Macpherson's own muse: the priest refers to the controversy surrounding the publication in 1762 of *Fingal, an Ancient Epic Poem, in Six Books* by James Macpherson (1736–96). Macpherson claimed the poem was a faithful translation of an early Scottish epic by Ossian but a committee investigating the literary mystery found that he had edited and greatly expanded Gaelic poems.

107 *John Fordun*: (d. 1384?), chantry priest at Aberdeen, author of Books i–v of the 'Scotichronicon', chronicles of Scottish history; Walter Bower wrote Books vi–xvi largely from Fordun's notes. Fordun is said to have made use of many Irish materials in his work.

Phœnicia: an ancient country on the coast of Syria.

Conquest: the Normans conquered England in 1066 and invaded Ireland a hundred years later.

108 *Erse*: the Gaelic dialect spoken in the Highlands of Scotland.

109 *Deucalion*: in Greek mythology, the son of Prometheus and Clymene. When Zeus destroyed the vice-steeped population only Deucalion and his wife were spared.

110 *solecisms*: things deviating from the proper, normal, or accepted order.

116 *'Mais un invincible contraint . . . Le desir seul ne suffit pas'*: 'But an invincible constraint | In spite of myself holds my steps here, | And you know that the desire alone | to go to Corinth is not enough.'

117 *purlieus of St James*: a fashionable neighbourhood in London.

    a portée: inclined.

118 *Marmontel*: Jean-François Marmontel (1723–99), French historiographer, playwright, and critic also noted for his moral tales.

    Bards, Fileas, and Seanachies: poets, storytellers, and historians.

120 *Carolan*: the Irish harpist Turlogh O'Carolan (1670–1738).

124 *hind*: a farm servant.

    rosinante: the name of the horse ridden by Don Quixote (see p. 43 above).

    rencontre: accidental meeting.

130 *St Crysostom*: St John Chrysostom (347–407), Greek church father, reformer, and patriarch of Constantinople.

131 *Hymeneal altar*: the marriage altar, after Hymenaeus, the Greek god who led the wedding procession and whose name was invoked at every wedding as a sign of good luck.

132 *les affaires du cœur*: affairs of the heart.

    'la langua Toscana, nel' bocca Romana': 'the Tuscan tongue in the Roman mouth'.

133 *Bœotian*: originally, of Boeotia in Greece; proverbially, the Boeotians were dull-witted.

    torpedo: a flat fish with a circular body that emits electrical discharges (*OED*).

134 *ass of Balaam*: a non-Christian prophet in the Old Testament whose talking ass tried to reason with her owner when he beat her (Numbers 22: 1–20).

    the golden-roofed temple of Solyman: Solomon (d. 922 BC), king of the ancient Hebrews and son of David, built the first Hebrew temple at Jerusalem. In 1 Kings 6 the temple is described as overlaid with gold.

    par hazard: by guesswork.

135 *Epaminondas*: (?418–362 BC) Theban statesman and general.

    'La solitude est certainement . . . une belle chose': 'Solitude is certainly a beautiful thing, but there is pleasure in having someone who knows how to respond, to whom one may say, solitude is a beautiful thing.'

    Monsieur de Balsac: Jean-Louis Guez de Balzac (1597–1654), French writer known for his letters, published in 1624 and expanded in the many editions that followed. He also wrote treatises on the moral and social ideas of his day: *Le Prince*, 1631; *Le Barbon*, 1648 and *Le Socrate chrétien*, 1652.

136 *cabaret*: a tavern.

    entre nous: confidential.

    à la Française: as do the French.

137 *malhereusement*: unhappily; unluckily.

cead mille a falta: *céad míle fáilte*—a hundred thousand welcomes; the conventional form of welcome in Irish.

138 *Hyperborean Island*: the land where Apollo lived for a time after his birth and to which he returned every year, a Utopia with a mild climate and inhabited by happy people.

Bacchantes: women who celebrated at the feasts of Bacchus, the Roman god of wine.

140 *Tempé*: a valley in Thessaly, an ancient region in north-eastern Greece.

Beheld her . . . could bestow: Milton, *Paradise Lost*, viii. 481–3.

votarist: devout or zealous worshipper.

143 *Hero . . . Leander*: in Greek legend Hero was a priestess of Aphrodite loved by Leander, a youth noted for swimming the Hellespont nightly to visit her.

144 *La Nouvelle Heloise . . . Chateaubriand*: *Julie, ou la Nouvelle Héloïse* (1761), Rousseau's popular story of the passionate love between a tutor and his pupil; *Paul et Virginie* (1788), Jacques Henri Bernardin de Saint-Pierre's (1737–1814) widely read romance (inspired by Rousseau) of two children brought up as brother and sister, raised outside society and according to nature's laws; Goethe's (1749–1832) *The Sorrows of Young Werther* (1774), the sensationally popular novel about a young artist in love with a woman engaged to someone else; and *Atala* (1801), François René Chateaubriand's (1768–1848) tragic romance of the Native American maiden Atala and her lover.

145 *Dr Burney*: music historian and father of Fanny Burney.

146 *alma*: dancing girl.

147 *supererogation*: performance of good works beyond what is required.

148 *bon ton nonchalance*: a fine nonchalant manner.

149 *'Le besoin de l'ame tendre'*: 'The need of a tender heart.'

150 *Collins*: William Collins (1721–59), English poet whose visionary and sacred verse influenced poets of the late eighteenth century. He is known for his *Odes on Several Descriptive and Allegoric Subjects* (1747), especially 'Ode to Evening', lines 5–8 quoted here.

151 *'Les ames humaines . . . de leurs force particulier'*: 'Human souls want to be fulfilled for the procurement of all their worth, and the combined energy of these souls, like that of the tears of an untrue lover, is incomparably greater than the sum of their individual power.'

'buvames à longs traits le philtre de l'amour': 'drank deeply of the potion of love'.

152 *St Columba*: Colum Cille, also called Columbkill (521–97), the Irish missionary to Scotland who established a great monastic centre at Iona in 563 and spread Christianity throughout Scotland.

sotto voce: softly.

153 *Hygeia*: Hygiea, Greek goddess of health, whose image at Sicyon was, according to Pausanias (*Description of Greece*), hung with women's hair and dedicated garments.

155 *'La confidence ingenû rapproche deux amis'*: 'Confiding frankly brings together two friends.'

157 *Etrurian*: relating to an ancient country in central Italy whose culture predated and influenced that of Rome.

158 *'Ces douces lumieres . . . les jours de la volupté'*: 'These soft lights | These sombre lights | Are the days of sensual pleasure.'

   Epicurus: Greek philosopher (342–270 BC) who argued that a life of pleasure regulated by morality, temperance, serenity, and cultural development ought to be the goal of humans.

159 *legislator of Lesbos*: Pittacus of Mytilene, whose assertion quoted here was criticized by Simonides in a poem cited at length by Plato, *Protagoras* 339A–346D.

160 *phasis*: aspect.

   the eternal qui vive: continual alertness.

   laquais: lackey.

   propria persona: in person.

161 *Hiberniana*: Irish lore or history.

   Philosophia Amatoria: lover's philosophy.

   Hindoo . . . Bramins: Horatio now listens to Irish with the same attention a Hindu might give Sanskrit, the language of India's classical and sacred texts.

163 *Breviare du Sentiment*: a breviary is a book containing prayers, hymns, psalms, and readings for the canonical hours.

164 *coxcomical*: like that of a fool, a fop, or a conceited foolish person.

165 *assymtotes*: an assymptote is a line to which a given curve approaches without their ever meeting (*not* a hyperbola).

   Weiland: Christoph Martin Wieland (1733–1813), German writer and forerunner of romanticism known for his espousal of the rational, sensual life. Among his works are light erotic poetry (*Komische Erzählungen*, 1765) and love poems (*Musarion oder Die Philosophie der Grazien*, 1768).

   climacteric: a major turning-point or critical stage (in human life).

   ignus fatuus: Lat. 'foolish fire'; a phosphorescent light seen flitting over marshy ground; hence, any delusive idea or purpose.

166 *Nimrod*: in the Bible, the son of Cush, a mighty hunter.

167 *palladium*: a safeguard.

170 *'Tout s'evanouit . . . de la vie'*: 'All vanishes under the heavens, | Each moment alters in our eyes | The shifting painting of life.'

   Eloisa . . . Wolmar: Rousseau's *Julie, ou la Nouvelle Héloïse* (1761) portrays the passionate love between a tutor and his pupil, Julie. Julie eventually marries another man, the Baron Wolmar.

171 *St Preux*: the name of the tutor in Rousseau's *Julie, ou la Nouvelle Héloïse*.

172 *doneur*: donneur, giver.

174 *Camden*: William Camden (1551–1623), English antiquarian and historian whose works include *Britannia* (1586).

Bede: Baeda or 'The Venerable Bede' (673–735), English scholar, historian, and theologian whose *Ecclesiastical History of the English People* describes the Irish clergy's important role in converting the English to Christianity.

Nido paterno: paternal nest.

178 *Doctor Warner*: possibly William Warner (1558–1609), author of a metrical history of Britain, *Albions England*.

palinode: retraction.

180 *old Brehon law*: the law prevailing in Ireland before the English occupation.

sept: a branch of a family, clan.

181 *'none of woman born can harm Macbeth'*: one of the riddling prophecies of the witches or weird sisters in Shakespeare's tragedy *Macbeth*. Macbeth was slain by Macduff, who was 'from his mother's womb | Untimely ripped.'

184 *the mother of Euriales in the Eneid*: when Ilium, the mother of Euryalus, learns that her son has been killed in battle and his head raised on a spear, she gives way to violent grief and asks that she be killed and her soul cast into the abyss; Virgil, *Aeneid*, ix. 473–502.

185 *osier*: any willow whose pliable twigs are used for furniture and basketry.

189 *Sir William Petty*: (1623–87) English political economist best known for his discussion of the economies of England and Ireland in *Treatise of Taxes and Contributions* (1662) and his descriptions of Irish people, politics, and natural resources in *The Political Anatomy of Ireland* (1691).

Mr Young: see note to p. 16 above.

'Si le pauvre . . . du desespoir': 'If the poor man saw clearly that work could better his situation, he would soon abandon this apathy, this indifference which is in fact only the habit of hopelessness.'

190 *House of Stuart*: the royal family ruling Scotland from 1371 to 1603, and Scotland and England from 1603 to 1714 except during the Protectorate of the Cromwells (1649–60).

British diadem: the British Crown.

191 *Balbec or Palmyra*: ancient cities known for their splendour. Baalbek (or Heliopolis) was the site of magnificent temples to Jupiter and Mercury. Palmyra, with its great Temple of Bel and Grand Colonnade, influenced

European neo-classicism when it was rediscovered in the eighteenth century.

192 *Laurentinum, or Tusculum*: cities in ancient Latium, Italy, the former named for the sacred laurel tree found on the site where the city was built, the latter home to many famous Romans, including Pompey, Brutus, and Cicero, before it was destroyed at the end of the twelfth century.

193 *a sentiment of St Paul*: 1 Corinthians 9: 11.

St Columbkill: Colum Cille or St Columba, see note to p. 152.

194 *Silenus*: in Roman mythology, the chief of the older satyrs and foster-father of Bacchus. Silenus is represented as cheerfully tipsy, bald, pug-nosed, and pimply.

195 *duenna*: a chaperone.

196 *battledore*: a game in which a shuttlecock is hit backwards and forwards between two players using a small racket.

197 *massacre of St Bartholomew*: on 23–4 August 1572, a general massacre of Protestants in France provoked by the marriage of the Protestant Henry of Bourbon, King of Navarre, with the Catholic sister of Charles IX, Margaret of Valois.

199 *hydra*: in Greek mythology, the many-headed snake of the marshes of Lerna, whose heads grew again as fast as they were cut off (*OED*).

wen: a lump or protuberance on the body (*OED*).

204 *Drumceat*: the ancient poem *Amra Coluimb Chille* gives Druim Cett as the site of a famous meeting where St Columba saved the poets of Ireland from banishment.

205 *Sir Philip Sydney*: Sir Philip Sidney (1554–86), English statesman, soldier, and author whose works include *Arcadia* (1590) and *Astrophel and Stella* (1591).

206 *Giants' Causeway*: a spectacular formation of basalt columns on the coast of Antrim, Northern Ireland.

208 *avant-courier*: harbinger, forerunner.

214 *cicatrised*: scarred.

219 *Elysium*: Elysian Fields, in Homer's *Odyssey*, a paradise populated by those favoured by the gods.

223 *pharos*: any lighthouse or beacon to direct mariners (*OED*).

226 *emolument*: profit or gain from station, office, or employment (*OED*).

227 *hoyden*: a girl or woman of saucy, boisterous, or carefree behaviour.

A SELECTION OF OXFORD WORLD'S CLASSICS

ANTHONY TROLLOPE

An Autobiography

Ayala's Angel

Barchester Towers

The Belton Estate

The Bertrams

Can You Forgive Her?

The Claverings

Cousin Henry

Doctor Thorne

Doctor Wortle's School

The Duke's Children

Early Short Stories

The Eustace Diamonds

An Eye for an Eye

Framley Parsonage

He Knew He Was Right

Lady Anna

The Last Chronicle of Barset

Later Short Stories

Miss Mackenzie

Mr Scarborough's Family

Orley Farm

Phineas Finn

Phineas Redux

The Prime Minister

Rachel Ray

The Small House at Allington

La Vendée

The Warden

The Way We Live Now

THE OXFORD SHERLOCK HOLMES

ARTHUR CONAN DOYLE

The Adventures of Sherlock Holmes
The Case-Book of Sherlock Holmes
His Last Bow
The Hound of the Baskervilles
The Memoirs of Sherlock Holmes
The Return of Sherlock Holmes
The Valley of Fear
Sherlock Holmes Stories
The Sign of the Four
A Study in Scarlet

WASHINGTON IRVING	The Sketch-Book of Geoffrey Crayon, Gent.
HENRY JAMES	The Ambassadors
	The Aspern Papers and Other Stories
	The Awkward Age
	The Bostonians
	Daisy Miller and Other Stories
	The Europeans
	The Golden Bowl
	The Portrait of a Lady
	Roderick Hudson
	The Spoils of Poynton
	The Turn of the Screw and Other Stories
	Washington Square
	What Maisie Knew
	The Wings of the Dove
SARAH ORNE JEWETT	The Country of the Pointed Firs and Other Fiction
JACK LONDON	The Call of the Wild
	White Fang and Other Stories
	John Barleycorn
	The Sea-Wolf
	The Son of the Wolf
HERMAN MELVILLE	Billy Budd, Sailor and Selected Tales
	The Confidence-Man
	Moby-Dick
	Typee
	White-Jacket
FRANK NORRIS	McTeague
FRANCIS PARKMAN	The Oregon Trail
EDGAR ALLAN POE	The Narrative of Arthur Gordon Pym of Nantucket and Related Tales
	Selected Tales
HARRIET BEECHER STOWE	Uncle Tom's Cabin

The
Oxford
World's
Classics
Website

www.worldsclassics.co.uk

- Information about new titles
- Explore the full range of Oxford World's Classics
- Links to other literary sites and the main OUP webpage
- Imaginative competitions, with bookish prizes
- Peruse *Compass*, the Oxford World's Classics magazine
- Articles by editors
- Extracts from Introductions
- A forum for discussion and feedback on the series
- Special information for teachers and lecturers

www.worldsclassics.co.uk

American Literature

British and Irish Literature

Children's Literature

Classics and Ancient Literature

Colonial Literature

Eastern Literature

European Literature

History

Medieval Literature

Oxford English Drama

Poetry

Philosophy

Politics

Religion

The Oxford Shakespeare

A complete list of Oxford Paperbacks, including Oxford World's Classics, OPUS, Past Masters, Oxford Authors, Oxford Shakespeare, Oxford Drama, and Oxford Paperback Reference, is available in the UK from the Academic Division Publicity Department, Oxford University Press, Great Clarendon Street, Oxford OX2 6DP.

In the USA, complete lists are available from the Paperbacks Marketing Manager, Oxford University Press, 198 Madison Avenue, New York, NY 10016.

Oxford Paperbacks are available from all good bookshops. In case of difficulty, customers in the UK can order direct from Oxford University Press Bookshop, Freepost, 116 High Street, Oxford OX1 4BR, enclosing full payment. Please add 10 per cent of published price for postage and packing.